WE DESERVE MONUMENTS

WE DESERVE MONUMENTS

Jas Hammonds

ROARING BROOK PRESS

NEW YORK

Published by Roaring Brook Press

Roaring Brook Press is a division of Holtzbrinck Publishing Holdings Limited Partnership

120 Broadway, New York, NY 10271 • fiercereads.com

Our books may be purchased in bulk for promotional, educational, or business use. Please contact your local bookseller or the Macmillan Corporate and Premium Sales Department at (800) 221-7945 ext. 5442 or by email at MacmillanSpecialMarkets@macmillan.com.

Library of Congress Cataloging-in-Publication Data is available.

First edition, 2022

Book design by Sarah Nichole Kaufman

Printed in the United States of America

ISBN 978-1-250-81655-9 (hardcover)

1 3 5 7 9 10 8 6 4 2

For Yasmin, who's read every word

NOW ENTERING BARDELL COUNTY, GEORGIA
POPULATION: 9,127
HOME TO THE RICHEST SOIL ON EARTH
A GREAT PLACE TO GROW!

1.

TEN.

That's how many bullet holes I counted puncturing the rusted brown Bardell County highway sign. There were probably more, but I lost count when it blurred past us as Mom accelerated into town. I turned to look through the rear window, wondering if I imagined them, but they were as real as the seat belt digging into my neck. Dreary sunlight streamed through the holes like an erratic cheese grater, and I couldn't think of a more fitting welcome to this wasteland.

"Richest soil on Earth!" Dad said from the passenger seat. "That's not foreboding whatsoever."

I bit back a grin as Mom sighed for the thousandth time since we crossed the South Carolina–Georgia border.

"Sam, please," she said. "Lay off. Bardell is a—"

"Diamond in the rough," Dad and I echoed. It was the same phrase she'd muttered the past few weeks as we packed suitcases and prepared for the trip down south. *A diamond in the rough.* Now, I pressed my forehead to the window to take in the flat fields and umber dirt. It was the same landscape I'd been staring at for what felt like years, and I saw no diamonds. Only rough.

"Besides." Mom shot me a terse glance in the rearview mirror. "You said you've been eager for a change of scenery all summer."

I swallowed my protests. *This* wasn't what anyone had in mind. Yes, I wanted a break from the DC nooks and crannies I'd known my entire life. I wanted an excuse to slip out of Kelsi and Hikari's carefully arranged summer plans. But in my imagination, this getaway entailed an escape to a charming beach cottage or an unfamiliar metropolis filled with taxis and overpriced tourist traps. More skyscrapers and fewer silos.

"We know, Z. Unsavory Avery and I are messing with you," Dad said, dusting off my childhood nickname. His hand was a slow smear of warmth across Mom's back, and her shoulders melted under his lanky fingers. I rolled my eyes and returned my attention to the window as Bardell, Georgia, unenthusiastically introduced itself.

At a red light, Mom studied her manicured nails against the steering wheel. An elderly woman in a sagging lawn chair on the corner motioned to the bulging basket of peaches by her feet and yelled something, but I couldn't understand her over the roar of the car's air-conditioning. Dad smiled his awkward white-dad smile and shook his head, and I sank against the leather back seat. All of our shoulders relaxed when the light flickered green and Mom cruised down Main Street.

"It's so different," Mom muttered. "Everything's so different."

Downtown Bardell unfolded all at once. The library, post office, pharmacy, and fire station were contained to one essential block. Across the street, a group of older white men in sun-faded denim leaned against the wall of a one-stop shop. The drooping banner above the entrance promised amazing deals on everything from cell phones to guns to wedding dresses in bright red letters, as if the convenience was something to be admired. The bar next door had a Confederate flag proudly draped in the window. My family said nothing. I could only stare at Mom's tight coils and wonder how in the world this place created her.

"Holy mural," Dad said. We slowed at a stop sign in front of an imposing brick building that towered over the street like a castle. A three-story-tall mural of a pale woman with a gleaming halo graced the side, staring serenely like the Mona Lisa.

"That's the Draper Hotel," Mom replied. The three of us watched as a trio of slim women in matching yellow yoga pants slipped through the revolving front door.

"Looks fancy," I said, and Mom hummed.

As we continued down the street, Mom muttered like a confused tour guide about gas stations long gone and snorted at a chic bistro with a sign claiming to have the best fried chicken in town. At the next stop sign, she switched off the GPS, and I silently lost hope that maybe, perhaps, somehow we weren't in the right place.

"It's so different," she repeated, followed by vague, clipped stories about how Mrs. Robinson used to live over there and that clothing store used to be a pharmacy called Easy Does It Drugs. She kept skirting over the real reason we were in Bardell, the one that had hovered over our family like a rain-heavy cloud for the past month.

It'd been five weeks since the wrinkled letter slid through the mail slot of our Shaw Victorian row house that quiet July morning. Saturday mornings had always been a bonding time for me and Mom. We'd wake up early, pick up bagels and fresh flowers, and hurry home to slip back into our sweatpants. For hours, she'd grade papers or work on grant applications, the clacking of her keyboard our only music. I'd run SAT prep questions or study successful college essays while the coffeepot slowly emptied between us.

But that Saturday morning was different. I could still see Mom clutching the letter, her slender brown fingers curling over the return address. The peeling American flag stamp on the envelope waved as she read it over and over.

That morning, Mom retreated to her bedroom before finishing her bagel. She didn't emerge until the late afternoon when the coffee was cold and stale and forgotten. At the time, she didn't tell us who the letter was from. She didn't elaborate on the cancer, didn't explain why *now*. She simply leaned against our granite kitchen island, the sharp scent of gardenias hanging heavy around us, and said, *I need to go home.*

And somehow, *I* turned into *we*, and now the three of us crossed over the murky Bardell River, heading deeper into the city's east side. We ended up in a neighborhood filled with scruffy houses and slumped trailers with tangles of weeds sprouting along their walkways. Old people lounged on front porches, fanning the August humidity away and staring curiously at our BMW. Bardell felt suffocatingly small, the complete opposite of DC. If I sank any lower, I'd be on the floor.

"Home sweet home," Mom said as she turned onto Sweetness Lane. The irony of the name wasn't lost on any of us as we crept down the pothole-riddled street and stopped in front of a weathered brown house. In the cracked driveway sat a faded indigo hatchback with missing hubcaps that looked like it hadn't transported anybody anywhere in a very long time. Mom cut the engine.

"Ready?"

"You and Avery go ahead," Dad said. "I'll grab some bags."

I unbuckled my seat belt and reluctantly followed Mom. Sweat dripped down my bare neck, and I wiped it away in disgust. I was tempted to strip off my jeans and run through the misty spray of the sprinkler next door but swallowed the urge with a grin. I could already hear Kelsi telling me a public indecency charge wouldn't look good on my Georgetown application.

"House looks the same," Mom said. "Do you remember it, Avery baby?"

We climbed the splintered steps to the front porch. A dingy white rocking chair and a hanging swing—both in desperate need of a paint job—were frozen in the muggy heat. I took it all in, trying to conjure decade-old memories of the last time I was here. There was nothing but haze and Christmas lights.

"Not really," I said.

Mom rang the doorbell and started fiddling with her dangly earrings, her signature nervous tic. "I guess it has been a while," she said quietly.

After a full minute went by with no answer, Mom knocked on the barred screen door, angling her palm so her nails didn't clip the rusted metal. Dad dragged a couple of suitcases down the sidewalk, his shoulder-length brown hair already damp with sweat.

"Don't tell me she's already dead," he said. "We just got here."

Mom glared. "Can you please refrain from making jokes about my elderly mother right now?" She continued to rattle the screen door, and I hid my smile by wandering over to the large picture window with a missing shutter. Through the cracked blinds, I made out a plaid sofa, wood-paneled walls, and a stack of newspapers piled high on a tasseled ottoman. But no Mama Letty.

"I'm calling the cops. She really could be dead," Mom said, pulling her phone from her leather handbag. Before she could dial, a booming voice echoed from the blue house next door.

"Zora? I'll be damned!"

A Black woman with long braids made her way across the lawn. Dad and I glanced at each other, then at Mom, expecting some kind of introduction, but her mouth stayed clamped shut as the stranger joined us on the porch.

"Can't say hi?" the woman asked. "Your family don't speak?"

Dad glanced at Mom, but she was frozen. He stuck his hand out. "Nice to meet you. I'm Sam Anderson, Zora's husband."

Finally, something flickered in Mom's eyes. "Carole . . . hi. I almost didn't recognize you with the braids."

"Gave up them perms a long time ago." The woman's gaze trailed Mom's chiffon sundress. "Nice to see you got my letter. How many years since you been home? Fifteen? Sixteen?"

"Not that long," Mom said swiftly. She clapped her hand over my shoulder and thrust me forward like a carnival prize. "Carole, you remember my daughter, Avery?"

"Hi," I said.

"She was a little thing the last time y'all were here." Carole's gaze lingered on my lip piercing, and my cheeks burned. It was a spur-of-the-moment decision I gifted myself in June, after Kelsi and Hikari vetoed me shaving my head. *Think about how it'll look,* they urged, although I had and it was exactly why I wanted to do it. The tiny metal hoop was supposed to be a compromise, but Hikari and Kelsi had regarded it with as much disdain as Carole was serving now. *It looks trashy,* Kelsi had said with a disappointed frown. Now, I ran my tongue over the metal and stared at the dirt peeking between the porch slats.

Carole moved on from her examination, asking Mom again if she was *sure* it hadn't been fifteen years since her last visit, surely it had to have been. Mom grinned and grunted, smiling in relief when Carole turned her attention to wondering why her daughter hadn't come out to say hi.

"Teenagers. Always on that damn phone." Carole sighed. "*Simone Josephine Cole!*"

The screen door of the blue house flew open and a short, curvy girl with shoulder-length locs and a bright tie-dyed shirt emerged. "I'm coming!" she yelled, yanking out a pair of earphones.

"I don't know who you talking to in that tone," Carole chided as Simone joined us on the porch. "Have you lost your mind?"

Simone sighed. "No, ma'am."

"You probably don't remember Ms. Zora since she ain't been home in about fifteen years. She Letty's girl. Y'all, this my youngest, Simone."

Simone shook Mom's hand. "Nice to meet you slash see you again." Her warm voice sounded like honey dripping off the comb. She shook Dad's hand before sliding her palm in mine. Like her mother, her gaze lingered on my lip piercing, and I heard Kelsi's voice again, calling it trashy.

"Lord, you know I wouldn't have written," Carole said, "if Letty's cancer wasn't eating her away. It's worse as I ever seen it."

Mom swallowed. "Well, that's why we're here. But she's not answering the door."

Carole waved her hand. "Poor thing probably taking a nap. She usually lay down around three." She pulled keys from the pocket of her frayed shorts and opened the screen door. Mom fiddled with her earring again.

The stench of old socks and stale grease greeted us in the living room. Simone left to wake Mama Letty, and I took in the piles of notebooks and faded newspapers crowding the ottoman and side tables. Flashes of my first and only visit to Bardell came to me slowly as I made a quiet lap around the room, surveying a stack of wrinkled catalogues on the floor and foggy glasses of water on the coffee table. There was an oversized floral armchair in the corner, and I had vague memories of my small fingers tracing one of the roses and wondering why the furniture was covered in plastic. I remembered a stack of gold-foil-wrapped presents in a pile near the rabbit-eared television. When I looked up and saw Mom's tear-rimmed eyes, I heard echoes of screams. But it was fleeting and faint, vanishing like a dream dissipating with sunrise.

"I should've come sooner," Mom said. "This is . . ." She bit her lip. Dad and I stepped forward to rub her back, and she shot us grateful smiles.

"Bless your heart, Zora." Carole clucked her tongue. "You ain't know how bad it was? After everything?"

Mom stayed quiet. A fierce protectiveness burned red-hot in my stomach.

"Shame that job of yours keeps you too busy to come home," Carole went on. "What is it you do again?"

"I teach," Mom said, swatting away her three degrees, her Georgetown tenure, her bestselling nonfiction book, and her superstar status as a nationally renowned astrophysicist as if they were yesterday's weather report. Dr. Zora Anderson enraptured auditoriums full of pensive students and eager journalists full of questions. She was able to make science sound interesting to even the most reluctant learner. She could describe the process of how a stellar black hole was formed and you'd swear you were floating among the stars, watching it happen for yourself. She was not the type of woman to wilt under anyone's words. Which is why Dad and I gaped when she turned away from Carole's taunting gaze and started flipping through a creased book of crossword puzzles.

"Well, good for you," Carole said. "Nice of you to make time to come home."

Those felt like fighting words, so I stepped forward. I'd had enough. But before I could say anything, Simone reappeared.

"Look who I woke up," she sang. The warped hardwood floor creaked behind her, followed by a series of low grumbles.

Mama Letty had arrived.

She wore a rumpled pink nightgown and a pair of ratty house slippers that might've been white ten years ago. She and Mom shared the same rich mahogany skin and high cheekbones, but Mama Letty's were more pronounced because of how thin she was. She blinked away crust as her eyes traveled over everyone in the living room. *Pissed* was the only word to describe her expression.

"Hey, Mama." Mom set the crossword book down. She met Mama Letty and wrapped her in the most awkward hug of all time. Mama Letty's arms hung limply at her sides before she patted Mom on the back twice. Mom peeled away, her face a mixture of hurt and confusion.

"Sorry we woke you," Mom said, tenderly giving Mama Letty's short gray curls a fluff.

Mama Letty waved her hand away. "No matter. I'm up now." We locked eyes, and her chilly gaze sent another memory ricocheting back.

I was six. Or five? Was it Christmas when Mom and I visited? Or New Year's? I only remembered the presents. I had a vision of Mama Letty throwing one of those shiny gold-wrapped boxes against the wall, fast as a shooting star. I heard the echoes of screams again. I saw a vast field of clouds outside of an airplane window.

"I know this ain't Avery," Mama Letty said now. She followed Carole and Simone's lead and zeroed in on my lip ring. "Out here looking like a fish caught on a hook. She a lesbian now, too?"

It was a thousand degrees in the living room, but a cold sweat gathered on the nape of my neck. I found the floor again, defenses hardening in my stomach. Any minuscule hope I had of this move being a good thing vanished. Mama Letty was nothing but a rude, grumpy woman. She was nothing like Dad's late mom, Grandma Jean, who would've baked me a cake if I'd come out when she'd been alive.

"Mama Letty," Dad started, "maybe a discussion about Avery's sexuality isn't appro—"

"No one asked your white hippie ass," Mama Letty snapped, not even looking at him.

Always the good sport, Dad ran a hand through his hair and shrugged. We had to be thinking the same thing: No wonder Mom left Bardell as soon as she could.

Mom's smile wavered. "Mama, what has gotten into you?"

"Oh, I'm sorry, Zora, would you prefer a little dance number to welcome you back?" Mama Letty shuffled over to the couch, dust pluming when she sat.

Carole chuckled in the corner, and I glared at her. *No one* ganged up on my mom. Not so-called family, and especially not people she hadn't seen in years.

"Mom, Dad, did you want to go grab the rest of the bags?"

I asked. Maybe outside of the scrutinizing gaze of Mama Letty and Carole, I could convince them that maybe this was all a mistake. Clearly, we weren't wanted.

"Make Simone go with you," Mama Letty said. "She need to work off all that cornbread."

Simone scoffed and pulled my arm before I could respond. Humidity slapped us in the face when we stepped outside.

"Come on, DC," Simone called as she sauntered down the sidewalk. My anger faded slightly when my gaze landed on her thick thighs; they filled every inch of her jean shorts. Of course I followed her.

"Um, sorry about that," I said to her back.

"Sorry about what?"

"My grandma. She's . . ." I searched for the right word, but I couldn't think of anything that could explain Mama Letty's rude comments. How do you apologize for someone you don't even know? In the Anderson family, shit was talked behind backs and closed doors. Mama Letty's snipes were as wide and outside as the sun. Then again, she wasn't an Anderson.

"She's what?" Simone prodded. "Stunningly beautiful? A grumpy old kook? A wolf in a pink nightgown? Take your pick."

I smiled, shook my head. "You don't need to work off any cornbread."

She laughed and it was all dimples. "Aw, she was basically telling me she loved me. Don't mind Mama Letty." My grandmother's name rolled off her tongue in one languid swoop.

I popped the trunk and hauled a duffel bag out. Simone

leaned to grab a suitcase, and our arms accidentally brushed. She jerked away; I tried not to take it personally.

"Do you know what school you'll be at?" she asked.

"Whichever one requires a uniform." Mom ordered the atrocious red plaid skirt and sad white polo before we left DC.

"Nice. You'll be at Beckwith. The more, the merrier!"

"More of . . . what?"

She tapped the brown skin of her fist. "Black people. African Americans. People of color. Y'all got a better term up in DC?"

Shame pinched my chest at the easy way she included me in the tally for Black people. It brought back the horrible, ugly fight that ultimately led to my breakup with Kelsi. I could still see her puckered pink mouth forming the words, *You're barely Black*. How I'd carried them for almost two months now, like a set of keys in my back pocket. Trying to brush the memory away, I joked, "What is this, 1955?"

"It's Beckwith." She said it as if it needed no further explanation and rolled the suitcase down the cracked walkway. I followed, actively ignoring her thighs this time. Instead, I focused on her locs. They were shoulder-length, black with electric-blue tips, and adorned with gold charms and shells. I was staring so hard, I nearly ran into her when she stopped and turned around.

"What's your sun?"

"My what?"

"Your astrological sun sign," she said impatiently.

"Uhhh . . . Capricorn?"

She hummed. "Good to know. Did that hurt?"

"Did what hurt?"

She ran her index finger over her plump bottom lip. "The piercing. Did it hurt?"

My tongue slid over it self-consciously. "Oh. Yeah. I guess." I braced myself for another reaction like Hikari's and Kelsi's, but then Simone smiled and told me she liked it. I momentarily forgot I'd been forced to this crappy town to reside with my cranky grandmother who hated everything that moved.

As we set the bags on the porch, Carole stepped outside and told Simone to go finish the dishes.

Simone cast me a sideways glance. "See you later?"

"Apparently."

She started for her house, leaving soft footprints in the wet summer grass.

"So," Carole said as we watched Simone head inside, "Avery. What you think of Bardell so far? You like it?"

"It's okay," I said stiffly. Saying as little as possible around her seemed like the safest option.

"It's been a long time since your mama been home."

My annoyance flared again. "Well, we're just here to help."

"Here to help." She rested her hands on her hips. Her fingers were empty of jewelry and full of scars, nails cut to the quick. She walked off with a laugh, mumbling to herself, "Here to help. Well, it's about time."

THE GHOST

THERE WERE APPROXIMATELY fifty people who resided in the sixteen homes that dotted Sweetness Lane, and all of them had heard the joke at one point or another. Out-of-town relatives, visiting friends, and mail carriers would examine the gaping potholes and pale patchwork lawns and homes that seemed to sag into the earth and ask, *Sweetness? Where?* Residents would laugh or roll their eyes or, if you dared to utter these comments in the presence of Letty June Harding, tell you to shut the fuck up. It didn't matter what Sweetness Lane looked like. Sweetness Lane was home. And home was always sweet.

Carole Cole had lived on Sweetness Lane since she was Carole Thompson. The blue brick ranch with the dogwood tree in the side yard was the only home she'd ever known. Darryl Cole had grumbled when he moved in after their wedding, complaining that grown men had no business moving into their mother-in-law's house. He promised one day they'd leave. But since the house was there and Darryl's funds were not, they stayed. They stayed after their first two babies were born, even though the eight hundred square feet became bloated with toddler screams. They stayed after Martha Thompson passed and left them the home in her will. They stayed even when the third baby took them by surprise. It wasn't until their three children became two that Darryl finally made good on his promise and left.

Through it all, Carole remained tethered to Sweetness Lane like a life raft. Seasons changed. People came and went. Her youngest daughter braided flower crowns under the dogwood tree. Usually, Carole would gaze upon the lane and think, *This is fine. This is good enough.* Occasionally, she thought about the girl who used to live next door and wondered what she was up to. Sometimes she thought about writing her. It wasn't until Letty's third round of cancer that she finally did.

By the time Carole devised a letter she was proud of, she'd burned through four days and half a notebook. After several weeks with no reply, she'd almost given up hope. On a particularly steamy August afternoon, Carole was sweeping her kitchen and minding her business when a fancy silver car arrived on Sweetness Lane. Fancy cars on this block were not a common occurrence, so Carole stopped mid-sweep. She paid attention. And when a ghost from her childhood emerged from the driver's side, she nearly dropped her broom.

2.

BY THE TIME I hauled the last bag inside, Mama Letty had retreated to her bedroom. I followed my parents' voices into the small, sun-drenched kitchen, mind still swimming from Simone's and Carole's comments.

Mom was leaning against the chipped tile counter, eyes trained on the peeling yellow diamond wallpaper. Dad sat at a circular Formica table shoved up against the window, drumming his fingers along a glass of water. Above his head was a creepy black cat-shaped clock, hands stuck at midnight.

"I didn't know," Mom said. She scrubbed a hand over her face and took deep, labored breaths. It was the same technique she always used before a big speech, the one she taught me when I was losing sleep over a public speaking assignment in eighth grade: inhale on the one, exhale on the two, continue to ten, lather, rinse, repeat. I cleared my throat, and my parents looked up with fake, stretched smiles.

"Hey, Avery baby," Mom said, too chipper. "Thanks for grabbing the rest of the bags."

"Don't mention it." I took a step closer. "You okay?"

She nodded. "I haven't seen your Mama Letty in a while, and it's hard. I'm sorry."

"You don't have to apologize," I said, but it was no use. She was already composing herself, wiping the emotions from her face like Windex on glass. Soon, she was Dr. Zora Anderson again—calm, collected, close to perfect.

"You're in luck," she said, pulling at one of my spiral curls. "You're getting my old bedroom. Best room in the house." She brushed past me before I could say anything and busied herself with the suitcases in the living room.

I looked at Dad. "What's going on?"

"What's going on," Dad said, "is that we lovingly agreed to take the luxurious pull-out couch in the back den to give you some privacy."

I narrowed my eyes. He knew that wasn't what I meant. "Dad, seriously. What is *up* with Mom and Mama Letty?"

His smile dimmed. "They'll be fine. It's going to be a trying time, but remember what we talked about?"

"We're here for support," I parroted. "And this situation is temporary."

"Exactly. All of this is temporary. We'll stay out of Mama Letty's way, and everything will be fine."

I wanted to press further, but based on Mom's disappearance and the return of Dad's wisecracking smile, I was out of luck for now. So I nodded, the ever-dutiful daughter.

Dad clapped my shoulder. "Anderson family motto?"

"Focus forward."

"Focus forward!" He pointed down the hall, past Mama Letty's closed door. "Your room's that way."

• • •

Entering Mom's old bedroom felt like stepping thirty years back in time. Dozens of textbooks and sci-fi novels crowded the built-ins along the wall. The dingy yellow carpet smelled faintly of mildew. Posters of Janet Jackson and Whitney Houston covered the wood-paneled closet doors. Above the bed was a glossy diagram of the solar system, poor little Pluto hovering at the edge, unaware of her fate.

I tossed my duffel bag on the floor and wandered over to the rolltop desk wedged in the corner. I gave the plastered window two strong pulls, sneezing as dirt and dust drifted into my nostrils. With a final push, the room flooded with sunlight. I had the perfect view of the side of the Coles' house. The image of Simone's finger trailing her lip flashed through my mind. I quickly shut it down and plopped into the desk chair.

I would not—*could not*—go down that road. Not after my breakup with Kelsi, not on this MAGA turf. Besides. Simone was probably straight. Probably dating some buff guy on the football team—if Beckwith Academy even *had* a football team. I took a deep breath and grounded myself like Mom taught me, replaying my conversation with Dad.

Focus forward. The Anderson family motto had gotten me through every roadblock in my life. When Grandma Jean died in eighth grade, I kept the sadness at bay by crafting the perfect life plan to make her proud. I set my sights on straight As and a Georgetown acceptance—focus forward. During the pandemic,

I gritted my teeth as I watched my high school experience slip away one canceled plan at a time—focus forward. I clung to the motto as I watched the nightly news in horror, telling myself things would eventually get better, that they had to. I had to keep my focus forward. Same as I had to see this stint in Bardell through.

Get in. Get out. No drama. Focus forward.

My phone buzzed in my pocket, and I rolled my eyes. Kelsi and Hikari hadn't stopped texting, even though I hadn't replied since a rest stop in Virginia. They were making good on their promise that our friendship wouldn't change after Kelsi and I broke up, even though things were clearly not the same. They were trying to re-create the magic that had glued the three of us together since freshman year, either unaware or choosing to ignore my icy aloofness. I scrolled through the new messages and felt nothing.

Hikari: Yooo I got Lentz for AP Comp fml.

Kelsi: She gives great rec letters tho.

Hikari: Avery where you at? Have you made it to the land down under?

Kelsi: I still can't believe you won't be here this year.

Hikari: Kels who did you get for AP Chem?

Kelsi: Jones for Chem. Toth for AP Physics.

Hikari: Can't believe you're taking both.

"Neck gone get stuck staring at that phone all day."

I looked up to see Mama Letty leaning against the doorframe. Her eyes combed over my new bedroom, somehow ending on my lip ring again. I awkwardly stood.

"Hi, Mama Letty. How are you feeling? Anything you need?"

"I need a lot of things," she said, crossing the room in light strides. "None of which yo ass can get." She stopped at one of the bookshelves and grabbed a small wooden box with a gold clasp from the top shelf. She didn't look at me as she ran a hand over the lid. Staring at the side of her face caused another splotchy memory to appear, as soft as a bubble blowing from a wand.

Christmas lights. Mama Letty's hair more black than gray. Her wrinkled brown fingers clutching a box like this one. Screams.

"What's in the box?" I asked.

She shot me an icy gaze. "Your mama raise you to be this nosy?"

I folded my arms over my chest. "Didn't realize it was a secret."

She snorted and left the room as quietly as she arrived. Her bedroom door slammed seconds later, and I slumped in the chair again. I had a nagging feeling that Dad's definition of a "trying time" wouldn't hold a candle to Mama Letty.

"Temporary," I whispered. "All of this . . . is temporary."

• • •

I spent the next two days unpacking and settling into the small, strange quiet of Bardell. In DC, my life was loud and expansive, full of Mom's domed planetarium lectures and Dad's jazz piano melodies padding every corner of our row house. The gridded streets of the city hummed with busy people, honking traffic, and pulsing energy, whereas the noises that comprised Mama Letty's home could be contained in a thimble. Crickets chirped all night. Mama Letty's coughs blended in with her groaning rocking chair. Mom sighed loudly from the den every fifteen minutes.

I was lonely. As an only child, I was used to finding ways to entertain myself. In DC, that usually meant going around the corner to Hikari's house to lounge by her backyard firepit. But in Bardell, there was nothing but me and my thoughts and a growing resentment toward Hikari and Kelsi I still couldn't name. My silence toward them finally broke when I texted them my class schedule the afternoon before the first day of school. They ridiculed my course load, like I knew they would.

Kelsi: 10th grade called, Hicktown High. They want their classes back.

Hikari: Only 3 APs???

Kelsi: you think Georgetown will still take you?

Hikari: Totally. It's not Avery's fault she had to change schools.

I thought about texting something snarky back. Something like, *hey bitches, my grandmother is DYING.* There were more important things to worry about than stupid AP classes. But I stayed silent because although they were annoying me, I understood why they cared so much.

COVID had taken a giant shit all over our grand high school plans. As starry-eyed freshmen, we imagined becoming officers in important clubs. We thought about the volunteer work that would push our college applications over the edge and made bets on who would get the highest PSAT score. Instead, what we got were clusterfucked virtual classes and half-hearted attempts at online extracurriculars. The experience ignited a fire that burned in the three of us equally to make the most out of senior year and beyond.

We had a plan. Three Georgetown acceptances, a triple room. Kelsi and Hikari were going pre-law, inspired after too many binges of *How to Get Away with Murder*. I was supposed to follow in my mother's footsteps and study the stars. But somewhere between the needle sinking into my lower lip and Kelsi's "We Should Just Be Friends" speech, my spark for academics—and Kelsi and Hikari—had extinguished.

There was a swift knock on my door, and Mom poked her head in. Her tight coils were covered in a gorgeous royal-blue headwrap. "Hey, Avery baby."

"Hey, Mom."

She swept into the room, ivory linen dress swirling around her ankles. "Love what you've done with the place," she said, and we laughed because there wasn't much that would improve the unremarkable room short of tearing it down and starting all over.

"No point in getting too comfortable, right?" I asked.

She looked around the room, eyes softening when they landed on the bookcases. She pulled a tall, skinny book from the shelf and joined me on the bed. She smelled like she always did—jojoba oil, vanilla, summertime. It was nice to have this small, familiar thing when everything else felt off-center.

"I'm surprised you haven't uncovered this yet," she said, leafing through the pages.

"What is it?"

She showed me the forest-green cover. *Bardell High School Yearbook, 1984–1985* was etched in silver block letters.

"Baby Mom!" I examined the senior class pages, hunting for Mom's perfect white smile and almond-brown eyes. After mistakenly searching for Zora Anderson, I found her under the Hs— *Zora Rayla Harding*. Over thirty years later, and she still looked the same. I traced her maiden name with my index finger. "It's so weird to see you with a different last name."

"What was weird was changing it when I married your dad. I was a Harding longer than I've been an Anderson, you know."

I turned the page, giggling at the hairstyles of decades past. "Is Ms. Carole in here?"

Mom didn't say anything as she flipped to the Ts. Carole Judith Thompson beamed proudly in the center of the page.

"I don't remember her from when we visited last time," I said.

"You were only five."

I thought about hazy string lights and shiny gold presents. "Did we come around Christmas?"

"New Year's." Mom frowned at Carole's picture and closed the book.

"What happened?" I asked. "During that visit? I don't remember much of it."

Mom exhaled and returned the book to the shelf. "Nothing really. We came for a quick visit so Mama could meet you."

"Must not have made a good impression considering she still wants nothing to do with me," I joked. Which I didn't necessarily mind. She responded to my passing greetings in the hallway with mild grunts, and I left her alone to do her crossword puzzles. Win-win.

Mom pursed her lips. "It's been two days. Give it time. In

fact, why don't you go keep her company while your father and I get dinner ready?"

"*You're* cooking?" That visual felt as incredulous as me and Mama Letty skipping hand-in-hand down Sweetness Lane. My parents didn't *do* cooking. At home, we had an entire drawer dedicated to Indian and pizza takeout menus and colorful magnets from every sushi restaurant in a five-mile radius decorating our fridge.

Mom flicked my lip ring, lightning-quick. "Don't be a smart-ass. It's not becoming of you."

"Ow! I was just saying!"

"Go keep your Mama Letty company while your father and I go *pick up* dinner."

"But—"

"Porch. Now."

I huffily followed Mom to the living room, and she pointed to the porch. Outside, Mama Letty eased back and forth in the rocking chair.

"Go talk to her," Mom said.

"Thoughts and prayers," Dad chimed from the kitchen. Mom shot him a look and told him to shut up and grab the keys.

I braced myself for Mama Letty's attitude and pushed open the screen door. Mom and Dad blew kisses and made a beeline for the car.

"Hey, Mama Letty." I sat on the hanging swing opposite her. "How's it going?"

Her eyes flicked up from her crossword puzzle. "Fine."

I watched reluctantly as the BMW made a slow U-turn and disappeared down the lane. I tried to calculate how much longer I had to stay before I could politely excuse myself. Even with the golden afternoon melting into evening, it was unbearably hot. The muggy air felt like a drenched washcloth waiting to be twisted.

"It's hot," I said.

Mama Letty grunted. I fiddled with my lip ring, patience waning. I tried again.

"I was telling Mom how I don't remember much from my first visit here."

She raised an eyebrow. "You were three. 'Course you don't remember shit."

"Mom said I was five."

"Same thing." She slipped a pack of cigarettes and a silver lighter from the pocket of her gray cotton capris. My eyes bulged.

"Do you think it's a good idea to smoke when you're . . ." I watched as her wrinkled fingers struggled to ignite a flame. When it caught, she inhaled deeply.

"Say it." She grinned through white smoke. "Dying? This ain't gonna change nothing."

I kneaded my fists into my thighs. The conversation suddenly felt way out of bounds of my light pre-dinner chat obligation.

"You gonna tell Zora on me, Fish?" she asked with a smirk.

"Fish?"

She motioned to my lip ring, and my cheeks burned,

remembering her earlier comment. *Out here looking like a fish caught on a hook.*

Words failed when I met her taunting gaze. My back stiffened against the swing.

"That's what I thought." She inhaled again. We settled into another uncomfortable silence. It was the complete opposite of the familiarity I used to have with Grandma Jean. Being in Mama Letty's presence felt like quaking under the scrutiny of a Newport-smoking Sunday school teacher.

I was debating between one more shot at conversation or running inside when a pearl-white Jeep rumbled down Sweetness Lane and stopped in front of the Coles' house. Seconds later, Simone bolted outside, locs flying behind her in an electric-blue whirl. The Jeep's roof and doors were missing, so Simone used the frame to haul herself into the passenger seat. There was a burst of laughter from the driver, a white girl with a mane of messy blonde curls. Mama Letty and I watched as the Jeep lurched forward, pop music and chatter amplifying, and stopped at the end of our driveway. Simone stood and gripped the frame of the roof.

"Avery! Come here a sec!"

I looked at Mama Letty. She looked at me.

"My name ain't Avery," she muttered before returning to her crossword.

"Come on!" Simone yelled. "We ain't gonna bite!"

The pop music dimmed to a dull roar as I made my way down the walkway. The driver studied me, ice-blue eyes shining behind thick, clear glasses. Simone sat and leaned over her.

"Jade, meet Avery, aka DC. DC, this is my best friend, Jade. Come hang out with us tonight."

Jade gave me a smile that teetered between polite and aloof. She looked like the type of white girl who lived for pumpkin spice lattes and had a pretty brown horse named Trinity or Diesel. A gleaming heart-shaped locket rested in the hollow of her neck.

"Nice to meet you," she said, voice as light as wind chimes. I imagined her around a bonfire, strumming a guitar, telling her youth church group to come on, y'all, sing along with her.

"Hi," I said.

"Come on, get in. Ya girl has a curfew," Simone whined.

I glanced over my shoulder. On the porch, Mama Letty penned in a crossword answer, cigarette still balanced between her lips. "I'm kind of busy."

Simone snorted. "Doing *what*? Capricorns aren't usually liars. What's your rising?" She leaned closer, and Jade sighed the sigh of someone who'd been through this a thousand times.

"I don't know," I said.

"She said she's busy," Jade said. "We should let her get settled in."

"But it's a new moon tonight," Simone said. "We're setting our intentions for the school year." She pointed to the junky back seat, which still had plenty of room for me. I had the slightest tingle in my chest when I imagined joining them.

"I—" I hesitated, remembering the mantra I told myself not even forty-eight hours earlier.

Get in. Get out. No drama. Focus forward.

"I'm good," I said firmly. "Thanks though."

Simone shrugged. "Suit yourself. You should definitely take the time tonight to set some intentions privately. New moon energy is powerful, boo."

I laughed, taking myself by surprise. Jade shook her head, a smile tugging on her lips. They waved goodbye and hit a U-turn at the dead end before peeling off, music returning to ear-shattering volume. I stood in their dust, heart skittering in my chest.

When I turned back to the house, I realized Carole had joined Mama Letty, much to my disappointment. I took my time walking back, in no rush to dodge more of her back-handed comments.

"Those girls," Carole was saying as I drew closer. She was pulling at the neck of her stiff white collared shirt. *Syrup* was embroidered in gold lettering above her name tag.

Mama Letty stubbed her cigarette out. "Can't believe you still let them hang out."

"What am I supposed to do, Letty? They been friends since they were girls." She frowned and looked at her watch. "I gotta go. Lucas will have my ass if I'm late again. Call me if Simone's not home by nine."

Mama Letty grunted. Carole's gaze flickered to me like she just realized I was standing there. She gave me a curt nod before heading to her car.

I sat on the porch steps and watched the sky slip into a purple-rose ombré. I could still feel the hum of the Jeep's engine in my chest. They seemed like such an interesting pair, Simone and Jade. Jade looked like she attended extravagant cotillions in fluffy white dresses, while Simone felt like the human equivalent of a rainbow. Jade seemed cool, calculated, skin as pale as her blonde curls. Simone was full of color, inviting, and probably capable of making people stop in their tracks. I ran my fingers over the worn rubber soles of my Chucks.

"Why doesn't Ms. Carole like Simone and Jade hanging out?" I asked.

When Mama Letty didn't answer, I tore my eyes from the sky and looked at her. She was studying me, twirling her pen between her lanky fingers.

"What?" I asked. "Is that another one of your 'secrets'?"

An unreadable grin bloomed on her face. "Be careful with all them questions you're asking," she said. "Might fuck around and actually learn something." And instead of explaining what she meant, she lit another cigarette.

3.

THE NEXT MORNING, I showed up for breakfast in an itchy white polo and an ugly red plaid skirt that fell past my knees—the official Beckwith Academy uniform. Dad chuckled into his coffee, clearly eager to tease. Mom was deep in focus, trying to make sure the sizzling pancakes on the electric griddle didn't burn. She spared a quick glance.

"You look cute," she said. "I'll hem the skirt later. Go wake Mama Letty so she can take her pills."

"Peace be with you," Dad whispered when my shoulders slumped. After our fizzled conversation on the porch, my decision to give Mama Letty a wide berth had become even more cemented. Dad saluted as I trudged out of the kitchen.

I knocked twice on her bedroom door. "Mama Letty? Breakfast time."

No reply. I placed my ear on the door. Nothing. I knocked again and, fearing the worst, slowly twisted the knob. "Mama Letty?"

I stepped into the empty room. It was barely big enough to

fit a lumpy full-sized bed and TV stand, but felt smaller thanks to a massive amount of clutter. The stained, graying carpet was covered in mounds of dirty clothes and Styrofoam containers. Piles of old newspapers overflowed from nearly every surface and the pink flowered wallpaper peeled and curled near the water-stained ceiling. I caught a whiff of something rancid and pushed down the urge to vomit.

"Hell you doing in here, Fish?"

I whirled around to find Mama Letty in the doorway, gripping her frayed yellow bathrobe closed. Her footsteps were *freakishly* quiet.

"Find what you were looking for?" she asked.

"Mom said it's time to take your pills."

Mama Letty grunted and shuffled into the room, maneuvering around the clutter with ease. She mumbled instructions to close the door. I cast a forlorn glance to the hallway before I obliged. She sat on her bed and pulled out a cigarette.

"Still haven't kicked the habit I see," I said.

"Over fifty years in the making." She shifted on the bed. A slew of crossword puzzles fell to the floor.

"Guess Mom didn't get her impeccable cleanliness from you."

Mama Letty smirked. "No. But I see you inherited her smart-ass mouth."

The air between us pulsed with tension. Then, miraculously, we laughed. I swiped a finger over her dresser, tracing a line through the dust.

"Seriously, Mama Letty, it can't be healthy to live like this. I can help you clean up."

She grunted. "I ain't worried about health."

"Well, Mom is. So come take your pills."

She flicked ash on her nightstand. "You stubborn. Like your grandfather." Her next inhale sent her into a coughing fit, and I cringed as she hacked into a blood-spattered handkerchief. She spotted the horror that flitted across my face. "Save your pity. I get enough from your mother."

"It's not pity," I said, although I wasn't sure if I was lying. Besides, I was still stuck on one word.

Grandfather.

I tugged at a curl. "What were you saying about my grandfather?"

"You stubborn like him."

"I thought . . ." I stopped because I realized how insulting the rest of that sentence would be. *I thought you didn't know him.* So I racked my brain, trying to recall anything Mom had shared about my grandfather, but there wasn't much.

She was always tense when June arrived and rolling fields of Father's Day cards sprouted in the aisles of Target. She'd begrudgingly helped me complete a family tree for an elementary school project. On the *Paternal Grandfather* branch, I drew roses for Grandpa Don, who'd passed away from liver cancer when I was two. Then, with my pencil hovering over the *Maternal Grandfather* branch, I looked to Mom for guidance.

Leave it blank, she'd said. *I didn't know him. Just . . . leave it blank.*

I'd freaked, fretting over an incomplete assignment, imagining the blank space on the top of the page where my gold star should've gone. But my teacher didn't care when I explained the situation. She told me not to be ashamed. *Some people aren't around, Avery.* I got my gold star anyway.

"I'm not surprised," Mama Letty said now, "that she didn't tell you."

"Tell me what?"

"About Ray." She puffed on her cigarette. "Your grandfather."

Curiosity took over. I traced an *R* in the dresser dust. *Ray.*

"What happened to him?" I asked. "Do you have a picture?"

She stubbed her cigarette in a chipped porcelain ashtray and shook her head. "Not now. Go get them pills."

"But . . ." I had so many questions. Who was this Ray? And why was this the first time I'd ever heard his name?

"The pills," she grunted. "Now."

I sighed. "Fine. Breakfast and meds for one grumpy lady coming right up." I left to the sounds of her chuckling.

In the kitchen, Mom was shoveling something in the trash with a sheepish smile. Dad pushed a box of Frosted Flakes across the table.

"There was an incident with the pancakes," he said somberly. "We don't want to talk about it. They were good men."

"Pancakes are beyond gender," I said, and Dad laughed. Mom sighed and handed me milk and an empty bowl.

"So, Unsavory," Dad said. "I have a proposition for you. How would you like to come to DC with me this weekend?"

I paused, milk carton in midair. "This weekend?"

"I have a gig. And some leftover flight credits thanks to Ms. COVID. You can join me if you want."

Dad was a founding member of Last Supper, one of the most in-demand jazz bands in the DMV. Weddings, reunions, bat mitzvahs—he played them all and then some. I pushed my spoon around my bowl, contemplating what I'd do with forty-eight hours back home. Sleepover at Hikari's, probably. We'd slather our faces in her mom's Korean beauty products and Kelsi would plead to take virtual tours of all the Ivies *again* and we'd gossip about how we *still* couldn't believe Amira Tankler didn't get into Yale last year even though she'd talked about no other college since middle school.

"Somehow I thought you'd be more excited," Dad said.

"I am," I said quickly. "Um, yeah. That sounds good."

"You *could* stay here and spend time with your Mama Letty," Mom added.

"And you could've *not* burned the pancakes." I made a show out of slurping my cereal. "Yet here we are."

• • •

Even though it housed kindergarten through twelfth grade, Beckwith Academy was less than half the size of my old school. And calling it an *academy* was a stretch—Kelsi's nickname, Hicktown High, was more accurate. It was a squat, single-story tan building with tiny windows. The only academy-worthy element was a giant bronze statue of some old man in the front courtyard, who held a notebook and gazed fondly at the school like a long-lost lover. Students lounged at its base, exchanging schedules and swapping summer stories. As I approached, I tried smiling at a few people. When the fourth person regarded me like I'd been dropped into Bardell via spacecraft, I reverted to full Resting Bitch Face, trying to ignore the awkward loneliness I was unfortunately growing accustomed to.

Get in. Get out. No drama. Focus forward.

"Yo, DC!"

Simone's voice sliced across the courtyard as a bell trilled. Students began trickling toward the front doors, shoulders slumped with the weight of the impending nine months of school. I stood in the middle of it all, searching for Simone's smile amid the sea of white faces and red plaid.

"Hey!"

There was a tug on the end of one of my curls. When I turned around, Simone smiled over a large iced coffee, eyes hidden behind aqua cloud-shaped sunglasses, complete with plastic-chained raindrops that brushed her cheeks. Jade was there too, swirling an iced green something around in a reusable glass thermos. The Beckwith uniforms looked much cuter on them than it did on me. Jade had an assortment of food-shaped pins on her polo collar while Simone's skirt hit above the knees, showing off her shapely legs. They both wore gold wire rings with crystals on their middle fingers, but Simone's had a craggy orange stone while Jade's was smooth, cloudy, and white.

"You getting acquainted with Richie?" Simone asked, nodding to the statue.

"Should I?"

Simone gasped. "*Should* you? Of course! Why, young

inquiring minds can't call themselves Beckwith students without paying homage to our founder, Richard Beckwith!" She pulled me toward the statue, ignoring Jade's insistence that we were going to be late for first period.

"Say hi to Richie," Simone said, rubbing her hand along his shoe. There was a shiny spot on his toe, like it'd been polished clean by thousands of students before her. Simone explained it was for good luck, so I followed suit. I needed all the luck I could get.

"First period," Jade repeated with a sigh.

"Say goodbye to Richie!" Simone sang.

"Bye, Richie," I said.

"Fuck you, Richie," Jade said, and Simone threw her head back in laughter. I looked between them, wondering where I went wrong. Simone looped an arm through mine, and we filed into the fluorescent hallways of school.

"Richard Beckwith," she said in a low voice, "was a giant, racist prick."

I paused. "Then why did we just do that?"

"The good luck isn't for *us*," Jade said.

"It's not?"

"Nope!" Simone said. "It's for him. 'Cause his ass is burning in hell. Coffee?" She tilted her cup in my direction. I shook my head. "Right, right," she said. "Germs, pandemic, got it. What's your first class?"

It was AP History. And as it turned out, it was also Jade and Simone's, and we barely beat the final bell. We slid into three seats in the front row just as an older white woman with bright red glasses ambled into the classroom. She wrote her name—*Mrs. Newland*—in neat block letters on the whiteboard.

She gave the usual speech about how excited she was for the school year, that she hoped we had a good summer. I tuned her out as she passed out the syllabus, choosing to examine the classroom instead. It was even smaller than I expected, maybe fifteen students total. They all seemed to have the easy familiarity of kids who'd known one another since diapers, swapping pencils without asking, answering Mrs. Newland's questions with ease. Simone and I were the only non-white faces in the room.

"Ms. Oliver," Mrs. Newland said, placing a syllabus on Jade's desk. "How is my star pupil?"

Jade beamed, and Simone snorted.

"All of you should take Ms. Oliver as an example," Mrs. Newland told the class. "While the rest of you were out partying all summer, Jade was volunteering with the Bardell Historical Society. The work that she put in—"

A piece of paper sailed my way. At the next desk, Simone wiggled her eyebrows. Of course she was bold enough to pass notes in the front row.

I waited until Mrs. Newland turned around before I opened it. Blue pen–scratched doodles of planets and stars decorated the top. Below, in sloppy cursive—*Did you make use of the new moon, DC?*

I shook my head and she frowned. Mrs. Newland was still talking about Jade.

"—so you *really* should consider volunteering with us at the society. Even a small city like Bardell has a fountain of knowl-edge to drink from! Now, who wants to help pass out text-books?"

"Hey, Simone," a guy in the row behind us whispered. From the corner of my eye, I noticed her tense up, but she ignored him.

"Come on," he said in a whiny whisper. "Si-moan-moan."

"What, Tim?" she hissed.

"Who's your new friend?"

"None of your business."

"She a lesbian?"

Now it was my turn to stiffen. I focused on the fresh page in my notebook, wishing I could magically transport myself back to DC where the faces were familiar and I wasn't the odd one out in a conservative wonderland. Dad's weekend proposal became more appealing by the second, especially when Tim didn't let up.

"Come on," he whispered. "She's gotta be a lesbian since—"

Jade whirled around and gasped dramatically. "Oh my God, Tim, you want to do *what* to Mrs. Newland?"

An awkward hush fell over the class. Mrs. Newland looked up from her computer with beady eyes and asked what was going on. No one answered.

"That's enough ruckus," Mrs. Newland said stiffly. "Let's get to work."

Jade flipped a page in her notebook and clicked her pen. Simone winked at me. Beneath the itchy polo, my heart warmed.

I learned Beckwith's ropes quickly, courtesy of Simone and Jade. They guided me to my next class, sandwiching me like bookends, and told me which bathrooms to avoid and the easiest route to the cafeteria, and warned me that my chemistry teacher was, in Simone's words, "an ole mayonnaise-looking bitch." They invited me to sit with them at lunch and were waiting at the small circular table near a window where they said they would be.

"And two becomes three," Simone said when I sat across from her. She eyed the selections on my red plastic tray and nodded in approval. "Stayed away from the country fried steak. Smart girl."

"Fries seemed like the safest option," I replied.

"You would be correct," Jade said. She was crouched over a napkin, doodling something in purple pen.

Simone promptly launched into a story about how she spent half of gym class going back and forth with her teacher over her hair color. She flipped her blue-tipped locs over her shoulder and sucked her teeth. "Kenslee Wilson had her whole-ass stomach out, but Mr. Donner want to whine about my hair?"

"Did you tell him about himself?" Jade asked.

"No. I put these bitches in a bun and kept it moving. He's not about to mess up my chances at Spelman."

I eased, slightly. Finally, a conversation that felt like familiar territory. "I didn't know you wanted to go to Spelman."

"You *could've* known if you hadn't been too chicken to hang out with us last night," she said.

I dragged a fry through my ketchup and shrugged. "I was busy."

"Hanging out with Mama Letty doing crossword puzzles ain't busy. Admit you were afraid."

I glanced at Jade, hoping for some backup, but her focus was still trained on her napkin doodle. I remembered Mama Letty saying she couldn't believe Carole still allowed Simone and Jade to hang out. Despite my plans to mind my business, I couldn't help but feel a little curious.

"Simone, lay off," Jade said without looking up. "If Avery thinks she's too cool to hang out with us then we have to respect that."

I ran my tongue over my lip ring, fought a grin. "You know that's not what I meant."

"Then prove it," Simone said. "Hang out with us this weekend."

"Can't. I'm going to DC with my dad."

Simone sat back, glossy lips parting in mock shock. "There you have it, Jade. We have not only scared Avery from hanging out with us but have completely run her out of town."

Jade added the final touches on her napkin doodle and spun it around. It was a freckled penguin, ice-skating in a striped hat. "You just got here and you're already leaving?" she asked.

I ate fries while Simone started drawing a scarf around the

penguin's neck. I didn't want to insult their hometown, but honestly . . . who wouldn't jump at the chance to get away from here? I decided to change the subject, hoping they would lay off me.

"What was up with that guy in history?"

Simone's face fell. "You mean Tim Joplin?"

"Ignore him," Jade said. "He's an asshole. Always has been."

"Clearly. I mean, I figured the lip piercing would give me away, but didn't expect that."

"Give what away?" Jade asked.

I vaguely gestured to my face. "That . . . I'm . . . gay?"

Surprise crossed their features, and dread settled in my stomach. I shoved my last fries in my mouth in case they were secretly homophobic and I was about to be banished from the table and left with nowhere to sit. I knew from movies that fries didn't taste too good inside a bathroom stall.

Jade's face softened. "You'll learn to ignore him. He likes to try and get under people's skin because he's insecure. Not everyone here is awful."

"When was the last time you climbed a tree, DC?" Simone asked abruptly.

I startled. Jade went back to her penguin doodle with a small smile, apparently used to Simone's subject changes.

"I don't know," I said. "Elementary school?"

Simone placed a hand on her heart. Her nails were neon green. I was sure they'd been bare this morning, which meant she must've applied a fresh coat sometime between second and fifth period. "Jade, we need to get Avery to the river because this makes no sense. Elementary school? How can you explain that? What the hell did you and your friends do in DC?"

I paused. What did we do, besides fawn over our grades? We ran 5Ks for charities because it would look good on college applications. We attended marches at the Capitol with hand-painted signs and joked about how we'd never see social security money and wondered if Florida would be underwater by the time we were fifty. During the pandemic, we read nonfiction books about diets and psychology and discussed them over video calls. On the rare nights it was just me and Kelsi, we would go for walks around our neighborhood and kiss in the shade of scarlet oak trees.

"I don't know," I said. "Hung out? Watched movies. Normal shit."

"Normal is boring," Simone said.

"So boring," Jade echoed.

The bell blared, and a symphony of scraping chairs filled the cafeteria. Jade handed me the napkin. She'd added two more penguins in the mix; one with locs, the other with thick glasses. On their sweaters were initials—*J, S, A. Welcome to Bardell!* was etched in the ice.

"This is for me?" When she nodded, I suddenly felt like a petty bitch for passing judgment on her so quickly yesterday. "It's so cute."

"It's not that big of a deal," she said, but her cheeks were tinged pink.

"I don't think you should go to DC this weekend," Simone said.

"Why not?"

She pulled her cloud sunglasses from her bag and slipped them on. She ignored a passing teacher who shot her a stern look.

"Do you really need a reason other than the fact we're amazing enough to stick around?"

THE FRESHMAN

THERE WERE TWO high schools that served the young minds of Bardell County, Georgia. According to search engines, there was Beckwith Academy and Bardell High School. According to locals, there was the white school and the Black school.

Bardell High suffered from underfunding, textbook shortages, and exhausted, underpaid teachers. Beckwith Academy had a sculpture studio, a robust study abroad program, and a history stretching back to 1971 when it was founded by white parents in response to school desegregation. Decades later, one school was still overwhelmingly Black; the other, 98 percent white. You didn't need a diploma to infer which school served who.

Simone Cole arrived at Beckwith Academy as a wide-eyed fourteen-year-old on a blistering August day, toes pinched in shiny Mary Janes. It'd been her dream for years to attend Beckwith. Simone had watched her older siblings complain about Bardell High's broken air conditioners and school clubs falling victim to budget cuts. From a young age, Simone thought that

Beckwith would take her to the places she wanted to go in life: Spelman or Howard, political office or med school. On the first day of freshman year, Simone stared at the school and tasted the honeyed sweetness of opportunity on her tongue.

She was accompanied by her mother, Carole, who warily read from the school brochure. They paused by the statue of Richard Beckwith and stared at the man's face, gleaming in the sun. *It says students rub his toe for good luck*, Carole said. And for the next four years, Simone did just that. She'd pass by this revered man who fought for his white children to be separated from her Black ancestors and brush her fingers over the bronze. But this ritual was not for good luck. It was a reminder to herself and Richard that his time was limited. Because one day, Simone would return to Beckwith and tear this man down, even if she had to do it with her bare hands, even if she had to do it alone. She wouldn't rest until the metal shards of this racist man made a home on the concrete where they belonged.

4.

NO MATTER HOW many times I reminded myself that making new friends was counterintuitive to my plan—and it was a lot—I drifted closer to Simone and Jade every day. We started our mornings together in AP History and crowded around the same table at lunch. On Thursday, Simone convinced me to ride home from school with them.

After final period, Jade pulled out of the student parking lot, Simone riding shotgun. I was squeezed in the back between hundreds of crumpled assignments, dried-up markers, and half-empty tubes of bright paints.

"Sorry my car's a disaster," Jade said, pushing her glasses up her nose. "I swear to God, I'm going to clean it up one day."

Simone leaned away, wind blowing through her locs. "Don't be swearing to higher powers while I'm in the car. You know damn well you haven't cleaned this thing since you got it."

As we sped toward downtown Bardell, I had the nagging sensation that I was actually starting to like them.

"Time for the town tour, DC!" Simone called over the wind. "Soak it up! Marvel in it!"

Jade caught my gaze in the rearview mirror. While Simone had been friendly from the moment she hopped onto my porch, it had taken Jade a little longer. What I'd initially thought was stuck-up aloofness was actually a calculated quiet. She was always listening, even when she seemed to be absorbed by drawing, even when it appeared she wasn't tuned into one of Simone's many rambling questions. I saw the way other Beckwith students regarded her, ogling her slim frame and blonde curls in the hallways. She could've easily eaten the attention up, but she only seemed interested in art and Simone. And now, apparently, me.

"Behold!" Simone boomed, gesturing to a grocery store wedged in the middle of a derelict strip mall. "Food Paradise, where I stole my first tube of lip gloss in seventh grade."

"Just the first?" I asked.

"Please save all questions for the end of the tour," Jade said.

Simone pointed to a small white building with a neon pink ice-cream cone blinking in the window. "There's Scoops, best ice cream in Bardell!"

"'Scoop me up, before you go go, try our ice cream and tasty fro-yo!'" Simone and Jade sang in unison. Simone swiveled around and lowered her sunglasses. Today, they were shaped like orange suns.

"One taste from Scoops and you won't ever wanna go back to DC," she said.

I laughed. "I'm going for a weekend."

"We'll see," they chorused.

Streets snaked through the city like arteries. Jade and Simone took their time, pointing out everything they deemed interesting. There was Slice of Bardell, the pizza shop Simone worked at part-time ("I stay with the free garlic bread connection!"), the ancient library ("Pretty, but smells like hot ass"), Stella Tacos ("Worst burritos in a fifty-mile radius, trust us"), and Bardell Lanes ("Friday is cosmic bowling night!").

Arriving in Bardell with my parents had felt like showing up unannounced on the doorstep of some second cousin twice removed. But with Jade and Simone, every corner held a story; all roads led somewhere familiar. Seventeen years of Bardell ran proudly through their veins, and I was nearly dizzy with facts by the time we stopped near a looming brick building. Simone drummed her hands on the dashboard and deepened her voice like a radio announcer.

"And finally, the heart of the town, the true showstopper—"

"Oh, *yes*, Simone, showstopper is right, indeed!"

"The Draper Hotel and Spa!" Simone held both hands out, fingers waggling.

Jade parked under the gigantic mural of the white angelic woman I'd noticed on my first day in town. Now that we were closer, I could make out the vibrant hues that formed the woman's wild blonde curls. Her sparkling blue eyes stared forward, and a golden halo shimmered above her head. Purple and blue stars surrounded her. Near the bottom, swirling letters dedicated a simple message:

Gone, Never Forgotten
Amelia Annabelle Oliver
"What a Wonderful World!"

Jade cut the engine, and silence filled the car as we took in the massive mural. Jade blew a kiss toward the bricks.

"Love you, Mom," she said quietly.

My face fell. "Jade . . ." I scrambled for the polite thing to say, even though I'd hated how people apologized after Grandma Jean died like it was their fault. Still, I felt the words, *I'm sorry* slip from my mouth.

"It's okay." Jade toyed with the locket around her neck. "It's been a long time. The mural was my gift to her."

My eyes widened. "*You* made this?"

"It was my design. I had some help. Paint needs a touch-up though."

"I can't believe it's been so long," Simone said. "You think the historical society is going to approve the statue?"

"I hope so," Jade said, and quickly explained to me that she'd been working with our history teacher, Mrs. Newland, and the Bardell Historical Society all summer, hoping to get in their good graces. The city was planning to construct five statues of Bardell residents who had an influence on the city, and Jade wanted Amelia to be honored.

"I hope you get it," I told her.

"Me too. It'd be a huge honor."

Simone threw open the passenger door. "Time to bug Mother Dearest for some happy hour snacks!"

We circled the imposing building, dodging couples with bulging suitcases. On the wrought iron benches outside, women in buttery leggings sipped fruit-speckled water with the easy, relaxed air of tourists. I had no idea who would willingly visit Bardell for fun, but when the revolving front door spilled us into the Draper's air-conditioned lobby, I got my answer. The hotel was not a reflection of the tired, humble streets outside.

The Draper Hotel & Spa was another world entirely.

A bellman in a pressed uniform greeted us. "Miss Oliver. Miss Cole. A pleasure as always."

"Hi, Tom." Jade shrugged off her school cardigan and waved Tom away when he reached for it, tying it around her waist instead. "Is my dad here?"

"Mr. Oliver just stepped out. But Mrs. Oliver is here, holding a meeting in the Peach Room."

Jade thanked him and led us through the marble-floored lobby. It was filled with chic artwork, sleek gray furniture, and leafy plants standing tall with importance.

"Jade's parents work here, too?" I asked Simone.

She smirked. "Her family *owns* the Draper." She pointed past a gleaming white baby grand piano to three photos on the wall in ornate silver frames. We slowed to study them.

In the first, a white man with slick hair and a serious face frowned with his arm around a petite blonde woman. *Founders Carl & Mary Oliver*, according to the plaque below. The next photo showed another couple—*Wallace & Elizabeth Oliver*—who looked equally as miserable. And in the last one—*Current owners Lucas & Tallulah Oliver with their three children*—there was

Jade, smiling between two young auburn-haired boys. Behind them, a tall, broad-shouldered man with a swoop of brown hair and a pale woman with a severe red bob beamed like proud parents.

"Great-grandparents. Grandparents. And dad and stepmom," Simone explained, pointing to the photos in order. She tapped the red-haired woman. "Tallulah married Jade's dad like two seconds after Amelia died."

"Are y'all seriously talking shit about my family when I'm five feet away?" Jade asked.

I stiffened, bracing myself for an argument. Then Jade rolled her eyes and added, "At least *tell* me so I can chime in." She looked at me, deadpan. "I apologize in advance for my parents."

"Literally the worst," Simone agreed. "Let's hurry and eat before they show up."

The lobby followed naturally into Syrup, a charming, sun-filled restaurant. Thanks to the pandemic, my comfort with dining out had been shaky for a while, so now I took the time to savor every small detail as a kind hostess showed us to a table overlooking a courtyard. Fresh-cut flowers bloomed like suns in the middle of each ivory-clothed table. Elegant jazz played overhead, creating a cozy, intimate vibe. We threw our backpacks on the floor and got comfortable in the emerald tufted chairs.

"So your parents own this entire hotel?" I asked Jade. "That's pretty cool."

Jade shrugged and helped herself to a glass of water from the crystal pitcher in the middle of the table. "It's fine."

Simone scoffed. "Fine? It's only single-handedly saved this town." She read from the back of the menu. "Without this 'cosmopolitan hotel and spa brimming with Southern hospitality' no outsiders would give a shit about Bardell."

"That's not true," Jade said. "There's so much history here that has nothing to do with this stupid hotel."

"No one cares about history!" Simone said.

"I think the people I spent working for all summer at the Bardell Historical Society would disagree with that statement," Jade said with a ghost of a smile.

Simone waved her hand. "People want sugar scrubs and mints on their goose-feather pillows. They want to take pictures of your dead mom's mural and catch glimpses of the rumored killer!"

"Uh . . ." I glanced between them with wide eyes. "Pause. Rewind. Explain."

Simone leaned in. "You haven't heard the rumors yet? People are *totally* convinced Jade's dad hired a hitman to kill Amelia."

"Holy—" I looked at Jade. She lifted a shoulder, like she was used to conspiracy theories about her murdered mother and the conversation now bored her. "Why would he do that?"

"Tallulah and my dad were having an affair," she explained, tracing the rim of her water glass. Bits of dried green paint were caked beneath her nails. "Tallulah was hired as the Draper's interior designer during the revamp. A few months later, my mother was murdered right outside the hotel. Police never found out who did it."

"They hired Tallulah to redecorate the guest rooms," Simone said, "and she ended up fucking the owner in one."

"Nice," Jade said wryly.

"Jade, I'm so sorry," I said. Suddenly, Mama Letty's and Carole's comments made sense. I wasn't sure I'd want my kid hanging out with someone whose parent had been accused of murder. I thought of Amelia's ethereal face gracing the bricks. "But if your dad had your mom killed . . . why would he let you paint that giant mural?"

Jade smirked. "Because he saw how many people posted pictures of it and hashtagged the hotel. Because people love a good mystery. Because death is good for business."

• • •

Jade insisted on ordering the appetizer sampler: cheesy mozzarella sticks, sizzling jalapeño poppers, jumbo lump crab cakes with rémoulade, and sweet barbecue pulled pork sliders. My mouth salivated when Carole approached the table, arms piled with the heaping plates. She shot Simone a stern look when Simone asked to add blackened oysters on the half shell.

"You're pushing your luck," Carole said.

"Put it on my dad's tab," Jade said sweetly, and Carole grunted and went to refill the next table's sweet teas.

"What a feast," I said, to which Simone replied this was a normal Thursday, and we all laughed and dug in. I hadn't realized how hungry I was, and everything tasted divine.

"This is why we put up with Jade's parents," Simone said with a mouthful of crab cake. "Syrup has the best food in Bardell."

"It probably has nothing on the fancy DC restaurants you and your friends go to," Jade said.

I helped myself to a golden mozzarella stick. The truth was, I rarely ate like this when I was with Kelsi and Hikari. The list of Hikari's food allergies was longer than my arm span, and one of Kelsi's favorite hobbies was trying out new diets while insisting they weren't diets. I could always count on her to inform me that avocados were superfoods, sugar was out to kill us all, wheat was Satan, wait, avocados were actually evil, too. When we broke up, she was in the midst of the Whole 30, cutting out sugar and carbs as easily as our eight-month relationship.

"It's better," I said, and Jade beamed.

We slurped tart lemonade and sugary sweet tea and picked at crumbs and cleaned our plates. Carole brought the oysters, and they tasted so good I wanted to go to the kitchen and personally kiss the chef.

While we dined, Simone and Jade assumed their tour guide roles again to give me Draper Hotel & Spa 101. The hotel was constructed in 1975 as a joint venture by Jade's great-grandfather and grandfather. After the Civil Rights Movement, most Bardell residents wanted to quietly tuck their prejudices away and pretend like the Jim Crow reign of terror never happened. But the Oliver men saw a golden opportunity: tourism.

"White people didn't want to visit the South and be reminded of all the evil shit they were responsible for," Jade said. "They wanted to be pampered. They wanted weddings on plantations. They wanted an idyllic Southern fantasy."

She then went on to explain that while the Draper started

as a humble bed and breakfast, it was Jade's mom, Amelia, who decided it would make a perfect country getaway for people seeking relaxation and good food.

"My dad didn't believe in her," Jade said. "He didn't want to pour a bunch of money into adding a spa. The hotel had been doing fine for years at that point. But Mom had a vision."

"A vision that *really* put Bardell on the map," Simone added.

I looked around Syrup, at the expansive wine rack behind the bar, the servers bustling around in pressed black-and-white uniforms, the glittering chandelier. It was a vision, indeed.

"The business exploded," Jade continued. "All it took was one feature in a home and garden magazine calling Bardell 'the new Savannah,' and people couldn't get enough. There was so much demand they had to add more guest suites. Especially after . . . my mom died." She fiddled with an empty oyster shell.

"Speak of the devil," Simone said. I was about to turn when she grabbed my arm. "Don't look, don't look. You'll turn to stone."

"Hello, girls!" a high-pitched voice boomed.

The red-haired woman from the Olivers' family photo— Jade's stepmother—arrived and loomed over the table. She was tall and skinny, and in her tan dress, she looked like a stick bug. I imagined her eyebrows drawing together to take me in, the pierced-lip, freckle-faced newcomer, but her features appeared too frozen with Botox to do so.

"Elizabeth Jade!" Tallulah placed her French-manicured hands on Jade's shoulders. Her smile was wide and white, lips puckered with fillers. "I didn't know you were coming in this afternoon!"

"We're here practically every day, Tallulah," Jade said, fixated on the oyster shell.

"Who's your new friend?"

"Avery." My name came out garbled. I sipped my lemonade, and my manners rushed in. "Um, the hotel is beautiful, Mrs. Oliver."

She tilted her head and clucked her tongue in an *Aren't you so sweet?* way. "Isn't it lovely?" she trilled. "Perfect mixture of Southern charm and world-class amenities. We're thinking of expanding to Atlanta. Business is *booming*! We barely had a vacancy all summer. We . . ."

My mind wandered as she continued to breathlessly boast about the spa and how some country singer I'd never heard of had once stayed for "*three weeks!*" She barely blinked, and I couldn't look away. She reminded me of Kelsi's mother, the kind of woman who volunteered at every PTA event and talked shit about other mothers' cookies at bake sales. She didn't seem like the type of woman to bust it open for her boss on the job, but then again, people were full of surprises.

Simone nudged me under the table, and I realized Tallulah had asked me a question.

"Sorry, what was that?" I stammered.

"I asked," she said, a bit stiffer, "what brings you to Bardell?"

I stared at her unblinking green eyes. This woman was *intense*. "My grandma is sick." I hoped that would be enough explanation, but Tallulah leaned in.

"God bless her beautiful heart. Sick with what?"

"Tallulah," Jade snapped. "Why are you being so nosy?"

Tallulah laughed, all hollow and tinkling and awful. "I'm trying to get to know your new friend. Speaking of, why don't you bring Grace and Maggie Elle by anymore? You ladies would all get along."

"I'd rather eat dirt than hang out with your friends' daughters." Jade said this like they'd had this conversation many times before. I snuck a glance at Simone and she nudged my knee under the table again.

Tallulah kept on laughing, paying no mind to Jade's sour expression. "But they're such *nice* girls." She said it as if Simone and I weren't. Her gaze lingered on my piercing, and it suddenly felt like it weighed a thousand pounds. I tucked it between my closed lips self-consciously, remembering Kelsi and Hikari's disdain.

There was a burst of chatter at the opposite end of the restaurant, and we all turned to see a tall, broad-shouldered white man enter the room.

"Oh, good." Tallulah ran her fingers through her razor-straight bob. "Your father's here."

Lucas Oliver's presence filled the entire room. He wore a tailored black suit, and a collared shirt open enough to expose a bit of his disgusting chest hair. He stopped at every table, asking how the food was, need any more wine? Tallulah watched him fondly while Jade spun the oyster shell around her empty plate like she was playing Spin the Bottle.

"Remember what we said," Simone whispered. "Literally the worst."

Lucas made his way to the table, footsteps echoing on the hardwood floor with a menacing weight. It wasn't hard to separate the man from the murderer rumors; as soon as I saw his greasy smile, I could see him under a shadowy overpass, handing a hitman a bag of money, telling him to make it clean. He kissed Tallulah and ruffled Jade's curls. Jade flinched, but he didn't notice. Like his wife, Lucas was too busy staring at me.

"Hello!" He thrust out a meaty claw of a hand, and I hesitated before shaking it. My skin crawled in his rough palm, and I imagined his fingers curling around a trigger.

"This is Avery," Tallulah said over his broad shoulder. "One of Elizabeth Jade's *new friends*."

"Pleased to meet you, young lady!" Lucas said. "What brings you to Bardell?"

"Not this again," Jade moaned under her breath.

I was getting ready to answer when a hand appeared over my own shoulder, snatching an empty plate with delicate speed. It was Carole.

"If you girls are finished, why don't you head on home?" Carole asked. "Dinner rush will be starting—"

"Carole," Lucas interrupted. "Come here."

The air stilled. Carole sucked in a breath.

"Yes, Mr. Oliver?"

He stepped closer and looked down his nose at her. I had the urge to jump in between them, but I was glued to my chair.

"I thought we had a talk about uniform compliance."

Carole stiffened. "I am in uniform, Mr. Oliver."

"It's wrinkly, dear," Tallulah said, frowning at Carole's white shirt. I didn't see any wrinkles, but Tallulah took her by the elbow. "Come on back to housekeeping and we'll get you straightened up."

Carole looked around the busy restaurant. "But my tables—"

"Hannah will take care of them," Lucas said. He winked at a petite college-aged girl who swiftly walked past with two sizzling plates. Gross.

Carole's jaw flexed as Tallulah headed for a side door and motioned for Carole to follow. She set the empty plate down with a clatter.

"Right away," she said.

"That's the spirit!" Lucas said. His gaze swung back to me, right before his gigantic hand grasped my shoulder. "And welcome to Bardell, Aster. You know, they say this town is a great place to grow."

My smile faltered, remembering the bullet-riddled welcome sign and the rumors of his dead wife. "I might've read that somewhere."

"It's *Avery*, Dad," Jade huffed. But Lucas was already off to the next table, ready to schmooze and delight more diners.

Simone waited until he was out of hearing range before steepling her fingers. When she spoke, her voice was radio-announcer deep again. "And there you have it, Aster. You have officially survived your first meeting with the Murderer and the Mistress. Marvel in it. Soak it up. And welcome to the fire."

THE BELLE

APPROXIMATELY SEVEN MILES from the Draper Hotel & Spa, on the outskirts of Bardell County, Georgia, were ten pristine acres that also belonged to the Oliver family. Since 1828, Ivy Rose Plantation had captivated visitors with its oak tree–lined drive and double balconies that wrapped around the entire house like a bow. The land had been passed down from one generation of Olivers to the next, wealth accumulating at the expense of Black labor with every turnover. The slave quarters weren't demolished until 1982, when Elizabeth Oliver deemed them unsightly. She told her husband, Wallace, that she didn't want distressing memories of *that ugly history* while she was out tending her rosebushes.

Amelia Annabelle Barnett was slightly uncomfortable when her future husband, Lucas Oliver, brought her to Ivy Rose for the first time. Coming from suburban Ohio, rural Bardell might as well have been Mars. Lucas nuzzled his lips against her ear and told Amelia to take a look around, soak it up, because all of this would one day be hers, too. And it was. As they moved through the motions of heteronormativity—a diamond engagement ring, a first dance to Louis Armstrong's "What a Wonderful World" in front of five hundred guests on Ivy Rose's grounds, a beautiful daughter named Elizabeth Jade—Amelia's discomfort of living in a plantation home eventually softened like snow in sunshine. It was a beautiful house, after all. It would be a shame to not revel in it.

And revel she did. Amelia made Ivy Rose hers, filling the rooms with rare antiques they didn't need and expensive art she swore they couldn't live without. She transformed the grounds into an official wedding venue, where brides sobbed at their first sight of their grooms under weeping willow trees and music from live bands intertwined with crickets every summer Saturday. She brought the same enthusiasm to work at the Draper Hotel & Spa, putting her art degree to good use by designing flyers for the hotel's fancy parties and renovating the interiors one stud at a time.

She knew about the affair. Of course she knew. But whenever she thought about confronting Lucas, Amelia would look around Ivy Rose and into her daughter's ice-blue eyes and imagine everything she would lose. So she swallowed the anger when Lucas would stay at the hotel until the sky bruised with dawn, swallowed the shame when her in-laws passed racial slurs around the dining room table as easily as they passed the salt, swallowed the embarrassment when her daughter began to ask why they lived in a house so big when so many people didn't have homes at all. Amelia convinced herself everything was fine, repeated it like a mantra, and believed her husband when he kissed her in front of their bedroom mirror and told her she was as beautiful as a painting. As pretty as a picture. The belle of the ball.

5.

JADE APOLOGIZED THE entire way home.

"I told you," she said as we sped away from the Draper, mural of her mother shrinking in the rearview. "My parents are the *worst*."

Simone laughed in the passenger seat. "I don't know why you're so upset. They were pretty light today."

I didn't say anything. I was still trying to shake off the disturbing hitman conversation, the murder conspiracy, and the way Lucas and Tallulah made Carole stiffen under their gaze. Pieces of a larger puzzle were slowly coming together: Mama Letty and Carole's conversation. Mom's decision to leave and never come back.

"I swear," Jade said, "I'm going to New York the second I graduate. I hate this place so fucking much." She swiveled around when we hit a red at one of the few stoplights in town. "I promise, if you want to hang out tomorrow, we will do it far away from my parents."

"Cosmic bowling night," Simone stage-whispered, slipping on her sunglasses.

Wind washed over us as we crossed the bridge over the Bardell River, entering the side of town where the houses shrank and the tourists were nonexistent. I appreciated Jade's gesture, but now I felt the urge to hightail it to DC without looking back stronger than ever. I thought of my original plan—get in, get out, no drama, focus forward—and saw threads unraveling. I was getting too close, learning too much. I now knew that Jade fidgeted whenever her stepmom was nearby and Simone preferred to dip her mozzarella sticks in honey mustard over marinara and Lucas Oliver may have hired a hitman to murder his wife.

"I'll think about it," I said.

"What's so important about DC that you have to go back after only a week of being here?" Jade asked.

"J, shut up. You were literally about to rip Tallulah's face off for being nosy," Simone said, laughing. Jade giggled and took her hands off the wheel to throw her curls in a sloppy bun. Simone leaned over to steer, a perfectly orchestrated dance. My heart panged at the relaxed ebb and flow of their friendship, how they could easily brush off their parents' interactions like they had nothing to do with them. I wondered if I ever looked like that with Kelsi and Hikari.

Moments later, Jade turned onto Sweetness Lane. The street was alive with children running around before dinner. Music bumped from someone's backyard, and the tantalizing aroma of barbecue permeated the air. Jade parked at the end of Simone's driveway, but no one moved. Next door—my house?—Mama Letty creaked in her rocking chair, attention on yet another crossword puzzle. For a moment, we simply watched her and baked in the evening steam.

"It must be hard," Jade said after a while.

"What do you mean?" I asked.

She motioned to Mama Letty. "You know . . . watching someone die slowly like that."

"Aren't we all dying slowly?" Simone mused. Jade smacked her shoulder and said we knew what she meant.

In the silence that followed, I realized they were waiting for my answer. The weight of everything that had happened in the past few months—from Mom's decision to uproot us to Georgia to the breakup to starting over in Bardell—suddenly felt as thick and gritty as wet cement.

"When my mom died, it was sudden," Jade said, turning around. "There one moment, gone the next."

"That's definitely worse," Simone said instantly. "At least Avery has a chance to say goodbye. With Amelia and . . ." She swallowed, and Jade squeezed her fingers. "With Amelia and Shawn . . . they were taken. Like that." She snapped. "There were no goodbyes. Nothing. One day you have a mother or a brother, and the next day you don't."

"I didn't know about your brother," I said quietly.

Simone barked a bitter laugh. "It's not really a great conversation piece. 'Hey, nice to meet you, did you know my brother was killed in a car accident and it completely wrecked my entire family?'"

"About as welcoming as, 'Hey, great to see you, did you know my mother was brutally murdered and now she's

memorialized forever on the side of my family business?'"
Jade added.

I sat back, mind reeling. Simone was right. What they'd both gone through was way worse. As we fell quiet again, I stared across the lawn at Mama Letty, the realization slowly dawning that one day, maybe soon, she'd be gone. Forever. I'd never hear her grumblings again; her crossword puzzles would forever be waiting for an answer that wouldn't come. I didn't know what to do with the guilt churning in my chest. On one hand, it still felt like Mama Letty was a stranger. When Grandma Jean died, my family had been at her bedside, holding her hands. Afterward, there were years of memories to sift through, so many good times to reference at her funeral.

With Mama Letty . . . there was so much I still didn't know about her. And she didn't exactly seem eager to talk about it, and pushing her to do so would go against my plan. But now, with the weight of this conversation and the memory of Amelia's halo glittering in the light, my plan felt hollow. Childish, even. Mama Letty was my last living grandparent, and all I'd been focused on was how quickly I could get out of town because feeling nothing was easier than dealing with hurt. I didn't know what to do now. My plan was a jumbled mess.

When Simone turned around, I realized I'd actually asked the question aloud.

"Enjoy the time you have. Soak it up. Marvel in it."

"Talk to her," Jade urged. "Get to know her, for real. If I could have one more afternoon with my mom, I'd honestly never stop talking."

"God, right?" Simone said. "I have so many things I wanna ask Shawn. He was supposed to teach me how to drive. How to fight."

I picked at the strands of my plaid skirt, and Jade and Simone delved into the shared pain of what it felt like to lose someone close. They talked about all the things Amelia and Shawn would miss. Holidays, college, weddings, births. As they ticked off each one, I stared at Mama Letty, thinking about how she'd already missed so much of that, and I'd never considered what it would feel like for her to miss the rest.

We stayed camped out in the Jeep until our limbs were damp with sweat and the sky turned gold. My mom's BMW sailed past us and parked in the driveway. Mom emerged with greasy bags of takeout and yelled for me to come inside for dinner. I said goodbye to Jade and Simone and crossed the lawn in slow strides, mind swirling with death and guilt, wondering where I fit in all of it.

"Look like you smelled some shit," Mama Letty said when I climbed onto the porch. Her crossword puzzle book was open on her lap, and I realized there was a tiny notebook filled with small handwriting tucked between the pages.

"What are you writing?" I asked.

She closed the book with a grunt. "None of your damn business."

I deflated slightly. Mama Letty changed the subject swiftly.

"Thought you were never gonna leave that car. Hell was y'all talking about?"

"You."

She squinted. "What about *me*?"

"About how much I want to get to know you better."

"If you trying to butter me up, just know I don't have life insurance, Fish."

During dinner, I studied Mama Letty. I watched how she pushed her pad thai around her plate and how her bony brown fingers struggled to hold chopsticks yet refused Dad's offer to grab her a fork. She looked so small sitting there, both of us silent as Mom rambled about a colleague she hated. I imagined Mama Letty at the table without us, years of solo dinners, the cat clock her only company. I had a creeping fear that she was about to die right there, just faceplant into her food, and I'd be left with so many questions only she knew the answers to. Like what was Mom like when she was younger? What did Mama Letty want to be when she grew up? What kind of music did Ray listen to? I was so deep in my thoughts, I didn't hear Dad when he asked about our DC trip.

"Sorry, what?" I asked.

"Are you all packed? I'm picking you up after school to head to the airport."

"Oh. Not yet."

"Do it after dinner," Mom said. "I'll check on you before bed."

I nodded and finished my food while Dad talked about the demanding bride he was going to be playing for over the weekend. I tried to catch Mama Letty's eye, wishing she would look at me, call me Fish, share an inside joke. But she just stared at her plate like she was searching for something in the ceramic.

The longer I looked at her, the louder Jade's and Simone's words echoed. Grief cracked open in the pit of my stomach when I realized how self-absorbed I'd been since arriving in Bardell, maybe even before then. So what if Mama Letty was grumpy? Who wouldn't be after so many years alone? We had everything we needed now to become a whole, complete family—time, proximity, bodies hugging the dinner table every night.

But that wasn't enough. If I was going to get to know Mama Letty, *I* was going to have to be the one to crack through her prickly exterior. She had to shed her loneliness, one layer at a time. Maybe I would be perfect for the job since I was dealing with my own version of loneliness after my breakup.

My mind was still turning in my bedroom later as I stared at my half-empty duffel bag. When Mom checked on me and asked how things were going, I had no idea how to answer her.

"Come here," she said. She sat on the bed with a creak and patted the space next to her. "Talk to me." I joined her, sinking into her jojoba oil sweetness. She stroked my frizzy, too-long hair.

"I feel like we haven't really talked since we got here," she said. "You've been so great, you know?"

"I'm okay, I guess."

She laughed. "There's no guessing. You *are*. Starting over senior year is hard, and you're taking it like a champ."

I snuggled into her deeper, feeling five years old. I had another flash of a memory—puffy white clouds outside of an airplane window, Mom holding me like this in a leather seat, crying into my hair.

"Mom?"

"Hmm?"

"What happened the last time we were here?"

"What do you mean?"

"I keep having these flashes of it. There was a lot of screaming. Something about an airplane?" I craned my neck to look at her. Her fingers absently trailed my arms.

"We left early because Mama and I got into a fight," she said. "We flew back to DC. It was your first plane ride. That's probably what you remember."

"Why did you never tell me about my grandfather? Ray?"

"What is this, twenty-one questions?" Mom pulled away.

"You made it seem like he wasn't in the picture. But Mama Letty said—"

"He died before I was born, Avery baby. I don't know much about him."

"You never told me he *died*. You made it seem like he wasn't in the picture. Like he was some deadbeat."

"I never said that."

"But you implied it. Don't I deserve to know about my own family?" I didn't add that I'd also never asked. But should I have had to?

She stood and paced to the dusty bookshelf. "It's painful, Avery. There are some things I don't want to get into, things that happened a long time ago."

"But you're the one who was telling me to get to know Mama Letty. How can I do that if no one is willing to talk?"

"I don't want to get into it." Her words were sharp and final.

But when she turned around, her smile was stretched like sticky bubble gum. I could see that she was preparing to launch into another one of her favorite speeches, the one where she quoted famed astronomer Carl Sagan and talked about the importance of always keeping the bigger picture in mind. She would say our time on the "pale blue dot" was limited, and there was no point holding on to fleeting things. And she did just that, pointing to Earth on the solar system diagram above her old bed for good measure.

"Life is short, Avery," she said. "We're here for a moment. Let's enjoy it and not rehash old family drama." Her words felt like stiff fondant stretching over layers of a rotten wedding cake. She gently lifted my chin up. "Focus forward, right?"

I nodded, even though it was the last thing I wanted to do. I wanted to demand answers. I wanted to tell Mom I was upset the only memories I had of Mama Letty were fuzzy ones. I had seventeen years of gaps where Mama Letty could've fit. I wanted to ask why the girl next door knew more about my grandmother than I did, but Mom's signature bootstraps attitude was in full force, and there was no shattering that armor. Dr. Zora Anderson muscled through sick days and shut conversations down with a single look. I knew she was going to change the subject, and seconds later she was asking me about my "new friends."

I pushed my frustrations away. "They're fine. They gave me a ride home from school. Don't know if that makes us friends."

"If Simone is anything like her mother . . ." Mom smiled,

but it was short-lived. "Well, I think she'd be a friend worth having."

I fiddled with my lip ring, ignoring the way my stomach dropped at the mere mention of Simone. I thought of her laughter, how her voice cracked when she sang a note too high, how I'd only known her a week and I somehow felt lighter around her and Jade than five years with Kelsi and Hikari.

"What about the other one?" Mom asked.

"Jade? She's nice. Her family is kind of intense though. They own that fancy hotel downtown."

Mom's eyebrows shot up. "Her family owns the Draper?"

Coughs from Mama Letty's bedroom rattled the thin wall. Mom and I shuddered, waited until it was quiet again.

"Yeah," I said slowly. "We met her dad and stepmom today."

"I see." Mom's lips pressed firm, her attitude doing a complete one-eighty.

"And yes, they told me the rumors."

"What rumors?"

"About her dad . . ." I mimed holding a gun. "Hired someone to kill Jade's mom."

Mom grabbed a book at random from the shelf, a thick sci-fi novel. "Those rumors are awful." She flipped through pages, reading nothing.

"So you've heard them, too?"

Her shoulders tensed. "People get bored in small towns. They like to talk."

"Do you think it's true?" I asked. She had to. Why else would she be acting so weird?

She shut the book and padded to the door. "I think you should get some rest, baby." She hesitated at the threshold, a faraway look in her soft brown eyes. "But . . . be careful."

"Careful about what?"

"This isn't DC." She closed my door, and I rolled back onto the bed and stared at the solar system diagram, my frustrations slowly melting back into guilt.

I'd been hearing Mom talk about Carl Sagan and his pale blue dot speech my entire life. And usually, it comforted me. It worked in tandem with her breathing exercises, reminding me what was truly important in life. Be kind to people, protect the planet, so on and so forth. It was supposed to be a reminder to let go of the little things. But as I stared at the small blue-and-green orb, suspended among all those stars, a minuscule speck in the grand scheme of the universe, all I could think about were the little things.

Mama Letty, alone in her rocking chair. Her chipped ashtrays, her unmown lawn. The broken clock in the kitchen and the bloody, balled-up handkerchief she kept shoved in her pocket.

I wanted to know how she took her coffee. I wanted to know how she felt when Mom left. I wanted to know her favorite foods. I wanted to know if Ray was funny or serious. I wanted to sit in Mama Letty's loneliness and maybe lay my head on her shoulder if she let me. I wanted to ask if she ever felt completely lost at seventeen and if so, what did she do about it? I thought about how Hikari's grandmother had died from COVID and how Hikari never got to say goodbye. How

Jade and Simone and so many people never got to say goodbye. And now I had the chance to be with Mama Letty, soak in all these small things, give her the best goodbye, and why in the world shouldn't I take it? Revel in it, in fact, as Simone would say.

My phone buzzed somewhere under my pillow. I rooted around for it, hoping it would be Simone or Jade. My shoulders slumped when I saw it was Kelsi, asking if Hikari wanted to go on another tour of Georgetown on Saturday and sending me a frown because she wished I could go. Maybe six months ago, I would've been sad, too. I would've sank into my loneliness, agonized that I was missing out.

Something had changed. Something I couldn't yet name. Maybe it was the way I'd been inching closer to exploring myself in DC and instead of encouraging it, Hikari and Kelsi had treated me like a toddler teetering too close to an electrical socket. Maybe it was the way Simone and Jade had pasts stained with painful deaths, but somehow they were living fully and authentically. Or maybe it was Mama Letty's coughs next door, reminding me she'd be leaving the pale blue dot soon, and there was nothing else to do but revel in the time we had left.

• • •

Dad dropped me off at school the next morning. When I told him my change of plans, he kissed my forehead and told me he was proud of me.

"We'll save the flight credit," he said, "just in case you want to come next time."

"Yeah," I said. "Maybe next time."

I waited by Richard Beckwith's statue, melting under the

sun, running my fingers over his bronze toe for luck. Yet when I saw Jade and Simone approaching, their mouths open in laughter, I realized I didn't need luck. I didn't need to force myself to not care or feel anything. I didn't always need to keep my focus forward.

I needed to get comfortable and look around and take in the view. I needed to let go and sink into the possibility of a new friendship. As we walked into school, they looped their arms around me, drawing me close like bees on lavender. It was a closeness that felt like a promise. A closeness that assured me I wouldn't fall through the cracks even if I tried.

6.

THE RIDE TO the Perfect Spot was long and winding and worth it. As soon as we emerged from the Jeep, Jade, Simone, and I headed for the slow-moving onyx waters, our arms piled high with barbecue chips and sour candy and sparkling cider. The moon reflected off the Bardell River's surface like a quarter sliced in half. Every few steps, Simone and Jade shared a shrewd grin, like they'd known all along I was going to change my mind.

I was nervous. I kept trying to silence the voice in my head that said maybe this was a bad idea, maybe I should've stuck to my script and gone to DC.

"Here we are." Jade motioned to the river, and her excitement slashed through my doubts. "The Perfect Spot."

We threw our bounty in the center of a splintered picnic table near the shore. Jade and Simone worked quickly, using a thin plaid blanket as a tablecloth and covering it with electric tea candles. Water lapped against the shore like a lullaby. We were the only ones there.

"So much better than Syrup, right?" Simone asked. "Close your eyes. Marvel in it!"

I closed my eyes and listened to nature's melody. The crickets and water sang in harmony, the perfect duo. A warm breeze washed over my face. An overwhelming sense of peace filled my chest. When I opened my eyes, Jade was rationing cider into three paper cups adorned with the Draper Hotel & Spa insignia.

"How did you find this place?" I asked. It was an obscure location; Jade had to go off-road for the last quarter mile. Now, we were hidden from the world, sheltered deep within the trees like three river fairies.

"My mom took me here once," Jade said. "She painted and I played on that tree." She pointed to an oak tree with sturdy branches that jutted over the river. "Simone and I found it again during one of our wanderings."

Simone pulled a stack of cards from her backpack and began shuffling. She was wearing glittery gold eye shadow, and every time she blinked it reminded me of dancing fireflies.

"We knew you weren't going anywhere," she said, and I sank comfortably in my decision to stay. I couldn't be hesitant when Simone sounded so confident. She paused from card shuffling to rip open the sour gummy worms, and the bag made its way around the table.

"I thought about everything we talked about yesterday," I said before munching on a blue-and-orange-striped worm. "About reveling in the time I had left."

"And yet," Jade said, "here you are, *still* not spending time with your grandmother."

"I'm still thinking of the best plan of action," I admitted. "She's my *grandma*, and I feel like I barely know her. I don't even know where to start."

Simone smiled as she cut the deck into three piles. "It'll happen. Mama Letty is like that cactus, the one that only blooms at night. You know the one?"

I didn't, but I nodded because I wanted her to keep going.

"Like. She looks prickly. And she is, she has every right to be. But there's still beauty. There's still blossom, no matter how rare, as long as you tend to it."

"And what kind of flower are *you*?" Jade asked.

Simone rolled her eyes. "Sunflower. Duh." She tilted her face to the sky, and even though it was black with night and sparkling with stars, I imagined warm rays washing over her. She *was* a sunflower. Beautiful. Standing tall, searching for warmth and expansion. The kind of flower whose fields you could get lost in.

"J, you are obviously lavender," Simone said. "Pretty, but useful. Resilient. And you smell good."

"Thanks?" Jade said, catching my eye. A grin tugged at my lips.

"What about me?" I asked.

Simone considered me. "Jury's still out."

Jade rummaged around in her backpack and produced a thick blunt. "Grabbed this from Tony. Figured we could use it right now."

"Tony's weed is always shit," Simone grumbled as she reached for it. She took a whiff and made a face. "Better than nothing. We should let DC have first hit since she's guest of honor." She passed it to me, and I held it in my palm like it was a grenade.

I'd never smoked weed. I'd been presented the opportunity once before, at a pool party I'd dragged a nervous Hikari and an irritated Kelsi to last summer. Sam Keller offered us a translucent green dinosaur-shaped bong under the shade of his diving board. Hikari panicked and swam away. Kelsi wrinkled her nose and asked, *What do you think we are, burnouts?* Weed wasn't for girls like us, same as alcohol. Experimenting was seen as shameful or a waste of time. I could still see Kelsi furiously drying off with a large yellow beach towel, grumbling about how she could've been studying instead of being offered bong rips at a "stupid" party.

"Never smoked before?" Jade asked gently. "Inhale slowly, like you're sipping through a straw. Don't take too much at once."

"That's what they said," Simone said with a snort.

I did as I was told. It burned going down my throat, a swampy, pungent aroma. I hacked into my shoulder and passed it off to Simone, my teeth already trying to scrape the rotting taste off my tongue. My eyes watered.

"Easy, tiger," Simone said. She took two hits like a pro before passing it to Jade, who held it between her middle and index fingers like it was a vintage cigarette holder. The white stone in her wire ring gleamed in the moonlight. Simone piled the cards together and started shuffling again.

"Tell me when to stop," she said.

"What is this?"

"It's best to not question it," Jade said lazily.

I watched the cards slide through Simone's hands like magic, my mind already softening. "Stop," I said, and Simone whipped a card out on the table, faceup. She hummed, the strange circle depicted on the card's face only something she could understand.

"Wheel of fortune," she said. She launched into a lengthy explanation I could only half follow while attempting another hit. Something about great changes on the horizon, new opportunities, fate. "The universe is working for you, DC. Major turning points ahead."

"That's cool." After my third hit, my mind was hazy, and I was having trouble focusing. But I kind of liked how everything felt soft and sharp at the same time. Every lick of wind felt delicious, every cricket chirp felt like a symphony. Hikari and Kelsi were really missing out, and the thought made me laugh.

"What's so funny?" Jade asked. Even in the dark, I could tell her eyes were red, too.

"I'm thinking about my ex. In DC."

"So *that's* why you wanted to go back so badly," Simone said.

"It's funny. I feel like she didn't know me at all. I feel like *I* don't know myself at all."

"That's some real shit," Simone said.

"Why did you break up?" Jade asked.

I didn't know where to start. Did our end truly begin with the fight in the museum or did we splinter before then? Maybe it was when I was excited to cut my hair and she wrinkled her nose. Maybe it was when I started to hate the way her voice sounded. Maybe it was when her jokes that used to make me laugh until I hurt could barely make me smile.

"We got into a fight," I said, "and it felt like there was no going back from it."

They listened intently as I set the scene. It was early June. School had ended, and everyone was cranky and ready for a break from computer screens. My mom had scored three tickets to the National Museum of African American History and Culture from a colleague. She dropped me, Kelsi, and Hikari off at the front, gave us money for lunch. It was supposed to be a beautiful day, full of learning.

The three of us had wandered through the exhibits, quietly taking in everything from Whitney Houston's American Music Award trophy to Chuck Berry's candy-apple-red Cadillac. I hid my tears from them in the domestic slave trade exhibit. I felt a full-bodied rage in the Jim Crow era section. And in the hip-hop collection, I felt my shoulders creep up to my ears when Kelsi started badly rapping "Party Up" in front of a photo of DMX.

"This bitch," Simone muttered.

"I told her to be quiet," I said, mind hazy with weed and memories. "She was so embarrassing. She wasn't even singing the right lyrics."

"White girls be like," Simone said.

"I'm sorry on behalf of white girls everywhere," Jade said.

I continued the story, recounting how Hikari had watched us go back and forth over whether or not she was allowed to mimic DMX, the argument not dissipating even as we moved on to a gorgeous navy-blue tuxedo once worn by Nat King Cole. She couldn't understand why it made me uncomfortable, couldn't understand why I thought it was disrespectful.

"I don't even know this bitch and I can't stand her!" Simone hit the blunt and smacked the table. Some of her tarot cards spilled onto the grass.

"I haven't even gotten to the worst part," I said, and they groaned.

I told them about how we moved to the education collection, me angrily leading the way, Kelsi sulking several yards behind, Hikari caught in the middle. I stopped at a photo of Howard University. I'd grown up practically around the corner from it, had witnessed the bustling excitement of their homecoming festivities and block parties. But I'd never seriously considered what it would be like to go there, and I made the mistake of asking the question aloud.

"I know this bitch didn't come for HU," Simone snapped.

I nodded, the memory still awkward and hurtful. I looked out to the river, and it slipped by so quietly it seemed like it wasn't moving at all. I felt like I was speaking in slow motion.

"She laughed," I said. "Said, 'Yeah, 'cause Howard is comparable to Georgetown.' And I told her Howard was a great school. So she told me to apply, and I said fine, maybe I would." I changed my voice for the next sentence, raising it slightly to match Kelsi's nasally, crisp tone. "'*You'll get in easily, just like you'll get into Georgetown easily.*' I asked her what that was supposed to mean. '*If you didn't already have the grades, you could just pull the affirmative-action card.*'"

Jade whistled. Simone sipped her cider and muttered "white people" into her cup.

After smoking, the endless shades of the blue night felt richer, deeper. The story that had once pained me to even think about now felt ridiculous. I saw myself moving through the museum, cheeks red, and didn't recognize that girl at all.

"I forgot why I even liked her." When I thought about the entirety of our relationship—from that first kiss on a blustery autumn night to making out in her room over winter break, sneaking kisses during SAT study dates in the spring—I felt nothing.

"I felt so lonely when I was with her," I continued. Jade passed me the bag of chips, and I devoured a handful, laughter bursting between crunches. "She was not a nice person. She made me feel so small. Anything I wanted to do, she shot down. I wanted to shave my head, she told me it would be ugly. I wanted to go to a party and she made me feel like a stupid, immature child. She just wasn't *fun*."

"And what about your other friend?" Jade asked. "Hikari?"

I laughed louder. "Hikari was the peacemaker! She hated when we fought. She never wanted us to date in the first place. When Kelsi and I were fighting at the museum, she wanted us to keep it down because we were embarrassing her. She didn't care *why* I was upset. She thought I was being dramatic, like

Kelsi. Even after Kelsi said what she said—" My breath caught. I realized I was crying. Simone came around the table and wrapped me in a hug. Jade rested her hand on my knee.

"You don't have to keep going," Simone said into my hair. "They sound like the worst friends ever."

"She made me feel so small," I repeated. I desperately wanted to get it together, embarrassed for Simone and Jade to see my tears so early, so soon. But my chest was twisting, and my eyes were watering, and maybe it was the weed, but I couldn't stop crying. The disjointed loneliness I'd been holding on to for months pooled around my feet. I'd given those girls five years of me, and now that they were gone, I barely recognized myself.

"She told me I had no right to be upset," I said. "She told me to get over it. She told me I was barely Black. Told me I couldn't police anything she said because I was half white. And afterward—" I gasped, coughed on the words. Simone rubbed my back in slow circles. "She wanted to act like the conversation never happened. She made me feel *so* dramatic when I didn't immediately let it go. Said it was a joke. Told me I needed to lighten up."

I hadn't told anyone this story yet, and the words unleashed like a lightning strike. In the silence that followed, I sat there like a scorched spot on the earth, stunned and dizzy.

Jade grabbed my hand; Simone grabbed the other.

"Tree," they said in unison.

• • •

We gathered the snacks. We left the blanket and candles. Jade led the way, her bare feet making imprints in the soft riverside grass.

"Avery," she said, "meet Tree."

It was the same one she pointed out earlier, the one that protruded over the river like a gnarled, leafy dock. In quick, calculated movements, Jade scaled a thick branch that hung low enough for her toes to graze the water.

"Go next," Simone instructed, voice like velvet. "I'll catch you if you fall."

I followed Jade's path. She extended a hand and guided me to the spot next to her. Simone followed with ease and looped the snack bag onto a branch above us. I started to sway and grabbed the rough bark before I tumbled into the water. My fingers landed on a set of jagged initials.

EJO
SJC

"Tree is special," Jade said. "We come here when we have serious questions."

I giggled at the image of tiny Jade and Simone consulting a wise old tree, searching for answers in her bark. My tears had subsided. Now, all I felt was warmth as I focused on the transcendent, steady rush of the river. Simone scooted closer, and her bare thigh rested against mine. We were perched like three birds on a telephone wire tuned into gossip, wrapped in a magic that only came out at night.

"You laugh," Simone said, "but that won't stop you from telling Tree your problems."

"What do I have to do?"

Simone trailed her fingers over the branch reverently. "Think about something you need clarity on. For example, what you want to do with your life now that you got rid of your old, toxic-ass friends?"

"Simone," Jade said, laughing. "Look, Avery, all you have to do is focus on your question. Then, when you're ready, take a piece of bark and throw it in the water. Like a wishing well."

"If I peeled bark for everything I needed clarity on, Tree would be naked."

I picked at the bark near my thigh until a small piece came off in my hand. I turned it over as I considered what was worthy of wishing. My mind swirled with thoughts of Kelsi and Hikari, my old life in DC, how I no longer recognized the old Avery who was obsessed with school and textbooks and college. Then I felt Simone's knee brush mine, and I instantly thought of her lips, her electric smile, how she truly was a girl made of sunflowers.

"Any day now," Simone said with a sigh. Jade giggled.

I closed my eyes and forced Simone from my mind, a hard feat since all I could smell was her.

"Breathe," Jade said calmly, "and let go."

I thought about my resolution last night to dig my heels into the earth, truly get to know Mama Letty. So I wished to learn how to revel in her, how to become a granddaughter she would miss and trust. I wished for her to eventually become comfortable enough to tell me about the grandfather I never knew. Most important, I wished to find my way back to myself, whoever she might be. I felt the bark slip from my hand, and I imagined the words Kelsi spat in the museum vanishing along with it, being swept away with the current, no longer mine to carry. When I opened my eyes, it was too dark to tell where the bark had fallen. I imagined the river carrying my wish all the way to the Atlantic.

Minutes passed. The branch dug into the soft fabric of my basketball shorts.

"You know what I wish?" Jade asked suddenly, pushing her glasses up her nose. "I wish I could run away to New York or San Francisco. Go somewhere where no one knows my name and I'm not the daughter of a murdered woman or the heiress to some stupid hotel."

"I'll be on the same bus out of town, headed for Atlanta to go to Spelman," Simone said.

I smiled, nudged her. "You going to major in tarot?"

She nudged me back. "That's simply going to be a side hustle, DC. I'm trying to go into political organizing like Stacey Abrams. When she helped flip this bitch blue, I knew that's what I wanted to do with my life. People said Georgia going Democrat was impossible, and she said bet." She unwrapped a chocolate kiss slowly and deliberately. "I got a whole plan. Spelman for undergrad, like her. Then a top grad school for public policy. All the while, doing tarot readings to keep my spirit in check, start a jewelry business, something fun. I don't know, haven't decided yet."

"You would actually fit in well with Hikari and Kelsi with all those plans," I said.

She wrinkled her nose. "Don't lump me in with them ever again in your life, okay?"

"Well, it's a lot more detailed than my plan," I said. "I don't even care about college anymore. The only thing I want to do is shave my head." It came off as a joke, but I was serious. My future felt as murky as the swirling, dark river below us.

"Sounds good to me," Jade said. "Plans are overrated anyway."

"Growing up is overrated," Simone said.

"Dating is overrated," I added.

"Yes!" Jade shook the branch overhead, and leaves rained down on us like snow. "Dating *is* overrated."

I suddenly felt emboldened. Maybe it was the moonlight filtering through the trees or the weed or the shedding of a two-month-old wound, but I wanted to know everything about them and now. So I asked if they were dating anybody. Strangely, the topic hadn't come up yet.

"We have a No Dating rule," Jade said.

"Why?"

Jade scoffed and made a vague motion. "For the exact reasons you told us. People suck, and there's so much more to life than dating."

"It's true," Simone said quietly.

"There's art and books and music and movies," Jade said, "and bowling and swimming and dancing—"

"And eating," Simone added, "and traveling and museums and flying kites—"

"—and berry picking and apple picking and roller skating—"

"—and watching clouds go by—"

"And coming here, to the Perfect Spot—"

"Okay!" I said, laughing. "I get it, I get it." Warmth pooled in my chest, and I wondered if that was what it felt like to fall in love.

Jade slipped off her glasses and stared at the water for a few silent beats. "It's like you said. We're seventeen. We're getting to know ourselves. Why tie yourself down to someone else who also has no idea who they are?"

"I know who I am," Simone said calmly.

Jade laughed. Then, after a moment, said, "It was my fault."

"J." Simone sighed.

"No, no, let me explain." Jade looked at me with an intensity that nearly sent me falling into the river. Watching her go from the quiet, studious observer to a red-cheeked and full-hearted lavender girl by the river was like witnessing winter melt into spring. "I dated this guy freshman year. I got kinda obsessed with him. I forgot about everything else."

Simone snorted. "Kinda?"

"Okay! I was literally obsessed with him." Jade shoved a blonde curl behind her ear. Her hair—much like mine—was haloed with frizz from the humidity. "He was my first love. We did everything together. And I completely spaced out of my friendship with Simone, even though I've known her since we were little. So when we broke up, I decided I'd never do it again. Dating makes you lose yourself. It makes you forget what's important."

"Yup," Simone said.

"What happened to the guy?" I asked.

Simone snickered. Jade winced.

"God, it was Tim Joplin!" she said, exasperated. "Do *not* judge me. I was fourteen."

I balked. "That gross guy in our history class? Lesbian guy?"

"It's not one of my finest moments," Jade said with a lift of her shoulder. "Tim was mad I broke up with him and started spending all my time with Simone again, so he thinks it's funny to call us lesbians. But we're obviously not, and he's a jealous idiot, and there you have it. All my relationship dirty laundry aired. You did it, I did it. Don't judge me."

I nodded, everything suddenly making sense. Of course Simone and Jade weren't gay. I didn't know why I felt disappointed. I shoved the feeling away and gently knocked Simone's knee. "Your turn. Before the No Dating rule, was there anyone?"

Simone's lips twisted up. "Nuh-uh. Not happening." She laughed and shook her head at our protests. "I said no, you vultures!" She grasped a thick piece of bark and sent it flying into the water.

"You cannot use Tree to get out of tough conversations," Jade said. "That's not how it works."

Simone's eyes sparkled in the moonlight. I couldn't help but smile with her.

"What'd you wish for?" I asked.

"For y'all to stay outta my damn business." In one swoop, she pushed off the branch and swung herself to dry land. Jade and I followed her back to the picnic table in a dizzy, sugary haze.

Now that my eyes had fully adjusted to the dark, I could absolutely see why this nook between the trees had been dubbed the Perfect Spot. I looked at the picnic table and saw a friend-ship blooming. I looked at the stars and saw hope. I looked at the water and saw wishes. Tall, knee-deep grass swayed by the river's edge. The Wheel of Fortune card was waiting for me on the table, promising a turning point. The sense of peace I'd felt when we first arrived had only amplified; the entire night felt like taking a giant, enormous breath.

"Can we come back sometime?" I asked. "I'm kind of in love with this place."

"The Perfect Spot is literally a monument to our friend-ship," Jade said, packing up the candles. "Of course we'll be back."

Simone scooped up three brown leaves as big as our faces and placed them in our hands. "A key chain to remember the night!" she belted like an opera singer. "A leaf so pretty! A leaf so bright!"

Our laughter followed us the entire way home.

7.

I **KNEW THE** news from Mama Letty's latest doctor's appointment was bad when I woke up to pots and pans banging. Still in my pajamas, I tiptoed down the hall, toward the muffled rapid-fire words drifting from the kitchen. I stopped right before the living room and listened to Mama Letty's sighs and Mom's clipped tone.

"They don't know"—*bang!*—"what they're talking about."

"Will you calm down?" Mama Letty asked. "You gone mess around and ruin my good skillet."

"You don't even cook."

Mama Letty said something under her breath. Then: "What are you so mad about?"

The refrigerator door slammed. "I'm not mad!"

Mama Letty chuckled. There was a tapping, Mom cracking eggs, a sizzle as she poured them into the pan. I imagined her staring at the whites slowly expanding, biting back whatever she really wanted to say. I was about to turn the corner when she spoke again, even harsher, despite her insistence she wasn't mad.

"I wish you would care more. I told you we should go back to DC, to a better hospital—wait, are you *smoking*?"

"It's my house."

"Jesus Christ, Mama."

"I'm dying, Zora! A goddamn cigarette won't change that. You and your daughter, I swear."

"Well, I know it must be disappointing to hear that people actually care about you."

"That's all we do, ain't it? Disappoint each other?"

Then there was just the sizzling and popping of eggs and bacon. I took the break in silence to enter the heavy fog of tension. I thought my appearance would cease the conversation, but Mama Letty looked directly at me, cigarette perched between her fingers, as she spoke again.

"Y'all knew I was dying. Y'all knew it was bad. You wouldn't have brought your asses down here otherwise."

"We'll talk about this later," Mom said. "Good morning, Avery baby." She slid a slice of bread into the toaster. "Breakfast is almost ready."

"What's going on?" My gaze fell on a stack of papers in front of Mama Letty. A pamphlet with muted colors entitled *Metastatic Breast Cancer: End-of-Life Care* sat on top.

"It's nothing," Mom lied. If her hands weren't so busy, she'd be fiddling with her stone earrings. "Don't worry about it."

I glanced between my mother and grandmother, wondering whose side to take. Mama Letty looked like she was still up for an argument, but Mom was burying the heated words, willing them to melt like the butter she slathered on the toast. She set a paper plate in front of me and muttered she needed some rest. Mama Letty and I listened as her footsteps disappeared into the den.

I looked at my food. The toast was burned in one corner and the eggs had hardened to rubber. I poked at them, keeping my eyes down so I didn't have to look at that awful pamphlet. The soft light filtering through the kitchen window felt too harsh after laughing well into the midnight blues with Simone and Jade.

"Damn shame," Mama Letty said. "Two Black women from the South and neither one of us can cook a damn." She puffed on her cigarette, and smoke curled near the cat clock's tail. "What about you, Fish? You cook?"

I pushed my plate away, shook my head. Mama Letty stared at the papers, mouth pinched like she'd bitten into a soft grape.

"What does it mean?" I asked.

"Cancer's spread to the lungs." She shoved the pamphlet across the table, and I reached for it like it was alive and capable of biting. On the front, surrounded by a fuchsia vignette, an old white woman gazed out a window with a tiny smile. It was like she'd seen Death across the street and was about to invite him in for tea.

"Is there anything we can do?" But I knew the answer was in Mom's frustration and Mama Letty's resolve. I flipped open the pamphlet, filled with an overwhelming desire to return to the Perfect Spot. By the river, words like *wills* and *hospice care* and *life insurance* and *the dying process* didn't exist. Only wishes and dreams and memories and nature.

"Don't start sniffling," Mama Letty said. "Already had to listen to your mother the whole damn car ride talking 'bout I can beat this if I keep on fighting."

"I wasn't going to say that."

She grunted. Inhaled on her cigarette, hard.

"I'm serious. I was going to say . . ." My eyes fell to the pamphlet again. I wanted to rip it into tiny confetti pieces and watch them rain down on the Formica table. "I was going to say if you wanted to talk about anything, I'd love to listen."

"What's talking gonna do?" she asked bitterly.

"It might make you feel better."

The cigarette shook between her fingers. The world moved on. Somewhere in DC, Hikari and Kelsi were oohing and ahh-ing at Georgetown buildings they'd seen a hundred times, and maybe a different Avery would've been there with them.

But I was here now. I chose to stay. I chose Mama Letty.

Revel in it, I heard Simone say.

"I want to do something," I said. "Let's go on a walk? Or sit on the porch?"

She stood, shaking. "Eat your food, Fish." She left me and the pamphlet alone at the table.

• • •

Mom and Mama Letty spent the rest of the day in hiding. I drifted around the house like an aimless ghost, hesitating at Mama Letty's door, backing away when my nerves talked me out of knocking. I hovered beyond the den during Mom's hushed phone call to Dad but didn't interrupt. The stack of papers from the doctor never moved from the table, so I grabbed a bag of chips and a bottle of water and avoided the kitchen for the rest of the day.

It was late when the tapping began. I was on my bed, bored, scrolling through my phone when a brown fist curled against my window and scared me half to death. When I realized who it was, I crossed the room with a wide smile and slid the window open.

Simone appeared like a bird springing out of a cuckoo clock. Her faded Slice of Bardell polo was smudged with flour.

"Hi." She held up a grease-stained bag. "You like cheesy bread?"

"Who doesn't?"

"Good answer. Cheesy bread is so good! Cheesy bread is so great! Cheesy—"

I watched in amazement as she hoisted herself inside, singing praises for cheesy bread, nearly tumbling headfirst onto the desk. I grabbed her arm to steady her, and her skin was warm and soft. I jerked away when I realized I was enjoying it a little too much.

"So *this* is what this room looks like," Simone said. She was so close I could smell her shea butter mixing in with the cheesy bread. It smelled like heaven. "You know, I've been in every room in this house except this one. It's cute. It's very you."

"Wood-paneled walls and stained carpet is me?"

She smirked and pointed to the napkin she and Jade had doodled on during our first lunch period. It was still resting on my desk, right next to the leaf from the Perfect Spot. "You have little touches. Subtle. Like you."

"Still haven't thought of a flower for me?"

"Don't rush the process, DC." She opened the cheesy bread bag, releasing a tantalizing steam. "I got extra marinara. Come on, let's have a picnic."

I grabbed a thick purple quilt from the foot of my bed and spread it over the carpet. We sat across from each other, knees brushing. While Simone launched into a story about her micromanager boss and annoying customers, she tore off pieces of cheesy bread and handed them to me for dipping. It was the first time we'd been together for an extended amount of time without parents or Jade, and I didn't know what to do with the giddy nerves that simmered when I realized this. She kept checking the time on her phone, wanting to make sure she was back home before Carole got off work.

"Does she usually work this late?" I asked. It was nearing midnight, but I was dreading the moment she had to leave.

"Yeah. Syrup's open till one on the weekends."

"Tips must be pretty good to put up with Lucas and Tallulah."

"Oh yeah. She loves those white guilt tips. Especially when she starts telling folks she's a single mother, trying to put her last kid through private school, wah wah wah. It makes them feel better about themselves." She tore off another piece of bread and watched as I dipped it for her. "One day, I'm gonna make enough money that she'll never have to deal with working for anyone else again."

"Why *are* Jade's parents so awful?" I asked. "Do you really believe those hitman rumors?"

She nodded seriously. "You've never seen her dad's temper, but it's *awful*. All the men in her family got that evil energy."

"And Tallulah likes that?"

"Tallulah likes his *money*. She likes being the boss of a luxury hotel. She likes living in a big-ass plantation house."

"Jade's family lives in a plantation house?"

Simone smirked, like I was a cute kid asking why the sky was blue. I twisted another piece of cheesy bread in the tangy marinara and thought about Amelia's mural.

"So you think he killed Amelia? Instead of getting a divorce?"

"Who knows." Simone leaned back on her forearms and wiggled her toes. Her feet stunk outside of her work shoes, but I found I didn't mind that either. "The timeline is suspicious. And *especially* since Tallulah hopped on him before Amelia was even in the ground? Tells you all you need to know."

"Jade seems nothing like them."

"She's not. She was a mama's girl all the way. She's Amelia's clone. Quiet at first. Super smart. Creative. Sees the potential in things. Her mom is the reason we're friends."

"Really?"

She nodded. "I used to spend so much time at Syrup and the Draper when I was little. There was such a huge age gap between me and my brother and sister, so I clung to my mom. Sometimes she'd take me to work, and I'd color or read in one of the booths. One day, Amelia brought Jade in, and the rest is history."

"You don't talk about your sister much," I said. I'd heard about Shawn, of course, and the awful car accident. But her older sister remained a mystery.

Simone twirled the end of a loc. "Sometimes I feel like I don't know her that well either. Shayla's twelve years older than me, so she was out of the house when I was really young. She's a hairstylist and makeup artist. She lives in Atlanta. What else is there to know?"

"I always wanted siblings," I said, and Simone groaned.

"They can be so annoying. Before Shawn died, he used to get on my nerves so much. He never let me play his PS3 and always hid the remote." Her lips parted in a quiet sadness, her sunflower face dampened by a rain cloud. I instantly regretted bringing it up, but she saved me by switching the subject and asking about Mama Letty.

"Not good," I told her. I didn't know how to form the words. So I walked nimbly into the dark kitchen, grabbed the pamphlet, and brought it back as an explanation. Simone's eyes widened.

"Shit. This is bad. I mean, I knew it was bad before, but this is *bad* bad."

I stared at her fingers clutching the pamphlet. She'd trailed a grease stain right down the middle of the dying white lady's forehead. I rooted around in the bag for cheesy bread, to give my hands something to do, but we were out.

"How's Operation Love on Letty going?" Simone asked.

"Like the *Titanic's* maiden voyage." I imagined myself as the iron ship, so foolishly confident, only to be met by Mama Letty's unstoppable frost. Soon, I'd be splitting and sinking to the bottom of the ocean. Simone burst out laughing.

"She can't be *that* bad."

"You've . . . met her, right?"

"Lived next door to her my entire life."

I stretched out onto my back and stared at the ceiling; Simone followed suit. From this angle, I noticed translucent stars stuck to the ceiling, so faded they blended in with the white paint. I smiled and imagined Mom at my age, staring up at the same stars.

"Why don't you tell me everything you know about her?" I asked. "It's probably more than I have. I barely remember anything from the first time I visited."

"Hmmm . . . let's see." I could hear her smile. "One time, I busted my ass playing on that dogwood tree in my side yard, and she laughed at me."

"Seems fitting."

"She's always been grumpy. As long as I've known her. She used to drink with my mom on the porch."

"Used to? What happened?"

"Shawn died." Her words, despite their weight, fell like grains of sand. "And then my dad left. Shayla was in Atlanta. And, I don't know, I guess my mom felt alone. She gave up everything. She started going to church, stopped drinking. I'm pretty sure she thinks all the awful shit that's happened in her life was because she wasn't a 'good person' before." She rolled over to her side and propped her head in her hand. Her brown eyes searched my face.

"Mama Letty was there for me after my dad left though. She brought me food."

"She *cooked*?"

"God, no. It'd be fast food, pizza, takeout. But still. When you're in middle school and your mom can't peel herself out of bed and there's nothing in the fridge but half-empty milk cartons, someone bringing you hot food is like a superhero." She smiled faintly. "That's why I say give it time. I know she's rough around the edges but . . . underneath. Underneath, there's more."

"But we don't have time." I motioned to the pamphlet. "She's going to die soon, and then what? I go back to my life, pretend like she never existed? I have nothing to hold on to." I took a deep breath. "All I know is that there's always been some rift between her and my mom. They had a really bad fight that I barely remember, and my mom never came home again. I know I have a grandfather named Ray that my mom *also* doesn't like to talk about. How am I supposed to work with any of that?"

"You have to." Simone's tone hardened. "Avery, you have to. None of that trivial stuff matters when someone dies. If your mom doesn't want to talk about it, then fine. You'll find your own way. Just don't give up. Promise?"

I hesitated, looking back up at the stars. That promise felt harder than any plan I'd ever made. It would be so easy to continue the way things had been going, mind my own business, focus forward. Trying to get Mama Letty to open up would require persistence. She'd reject me some more. We'd both be lonely together.

"I promise," I said.

Simone sat up, satisfied. She yawned and stretched, exposing a strip of brown skin beneath her polo. When she caught me looking, she cocked her eyebrow. "Tryna catch a peep, DC?"

My cheeks burned, all thoughts of Mama Letty vanishing. "No, I'm not—"

"Can I ask you something?" she interrupted.

My heart picked up speed. "Yeah?"

"It's about your ex."

Annnd everything deflated. I cringed, thinking about Kelsi's twisted pink mouth in the museum. I nodded slowly.

"Was she your first girlfriend?"

"Yeah."

Simone dragged a finger over the quilt. Her name tag—HI! I'M **Simone**! FEELING CHEESY?—quivered on her shirt. "And your parents were cool with it? With you being gay?"

"Yeah. For the most part." I smiled, thinking about that nerve-racking day when I was fourteen. My newfound identity had kept me up at night for weeks, tracing the words *lesbian* and *pansexual* and *queer* into my sheets. When I finally told my parents, Dad promptly burst into song, much to my horror. Mom kissed my forehead and told me she was proud. But later that same day, I heard her crying in the shower. I never brought it up to her, told myself those tears weren't about me.

Simone fiddled with the ring on her middle finger, twisting the orange stone around and around and around. "That's cool. I mean, my parents would—they would—" She kept stumbling over her words. I waited patiently. "That's good that you were supported."

"Why do you ask?"

"No reason."

I pulled at a curl and played with the split ends, hoping my casual exterior would calm her. My nerves were actually in overdrive, recalling the way Simone's jaw flexed at Tim's lesbian question. But then there was Jade's explanation about their breakup, Tim's jealousy. They weren't lesbians. Obviously. But there was something about the way she kept nervously digging into the carpet, the way she danced around the questions. Something familiar.

"I should go," she said abruptly. "I work lunch shift tomorrow." She gathered her things without looking at me, and I pushed away the disappointment. Because although my original *get in, get out* plans had shifted, they'd been replaced by something else: Simone and Jade's insistence that friendship was more important than anything. The No Dating rule. And I wasn't going to be the one that screwed up a new friendship over hoping Simone was something she wasn't.

She left my bedroom window more gracefully than she entered and crossed the lawn, hips winding with every step. She smiled at me before she disappeared inside.

Even at midnight, the girl made of sunflowers lit up the entire world.

• • •

I didn't notice the letter until I was getting ready for bed. On the floor, tucked beneath the purple quilt, was an envelope, my name on the front in graceful swoops. I pressed it to my chest like a long-lost treasure map, wondering when Simone had slipped it there unnoticed.

Inside was a heavy piece of aqua cardstock paper. When I unfolded it, I recognized Jade's calligraphy letters and her familiar doodle style in the sunflowers and lavenders gracing the corners. The letter was short, ink on the last couple of words smudged.

Dear Avery Anderson,

Your presence is requested at a secret location at midnight, next Friday, the ninth of September. Transportation will be provided from your home promptly at 9:30 p.m.

This invitation admits you and only you.

J&S

P.S. Please bring sour gummy worms since you ate them all the last time.

8.

IF I WAS a ship and Mama Letty was the iceberg, then Mom was the rocky, unforgiving ocean. I figured the heat from their argument would've cooled by the next morning, but I woke up to screams. The family boat had been rocked. Again.

I found them in the living room, Mama Letty's mouth twisted into a scowl, Mom clutching a stack of papers with tears in her eyes.

"I wish you would at least check it out," Mom was saying. Mama Letty snatched the papers and, in one fluid motion, ripped them in half and threw them at Mom's feet.

"I don't need to check out shit," Mama Letty snapped. "If I had known you was gonna bring your ass down here to try and shove me into a nursing home, I woulda told you to stay in DC."

"It's *not* a nursing home!" Mom said, exasperated.

I wiped crust from my eyes, still trying to make sense of what was happening. Mom went on, talking about how Blue Meadow was one of the nicest facilities in Georgia.

"They provide around-the-clock nurse care, gourmet meals, activities—"

"The only way I'm leaving this house," Mama Letty interrupted, "is in a body bag. I've lived here over fifty damn years, and you not about to shove me into the goddamn morgue before I'm dead!"

"Morgues don't have tennis courts," Mom said dryly. "Or an Olympic-sized swimming pool. Or—"

"So I got diagnosed with cancer, and you thought, 'Gee, bet she'd really love to pick up tennis!' Thought you was supposed to be the smart one."

"Why won't you let me help you?"

"I was doing fine before you brought your ass back down here," Mama Letty snapped. "Carole was able to take good care of me without once bringing up a goddamn nursing home."

"So *now* you like Carole," Mom muttered. "How convenient."

"Here you go. How many times do I have to apologize—"

"I can't deal with this right now." Mom spun on her heel and stormed off to the den. Mama Letty stomped out to the porch. The shredded papers lay tattered and wrinkled on the braided rug, and I cautiously scooped them up. *Blue Mea* was on one half; *dow Hospice Lodge* on the other. When I pieced them together, my heart sank.

I glanced between the den and the porch. There was clearly a line being drawn down our family tree, and even still half asleep, I knew which side I was choosing.

Mama Letty didn't look up when I stepped outside. She was glaring at the thick knot of trees across the street. The day was already blooming into a sticky heat, the kind of weather that drives people indoors and makes tempers burn brighter. There wasn't a cloud in the sky.

"Hey, Mama Letty." I eased onto the porch swing. "What's going on?"

"Other than the fact my good-for-nothing daughter wants to shove me into an old folks' home?"

"I'm sure that wasn't her intention."

"I'm not leaving," she snapped. "I'm not going nowhere."

"Okay. So you won't leave."

She gazed at me warily. I pushed back against the swing, trying to appear casual although an idea was blossoming in my head that terrified me a little. I looked over Mama Letty's shoulder, to Simone's house, and the thought of her knees brushing mine during our carpet picnic propelled me.

"Do you want to hang out today?" I asked. "Like, away from the house?"

"So you can trick me into getting into a car so you can drive me to that nursing home?"

"Do you really think I'm capable of that?"

"I don't know," Mama Letty said, but it sounded like she really meant *I don't know* you. And she didn't. Not really. And that hurt.

"Let's go for a drive," I said, trying to remain upbeat. "You can show me all your favorite Bardell spots."

"I don't have any favorite Bardell spots."

"Then we'll drive around aimlessly in circles. At least we'll get away from Mom for a bit."

Mama Letty considered it. Then, slowly: "You know how to drive, Fish?"

"Yup. Wanna see my license?"

She grunted, waved the suggestion away. She stood, and just as I thought she was going to head inside, she started toward the faded hatchback in the driveway and told me her keys were on a hook near the stove.

• • •

I quickly discovered Mama Letty's penchant for critique extended beyond the bounds of Sweetness Lane. As I navigated through the streets of Bardell, Mama Letty happily slipped into the role of grumpy passenger seat driver.

Too slow, she barked as I eased over a speed bump. *Put the blinker on*, she demanded while paused at a stop sign with no one in front or behind us. *Jesus Christ, are you trying to kill me?* she yelled when I braked too hard at a yellow light.

"Would you like to drive?" I asked sweetly. "I'm trying to be gentle since this car is literally an ancient artifact."

"This is a 1984 Ford Escort, and you will respect it. And the light changed. Go on, hurry up!"

We chugged along, the only music option a scratchy Ray Charles tape that Mama Letty refused to change or turn down even though it skipped every ten seconds. As we cruised through downtown, she pressed her nose to the window to take in all the sights. When we stopped near the Draper, she gazed at the mural of Amelia. Her halo glittered in the sun.

"You know that's Jade's mom?" I asked.

Mama Letty grunted. "Light changed."

As we drove away, I glanced at the mural in the rearview. "You know, Jade is trying to get the Bardell Historical Society to build a statue for her."

"Like the world needs any more statues of white people."

I laughed. Mama Letty didn't.

"You know, Jade's not that bad," I said. "Her family is shitty, but she's really nice." I was hoping Mama Letty would take the bait and open up about those comments she and Carole made the night I first met Jade, but no luck. She stayed silent, I kept on driving, and downtown fell away.

A few minutes later, Mama Letty directed me to a small red-brick building across from a shuttered pharmacy and told me to park near the entrance.

"Don't hit that truck," Mama Letty scolded as I steered into a space.

"That truck is two miles away. You know, I really think *you* should drive home since you want . . ."

My voice trailed when I saw her glistening eyes. She was on the verge of tears.

"Mama Letty, what is it?"

She didn't answer. She was staring at the sign on the side of the building. Faded blue letters spelled out BARDELL STATION. And below: THANK YOU FOR CHOOSING AMTRAK!

"Are you okay?" I asked quietly.

"This is where I met your grandfather," she whispered.

The Ray Charles tape skipped and scratched.

● ● ●

Besides a sleepy-looking receptionist at the ticket counter and a hunched man sleeping in a plastic seat, the train station was empty. Mama Letty and I slipped through the waiting room unnoticed and onto the platform. Two tracks with weeds sprouting between the rails stretched north and south as far as we could see. I helped Mama Letty onto a bench, and she marveled at the tracks like they were made of gold.

"I ain't been here in so long," Mama Letty said. "Building ain't changed a bit."

"My grandfather used to work here?"

"He used to work *there*," she said, and pointed to the rails. "He was a porter for Amtrak. I met him right over there." She pointed to the far end of the platform where a wastebasket was bolted to the ground. "I was on my way to Orlando to visit my Aunt Regina. He helped me with my bag."

My heart melted. "Mama Letty! That's so romantic."

"Oh, Ray was a romantic. He fell in love the moment he saw me even though I thought he was annoying. But he eventually won me over. He was so handsome and whew, that uniform!"

"Tell me everything," I said, and she turned to me like a giddy schoolgirl. I'd never seen her face light up like this, and I thought about Simone's cactus analogy. How prickly could still bloom.

"Oh, we were so in love," she said. "And it was *real* love. Not that bullshit y'all call love nowadays. Ray was romantic. A real gentleman. A gentle heart and a kind soul. And he could *sing*.

He always used to call Ray Charles the 'second-best Ray.'" We laughed, and Mama Letty brought her wrinkled fingers to her lips, like she could still feel his kiss. "I thought for sure I would never see him again after that first trip."

"What happened?"

"We wrote letters. Two years of letters. I still have most of them."

"Can I read some of them one day?" I asked hopefully.

She gave me a look that wasn't a yes, wasn't a no. "I'll think about it," she said. "But one day he showed up at this train station and told me he was here to stay. He wanted to marry me."

My eyes widened. "He gave up his job for you?"

"He was tired of always being gone. The pay was good, but Ray wanted a family. He wanted to settle down. That was all he'd ever dreamed of."

Knowing how the story ended, knowing that Ray's dream had been cut short before he ever laid eyes on my mom, made my stomach cave inward. I looked at the railroad tracks and imagined a gleaming train pulling into the station. A handsome man stepping off. A young Mama Letty catching his eye.

There was no easy way to wrangle a life into a simple story, and Mama Letty had no intention of trying. She skipped around in their timeline, rewinding to that first train ride when Ray checked on her repeatedly, listening raptly while she told him what was bringing her to Orlando.

"You woulda thought I was some Hollywood starlet heading to a premiere with the way he was doting on me," Mama Letty said, lifting her chin. She ran a hand through her short gray curls. "He was so sweet. Gentle. I thought for sure your mama would get some of that gentleness, but she's always been all hard edges."

I thought of Mom in her fitted suits and her business class flights to speak at science conferences. She always told me she had to work twice as hard as the white women in her field, ten times harder than the white men. There was no room for gentle on her climb to the top, but I didn't want to interrupt Mama Letty to make that point. She was in a zone I'd never seen before. Being at the train station and talking about Ray had brought her to a transcendent place I felt lucky to witness. While she spoke about Ray's romantic letters and his proposal overlooking the Bardell River, I silently pleaded for the weather to not get any hotter, hoped the receptionist wouldn't tell us the platform was for ticketed passengers only, prayed for no interruptions, just so I could stay and have this story to myself.

Mama Letty said Raymond Harding was from Miami, and she never met his parents, even after they were married.

"Can you imagine?" Mama Letty asked. "Not wanting to meet *me*?"

"Never," I said, and we laughed again.

She told me that before her, Ray was engaged to someone else. "Some light-skinned girl. *Vivian*." She gripped the seat of the metal bench like the memory still pained her. "His parents didn't want him to be with me. They thought I was nothing but a dumb dark girl from the sticks. But bet if I passed the paper bag test, they would've had no problem with me bein' from here."

"That's awful," I said.

"All skinfolk ain't kinfolk. But I know they blamed me for his death. We hadn't been married even a year before it happened."

"Before what happened?"

She tore her eyes away from the tracks. By now, the sun was high, and even the shade of the platform didn't help matters. Sweat dripped down her temple, and she looked like she was debating something in her head.

"You can tell me," I said. "I want to know."

"Why do you think your mama hasn't told you?"

"Because she avoids everything. Anything remotely uncomfortable, she barrels through and focuses her attention elsewhere." It was a trait I'd once admired. It was a trait I'd inherited.

Mama Letty pulled a cigarette from her pocket and lit it. I hated the way the smoke smelled, hated knowing her lungs were dying and this obviously wasn't helping, but I said nothing.

"Your mama feels guilty," she said. "And it's eating her up."

"Guilty about what?"

"For not visiting."

"We visited once. Seemed like it didn't go well."

She smirked. "That was over a decade ago. She could've made time since then."

My eyes watered as smoke wafted my way. "She never told me why she never wanted to come back. She's always busy with work."

"Busy," Mama Letty echoed. "She sure was busy when y'all

went on that family trip to Florida. And Colorado. Or California. Or all them summers you spent at Grandma *Jean's*. I can't keep track. No wonder you grew up all lopsided."

"What do you mean?" But part of me knew what she meant. It was the same part that cowered in the museum when Kelsi's words seeped into my veins like venom. The part of me that always ached when I was little and couldn't find myself in either of my parents' faces. The empty, gaping branch on my family tree.

"You tell me," Mama Letty said. "You don't know shit about me. You ain't even know your own grandfather's name until last week. Ain't that odd?"

"I'm trying to get to know you. But you aren't exactly making it easy." I was sweating at this point. The cigarette smelled, and my throat was dry with thirst. "You hole yourself up in your room. Mom always shoots my questions down. But I'm trying. Mama Letty, I'm trying."

At that moment, the receptionist stepped out onto the platform, shaking a cigarette from a cellophane-wrapped pack. She glanced at us, opened her mouth, then shrugged and leaned against the building.

"I'm hot," Mama Letty said, voice hard. She stood slowly, and I grabbed her hand and helped her. The spell was shattered. The moment, gone.

In the car, I cranked the air-conditioning, but it was barely a sputtering breeze. I put the car in reverse, my cheeks hot. It felt like all the progress we'd made had evaporated on the platform.

"Avery."

My hand hovered over the gear stick. My real name, not *Fish*, sounded strange in her mouth.

"You really want to know about Ray?"

I swallowed past the lump in my throat. "Of course I do."

She pursed her lips and looked at the Bardell Station sign. Then she nodded.

"Fine. I'll tell you some things. When I'm ready."

"When will that be?"

Her smile was small. "I'll let you know."

THE PORTER

THERE WERE SEVERAL ways to get to Bardell County, Georgia, and Raymond Harding knew them well. You could drive, of course. Or fly to Savannah, but cab fare from the airport would surely clean the pockets. The bus was least preferable, albeit the most affordable. But if you asked Raymond his professional opinion, he'd tell you the only way to arrive in Bardell, if you wanted to arrive in style, was to go by train.

Raymond had worked on the Silver Meteor for a mere two years when he met Letty June Prince. Unlike his proud Pullman Porter father, Raymond's ability to appear simultaneously present and invisible to the white passengers did not come naturally. He was clumsy, for starters. He talked too much, and his jokes usually fell flat. He was easily distracted by the passing landscapes, being admonished multiple times for marveling at a pink DC sunset when he should've been turning down beds or admiring a tangerine Lowcountry sunrise when he should've been preparing coffee orders. Raymond's father had always told him working for the rails was a Good Black Job, but Raymond struggled to believe it until the day Letty June Prince asked if he was going to help with her battered suitcase or just stand there all day.

In the six hours between Bardell and Orlando, Raymond made Letty June laugh five times. He counted because it wasn't an easy feat. She called him unprofessional the first time he told her she was beautiful. She scowled when he asked for her phone number. It wasn't until Raymond accidentally stepped on a white woman's foot that Letty finally cracked a smile. When Raymond noticed it, he felt a detour carving its way through the careful plan his pretentious upper-middle class parents had pushed on him for twenty-three years. As he watched Letty June disembark in Orlando with his phone number tucked in her purse, he felt his life trembling like steel rails bracing for an incoming train.

His parents didn't understand when Raymond broke his engagement to Vivian Roberts. Vivian was such a *nice* girl, his mother insisted when Raymond would check the mail, desperate for one of Letty June's letters. Wanda Harding couldn't understand why her handsome son would rather be with a poor girl from some pit stop between Jacksonville and Savannah over wealthy, caramel-skinned, apple green–eyed Vivian. Raymond tried to persuade his parents to visit Bardell, confident they would fall in love with Letty June as easily and effortlessly as he did. They refused, believing Letty June was the wrong direction, a detour, a dead-end street Raymond would U-turn out of. They hoped Raymond would eventually move on, full-steam ahead. They did not understand that Letty June's slow-simmer heart and firecracker mouth and sparkler fingers were the only reasons Raymond needed to stay put.

9.

"ARE WE ALMOST there?"

"Shhhh!"

"Ouch! What the—"

"Sorry, sorry! That was my bad!"

"This blindfold is excessive."

"*You're* excessive."

"Y'all, I'm serious, *shut up.*"

"I feel like I'm going to puke."

"Almost there . . ."

"Okay . . . now."

I knew it was Simone unwrapping the bandanna around my eyes because her jagged stone ring kept brushing the back of my neck. There'd been nothing but darkness for half an hour, and when the cloth fell, I had to squint against the soft light of a table lamp. We were in a hotel room.

"Surprise!" Jade stood in front of me, wild curly hair fanning her face. "Welcome to your party!"

I rubbed my eyes, trying to erase the fuzzy stars. "My party?"

"I guess the blindfold was a little extra," Simone said as she dropped a bulging backpack on the ground. "Or *excessive*, as you said."

"I could handle the blindfold. But that was literally a hundred stairs. At *least*."

"I couldn't risk us getting caught in the lobby," Jade said. "For obvious reasons." She tossed a duffel bag on the massive king-sized bed. The room matched the Draper's lobby, tastefully decorated with sleek, modern gray furniture. There was a plush love seat nestled in the corner near a stocked minibar and a giant flat-screen TV. Large windows overlooked the dark and winding Bardell River.

"Another perk of being the owner's daughter?" I asked.

Jade smirked. "My dad doesn't know about this. One of the front desk clerks owed me a favor. Long story short, this is ours for the night as long as we're out before housekeeping comes at ten."

"And don't worry about your parents," Simone told me. She pulled clothes from her bag and tossed me a pair of soft yellow shorts and a faded Atlanta Falcons tank top. "They think we're spending the night at Jade's."

"And *my* parents think I'm at Maggie Elle's," Jade said.

"Don't you think that's a little risky?" I asked. "Since both of your parents—"

"Good Lord, DC, would you lighten up and live a little!" Simone interrupted. She grabbed my arm and ushered me to the bathroom. "Go change, we have a party to start!" Her dimples were the last thing I saw before she slid the bathroom door closed.

The bathroom was even more impressive than the bedroom. Gleaming marble floors led to a claw-foot bathtub and waterfall shower. I slipped out of my jeans and hoodie and put Simone's clothes on, smiling ridiculously when I realized they smelled like her almond lotion. Afterward, I studied my face in the mirror, trying to make the red in my cheeks go away. My curls were a tangled mess—as usual—so I took my time readjusting my frizzy ponytail to calm myself down.

This was not what I had in mind when I thought of all the things Simone and Jade could've been planning all week. I had envisioned another night at the Perfect Spot, maybe even cosmic bowling. Definitely not being shoved blindfolded in the back of Jade's Jeep for half an hour and sneaking into the fanciest hotel I'd ever been in. After my conversation with Mama Letty at the train station and a full week of awkward, icy silence between her and Mom, a party felt like a welcome relief.

"DC! Did you fall in the toilet?" Simone's and Jade's giggles were muffled through the door.

When I emerged, they were also in pajamas—Simone in a faded T-shirt and shorts like me, Jade in a lacy boxer set. Simone was setting electric tea candles along most of the surfaces in the room while Jade unwrapped a bottle of whiskey. Three paper crowns rested on the coffee table, surrounded by bags of kettle chips, miniature chocolate bars, and the sour gummy worms I'd been instructed to bring.

"What are we celebrating?" I asked.

"You," Simone said simply. Jade twirled the cap off the whiskey and rationed it into three glasses with soda.

"Me? My birthday isn't until December." But my throat tightened when I walked closer and saw the crowns didn't say HAPPY BIRTHDAY. They were covered in rainbow glitter and royal rhinestones and gold sparkles. Bright pink letters spelled out BEST FRIENDS!

"It's not a birthday party." Jade put her crown on, and her curls sprang in every direction. "It's a celebration. Of a new friendship."

I stared at the crowns and snacks like they were expensive caviar, at a complete loss for words. When I looked over at Simone, she was holding a gold wire ring with a marbled dark blue stone in the middle, similar to the ones she and Jade wore all the time.

"It's a sodalite stone," Simone explained. "It's helpful for enhancing self-acceptance and confidence."

"This is for me?" I asked.

"Yeah," Simone said, sliding it onto my middle finger. It was a perfect fit. "Jade's is selenite for peace. Mine is citrine. It stands for joy. Delight."

My throat burned as I stared at my stone.

"In all seriousness, we wanted to officially welcome you into our circle," Simone said. Jade swooped in with two heavy crystal glasses filled with whiskey and soda. "I should add that you shouldn't take this lightly since we pretty much hate everyone."

"Hear! Hear!" Jade held a glass in the air.

"We're sorry your friends in DC were horrible, no-good, rotten poop faces," Simone continued, "and we know Bardell can seem pretty damn bleak. But we can offer our friendship, if you want."

They both stared at me expectantly, but my confusion must've been apparent on my face.

"Hey, my arm is getting tired," Jade said. "This is the part where you say yes or no. But preferably yes since Simone just put a ring on it."

I laughed and raised my glass. "Of course I say yes. I thought we were already friends!"

"To us!" Simone exclaimed, and we clinked our glasses and sipped. The whiskey burned going down in a good way.

"Before we get too drunk," Jade said, "we have a surprise for you."

"Another one?"

"Close your eyes," Simone said, and when she told me to reopen them, she was holding a pair of scissors and an electric razor.

"I'm . . . frightened," I said.

They pulled me into the bathroom in a wave of laughter and stood in front of the large mirror. With me squished between them, we made a perfect slope—Jade slightly taller than me, Simone several inches shorter. It was such a change from being with Hikari and Kelsi. With them, I'd been the short one while the two of them were skinny and tall, all points and angles.

"Ms. Anderson, we do believe you're overdue for a haircut," Simone said.

"Shall we go nice and short?" Jade asked. "Shave the whole head?"

I thought of Kelsi and Hikari, their concerned faces when I approached them with the idea months ago. I burst out laughing. "Oh my God, my ex would hate it."

"That's kind of the point," Simone said, resting her chin on my shoulder.

"You know how to cut hair?" I asked their reflections.

"Totally," Jade said. "I've watched so many tutorials. Plus, I cut my little brothers' hair all the time."

"She does," Simone chimed in.

"This is wild," I muttered. I stared at my limp curls. Then my new sodalite ring. I wanted to believe Simone's promises that it would bring me confidence and self-acceptance. Three months ago, I'd been too afraid to make this change, scared of not living up to Kelsi and Hikari's expectations of what I should look like. How I should act. Who I should be.

But what did I want?

I picked the gleaming scissors up from the quartz counter. Then, before I lost my nerve, I grabbed a handful of curls near my temple and chopped them off. They rained like confetti into the sink, and Simone and Jade whooped with delight.

"Let's do it," I said.

Simone ran a hand through my hair, knuckles brushing my earlobe. "Get in the tub."

• • •

Jade wielded the scissors like a magician, swiftly cutting away curls with gentle snips. Simone had the job of brushing stray hairs from my lap, and I didn't know if it was the whiskey or the adrenaline, but time seemed to slow when her fingers brushed my thighs. We took turns DJing, and our musical tastes couldn't have been more different. Kelela turned into Kacey Musgraves, Megan Thee Stallion followed by Taylor Swift. At the Perfect Spot, I'd wondered if I was falling in love with this friendship, but in the tub I knew. Jade and Simone weren't the kind of people to wrinkle their noses at an unfamiliar song, they didn't ask *who is this?* with disdain like Kelsi had when I put on Be Steadwell. I played "Love Song for a Dom Stripper" and Simone screamed "*Yessss!*" and twerked in the tub, flipping her locs and shaking her ass while Jade and I cheered her on. Everything was beautiful and tinged with glitter, my face was warm and the tub was cold against my thighs.

Jade pressed the razor to my scalp, and I gasped when my spirals sprinkled in my lap.

"It's okay," she assured me. "It's going to look great!"

"Do you want a full shave?" Simone asked. "Because now I'm thinking a side shave would actually be so badass."

"You'll look good either way," Jade said.

I told them to do half now and if I hated it, I'd shave the rest off. My heart pounded wildly as my head grew lighter. Soon, most of the hair on my left side was gone. There was silence as Simone paused the music and Jade turned the razor off.

"How do I look?" I asked cautiously.

"So cool," Jade said.

"Fucking amazing," Simone added.

Simone and I climbed out of the tub, brushing stray curls off our laps. I squeezed my eyes shut as they led me to the mirror, and they did a dramatic countdown in their radio announcer voices. When I opened my eyes, I was speechless.

"Do you like it?" Jade asked.

"A little too late if you don't," Simone teased.

I turned my head in all directions, biting down on my lip ring. I was horrified to find my eyes welling up. Jade's mouth dropped.

"Oh my God, you hate it. You hate it. I'm so sorry—"

"No," I said. "I don't hate it. I've never . . . seen." I swallowed and took a breath. "I look like . . . me."

"I think that's a good thing!" Jade insisted.

"I think it's a great thing," Simone said.

• • •

We toasted to my new hair with whiskey shots. Then Jade played bartender and refilled our drinks while Simone and I jumped on the fluffy king-sized bed and created our own lyrics over Cardi B beats. We sang, "Sleepovers are so much fun, so much fun, let's fling ourselves into the sun!" and laughed because it made no sense and we were offbeat. At one point, I almost cried because I loved my hair so much and everything felt so perfect and there was glitter in my whiskey soda and sodalite in my gold ring and Simone looked so beautiful in the dim light and Jade's hugs were so warm, but I blamed the alcohol when they asked me why my eyes were red because I didn't know how to say any of that. I drunkenly thought of my mom and her pale blue dot speech, and all I could think about was how lucky I felt to have found these two humans in my tiny corner of the universe, and we had somehow created this perfect night together.

We greeted midnight with a rousing game of Truth or Dare. Simone and I dared Jade to call Tim Joplin, which she happily did. She told him his balls smelled like rotten fish and had to hang up quickly because Simone and I were laughing so hard. Jade and I dared Simone to knock on half the doors on our floor and she obliged, dancing and twirling down the hall in her doughnut socks, knocking on doors and sprinting back to the safety of our room before anyone could catch us. When I picked Truth, they asked me if I'd ever had sex, and I recounted the one awkward time Kelsi and I had tried but her mom came home early.

By one a.m., we were whiskey drunk and ravenous. We flipped through Syrup's twenty-four-hour dining menu, arguing over what we should get. Jade texted an order for a large pepperoni pizza to the night line cook. He told us to come down to the kitchen to pick it up, but Jade didn't make it that long. After setting her phone down, she promptly fell asleep in the middle of a sentence, blonde curls splayed across the down-feather pillows.

"Typical," Simone said, poking Jade's side. She snored and rolled over.

"We'll get it ourselves," I said.

We shoved jeans over our pajamas and trudged to the stairwell. I squinted against the harsh light and gray concrete. My head spun as we made our way down the steps, carefully gripping handrails and cackling when I almost slipped.

"Your hair looks good," she said when we paused on a landing. "Like, *really* good." She leaned in to inspect Jade's work. She was so close, too close; all I could smell was her. I was drunk on not only the whiskey, but Simone's almond butter body, her spicy chocolate breath.

"It was a great idea." The words fell from my mouth like sap. She was still so close. Why was she so close and moving closer?

"I wanted to tell you," she whispered. "The other night. Cheesy bread night? I wanted to tell you my secret, but I got scared." Our foreheads were almost touching. Her unblinking eyes held galaxies. They were so pretty, pretty like the stones she used to make rings. Dark brown, flecks of gold.

"What secret?"

"I'm gay. I'm a lesbian, I think. No, no, no, I know, I—" She clamped her hands over her mouth. "Oh, shit. I'm sorry. I'm on my period, I'm emotional, I don't—"

Then she started to cry.

"Hey, hey, it's okay." My words were muffled in her locs as she leaned into me. "It's okay."

"It's scary." Her voice was smaller than I'd ever heard. Her breath was hot on my neck, rapidly picking up speed. I guided us down on the steps.

"Breathe with me," I said. "It'll be okay. One . . . two—"

"No!" she snapped. "It won't be okay. It's not—" The rest of her sentence drowned in a wave of hiccups.

My panic rose. I didn't know what to do with my hands. Her words sank in slowly before hitting me like a sucker punch.

I *knew* it.

"It's not going to be okay," Simone said. "Not for me. You have *everything*, Avery. Parents who accept you. You're from a big city filled with people who couldn't care less about who you date. You'll have so many girlfriends and—"

"You can have that, too. Atlanta is full of queer people."

Her eyes hardened and she scooted down two steps.

"You don't get it," she said coldly. "I'm not going to Atlanta. I never was."

"What are you talking about?"

"Seriously, Avery? In what universe could I up and leave my mom? I can't leave her alone in Bardell. Atlanta is a fantasy. A game."

I gripped the handrail and closed my eyes. The stairwell felt like it was caught in a tornado. "I don't get it," I said slowly. "You have the grades. You'll get into Spelman. This is your dream."

"That's rich. *You* giving me a speech about following my dreams."

Her harsh tone made me reel away. I had no idea where we went wrong. If we went back to the room, back to the soft light and glitter and whiskey, would that make everything better again? The stairwell was cold and grimy, and the concrete was rough beneath my palms. This was nothing like the party. Simone slipped down another step.

"I'm all my mom has, Avery," she said, staring at the bold LEVEL FIVE on the wall. "I can't leave. My dad left, Shayla left, Shawn died. It's just me, and I'm so fucking lonely."

"You have Jade," I said. "You have me."

"Jade's straight," Simone cried, "she's white. And you're

already out, and your parents accept you. Do you know how lonely I feel sometimes? Listening to all the fucking white boys in school call me fat? Fucking Aunt Jemima? Can you imagine how much worse it would be if they knew I was a lesbian, too?"

"Fuck them. They're idiots, Simone. You're beautiful. You're stunning. You're—"

"I know!" Her voice bounced around the empty stairwell like a boomerang. "I know that! But it's still exhausting, and you will never understand. So I tell myself I just have to make it to the end of the year, just have to make it until I get my Spelman letter and then I'll be out of here, but it's not real, Avery. None of it's real."

I scooted down so I was next to her again. "It can be."

"My mom would never accept me if I came out. *Never*. So I'm stuck here in fucking Bardell for the rest of my life while you and Jade get to run off and chase your dreams and be yourselves." Her face collapsed and she buried her head in her hands. The sunflower girl was wilting. When I tried to put my arm around her, she shrugged me off and told me she needed a moment.

"Okay. I'll . . . go get the food." She didn't stop me as I slowly walked down the steps, mind and heart reeling. I wondered if I was about to wake up, nestled right next to Jade, still in our dizzy slumber party dream because this couldn't be how this night ended. It couldn't.

I somehow found my way to Syrup's side door. The restaurant was dark. Bottles glittered behind the bar. Besides the low hum of a radio from the kitchen, it was eerily quiet.

The line cook slipped out of the kitchen and handed me a large pepperoni pizza. "Tell Jade she better put in a good word with her dad," he said. He went on about how he really, *really* could use a raise, but I was only half listening, still stunned from the sharp turn the night had taken. I nodded numbly, and he disappeared back into the kitchen. I was left in the dark, holding the too-hot pizza and wincing against the gust of air-conditioning on my newly shaved head.

I was about to return to the stairwell when there was a loud, muffled burst of laughter. I backed into a shadowy corner, mind running wild with thoughts of Lucas and Tallulah catching me, maybe putting a hit out on *me* for breaking into their hotel. But then the person laughed again, and I realized it was coming from outside.

On the street, leaning against the hood of a very familiar car, were two women. When I realized who they were, I almost dropped the pizza.

Mom and Carole were laughing, the loud, gut-wrenching kind. I watched as Mom leaned against Carole with a familiarity like she'd known her all her life. It took my foggy brain more than a couple of seconds to remember she had. The two of them were washed in the streetlight's warm glow, Carole still in her Syrup uniform, Mom in a loose white sundress with one of Dad's blazers draped over her shoulders. Mom said something, and that made them laugh even harder. My brain told me to go, leave before I got caught.

But I couldn't look away. I stayed rooted, watching in disbelief. It was like all those petty snipes they'd exchanged on our first day in Bardell didn't matter. Clearly, they didn't hate each other, not even a little bit. It felt weird seeing Carole without a frown or a sneer. And Mom . . . I could tell there was a lightness about her, a tenderness, even from far away. I'd never seen her look at anyone the way she was looking at Carole. Even my dad.

A weird sensation crawled up my spine that had nothing to do with the whiskey or the conversation with Simone. A voice in my head was screaming for me to leave, but I shook it away. They weren't going to catch me. They didn't even notice me. I could tell by the way they were looking at each other; they couldn't see anything else. A spaceship could've landed on top of the Draper, and they would've been oblivious. They were the only two humans alive, and I could've stayed there watching them for an eternity.

But then Carole rested her head on Mom's shoulder, a move so intimate that I had to look away. I slipped back into the stairwell, heart pounding like a wild animal entangled in a trap, stunned to have been caught in the wrong place at the wrong time.

10.

WE WOKE UP to a cold pizza, a tub full of clipped hair, and three massive hangovers. When Jade saw the time, she leapt out of bed.

"Rise and shine! We gotta be out in twenty minutes!" She fluttered around the room, shoving candles and clothes into her duffel bag. Her absence left a wide gap in the rumpled sheets, and when Simone caught my eye, she rolled over and left me staring at her fading blue–tipped locs.

Last night, I'd stumbled up the steps, woozy but ready to continue our conversation. I imagined we'd share the pizza and I'd listen if she wanted to cry or talk some more. I'd tell her about the closeness of our mothers and the strange feeling it gave me.

But when I returned to the landing, she wasn't there. She'd retreated back to the suite and was already curled up in bed by the time I arrived. I whispered her name, but she was asleep—or at least was pretending to be. So I sat on the floor and half-heartedly ate two slices, my mind slipping between thoughts of Simone's confession and Carole's head on my mom's shoulder.

"Come on, beauty queens." Jade yanked the fluffy down comforter off in one motion. "Unless you want to have to explain to my parents what we're doing here, I suggest you get up now."

I peeled myself out of bed and went to the bathroom to change. When I handed Simone the pajamas, I smiled at her, but she looked away. Dread curled in my stomach.

"Are you okay?" I asked.

"Hangover," she mumbled, but she still wouldn't look at me. Jade moaned in agreement from the other side of the room.

When Jade dropped us off on Sweetness Lane, Simone took off across her lawn without a backward glance. Jade waved and drove off, leaving me on the sidewalk in the warming sun. Mama Letty was on the porch, as usual, smoking a cigarette, as usual.

"Hey, Mama Letty," I said as I plopped onto the porch steps.

The rocking chair squeaked to a stop. "What the hell did you do to your head?"

"You don't like it?"

"I ain't say that."

"You can if you want."

"Must've been one hell of a slumber party."

"You have no idea."

She snorted and returned her attention to a small notebook on her lap. I leaned back on my forearms and looked at her upside down, staring until blood rushed to my head. She lowered the book and sighed.

"What is it, Fish?"

"What's in the notebook?"

"None of your damn business."

"Okaaaay. You want to go for a walk? Or a drive?"

"Not particularly."

I looked over at Simone's house and felt the chasm in my heart split wider. I had to get away from here. I crab-walked backward onto the porch until I was at Mama Letty's feet. She slapped the notebook shut and laughed.

"Something wrong with you," she said.

"I know."

"Your mama do drugs when she was pregnant?"

"Not that I know of. Speaking of Mom." I swiveled around and leaned against the porch rail. "Where is she?"

"She and your hippie-ass father went for a drive," Mama Letty said, taking a drag from her cigarette. "You know, because taking care of me is so *exhausting*."

I thought of Mom and Carole, leaning together in the quiet dark, laughing together without a care in the world. Those thoughts ultimately looped back to Simone and her eyes in the harsh concrete stairwell. Her admission delicately hanging between us as if the words were spun from spider's silk.

"Let's go for a drive," I said. "You can boss me around and tell me I brake too hard."

"No."

"Please?"

She grunted. "Get the keys."

• • •

At the train station, the same man was slumped in a plastic chair, snoozing with a gaping newspaper on his stomach. The woman behind the ticket counter watched as Mama Letty and

I headed for the platform, but returned her attention to her phone without saying anything.

Outside, we sat on the same bench, stared at the same tracks, baked under the same heat. I pressed a chilled water bottle into Mama Letty's hands.

"Please drink this," I said. "Would hate for you to keel over and die from heat exhaustion."

Mama Letty laughed. "So you got jokes."

"Trying to keep up with you."

She eyed my hair. "Simone and that white girl do this?"

I nodded.

"Looks nice."

"I can get them to do yours, too," I said. "We can match."

"Girl, don't press your luck."

We sat and let the world go by for a bit. The quiet that once felt suffocating when I first arrived in Bardell now felt comfortable. Mama Letty and I listened to the drone of insects and I tried not to think about Simone. If it weren't for the sodalite and my side shave, I would've sworn the entire night was a dream.

"Can you tell me more about Ray?" I asked.

"What about him?"

"Anything you want."

Mama Letty stared at the tracks. Condensation dripped down the water bottle and onto her hands. "I don't know what you want me to say."

"Anything! You promised me you'd tell me more about him."

"I never promised nothing."

"Mama Letty!"

She chuckled and leaned back, crossing her feet at the ankles. She was wearing scuffed flip-flops, and her toes were cracked and unpainted. "It's not a pretty story. You still want to know?"

"Of course I do."

"Ray was murdered," she said, as simply as someone saying the sun was hot or the moon was a quarter of a million miles away. She said it with the finality of someone who'd had time to grapple with the weight of the words and understood there was nothing she could do about it.

"Murdered?" I asked. "Are you serious?"

"Let me tell you a goddamn thing, Fish. If you'd been lying on the ground four months pregnant watching the love of your life get dragged into the back of a cop car by three white men, you'd never be so sure of anything in your entire life. It will stay with you. Every day, it will stay with you."

I covered my mouth with my hand. "Mama Letty, I didn't know. I'm so sorry, I didn't know."

"It was the worst day of my life. Never forgotten it. And folks don't like to talk about it because it's so damn ugly. Now I don't blame your mama for wanting to bury it. Of course she ain't tell you. You a child. How is anyone supposed to know the right age for carrying all this shit?" Her hands were clasped in her lap, and all I wanted to do was reach over and braid our fingers together.

But I didn't. I couldn't. I pulled at the end of my curls instead, desperate to give my hands something to do. I heard the echoes of screams again. Saw the gold-wrapped present shooting across Mama Letty's living room like lightning.

"They were bad men," Mama Letty said. "Evil men. Shoved Ray in a patrol car, and that was the last time I ever saw him. They killed him."

"Who?" I pressed.

"The goddamn sheriff and his men! They all had connections to the Klan back then. They killed him and covered it up so good no one ever found his body. And people had the nerve to say he left me, that the pregnancy was too stressful, he went back to Florida. But Ray would never leave me on his own."

The sun was blazing through the platform roof, sinking into my bones. I was lightheaded and dizzy, but I forced myself to keep it together. I told her I could handle it. I told her I wanted to know.

"It was my fault," she said, quieter. "If I hadn't said anything, Ray would still be alive."

"Said *what*?" I demanded because there was no world in which any words could've justified this. Mama Letty reached for her pack of cigarettes, and for the first time, I didn't have the urge to scold her.

"After Ray quit working for the train, he moved to Bardell to be with me. Got a job at the general store. It damn sure wasn't as fancy as the other job, and his parents hated it, but we were together. We were happy. I was pregnant with your mama. We had so many plans. And they were all taken, snatched away in one day. Help me light this."

She dropped a lighter into my palm. She could barely hold

the cigarette between her fingers because she was trembling so hard. I lit it and she leaned back against the bench.

"If he hadn't been working at that goddamn general store, he'd still be here. If we'd closed moments earlier, he'd still be here. But no. I was helping him close up when the sheriff pulled up with two other officers. They looked drunk, even though they was supposed to be on duty. They wanted some food, some more cigarettes. And Ray told 'em he was sorry, but the store was closed for the night." An amused look crossed her face. "You should've seen their faces! How dare a Black man talk to them like that? Never mind we closed at six thirty every goddamn day, Monday through Saturday. Nothing new. But they was looking for trouble. I remember, I was wearing this pretty light blue dress I'd sewn over the summer. Your mama ever tell you I used to sew?"

I shook my head.

"'Course she didn't. Well, I did. And I was pretty damn good, too. It was blue. Ray loved me in blue." There was a flash of a smile, but it was gone within seconds. "I thought Ray would give in. He was always the *nice* one between us. So I spoke up."

My stomach dropped. I felt all the whiskey and sugar and pizza stirring in my stomach, desperate to reappear. "What did you say?"

"I told them we were running late for a dinner. And when that sheriff looked at me, I swear to God I was looking at the devil." Mama Letty lowered her voice, imitating a deep

Southern male twang. "'*So I guess your dinner is more important than ours! Is this any way to treat your local law enforcement?*'" Her lip curled. "Punk ass. At that point, he knew he was getting under my skin. Ray pulled me back before I could say anything else. He told them he'd get them their sandwiches. Typical Ray. Always so nice to people who didn't deserve it."

I knew how the story ended, but my eyes welled with tears anyway. I knew about the Klan. I'd felt my blood boil learning about them in museums and history books. There were so many people who liked to believe the Jim Crow era was ancient history, but Mama Letty was talking about it like it was yesterday. I stared at the train tracks, trying to focus on something so I didn't heave.

"They started taunting us. Saying things like how pretty they thought my dress was. Could I make something like that for their wives? Ray was fumblin' around with his keys, trying to get that damn store open. But then that son of a bitch sheriff reached for me. I think he was trying to put his hand up my dress, but he never made it that far." Mama Letty mimed slapping someone, her face twisted in rage. "I cracked him across the face like a cat in heat. I know I shouldn't have done that. I know that. I think about it every day. How differently that night might have gone if I had let him feel me up. Swallowed my pride. But I was fiery when I was young, too fiery."

She took a long drag on her cigarette and almost immediately began to cough. She reached into her purse for her handkerchief and hacked up blood.

I stood. "We should go."

"No," she snapped. "I ain't done."

"Mama Letty, please," I begged. "It's hot and you shouldn't be out here."

"Let me finish the damn story."

The ferocity in her tone forced me back down. I looked away, my eyes burning and stomach twisting harder and tighter and faster.

"Ray begged and pleaded and apologized," Mama Letty continued. "Can you imagine? Apologizing to the man who was trying to feel up your woman? But that was the way of the world back then. You apologized to white people for everything. Sorry, sorry, sorry. Sorry for brushing against you on the sidewalk. Sorry for standing too close to you at the bus stop. Sorry for trying to go to school with your little white children. Sorry for existing."

Her words suddenly felt so far away. Heat rushed to my forehead. Another stomach twist.

"Ray was damn near in tears, apologizing for my actions. He told those men I was pregnant and emotional. That really got them going! They kept taunting us, having a grand time. Ray kept saying he didn't want any trouble. But it was too late. They were all laughing, but nothing was funny. They were sick men, Avery." She coughed again, spat on the concrete.

"When they shoved Ray in the back of their car, I didn't understand. Didn't understand why they were taking Ray and not me. *I* was the one mouthing off. I thought they were going to come back for me. But once they got Ray in the car, which was *not* easy, Lord you should have heard him yelling, they took off. Left me in the middle of the street—"

The door to the station flung open, and the woman from the ticket counter stepped out with the heavy sigh of someone who hated their job.

"Look, I don't know why y'all wanna hang out here," she said, pulling out her own cigarette. "And I usually wouldn't give a damn. But my boss coming in a bit so y'all gone have to go unless you're ticketed passengers." She squinted. "Are y'all ticketed passengers?"

Mama Letty grumbled and said something along the lines of no, of course we weren't no damn ticketed passengers, but I didn't catch it all. Suddenly I was standing, heading toward the tracks in a sun-hot daze, tears streaming down my face, bile rising in my throat. I hunched over the platform and vomited directly onto the tracks, barely registering the ticket counter woman's disgusted, "Oh *hell* nah!" The last thing I saw before I squeezed my eyes shut, bracing myself for the next wave, was the silver steel of the rails, glinting in the sun.

• • •

When we got home—Mama Letty shakily driving because I could barely walk—Mom and Dad were waiting on the porch.

"Not looking too hot, Unsavory," Dad said, nose wrinkling as he caught a whiff of me. "Everything okay?"

"Where the hell were you?" Mom scolded. "Mama, you know you shouldn't be driving."

"What you gonna do, Zora? Shove me into a nursing home? Oh wait." Mama Letty breezed up the porch steps and into the house.

"It's *not* a nursing home," Mom said through gritted teeth. She looked me over, shook her head. "What happened to your hair?"

I groaned and pushed past her, following Mama Letty into the house. Mom was right on my heels.

"Excuse me, young lady, I am talking to you!"

"Mom, *please*."

"'Mom, please' what?"

"Not now." I sighed, barreling down the hall. "I don't feel good."

"And you're gonna feel a whole lot worse if you don't start talking."

I threw open my bedroom door and collapsed onto the bed. The pillow was cool against my forehead. I groaned when Mom sat next to me and ran her hand over my newly shaved scalp.

"Why did you do this?" she asked.

"Because I felt like it and thought it would look cool," I mumbled into my pillow.

"And *why* did you have your Mama Letty out there driving in this heat? She's supposed to be *resting*, Avery. Not going on joyrides."

"Excuse me for trying to spend time with her before she dies, unlike you."

Mom pulled her hand away. "Excuse me?"

I rolled onto my back and stared at her. Despite her expertly applied eyeliner and nude lip, she looked so tired, so sad. I knew she didn't need my attitude, but between the hangover and Mama Letty's story, my filter was nonexistent.

"That Blue Meadow Hospice Lodge thing," I said. "How could you ever think she would want that?"

"I've been through this a million times. Blue Meadow is a luxury facility with good doctors and the best amenities. It's supposed to be *nice*."

"Well, Mama Letty doesn't want nice. She wants to be home."

"Well, fine," Mom said stiffly. "If you're so full of ideas, what do you propose we do?"

"I don't know! Spend time with her! Take her out to nice places! Ask her what she wants to do!"

"That's enough." Mom stood and strode to the door in a huff. "I can't deal with this right now."

"You say that all the time," I muttered, and she was back at my side in a flash.

"You wanna say that again, little girl?" Her face transformed into the soft, terrifying calm she usually reserved for men who asked her condescending questions on panels. I had rarely ever been on the receiving end, and for a split second, I thought about biting back the words, saying never mind, never mind, never mind. But something pushed me forward.

"You always say you can't deal with something," I said slowly, "and then we never end up talking about it again."

"That's not true."

"It is true! Like how could you never tell me that my grand-father, *your father*, was murdered? By the Klan! Don't you think that's something I should know?" All those stories I learned in school about the Civil Rights Movement, all the horrors I knew about the deep-rooted history of the Klan in the South. That violence ended Ray's life. *My* grandfather's life.

How could Mom not tell me?

Mom's eyes widened like she'd been slapped. She took a giant step back, arms rigid at her sides. In her cobalt-blue maxi-dress and white headwrap, she looked like a royal statue, frozen in time.

"She told you that?" she asked quietly.

"Yeah. Thank God. Because it's not like you were ever plan-ning on it."

Mom pinched the bridge of her nose. When she dropped her hand, her eyes were shining. We were silent for the longest minute in the world.

"There are things I didn't want you to know," she said, "because they are painful. Do you understand that?"

"I think I should be able to decide that for myself."

She smiled unkindly. "Oh, because you're grown now?"

"No, because this is my family, too."

My hands were trembling; so were hers. She brought one up to scrub over her face.

"She's an old woman, Avery. She's dying. Those memories are painful, and I want the last bit of her life to be joyful and relaxing. Not focused on the dredging up of old memories."

"Joyful and relaxing?" I laughed. Had she met Mama Letty? "Why don't we just book a first-class flight to Paris or—"

"That's enough with the attitude."

"You still should've told me."

"Well, now you know."

She slammed the door when she left.

11.

THE PERKS OF becoming an official member of Simone and Jade's inner circle apparently didn't end with extravagant parties at the Draper Hotel. On Monday morning, seven thirty on the dot, Jade arrived in her pearl-white Jeep to chauffer me and Simone to school. I was grateful I didn't have to spend twenty agonizing minutes in the car with Mom since we still weren't speaking. But Simone didn't even look at me when I slid in the back seat, and it was a crushing realization that I wasn't exactly on good terms with her either.

"Iced white mocha extra shot for you," Jade said, passing Simone a delicious-looking concoction with a whirl of whipped cream on top. "And cappuccino for Avery."

"How'd you know I liked cappuccinos?" I asked as she handed it to me.

"You mentioned it during lunch last week," Jade replied, shifting into drive. A glimmer of our dizzy Friday night magic warmed my heart, but it cooled instantly when Simone stayed quiet. Her sunglasses were black cat-eyes, even though gray clouds were hanging low.

We drove through the neighborhood and into downtown, a bouncy Ariana Grande song playing. When we passed the road that led to the train station, I had a flash of Mama Letty's grim face, recounting the story of Ray's murder, and shivered. It was time for a subject change.

"How was the rest of your weekend?" I asked.

"Ugh, I had to listen to Tallulah talk about the stupid winter formal nonstop," Jade said. "She somehow managed to wrangle the PTA into hosting it at the Draper, so I'm sure she's not going to shut up about it for the next three months."

"What's the winter formal?" I asked.

"It's *usually* a sad little dance held in the gym before winter break that no one really cares about," Jade said. "But since it was canceled the last two years, Tallulah and the PTA wanted to go all out. Hence the Draper."

"Sounds fun," I said, glancing at Simone. She sipped her mocha and rested her head against the window.

"If your idea of fun is standing around in sequins to watch our ugly classmates dry hump each other, then sure," Jade said lightly. "Loads of fun."

I imagined dancing with Simone in front of the entire school, foreheads pressed together. I pictured us laughing like we did during the slumber party, draped in glitter and strobe lights.

"Well, maybe we should go. You know. Last year of high school. Make the most of it?" I tried to sound casual, but my voice was trembling. I sipped my cappuccino and savored the burn.

Jade stopped at a light near the Draper and cast a glance in the rearview. "Maybe. It could be fun to go as a group. I would ask Simone, but"—she dropped her voice to a whisper—"she has a rough time forming sentences on Monday mornings."

Simone snorted and sipped her drink. I stared out the window and tried to focus on a sign outside of the Draper promoting half-off massage deals, but I felt myself shrinking, caving in, wondering what I could do to make everything feel normal between us again.

When we reached the student parking lot, Jade took off, saying she needed to visit her guidance counselor before first period. Simone and I walked into school slowly, sipping our drinks, staring up at the cloudy skies. When we passed Richard Beckwith's statue, Simone rubbed her fingers over his toe absentmindedly.

"Are you okay?" I asked.

"I'm tired. I worked all weekend." I couldn't see her eyes behind her sunglasses. I couldn't tell if she was lying.

"If you wanted to talk about Friday night," I started slowly, "I would—"

"I was drunk," she interrupted. "We were all drunk. Really drunk."

I stared at the wire ring on her finger, then my own. I felt the urge to vomit, like I did at the train station. "I'm sorry," I said, even though I wasn't exactly sure for what. "If I said something to offend you."

"You didn't do anything. We don't have to talk about it."

"But I don't want things to be weird between us."

"They're not weird," she said, and when she smiled I wanted to cry because everything felt wrong and nothing like Friday night. My summer loneliness was threatening to return and cocoon me.

Simone nudged my shoulder and laughed, too loud. "I'm serious, DC. I said some things I shouldn't have, that's it. Let's drop it. It's cool."

The bell rang and we went about our day, moving through the motions like everything was fine. Every time I thought of our conversation in the stairwell, I had felt a shameful, embarrassed lurch in my stomach. I couldn't stop myself from retracing that entire conversation, trying to figure out where I took a wrong turn. Was it when I told her she could chase her dreams? Was it when I told her she was beautiful? Would it have been better to not let myself be vulnerable like I'd originally planned?

When we met at lunch, Simone was her usual bubbly self again, talking shit about a girl in her gym class and adding her silly touches to Jade's signature napkin doodles. And I played along, not wanting to rock the boat of this new delicate friendship any further. I ate my fries and laughed too loud and chose my words as if they were capable of breaking something again.

• • •

At home, my family fell into a routine, too. Dad continued to split his time between Bardell and DC. He always offered me the chance to join, but I never did. I was still getting the occasional text from Hikari and Kelsi, saying they missed me, asking when I'd be coming home next, but they began to taper off when I stopped replying. I imagined them talking about me during sleepovers, clucking their tongues, wondering what my deal was before returning to their favorite topic of college applications.

Mom asked about the status of my Georgetown application nearly every day, constantly reminding me of the impending Early Action deadline. I always lied and told her yes, I was working on it, everything was fine, just fine, when in reality, I hadn't even started and I didn't even care. I didn't know how to explain to my high-achieving mother that my interest in studying the stars had taken a back seat or maybe had been left on the curb altogether. I didn't know how to explain to a woman who left Bardell without looking back that I was beginning to love everything she claimed to hate about it. While Mom bemoaned being in the middle of nowhere, I liked how the small city felt manageable. Predictable. Peaceful, even with Mama Letty's and Mom's snipes and silence. After years of college prep and bustling DC streets and jam-packed school schedules, being in Bardell felt like taking the biggest breath I'd taken in years.

Meanwhile, Mom and Mama Letty reached a shaky compromise where any mention of Blue Meadow Hospice Lodge was off-limits. Mom shifted gears and, in the span of one week, interviewed and hired a staff of rotating nurses that began to drift in and out of the house like clockwork. Isaac, a younger Black guy with oversized glasses and an affinity for horror movies, seemed to be Mama Letty's favorite because her attitude didn't bother him one bit. Only a few days after he was hired, I came home from school to find him and Mama Letty watching *The Shining*, their feet propped on the coffee table.

"Greetings, young one!" Isaac chirped. "Popcorn?" He thrust a metal bowl in my direction, and I happily obliged. I sank into an armchair, tugged my itchy school cardigan off, and let myself sink into a fictional world full of characters with much bigger problems than me.

"This is my favorite part," Isaac gushed as a crazed-looking man chopped through a bathroom door with an ax. Some white woman started screaming, and Mom emerged from the back den, reading glasses perched on her nose.

"Is this really the best thing to be watching right now?" she asked only to be met with shushes from Isaac and Mama Letty. Mom rolled her eyes and headed for the kitchen, hooking her finger in my direction. I sighed and followed her, slumping in a chair at the Formica table.

"How was your day?" she asked. "Have you thought anymore about safety schools?"

"Yeah," I answered, automatically rattling off the names of five colleges I had no intention of applying to.

"*Here's Johnny!*" Isaac screeched from the living room.

Mom made a face. It'd been over a week since our argument, and the tension between us was still swamp-thick.

"I've been thinking about what you said. About treating Mama Letty to a nice outing," Mom said. "And I think you're right."

I perked slightly. "Oh yeah? What did you have in mind?"

"That's what I was going to ask you."

I shrugged. "I don't know. Something relaxing. Maybe a spa day?"

Her face lit up. "A spa day, huh? That sounds like a great idea actually. I think she'd really like a massage."

"I could ask Jade about getting a deal at the Draper," I suggested, remembering the sign outside the hotel last week. I wasn't sure if they were the only spa in town, but they definitely had to be the nicest.

Mom's face hardened. "Absolutely not. We're not going to the Draper."

"Why not?" I asked at the exact same time as Mama Letty. She had appeared in the kitchen's arched doorway, arms crossed over her chest.

"It's out of the question," Mom said firmly, and my mind flashed to the night of the slumber party. Her and Carole, outside the hotel. Laughing. Carole's head on Mom's shoulder.

"So I guess what I want is out of the question," Mama Letty said, amusement laced under her usual cold mask.

Mom leaned against the refrigerator. She looked like she wanted to scream. "There are plenty of other spas." She fiddled with her earring and began rummaging through the refrigerator. Mama Letty and I stared at her back, then at each other.

"But why go out of our way?" Mama Letty asked. "When we have such a *fine* establishment in our own backyard?"

Mom pulled out a bottle of white wine and poured herself a large glass. When I noticed her hand shaking slightly, my stomach dropped. She was nervous. She *really* didn't want to go, and it had to be because of Carole. What happened between the two of them that night? How did she go from offering Carole a ride home with big smiles to not even wanting to be in the same building?

"I'll think about it," she said finally. She took a giant sip of wine and retreated to the den.

Mama Letty and I exchanged a quiet, knowing look. It was a look we'd been sharing since the train station, since the story of Ray, since I threw up on those tracks. She sat across from me, and we listened as Isaac gasped as the movie came to a close.

"Surprised Mom hasn't fussed him out yet for watching movies instead of working," I said, nodding to the living room.

"He's a good kid," Mama Letty said. "He deserves a break."

"So do you," I said, and she grunted. "Do you really want to go through with this spa date? We don't have to if you don't want to."

"I want to."

"Good. Then that's what we'll do."

She nodded and gazed over my head at the creepy cat clock. The hands were still stuck at midnight.

"We should get you some new batteries," I said. "Or a whole new clock, honestly. This thing freaks me out."

"I always thought it was ugly," she agreed.

I laughed. "Then why did you pick it?"

"I didn't. You did."

"Me?" I looked up at the clock, trying to recall a moment where I picked it out, but there was nothing.

"It was your Christmas present to me," Mama Letty said. "When you and your mama came to visit when you was seven."

"I thought I was five."

"Same thing."

I propped my chin in my hand. "I wish I could remember that visit."

Mama Letty shook her head. Pulled out her pack of cigarettes and surreptitiously looked over her shoulder to make sure Isaac wasn't coming. "No, you don't. All me and your mama did was fight. She won't here but two days."

"Fight about what?"

She fumbled around in her pocket for her lighter. "Same shit we always fight about. I was a horrible mother. So on and so forth." She was about to spark the lighter when Isaac waltzed in the kitchen and swiped the cigarette from her fingers smoothly.

"Aht, aht, Ms. Letty," he said. "You know better than that."

She rolled her eyes. "I take back what I said about you being a good kid."

Isaac and I laughed, and he left to grab a blood pressure cuff. I glanced at the cat clock again and cringed.

"Well, I'm sorry my five-year-old brain wanted to buy you an ugly clock that no longer works," I said. "Hopefully a Draper spa date is a much nicer present."

Mama Letty smirked and pulled out another cigarette. "It's the least that family could do." She lit the cigarette but only got one drag in before Isaac returned and snatched it from her hand.

THE CON ARTISTS

IF THERE WAS one thing Lucas Oliver knew, it was how to get what he wanted. He fell in love with Amelia Barnett as soon as he spotted her at an Atlanta Braves game, so he made her his wife. He fell in lust with Tallulah Walters when he caught a glimpse of her black lace bra during her interview, so he made her his mistress. His father and grandfather clapped him on the back when Lucas hinted at the affair on a boys-only hunting trip. *The more the merrier,* his dad had said before toasting him with his Bud Light. His grandfather Carl beamed with such pride, one would've thought Lucas was a baby who'd taken his first steps. He tipped his hat to his grandson and gave him a light reminder across the crackling fire: *Make sure you don't get caught.*

Lucas never worried about Amelia finding out; he knew from history that when Oliver men screwed up, they never stayed in trouble for long. Oliver men didn't get speeding tickets, not when they *were* the law. Oliver men didn't face consequences for boyhood pranks or violent bar clashes, of course not, not with the klavern on their side. And Oliver men certainly didn't get divorces. Their wives knew their husbands having a little something extra on the side was a small price to pay in exchange for the comfort Ivy Rose Plantation provided and the wealth that the Draper Hotel & Spa brought.

I am a genius, Carl Oliver thought to himself on occasion, usually after a few beers and watching the sunset from Ivy Rose's back porch. All this wealth accumulated, this beautiful life his family lived. None of it would've been possible if he hadn't made the decision to invest in Bardell County's future way back in 1973. The Olivers had never once wanted for money, but the Draper's success cemented them as the richest family in Bardell. Carl gambled that people would happily spend their money in an idyllic Southern fantasy straight from *Gone with the Wind*, one that let them forget the ugliness of the Jim Crow era.

Decades after Carl's fateful and fruitful decision, five-year-old Avery Anderson arrived in Bardell on a gray December day for a visit she would barely remember. The details of this trip would quickly fade in her memory, leaving only a few key pieces behind: snippets of her first plane ride, post-Christmas lights and deflated decorations, a family fight that wouldn't be revisited for another twelve years. She wouldn't remember the tears her mother shed. She wouldn't remember idling in a taxi near the Draper Hotel & Spa, wouldn't remember the police tape crisscrossing the nearby bridge where a body had just been discovered. She wouldn't remember the sign outside the Draper, proudly promoting a new slogan the Oliver men had jointly created: BET ON BARDELL! It was supposed to show guests that Bardell was a town worth visiting—and more important—worth spending their money in. After all, the Oliver men would know best. Because the Oliver men did bet on Bardell.

And they always won big.

12.

SEPTEMBER BLED INTO October with one lazy day after another. When I told Jade about the Draper spa date idea, she lit up like a firecracker and said she'd work some magic with Tallulah. Before I knew it, we had a whole day of pampering booked for me, Mom, and Mama Letty.

"It's on the house," Jade told me when she handed me the itinerary one day at lunch. "Two weekends from now! Consider it Tallulah's white guilt gift."

"That woman loves to feel good about herself," Simone said, picking at her fries. She'd recently re-dyed the tips of her locs a burnt orange fit for fall. When I told her they looked amazing, she mumbled a thanks and looked away. Despite her insistence that things weren't weird between us, our interactions hadn't been the same since that night in the stairwell.

I tried not to think about it, I really did. I tried not to think about how she hadn't touched me since the night of the slumber party, not even a hug. Whenever she'd get close, she'd jerk away as if I were a virus she was afraid of catching.

And yet.

I still loved the way her name sounded. I whispered it to myself when I was alone in my bedroom in a cave of blankets, trying and failing to squash the butterflies that appeared whenever my mouth cupped the syllables. *Simone. SImone. Simoooone. Simone Cole.* How they felt as slick as ice cubes sliding down marble counters. At night, I twisted my sodalite ring around my finger and traced our initials—*SC & AA*—in my sheets so they'd leave no evidence. My crush on her was bigger than anything I'd ever experienced. I half hoped it would go away on its own, like a lightning bug whose ass eventually putters out.

On the surface, I was business as usual. I did my homework with bare minimum effort and watched horror movies with Mama Letty and Isaac and lied to my parents over and over again when they asked about college applications. At school, Simone, Jade, and I talked about how the winter formal would be stupid, but we'd probably go anyway. We planned a group Halloween costume after unanimously voting on pirates. On the weekends, we went to the Perfect Spot and got high and listened to music and tossed wishes into the river. They even took me to Bardell Lanes on cosmic bowling night, and Jade rolled nothing but gutter balls, and Simone beat me by nearly double. The bowling alley smelled like hot dog water and feet, but Simone's brown skin shimmered under the black lights and made my heart flutter so I said yes, of course, when they asked if we should play a second round. And when Simone chose to sit across instead of next to me, I stared at the glow-in-the-dark planets on the carpet and heard my mom telling me not to worry about it because life was short. We were only here for a moment. I had my focus forward, but I no longer knew what I was looking for.

• • •

On the morning of the spa date, under heavy slate skies, Mom, Mama Letty, and I pulled into the parking lot of the Draper and parked near the base of Amelia's mural. Mom cut the engine and craned her neck to read the inscription. A clap of thunder rumbled in the distance.

"Your friend is really talented," Mom said. "She painted this, right?"

She was stalling. But at least we were here. On the way over, I'd half expected her to drive right past the Draper and not stop until she reached the ocean.

"Yep," I said. "She's hoping to get the town historical society to build a monument in honor of her, too."

Mom stared at the mural for a bit, saying nothing. Fat raindrops plopped on the windshield. "I guess we better go inside." She said it as if we were about to ship off to war.

I led Mama Letty around the building, Mom trailing reluctantly. It took a lot of convincing to get her to wear it, but Mama Letty's *Queen for the Day* neon pink sash I bought at Walmart popped against her gray sweatpants and worn hoodie. Tom the bellman greeted us when we entered the lobby.

"Ah, yes, Miss Anderson. Miss Oliver informed me that you'd be arriving soon." He nodded at Mama Letty's sash. "What are we celebrating today, ladies?"

"My death," Mama Letty replied, and Tom turned beet red.

Mom ushered us in the direction of the spa, throwing apologies over her shoulder.

The spa manager was a kind, wrinkled woman named Ethel. While we sipped cucumber water, Ethel went over the deluxe spa package details and handed us intake forms. Mom's shoulders melted at the mention of a hot stone massage, smiling for the first time in what felt like weeks. Squished between me and Mom, Mama Letty glanced around the waiting room, her small feet rubbing over the plush blue carpet. A soft soundtrack of peaceful garden noises was playing.

"I hear you're the woman of the hour," Ethel told Mama Letty. "How long has it been since your last massage, dear?"

Mama Letty snorted. "My last massage."

"Mama," Mom said with a sigh. "Just answer the question."

"Would seventy years suffice?"

Ethel's eyes lit up. "So first massage, then? How exciting!"

Mama Letty adjusted her sash, expression unreadable. And even though I'd planned this entire day, guilt seeped into my chest. Because one spa day wasn't enough to make up for everything I'd missed. Not by a long shot.

• • •

My guilt didn't stick around for long. Ten minutes into our hot stone massage, I fell asleep to the peaceful Zen garden soundtrack. When I woke up in a daze an hour later, the first thing I saw was Mama Letty's blissful smile as she was rubbed down on the table next to me. On my other side, Mom sighed in contentment. Everything was peaceful and wonderful. There was no talk of hospice or doctors, no arguments over past mistakes. Just the three of us in total relaxation. Afterward, we snuggled into fluffy white robes and slippers and headed to our facials. None of us could stop smiling.

There was a break in the pampering for a late brunch. After we changed, Ethel led us to a cozy booth in the corner of Syrup. Even with heavy rain slapping against the windows, most of the tables were full. Across the room, Carole hustled through the kitchen's swinging door, arms loaded with orders of chicken and waffles and sizzling steak and eggs. I snuck a glance at Mom to see if she noticed, but she was too absorbed in her menu. Mama Letty had been quiet since we left our facials.

"Well?" I nudged Mama Letty with my newly scrubbed elbow. "What do you think of your first spa experience?"

Mama Letty's eyebrows raised. "It was nice. I see why this place is famous."

Mom set her menu down. "Why, Mama, I think that might be the first thing you've said in years that isn't sarcasm or an insult."

"If you don't hush your damn mouth." Mama Letty flicked her napkin in Mom's direction, and we all cackled. We were laughing so hard we didn't see Carole approaching the table.

"Isn't this a sight for sore eyes," she said, whipping her order pad out and smiling at Mama Letty. "Nice sash. Never thought I'd see the day you'd wear something pink and sparkly."

"Thank my granddaughter," Mama Letty said. She placed a hand on my arm, and I nearly dropped my water glass at the rare touch of her soft hand. "It was her idea."

"Isn't that nice?" Carole said, eyes briefly combing over me before settling on Mom. "Looks like the spa has been treating you well, Zora."

Mom nodded, unsmiling. "It's lovely."

"I wouldn't know," Carole replied. She tapped her pen against her order pad and asked what we wanted to eat.

Before Mama Letty or I could speak, Mom ordered three pancake specials—clearly the first thing that popped into her mind. It was like she wanted Carole to get away from the table as quickly as possible. Mama Letty and I watched as Carole jotted our order down with a smirk and left. Mom's shoulders heaved.

"You okay?" Mama Letty asked.

"I told you both I didn't want to come here," Mom said.

"Because of Carole?" I asked.

"*Ms.* Carole," Mom snapped. "And yes. Don't you see how it's rude?"

"What's rude? We're having lunch."

"These spa packages are ridiculously expensive," Mom muttered, so low I could barely hear her. "It's like we're rubbing it in her face."

"I think you're reading way too much into this situation," I said, and Mom's sharp look made me regret the words immediately.

"Listen to your daughter," Mama Letty said. "You too damn uptight. Holding on to things you should've let go thirty years ago. It's a free spa day, who wouldn't take it?"

"I don't think you have the right to tell me what to hold on to and what to let go," Mom said evenly. Mama Letty sighed.

"Zora, if you don't—"

"Stop!" I slapped my hands on the ivory tablecloth, startling the couple toasting mimosas the next table over. I mouthed an apology and leveled my gaze at my mom and grandmother. "This is supposed to be a *nice outing*. Can you stop bickering for ten seconds? Weren't we just saying how nice this all is?"

"She started it," Mama Letty said.

Mom pinched the bridge of her nose. "I can't—" She caught herself before the rest of the sentence slipped, before she proved that she did, in fact, lean on her *I can't deal with this right now* excuse all the time. Instead, she excused herself to the restroom and left in a huff. Mama Letty fiddled with the saltshaker.

"I don't get it," I said. "I don't understand why you both can't get along. For *one* day?"

"She's still so angry. All these years later, and she's still so angry."

"Angry about what?" I asked, exasperated. "That fight you two had during the last visit was over *ten years ago*. Can you please get over it?"

"I been over it."

"Yeah, right." I sat back against the emerald tufted booth and rang my tongue over my lip ring. "We need to get it all out on the table and talk. When Mom comes back, we're going to hash all this out and get it over with."

"No," Mama Letty said.

"Why not? If you've been over it, why not?" A heat crawled up my neck. I poured myself a glass of water from the crystal pitcher and resisted the urge to throw it against the wall.

"There's some things you don't understand," Mama Letty said, and I set the glass down with so much force that water spilled onto my hand.

"Great. First Mom treats me like a child, then you do."

"This not about you."

"How can you say that?" I asked hotly. "How can you think for one second that the relationship you two have doesn't affect me?"

Mama Letty stared off into space. For several moments, there was only soft jazz playing overhead and clinking silverware. I reached for her hand.

"Mama Letty?"

When she started to cry, I was so shocked I nearly jerked my hand away. Tears rolled down her cheeks, and I scooted closer, unsure of what to do. I repeated her name over and over, asking what's wrong, but she shook her head. The people at the surrounding tables tried not to stare, but they were doing a really bad job.

"Tell me what's wrong so I can fix it," I pleaded in a low voice.

Mama Letty wiped a wrinkled hand over her face. "You don't need to know everything. You can't fix this."

I couldn't think of anything else to say. All I could do was hold her hand. By the time Mom came back to the table, Mama Letty's tears had subsided, and she was looking around the restaurant like she was searching for an escape route.

"Everything okay?" Mom asked.

"No," Mama Letty said. "I'm tired. Take me home."

"You don't want to stay for our food?"

"There's manicures after lunch," I added.

"I said *take me home*."

"I can walk her to the car if you want to get the food to go," I offered. Mom sighed and handed over her keys.

Mama Letty and I slowly made our way between tables full of smiling people. There was a flash of envy as I passed them, jealous over the fact that their biggest problems were what flavors they wanted for mimosa flights or what style they took their eggs. As far as I knew, they weren't worrying about their grandmother's cancer or their mother's decade-old resentment or news about their grandfather's murder or crushes on girls who didn't like them back.

Tom offered to bring the BMW around front, so Mama Letty and I waited near the revolving glass door as heavy rain pelted the windows. Her queen sash was rumpled in her pocket, and I swallowed away guilt, trying and failing to not beat myself up for the day going sideways.

"Avery?"

I looked up to see Tallulah making her way across the lobby, high heels clicking on the marble floor. Her smile was as white as the baby grand piano, but it was her garish lemon-yellow suit that commanded the most attention. Against the gray furniture and green leafy plants, she looked like a giant corn on the cob. I forced a smile anyway, remembering she was the one responsible for our free day of pampering.

"Hi, Mrs. Oliver." I tried not to cringe as she hugged me.

Her flowery perfume was heavy enough to choke on. "Thank you so much for the spa day."

"Our pleasure! As you know, the Draper Hotel and Spa has been committed to providing top-notch hospitality since 1975." Tallulah thrust her hand out to Mama Letty, her sharp green eyes lingering on Mama Letty's sweatpants. "This must be your grandma. I'm Tallulah Oliver, proud co-owner of the Draper Hotel and Spa. How did you enjoy your morning? The deluxe spa package is one of my favorites. Did Jamie do your massage? She's my absolute favorite."

"It was nice," Mama Letty said. Her hand was limp in Tallulah's, and I struggled to contain my laughter at the pinched look on her face.

"I'm so glad to hear it!" Tallulah gushed. She finally dropped Mama Letty's hand and ran her fingers through her red bob. "Who's up for the grand tour?"

"We're fine," I said. "Mama Letty's not feeling well, so we're headed home."

Tallulah clucked her tongue. "Oh, yes, I heard you were sick, God bless your heart. I'll be praying for you . . . I'm sorry, remind me of your name again, sweetheart?"

"Letty."

Interest piqued across Tallulah's face. "Letty . . . that sounds so familiar. Why do I know that name?"

Mama Letty shrugged, a glazed look in her eyes. Tallulah was still trying to place her when Tom walked in and handed Mama Letty the car keys.

"Well, it was nice to see you," I told Tallulah. "Thanks again for the spa services."

"My pleasure." Her tone had grown chilly. "Hopefully I'll see you again before the Cotton Ball."

"The Cotton Ball?"

Tallulah explained how the Beckwith Winter Formal was named the Cotton Ball for many years before *certain* people started to get so offended at everything. "It's tradition," she said. "It's honestly offensive that people are so offended by it. It's part of Bardell's history, you know."

"Right," I said uneasily. Over her shoulder, I spotted Mom approaching, toting a plastic bag full of food. "Well, thanks again."

In the car, Mom thrust the food in the back seat with a glare. The fury in her eyes was raw.

"We are never coming back here again. Do you understand me?" When a response died in my throat, her voice raised. "Avery. You are not to come back here, even with Simone and Jade."

"But *why*—"

"Because I said so. Do I make myself clear?"

I nodded. My fingers curled into fists, the veins in my neck tightened. I waited for Mama Letty to stick up for me, but she was staring out the windshield. The rain-swept wind had the stoplights dancing on their wires.

"This was a bad idea," Mom said, and no one argued with her as we drove off.

I willed myself not to cry, but my eyes were burning, and it was only a matter of time. I wanted to fling myself out of the car, away from Mom's intense gaze, away from her *I was right* face, away from the disastrous day.

Mom turned on the satellite radio, and a group of men from the seventies crooned about only having eyes for one woman. It was hard to hear the music over the furious swish of windshield wipers, but I knew it was one of Mom's favorites, and it still wasn't enough to loosen her grip on the steering wheel. There was only miserable silence and Amelia's mural, her serene gaze following us as we drove away.

13.

WHEN JADE CALLED the next morning to hang out, I didn't care that Simone was at work and wouldn't be able to join us. I said yes immediately because I wanted to get out of the house and away from Mom and Mama Letty.

I was so sick and tired of the teasing dance of my family's dynamics. After the failed spa date, Mom stuck to her usual script. As soon as we got home, she immediately retreated to the den to whine to Dad about how horrible Bardell and Mama Letty were. Mama Letty holed up in her bedroom, the only proof of her existence the muffled coughs through the wall. And I—as usual—was left in the living room with nothing but unanswered questions and building resentment.

All night I thought about how Mom uprooted our entire lives to move down here, and now all she did was swat away my questions in a half-baked attempt to pretend like everything was okay. Mom had always raised me to be mature and inquisitive. But when it came to our own family, all of that was out the window and replaced with her *Don't worry about it! Life is short! The universe is big and our problems are not!* bullshit. I'd gone to sleep annoyed and woken up angry. By the time Jade arrived, I was fuming.

"Where are you going?" Mom asked before I stepped onto the porch.

My skin bristled. "Out."

"Excuse me? What do you mean, 'out'?" Mom's eyebrows shot up. Sensing a brewing fight, Dad sipped his coffee.

Alarm bells went off. I had been nothing but a respectful daughter for seventeen years. Now, there was only anger. I felt nothing like the well-behaved girl who used to quietly spend my Saturday mornings reading next to her. She had been treating me like a child. I was going to act like one.

"Apparently you don't have to answer any of my questions. So why do I have to answer yours?"

"Okay, smart-ass." Mom narrowed her eyes. "Someone woke up on the wrong side of the bed this morning."

"I'll be back later." Before she could answer, I threw open the screen door and let the crisp autumn air hit me in the face. The Jeep idled at the end of the driveway.

"Please get me out of here," I said as soon as I climbed into the passenger seat. Mom glared at us through the screen door.

"Seriously," I said. "Just go."

Jade pressed the gas, and we drove down Sweetness Lane. I didn't allow myself to relax until the little brown house disappeared from the side-view mirror. I turned my phone off when Mom started calling.

"Everything okay?" Jade asked warily.

"Nope."

"Family stuff?"

"Yep."

She shoved her glasses up her nose. "Say no more."

● ● ●

"That . . . is your house?"

Jade's cheeks flushed scarlet. "Yeah."

"But . . . it has a name?"

She sighed. "I know."

"A *name*!"

"Yep."

I gawked as Jade steered the Jeep under the arched sign canopying her driveway. *Ivy Rose Plantation* was carved into the wood with swirling, ornate letters. Words failed as we glided through a wall of oak trees toward a massive, white three-story home with soaring columns and a wide porch bursting with Halloween and harvest decor. I suddenly felt eight years old again, gawking at the White House's vastness for the first time on a field trip. It was one thing to hear from Simone that the Olivers lived in a former plantation home; it was another to see it up close and gawk at the ornate monstrosity.

"Tell me again why we never hang out here?" I asked as Jade parked behind a colossal silver pickup truck with a gunrack in the rear window.

Jade said nothing. She merely nodded toward a drooping flag on her front porch, and I could tell, even from far away, that it was a MAKE AMERICA GREAT AGAIN! flag.

"That's why," she said. "But my family's at church now so we'll have the house to ourselves."

"Why aren't you with them?"

"I'm studying for my SATs," she said innocently, and we smirked at each other.

It was too chilly for the pool but the perfect temperature for the hot tub. Jade let me borrow a plain black one-piece, and we brought a bag of chips and a portable speaker to her sprawling backyard. The sky was crystal blue and cloudless, yesterday's rain a memory. As we soaked in the jets, I couldn't stop gawking at the Olivers' immense wealth on display. Apart from the pool and hot tub, they had a line of mud-crusted ATVs outside the garage, a botanical garden that could probably get away with charging admission, and a long white tent on the sloping grassy lawn that was rented out for weddings and special events. Jade blushed as she spoke of these things, as if her family's money was something she was deeply ashamed of. She changed the subject the first chance she got, telling me she guessed Mama Letty's spa date was a bust.

I snorted. "What gave it away?"

"I kind of overheard Tallulah talking about it last night. She sounded weird."

"What do you mean?"

Jade shrugged through the foamy bubbles. "She said y'all left early. You didn't even want to finish the rest of the afternoon."

I told her about Mama Letty not feeling well while she dragged her fingers through the water. The memory of the brunch argument and Mom's demands to stay away from the Draper for no good reason annoyed me all over again. I frowned at the sky.

"I feel like my mom is a hypocrite. She says we need to let go of little things, to focus on the bigger picture, but she obviously can't get over whatever happened with Mama Letty so many years ago." I sighed. "Don't you ever wish your family was normal?"

Jade laughed. "Are you kidding me? I've spent the last decade wondering if my deranged father put a hit out on my mother. Of course I wish my family was normal."

"So you actually believe it?" I asked. "About your dad?"

She sighed. "I don't know. Maybe? Not really. But isn't it sad enough that I wouldn't be surprised if it was true?" Her face clouded over. "I'll never know what truly happened. I was just a kid when she died."

"I'm sorry," I said quietly.

She shrugged. "Enough about me though. Tell me about *your* family drama."

All my frustration spilled over. I started from the beginning, telling Jade about how I barely knew Mama Letty or my grandfather growing up and how Mom was never eager to talk about them. I told her that Ray died but spared her the gory details. I told her about Mom refusing to acknowledge whatever past hurt she still harbored and how it ultimately led to fights whenever she and Mama Letty seemed to be in the same room for too long. The entire time, Jade listened quietly, nodding along in all the right places.

"I'm so over it!" I finished. "I'm tired of them treating me like a little kid or like I can't handle whatever it is that broke them. Like, get over it! Mama Letty is about to die and they're still fighting like cats over petty little things."

"Maybe they're not petty little things."

"It's been years since my mom left, Jade. *Years!*"

"Exactly. It's been years, and whatever broke them is still bothering them. That means it must've been serious."

"Serious enough that Mama Letty is literally about to die and my mom still can't let it go?"

Jade shrugged. "Trauma is a bitch who keeps on giving. It's hard to let go of something you haven't worked through. Some would argue it's impossible."

"Okay, Ms. Therapist."

"I'm an unwilling member of the Dead Mom Club," she said with a wry smile. "I've had a lot of therapy."

I sat back with a frown, thinking about the stories Mama Letty shared at the train station. How she told me she used to look at Mom and hate her because she resembled Ray.

"Death changes people, Avery," Jade continued. Her fingers flew to the locket resting in the hollow of her neck, which I now knew once belonged to Amelia; I'd never seen her without it. "My dad used to be funny and silly and romantic. I remember how he used to dance with my mom all the time. He'd brag about her paintings to anyone who would listen. Then he met Tallulah, and I'm pretty sure she sucked his soul out."

I flicked water in her direction. "She's not *that* bad. She hooked us up with three deluxe spa packages."

"Yeah, and she's going to hang that over my head for the rest of the school year to guilt me into doing whatever she wants. '*Elizabeth Jade, wear this horrible ruffled thing to the Cotton Ball. What do you mean no? Well, maybe I should've said no when you begged for free spa services for your friends . . .*'" Jade rolled her eyes as sweat trickled down her temple. "See where I'm going here? She's a master manipulator."

"If I'd known that, I wouldn't have asked."

She waved her hand. "Whatever. I've got the connection, so I'm gonna use it. My point is that death can bring out the worst in people. And it sounds like when your grandfather died, Mama Letty was never the same and she took it out on your mom." She made a circle in the air, water dripping from her pruned fingers. "Cycle of trauma. So many people never escape it."

I thought about it. "Do you think you have? With your family, I mean?"

Jade closed her eyes and, tilting her face to the sky, told me to check back in a couple of years.

• • •

We spent the rest of the afternoon on pool loungers wrapped in fluffy towels, basking in the sun. While I found shapes in the clouds and daydreamed, Jade drew cartoon versions of me and Simone in her sketchbook, expertly crafting my side shave and lip ring and Simone's dimples and round face. I kept my phone off, trying to delay Mom's fury for as long as I could. But our relaxed spell was broken anyway when Tallulah arrived with

Jade's younger brothers, Johnny and Nolan. The boys made faces behind Tallulah's back as she stared disapprovingly from the deck.

"Elizabeth Jade! It's almost dinner and you're in your bathing suit?" Her annoyance transformed to composed Southern charm as she turned her attention to me. "Hello, Avery, lovely to see you again."

I waved, and Jade slapped her sketchbook closed. Her feet literally dragged as we headed inside.

"I'm glad to see you skipped church this morning to doodle," Tallulah said as we joined her in the kitchen. Her face was almost as red as her hair. "Please go take a shower and get ready." Nolan and Johnny snickered quietly while they put groceries away. With its stainless-steel appliances and busy granite countertops, the Olivers' kitchen appeared to have been plucked out of one of those fancy home-makeover shows.

"I have to take Avery home," Jade said.

Tallulah shook her head. "Avery is more than welcome to stay for dinner or have her parents pick her up, but you are getting ready *now*."

Jade cast an apologetic glance my way, but I only felt relief. At this point, I'd rather be around someone else's messed-up family instead of my own.

Jade's grand bedroom matched the rest of the house. She had a king-sized canopy bed with a million bedazzled pillows, her own bathroom with a soaking tub, and one of those hanging egg chairs my parents refused to buy me when I begged for one in elementary school because of "safety concerns." After we changed in her walk-in closet, Jade placed her hands on my shoulders and gave me a serious look.

"If at any time you want to leave, we're out of here," she said. "My entire family can be . . . a little much."

"Have you met my grandmother? I can handle them," I said, but she looked doubtful.

In the kitchen, Dolly Parton blared from a speaker on top of the refrigerator. Tallulah put us to work chopping vegetables for a salad. I was slicing through a carrot when Lucas arrived with the rest of the Oliver clan. I discovered that Jade's grandparents and great-grandparents actually lived in Ivy Rose, four generations housed under one roof. They were all polite but way too loud, talking over one another in booming drawls. There were too many names to remember. There were aunts and uncles, bored-looking cousins buried in their phones, and a tornado of a child named Bubba who broke one of Tallulah's marble coasters almost immediately. I recognized Jade's grandparents, Wallace and Elizabeth, from the photos at the Draper. Jade introduced me to Carl, her great-grandfather who had knobby fingers and a crooked smile with several missing teeth. He pulled me in for a shaky hug, and I tried not to flinch when his cracked hands scraped my forearms.

"Lovely to meet you!" he said. "Aren't you pretty as a picture!"

When he let me go, the rest of the family eyed my lip ring and side shave with curiosity. Dread curled in my stomach as I anticipated a tidal wave of nosy questions, but I was saved when an uncle announced a NASCAR race was starting and mostly everyone rushed to the family room.

"Well, Avery," Tallulah said as she checked on a pot roast in the double oven. "You survived your first Oliver ambush."

Across the counter, Jade snorted as she squeezed lemons for fresh lemonade.

"Everyone seems very nice," I said. "Actually, I'm kind of jealous of how big your family is. It must feel like a mini family reunion every day."

Tallulah's arm was working overtime as she whipped a giant bowl of mashed potatoes. "It is. It makes me miss my family in Texas. We used to have big family dinners like this every weekend. Hand me that butter, sweetheart."

"I'm jealous of small families," Jade said with a sigh. "Ten people living in one house is too much. Must be nice to have some peace and quiet."

I shrugged. "Sometimes too quiet."

Tallulah tapped her mixing spoon against the bowl. "Speaking of families. I've been thinking about yours, Avery."

"Mine?"

"I couldn't get Letty out of my mind yesterday after I saw y'all," Tallulah said. "She looked and sounded so familiar."

"There's, like, two people that live in this town, Tallulah," Jade said. "Everyone looks familiar."

Tallulah ignored her. "She used to work at the pharmacy, didn't she?"

"I'm not sure?" I honestly hadn't really thought about what

Mama Letty did for money before Mom started sending her monthly checks.

"She did," Tallulah said with certainty. "On the corner of Main and Juniper. I used to pop in there sometimes to grab a soda when I needed a break from all that construction at the hotel about eight years ago. That was when we were updating the guest rooms and putting in the claw-foots."

"Claw-foot tubs? Sound fancy." I subtly ran a hand over my side shave, recalling the night of our party. A lemon slipped sideways in Jade's hand as she tried to hold in her laughter.

"Oh, they're beautiful," Tallulah said. "Acrylic with imperial feet, just breathtaking. Anyway, I used to pop into that pharmacy all the time until I had the worst experience with one of the new cashiers there. Hadn't seen her in years until yesterday."

The smile dropped from my face. I set the knife down. "It was Mama Letty?"

"Sure was! Jade, could you grab the deviled eggs and take them into the family room? It's only a matter of time before they come back in here whining about being hungry."

Jade glanced at me, but I gave her an imperceptible nod. Anything anyone had to say about Mama Letty, I wanted to hear it. Jade slid off her barstool, grabbed a platter of deviled eggs, and disappeared into the family room. Tallulah handed me a large cucumber to slice.

"That's why I didn't recognize her yesterday," she continued. "She looked happy! I don't think I ever saw her smile a single time I went into that pharmacy."

"She's been through a lot." I tried to keep my voice even.

Tallulah hummed. "She used to be the meanest woman. Last time I saw her, she seemed like she'd had a bit too much to drink. They fired her after someone complained."

My jaw clenched. There was nothing in me that doubted Tallulah herself was that "someone." I focused on the cucumber, trying to get perfectly even slices while she rolled out biscuit dough.

"I was nearly eight months pregnant with Nolan, and I went in for a soda. That was my biggest pregnancy craving. With Johnny, I couldn't get enough pretzels and mustard, but Nolan only wanted soda. Lord, I swear that's why he's so hyper now. Anyway! I went in for a soda, but I forgot my wallet in my office. Your Mama Letty was working the register that day. And I tried to explain to her that I would come back with the money, that I worked right across the street. I was *so* thirsty, it was so hot that day, the middle of summer. July, I think. And she said no!" Tallulah laughed, but she pressed on the rolling pin harder like the memory angered her. "I couldn't believe it! I'd been coming into that pharmacy darn near every day. I knew the owners personally! But I could tell your Mama Letty had been drinking. Lord, she was mean as a python. That's why when I saw her smiling yesterday, I couldn't even place her! It was like she was a different woman."

"She's dying of cancer." I set the knife down and walked over to the sink to wash my hands. Anything to put some distance between us. Being around her made me feel like I had fire ants under my skin. The more she talked, the faster they scurried.

"Bless her heart," Tallulah said with a sigh. "God works in mysterious ways. Does your Mama Letty go to church?"

My shoulders clenched. "I don't think so."

"Well, I'll be praying for her. I even prayed for her back then, you know. She seemed very disturbed."

"Disturbed?"

The voice wasn't mine. It was Jade's. When I turned around, she'd resumed her place at the juicer, eyes narrowed at Tallulah. "Who was disturbed?"

"Avery's grandmother. I was explaining how the power of prayer can heal so much. Even if you're not the one that did the praying!"

I couldn't help but laugh. "I'm sorry, but are you saying you *healed* my grandmother? Because you prayed for her after she was mean to you?"

"Good Lord, no!" Tallulah's cheeks flushed, and she wiped her hands on her polka-dot apron. "That's not what I'm saying at all."

"That's what it sounds like," Jade deadpanned.

There was a crash in the family room, followed by a wail from Bubba. Tallulah's shoulders slumped as she excused herself before responding.

In the now-empty kitchen, Jade came to my side, eyes laced with guilt. "Let's go. I'm so sorry."

I released a shaky exhale. "No . . . it's okay."

"Are you sure?"

I nodded, even though I was torn. Part of me wanted to run

out of Ivy Rose without looking back. But the other half—the half so desperate for any information about my family—had to stay and hear the rest of Tallulah's story, even if I did feel like sticking her head in a blender. I resumed my slicing and tried to calm my shaky hands.

When Tallulah returned, Jade's grandmother, Elizabeth, was with her. She had a face that'd seen the end of too many Botox needles and gray roots peeking out, but I could tell she used to be stunning when she was younger. Her ice-blue eyes reminded me of Jade, but her frown reminded me of Tallulah, even though they weren't blood-related. She settled onto one of the tall barstools along the granite island and helped herself to a glass of lemonade.

"So," Elizabeth said slowly. "Avery, is it? You go to Beckwith as well?"

I nodded. "Yes, ma'am."

"What brings you to Bardell?"

I gave her the same condensed version I gave Tallulah. Elizabeth looked intrigued.

"What's your grandma's name? I grew up here. I know everyone in this town."

"Letty Harding."

Elizabeth's face morphed into recognition. She smiled like she knew something I didn't. "Yes, I know Letty. Well, *of* her."

"I was telling Avery about the pharmacy," Tallulah went on, setting biscuits on parchment paper with a delicateness that didn't match her tone. "Remember when I was pregnant with

Nolan and that drunk cashier screamed at me, and I had to get the manager? Over a dollar!"

"Good Lord, yes, I remember that," Elizabeth said with the horrified reverence of someone recalling a deadly hurricane or mass shooting. "How awful."

Jade searched my face across the room. My cheeks were growing hotter by the second, but Tallulah and Elizabeth didn't notice.

"She was going on and on about how horrible my family was," Tallulah said. "This woman didn't even know me, and she was so mean! I remember standing there in shock with my big ol' pregnant belly. Thank God she's doing better now. I was telling Avery I prayed for her."

"Prayer works miracles," Elizabeth said, clucking her tongue. "She had such a mean reputation back in the day."

Tallulah beamed, validated. And that was all I needed to go from annoyed to straight-up pissed. An unfamiliar fury stoked in my stomach before crawling up to my throat.

"You want to talk about reputation?" I asked, smoothly setting down the knife. "Because we can absolutely do that."

"I beg your pardon?" Tallulah brushed her hands over her apron.

"Word on the street is you were putting in overtime at the Draper before Amelia died. Does that sound about right?"

"Now, that's enough," Elizabeth said. Tallulah was dumbfounded, staring at me with a frozen smile. The fire in me burned brighter, sparking and hissing and smoking. Out of the corner of my eye, I could see Jade's mouth dropping, but I was in too deep to turn back now.

"Let's do it," I said. "You want to talk about my grandmother's mean reputation? I don't see why I can't also bring up the rumors I've heard about *you*. Because sleeping with a married man and then arranging for his wife to be murdered is, well, pretty mean, too."

A bone-chilling silence settled over the kitchen. Tallulah's smile dropped, one centimeter at a time, revealing the wicked expression of a woman who absolutely looked like she would happily hire a hitman to take care of someone she deemed a problem. She leaned close, green eyes flashing like evil emeralds.

"You will get out of my house with that filthy, disgusting mouth," Tallulah hissed. "Elizabeth Jade, take her home *now* before I get your father in here."

"What, you gonna kill me, too?" I asked, laughing. I vaguely felt Jade pulling me away, vaguely heard Elizabeth gasping, vaguely felt the erratic, furious pounding of my heart. My tunnel vision could only focus on Tallulah's shocked face and her big, stupid mouth.

"Cannot *believe* I welcomed you into my home," she was saying. "And I'll be expecting payment for those spa packages I generously provided! You are so ungrateful!"

"I'm sure you'll pray for me," I spat, and that was the last thing I could say before I was pulled in the dark, damp quiet of the Olivers' garage. Jade slammed the door and locked it. When she faced me, her eyes were wild and wide behind her glasses.

"Um" was all she could say for a full ten seconds.

The sharp scent of gasoline and garden soil broke through my furious stupor. I blinked hard, trying to decide if that really went down or if it was something out of a daydream.

"I think we should go," Jade said with a firmness that clarified yes, that really happened. "*Now.*"

Somehow, I ended up in the Jeep. I was in too much of a daze to buckle my own seat belt, so Jade reached over and did it for me. She started the engine, and we idled in front of the massive house for seconds, minutes, hours, days, I didn't know. I felt my mouth form the words *I'm sorry.* When I looked over, Jade was gaping at the steering wheel.

"I don't know what got into me," I said. "I got so mad—"

"You don't have to apologize," she interrupted. She glanced past me, and we both turned to see Tallulah and Elizabeth glowering at us from the porch. Jade pressed the gas, but we were still in park, so the engine only revved. She threw the gearshift into drive, and we peeled off with dizzying speed.

Down the long, winding driveway, evening shadows of oak trees sliced across the Jeep's hood in a calming, steady rhythm. I heard my mother's voice, telling me to inhale on the one, exhale on the two. By the time we reached the arching Ivy Rose sign, I felt like myself again. And I was horrified.

"I'm *so* sorry," I blurted. "I have no idea what came over me! I *never* get that mad. I couldn't help it."

Jade shot me a glance as we turned onto the main road. Then she burst into laughter so hard she had to pull onto the shoulder. I sat in stunned silence as she released gut-wrenching, full-body laughter, and before I knew it, I joined in. Through tears and gasps, we screamed, *I can't believe you* and *Did you see her face?* and *holyshitholyshitholyshit* until we couldn't breathe.

"Oh my God," Jade said, wiping away tears. "Simone is going to be *so* pissed she missed this."

THE CASHIER

IN DOWNTOWN BARDELL, on the corner of Juniper and Main, there was a charming brick building that perpetually lived in the Draper Hotel & Spa's shadow. Before it was bought out and gutted into a clothing boutique, the building was home to Easy Does It Drugs & Soda Shoppe for nearly sixty years. Many older Bardell residents had fond memories of sipping chocolate malts on the swiveling red stools and chatting up friendly Mr. Wilson while picking up prescriptions. But locals privy to gossip would always know Easy Does It as the site of the Letty Harding and Tallulah Oliver Dollar Debacle.

Letty June had been working at Easy Does It for one mind-numbing month when Tallulah Oliver waltzed in and asked for a soda on the house. It was July, and that particular afternoon was a sweltering ninety-nine degrees. The air conditioner was on the fritz. Mr. Wilson's breath smelled like garlic, and Letty had a nasty, splitting hangover. All of these details were minor annoyances by themselves. Together, they were sticks of dynamite, and Tallulah's doe-eyed *I forgot my wallet* and *Let me speak to your manager* were the matches that lit the fuse.

Dottie Henderson had been enjoying her weekly root beer float when she overheard Letty June say, *Let me tell you one damn thing* before proceeding to berate poor, sweet, pregnant Tallulah Oliver. Dottie had never been known to keep anything to herself, and by the end of the day, half of Bardell County had heard the news. *It was awful*, folks said before launching into a version of the story that snowballed every time it was told. *That cashier down at Easy Does It was a raving lunatic. A cashier lost her job after verbally assaulting Tallulah Oliver. An unhinged cashier threw a soda on Tallulah and pulled her hair. The cashier punched Tallulah in the nose. Lord, I heard Tallulah Oliver might lose her baby after that cashier down at Easy Does It pummeled her in the stomach.*

The truth, which often went ignored as it was much less exciting than the rumors, was that Letty June Harding never laid a finger on Tallulah Oliver. It was true she was fired immediately when Tallulah cried to the owner, Mr. Wilson. And it was also true that Letty gathered her things in a stream of expletives and, oddly, a demand that Mr. Wilson *brush his goddamn teeth* every now and then. Tallulah was too emotional to register when Letty June added, *It's not about the fucking dollar and it never has been* before leaving the building. These words, this seemingly insignificant detail, became forever lost to time mere seconds after they were uttered.

14.

THE JOY AND adrenaline of putting Tallulah Oliver in her place was quickly extinguished when I arrived home to find out I was grounded for two weeks on account of my "disrespect" and "disobedience." It was a generous offer, according to Mom, who slapped me with the punishment as soon as I emerged from Jade's Jeep.

"I'm *so* disappointed in you," Mom said before disappearing into the house.

In the silence that followed, Dad whistled and motioned for me to join him on the porch swing. I sank down, rested my head on his shoulder.

"I thought we had a plan, Unsavory," he said in a low, teasing voice.

Right. The Plan. *Get in, get out, no drama, focus forward*. It felt so long ago that I actually cared about it. "The plan is stupid," I muttered.

Dad gasped in mock offense. "Stupid? Now the Anderson family motto is stupid? You really have been unsavory lately, haven't you?"

"And you haven't been here at all. You have no idea what's happening."

"Enlighten me then, young one."

"Other than the fact that my last living grandparent is dying and instead of making the most out of our time, we all just keep fighting?" I craned my neck so I was looking at the underside of his chin. "And all you've been doing lately is flying off to DC every chance you get."

"I still have to work, Ave. These gigs were booked before your mom decided to move down here. But I can assure you you're not the only one who cares. You know I love you and your mother from A to Z."

"Did Mom tell you about the spa? How their argument ruined everything? They can't put aside their differences for *one* afternoon. The day was supposed to be perfect." My throat tightened, and Dad sighed.

"They aren't arguing because they're trying to make you upset. They've been through a lot."

I pushed away from him. "Exactly! Right there. *What* have they been through? And why are they not fixing it? Mom can afford the best therapist in the world to help them get over whatever it was, but they're so stubborn! Did you know about my grandpa Ray? How he was murdered?"

Dad's eyes were sad. "Yes, Avery. There are some things people don't 'get over.' And there's nothing we can do about it. You can't force people to forgive."

"Then what's the point of all of this? Why did Mom move us down here? To waste our time?"

"We're a family," Dad said. "And that means supporting one another. Loving one another, even when things aren't working out exactly like we planned."

"I thought . . ." My voice cracked as tears pressed. "I thought everyone would get along. It wasn't like this when Grandma Jean died."

"And your Grandma Jean wasn't perfect either. She wasn't exactly the most accepting of your mom when they first met. People are messy, kid. Families are messy."

This new detail pushed me over the edge, and the tears arrived. Dad let me cry against the soft fabric of his shirt. I cried because I felt guilty. And helpless. And lonely and frustrated and angry. I cried because I couldn't tell if everything was changing or nothing was.

• • •

Dad stayed by my side for a while, only moving when Carole's sedan chugged into the Coles' driveway next door. When he noticed Simone look over at us longingly, he stood.

"I'll give you some privacy," he said. "But if your mom asks if I let you hang out with your friend after she said you were grounded, no, I didn't."

He disappeared inside, giving me little time to prepare myself as Simone crossed the lawn. The night was coming alive with crickets and a navy sky. I hoped my face wasn't puffy from crying.

"Hey," Simone said, stopping at the porch steps. She tugged at her Slice of Bardell polo awkwardly. "Can we talk?"

"That's about all I can do since I am now officially grounded," I said.

She joined me on the swing with a smile that reminded me of when we first met. Before the admission in the stairwell, before her silent treatment.

"Jade texted me about the Oliver family showdown," she said. "She told me about how you absolutely dunked on Tallulah." She laughed and tugged on the end of a loc. "I'm so sad I missed it."

"Maybe we can reenact it for you."

"Promise?"

I nodded, finally meeting her gaze. Her eyes darted away nervously.

"Can we talk?" she asked again. "About that night? At the Draper?"

I stiffened. "I thought we already did."

"I have some things I need to get off my chest, and I want to do it now before I lose my nerve. I'm braver when I smell like marinara sauce." Her smile faltered when I didn't laugh. "Can we take a walk?"

"I'm pretty sure my mother's punishment means I can't go past the porch."

"Right. Okay." She took a deep breath and faced me. "I freaked out. Okay? I've literally never told *anyone* what I told you that night. Not even Jade. I've never even said it out loud." She closed her eyes. "But I meant it. And I don't know what to do about it." Her fingers trembled on her knees in a desperate dance. "What am I supposed to do, Avery?"

My throat felt raw. There were too many emotions all at once, crowding and demanding my attention. I felt relief that Simone wasn't mad at me anymore. Leftover sadness and guilt from my conversation with Dad. Anger from my time spent at the Olivers'.

"My mom would hate me," she whispered. "She'd tell me I'm going straight to hell."

"How do you know?" I asked.

She snorted. "Because I know my mom. Out of all the sins in the Bible, nothing upsets her more than the gay shit. If I came out to her, she'd never speak to me again."

I was thrust back to the night at the Draper. To that dark corner where I cowered behind a potted plant, watching Carole rest her head on my mother's shoulder. I didn't know what that moment meant, but I still couldn't shake the weird feeling I had when I saw it.

"How did you know?" Simone asked. "Have you always?"

I shook my head, forcing the thought away. I couldn't deal with that memory now. Not on top of everything else.

"You didn't?" Simone asked.

"No. No, that's not what I'm saying. Yeah, I think I've always known."

She scooted closer until there was no room left between us. "I've always known, too. I knew whenever Jade and I were younger and we used to watch movies and she'd be dying over the prince, saying how cute he was, but all I ever wanted was to be in his place. So *I* could kiss the princesses. And every moment since then. When I read about gay celebrities, I'd get so jealous that they get to openly be with whoever they want. So far away from Bardell." She flipped her locs over her shoulder and stared down Sweetness Lane. I followed her gaze, visualizing how the street eventually turned into Maple Drive. And if we kept going, we'd end up on Main Street. If we kept going, we'd leave town.

"And then you showed up," Simone said, "and I knew you were gay from the moment I saw you."

"The lip ring," I said, running my tongue over it. She giggled and pushed me, and her touch was electric.

"It was that *and* the way you kept checking me out. Don't think I didn't notice." She laughed at my hesitation. "You don't deny it!"

"You're pretty, okay?" The smile that burst on her face sent me into a tailspin because oh my God, we were actually flirting. Like, out in the open. And no one was drunk. All my worries suddenly faded, slipping away like the sun sinking below the horizon. The night had brought back the magic of us. It brought back the sunflower girl. I looked at my ring, and for the first time in days, the sight of it didn't make me sad.

"That night at the Perfect Spot. At the river. Do you know what I wished for?" Simone asked.

"Isn't telling me against the rules of Tree?"

"Nope. Not when it's already come true." She looked up at me through her long lashes. Her eyes were black in the night. "I wished to come out. I didn't specify how it would happen or who I'd tell, but a week later we were in that stairwell, Avery. And I felt like I had to tell you."

"I'm glad you did."

"And . . ." She tucked her bottom lip in, hesitating.

"What?"

"I wanted to kiss you."

My heart pounded. I gripped the swing's splintered wooden edge to steady myself. I swallowed, trying to respond, but all that came out was a garbled hum. Simone scooted closer.

"I wanted to kiss you," she repeated. "But then I started thinking about how it could ruin things because I'm not out, and *then* I got angry with myself that I wasn't and I lost it. I thought I ruined everything. I just want to be a good person."

"Coming out doesn't make you a bad person," I said, voice hoarse. "I'm out. Do you think I'm a bad person?"

"No. Not at all." Her face was inches from my own. "But what if I *still* want to kiss you? Am I still a good person then? After knowing what happened to you when you started dating your friend back in DC? Even with me and Jade's No Dating rule?"

All the logic, all the reasons not to—they were gone. The only thing in the world that mattered in that moment was Simone. Blood rushed to my head so fast I heard it roaring in my ears.

"Absolutely," I said. "Better than good."

There was still a chance to pull away, but neither of us did. Instead, I closed my eyes, and her lips met mine.

The kiss was hesitant at first, our lips just barely grazing. Then she leaned into me, and my entire body erupted in goosebumps, all of them screaming, *Yes! Yes! Yes!* Kissing Simone felt like biting into a wild blackberry—surprise, taken aback by the ripeness before sinking into sweetness. Her lips were soft and full and tasted like sugary soda. It was perfect. She was perfect.

Then, abruptly, she pulled away, and my lips didn't know how to make sense of it. I immediately wanted her to kiss me again, leave some evidence of this honeyed moment behind, like seeds stuck in teeth. She scooted to the end of the swing, and it was time for panic mode.

"Are you okay?" I asked, already prowling through a mental filing cabinet of excuses.

I'm sorry.

I promise I won't tell anyone.

We can pretend like this never happened.

All she could say was "Um."

"I'm confused," I said. My happiness deflated like a star collapsing on itself.

Simone was staring at her house. "Do you think anyone saw?"

I followed her gaze to the little blue house where the kitchen windows were a bright outline in the night. I braced myself for Carole to burst out onto the porch with a crucifix, but she passed by the window seconds later, not even looking our way.

"Looks like she's cooking," I said. "I think we're okay."

"I should go."

My heart dropped as she stood. *Not again.* I really didn't want to go through another silent treatment. But there was a flicker of hope when she extended her hand to help me up. Her palm was warm and slick with sweat. We faced each other, electricity and warmth humming in the space between us.

"I can't believe this," she whispered.

"Me either."

"That was my first kiss. Ever."

I froze. ". . . And?"

"I feel like there should've been a parade coming down the street. Or a full band in the front lawn. Fireworks at least."

"Wasn't there?"

She shoved my shoulder, and I melted. "Real smooth, DC. No wonder all the ladies loved you."

"If by 'all the ladies' you mean one girl, then yeah, sure." I wanted to add I was pretty sure Kelsi had never loved me, not even close, but this moment was too perfect and I wasn't about to ruin it. Everything felt so wonderful and so unreal I was certain an alarm clock was about to yank me out of a dream. But the porch groaning beneath our feet and the symphony of crickets ensured me of our reality.

"We should . . . do this again sometime," she said.

"Sounds like a marvelous idea."

"Let's not tell Jade?"

Everything fell at once, as if we'd been floating without gravity among the stars and were now being pulled back into Earth's atmosphere. All my problems returned: the ruined spa date, Tallulah, my grounding. Simone reached for my hand, interlaced our fingers.

"It's not because of you. I don't know how to explain it yet," she said. "Jade and I have been friends forever, and I haven't come out. I don't want to hurt her."

I considered it. Maybe she was right. Maybe it was for the best. Everything else in my life felt so big, so impossible to tackle. Maybe having a small secret, a tiny joy tucked away from the rest of the world, was the best course of action for now. A marvel for only our eyes.

"Okay," I said. "We'll keep it between us."

Her smile returned hesitantly. "I'll see you tomorrow?"

"Of course."

She hopped off the porch and cut through the grass. "Good night, DC," she said over her shoulder. "Try not to read any more people for filth tonight."

"I make no promises," I called. "And Tallulah deserved it!"

With a laugh, she went inside. I watched her silhouette pass the kitchen window. I traced my bottom lip with my fingers.

We kissed.

Simone and I *kissed*. On a day that felt so awful, the universe was giving me a gentle nudge, reminding me that not everything was shit. Sure, I was grounded and my family was a disaster and I'd aired my friend's stepmother's dirty laundry in her own home. But!

I kissed the girl of my dreams. And it was absolutely, positively, undeniably earth-shattering. I thought of Simone pulling the Wheel of Fortune for me on the banks of the Bardell

River and wondered if she knew then that she would ultimately become that turning point she spoke of.

I had a smile the size of Georgia when I stepped inside. The living room was dark and quiet, but it wasn't empty. Mama Letty sat on a couch, fiddling with her lighter.

"Jesus," I said, bringing my hand to my heart. "You scared the crap out of me."

Mama Letty said nothing. Her face was eerily blank. And then the horrifying realization dawned on me. Me and Simone's kiss.

Carole might not have seen it. But Mama Letty sure as hell did.

I took a cautious step forward. "Um, Mama Letty? What you saw—"

"You went to that white girl's house?" Mama Letty interrupted.

I paused by the worn armchair, wondering how this connected to the kiss. "Huh?"

"That white girl. The Oliver girl. You went to her house?"

"Yeah?" I said. "I . . . might've gotten into it a little with Jade's stepmom. But I promise it was for a good reason! She was saying all these rude things—"

Mama Letty stood shakily, waving me away when I tried to help her. She glared at me, and the rest of my explanation died in my throat.

"Those evil men," she said, voice thick and gritty. "The ones who took Ray. Who do you think they are?"

I froze as a mean grin graced her lips.

"Well?" she asked.

"I don't . . . What do you mean?" My mouth was dry.

"Cops. Hotel owners." She leaned close, and I could see every wrinkle, every mole, all her anger. "*Family men.* Any way you dress them up, a murderer is still a murderer, Avery."

15.

"*. . .* **FINAL TOUCHES ON** my Pratt application. '*I'm going to ride a train out of town. I'm gonna make some art and make my mom proud. I'm gonna—*'" A pause. Then: "Well, fuck my backup vocals then. Let's not all cheer at once."

I snapped out of my thoughts in time to see Jade shove a frizzy curl behind her ear.

"Sorry," Simone said, startling next to me. "What did you say?"

Jade sighed and pushed her lunch tray away. "Just detailing my grand escape from Bardell, no big deal. What is *with* y'all? You've both been in outer space all morning."

Where did I start? The kiss with Simone? Or Mama Letty's words that had seeped into my skin last night, burrowing deeper every passing second?

A murderer is still a murderer.

The Oliver men. Jade's family. Her father, her grandfather, her great-grandfather. Mama Letty was saying these men—the same men whose home I'd been in, whose hands I'd shaken—were the same men who killed *my* grandfather.

How the fuck was I supposed to explain that?

"I'm worried about the SATs," I said instead, and quickly realized it was the flimsiest lie ever. I wasn't even taking them again. Jade arched an eyebrow and looked at Simone, waiting for her excuse.

Simone prodded a wilted lettuce leaf in her sad salad. "Shawn's death anniversary is coming up."

Jade shrank in her seat. "Right. Shit. Sorry."

"It's fine." Although Simone had carefully been avoiding my gaze all lunch period, her fingers kept brushing my thighs under the table. "Talk about something else, please?"

Jade hesitantly obliged and started talking about her proposal for Amelia's statue for the Bardell Historical Society. The deadline was in December, and Jade seemed more concerned about it than her actual college applications.

"I want to make her proud," Jade said. "And *really* piss Tallulah off." She looked at me, and I managed a shaky smile, remembering her stepmother's and grandmother's dumbfounded faces. "Simone, you really should've been there."

"I heard all about it," she said.

"Her jaw was on the floor for, like, six hours after you left," Jade told me. She went on to say she was pretty sure she'd never seen Tallulah be put in her place like that, how badass it was. But my mind was wandering again, thinking about Mama Letty's words. She'd dropped a bomb on me last night and then left me alone to pick my way through the rubble.

• • •

During last period chemistry, I was so deep in my thoughts that my teacher had to call my name twice to get my attention. He thrust a hall pass in the air, clearly annoyed his kinetics lecture had been interrupted.

"Early dismissal," he said with a huff. "Gather your things."

My heart dropped as I anticipated the worst. I gathered my books with trembling hands, mind already filled with thoughts of Mama Letty in a hospital bed or a casket. As I drew closer to the main office, I could see my mom's grim face through the glass windows.

"Is it Mama Letty?" I asked as soon I burst into the office. "Is she okay?"

Mom plastered on a fake smile. "Of course she's okay, Avery baby."

My shoulders slumped. "Then what is it?"

"You have that dentist appointment, remember?" She gripped my elbow and pulled me out into the hallway with a wave to the secretary. She pushed open the front door, and we stepped into the warm late October sunshine.

"What dentist appointment?" I asked.

She said nothing. She only dropped my elbow and headed toward the BMW in the circular drop-off zone.

• • •

I didn't ask questions. Not when we were idling at a stoplight downtown by the Draper. Not when we headed for the

highway. Not even when the bullet-riddled WELCOME TO BAR-
DELL sign blurred past. The radio played one seventies hit after
another, and Mom kept driving, her knuckles tight on the
steering wheel.

Just when I was convinced she was about to drive back to
DC, she made a sharp turn onto a dirt road that seemed like
it was heading directly into a thick line of trees. A mixture of
amusement and terror bloomed in my chest.

"Is this the part where you kill me?" I asked.

She rolled her eyes. "Hush."

We drove under drooping willow trees, branches grazing
the car roof like sweeping drum brushes, and entered a shaded
clearing. It almost reminded me of the Perfect Spot. But instead
of Tree and a flimsy, splintered picnic table, there was a squat,
two-story house with faded blue aluminum siding perched on
tall stilts. There were a couple of crookedly parked cars near the
stairs, and Mom stopped next to a rusted pickup truck with
a million faded stickers on its bumper. When she opened her
door, I could hear the slow rush of water. The Bardell River
was close.

"Uh, Mom? What's going on?"

She looked at me seriously. "I overheard what Mama Letty
told you last night."

My fingers twitched on my plaid skirt. *This* was not what I
was expecting.

"You wanted answers," Mom said. "I'm going to try to give
you some. Come on. I hope you're hungry."

• • •

The Renaissance was unlike anything I'd ever seen. It was the exact opposite of the Draper Hotel and Syrup. Instead of fresh-cut flowers and candles, sticky plastic checkerboard tablecloths adorned every table. Multicolored lights crisscrossed the ceiling, illuminating the dim house in a soft pink glow. It smelled like fried chicken and pie, and blues music thumped low and deep. And as soon as me and Mom stepped inside, I could tell it was someplace special.

"Are my eyes deceiving me or is that Zora Harding?"

An elderly man with wrinkled brown skin and a dusty black fedora pushed off a stool and lowered his sunglasses. Mom's smile lit up the entire room.

"Hey, Mr. Arnie," she said. "And it's *Dr.* Zora Anderson now."

The man hurried across the room and embraced Mom like a long-lost family member. They squealed like children, tears in their eyes.

"I don't care what you called. It's been years, girl!" Mr. Arnie cried. "Let me take a look at you!" Mom spun in a slow circle, laughing the entire time. "It's *you*! In the flesh! Not one of those postcards. Oh, you was just a girl the last I saw you! Thank God you grew out of them awful hats!"

"I see you didn't," Mom teased, flicking the brim of his fedora. Then, seeming to remember I was standing next to her, she pulled me close. "This is my daughter, Avery."

Mr. Arnie crushed me into a hug. He smelled like a mixture of sweat and grease, something fried and something sweet. "A daughter!" he cried, pulling back to get a good look at me.

"Oh, Lord, she look *just* like Letty. Even with this shaved head and these piercings! And look at all them damn freckles!"

"Don't I know it," Mom said.

"Sit, sit, sit!" Mr. Arnie flapped his hands toward the only empty table. "I'll grab y'all two specials. I hope you're hungry because the chicken is fresh and the grease is hot, okay?" We sat and Mr. Arnie plopped two glasses of water and an array of hot sauces on the table before disappearing into the kitchen.

"Well," Mom said, looking around the room, "this is the Renaissance."

My eyes widened as I took in details I didn't notice before. We were in what might've been considered the living room in a normal house. But where a regular family would've had boring art or school photos on the walls, Mr. Arnie had decorated with blinking string lights, stuffed animals with cotton bursting from the seams, and license plates from every state. Along one side of the room was what appeared to be a makeshift stage with hundreds of names and initials carved into the wall behind it. Every table was filled with Black folks enjoying the soul food spilling off their plates, singing along to the music, laughing open-mouthed. The sign above the kitchen announced, No Assholes Allowed!

"What is this place?" I asked in awe.

"My favorite place in the world. I'm happy it still exists."

"You used to come here a lot?"

She nodded, taking a sip of water. "We used to come here all the time."

"We?"

Mom's face softened, and I had the sudden, overwhelming urge to talk like we used to. Like before we moved to Bardell and our relationship was thrown off its axis. Like when we shared coffee on quiet Saturday mornings. Maybe she wanted that as bad as I did. She wouldn't have pulled me out of school if she didn't.

I leaned in so she could hear me over the music, which was reaching a scratchy crescendo. "Mom. Who's 'we'?"

"Me and Carole."

"Oh." I watched as she fiddled with an unlabeled bottle of hot sauce, and it was there. In my chest, there was That Feeling. The same familiar feeling I had when Simone was in my bedroom, tentatively dancing around the topic of sexuality. That Feeling that kept me up so many nights myself. My mind flashed to Carole's head on Mom's shoulder, and the realization was harsher than the baby's screams at the next table over.

"*Oh,*" I said again, quieter this time.

"I took you here because I trust you," Mom said swiftly. "And I know you have a lot of questions. I don't know if I'll be able to answer all of them."

"You overheard everything Mama Letty said last night?" I asked.

She nodded, and an overwhelming relief flooded me. I'd had to grapple with Mama Letty's words alone for only one night, but that was more than enough.

"Mama Letty," Mom began shakily, "has always claimed the Oliver men were the ones responsible for killing Ray. Ever since I was a little girl, she told me that story."

I suddenly felt sick. All the time I'd spent with Jade. Dining at the Draper, being in their *plantation* home. I was humiliated when I pictured the three of us in Syrup during the spa day. How annoyed I'd been that they couldn't enjoy the afternoon when the reality was a lot more complicated. "So it's true?" I managed to ask.

Before she could answer, Mr. Arnie reappeared with two plates loaded with crispy chicken, collards, fried okra, macaroni and cheese, and hefty slices of cornbread. He set them down and joined us at the table.

"Two Renaissance specials!" he proudly declared. "Same recipe, same great taste!"

Mom cleared her throat. "This looks amazing. Like always."

The feast eased the disappointment of our conversation being interrupted. Mr. Arnie laughed as I shoveled pieces of fried okra into my mouth.

"Good appetite," he said. "She's your only kid, right?"

"The one and only."

"God, she look like Letty," Mr. Arnie said again, propping his chin in his age-spotted hand. "Them eyes! How's Letty doing, anyway?"

Between bites of food, Mom filled him in on Mama Letty's health and our life in DC. She told him she became a professor, to which Mr. Arnie cackled and said he wasn't surprised.

"You've always been a damn know-it-all," he said.

We ate and laughed and nodded along to the music, and I decided the Renaissance could be my favorite place in the world, too.

Just when I thought I couldn't eat anymore, a waitress replaced our empty plates with bowls of banana pudding. Mom groaned and pushed hers away.

"You too good for banana pudding now?" Mr. Arnie asked. "You and Carole used to eat me out of house and home."

Mom lowered her eyes at the mention of Carole's name; Mr. Arnie and I both noticed it. He rubbed Mom's back.

"How is Carole doing, by the way? I ain't seen her in a long time either."

"She's okay," Mom said. Then, more hesitantly, "I think she's okay."

"When you see her, you tell her I miss her. The way you two used to dance, chile! You know we still have live music and dancing every Saturday. Y'all should come down."

Mom dragged a spoon through her banana pudding and said, "Yeah, maybe," with the nonchalance of someone RSVPing to an event they didn't have any intention attending.

Mr. Arnie left to bus tables, and I finished off my pudding, spoon clanking on the side of the bowl. Mom pushed hers in my direction.

"Don't let it go to waste."

I was so full my uniform skirt was digging into my stomach. But I figured the longer we sat there, the greater chance there was Mom would open up and tell me everything. A blues song wailed, then abruptly started to skip. Mr. Arnie, walking toward the kitchen with one hand loaded with dirty dishes, gave the speaker a good whack, and the record began to play smoothly again.

"That man," Mom said, "is like a father to me. I'm so sorry neither of us will ever get to meet Ray. But Arnie might as well have been my dad how he was always looking out for me. This was my second home."

I stayed quiet, my heart aching for something I couldn't name.

Mom fiddled with her napkin. "I'm not saying what Mama Letty told you was a lie. I wasn't even alive. Only she was there. But it's never been proven."

"She shouldn't have had to *prove* anything," I said. "Her word is proof enough."

"I agree. But you have to understand what it was like growing up in a house with her. Losing Ray changed her, Avery. If there was ever a soft side to her, I never saw it. She was drunk my entire childhood. Always yelling at me. Always making me feel awful for existing." Her eyes pooled with tears, and I reached for her hand.

"I want to forgive her so bad, Avery," she said, "and I'm trying, I really am. But you have to understand there is a long, long history of abuse and neglect and pain." She took a deep breath. "I'm *still* trying to forgive her. She made me believe I was unlovable for so many years."

"Mom," I started.

"Do you see why it's hard for me to talk about this?" she asked, wiping her eyes. "It's not because I don't care. It's because it's deeply painful. Every time I have to revisit those old memories, it's like a stab right to the chest."

"I'm sorry," I said quietly. "I didn't know."

She squeezed my fingers and shot me a shaky smile. "This was one of the places where I could be free. Arnie opened his door to me. He loved me without question, without hesitation. This was the only place me and Carole were safe."

"You had feelings for each other," I said quietly.

Her deep brown eyes flashed as she looked away from the disco ball. "How . . . ?" Her question dangled in the air, riding the final notes of the R&B song.

"I saw you two. At the Draper. When you picked her up from work." Her face morphed into confusion, so I told her about the sleepover. She was exasperated by the time I finished.

"You lied to me and your father about where you were?"

"Yes," I said slowly, "but since I'm already grounded, can we pretend this is one of my crimes and let me off the hook?"

She swiped a tear with the back of her hand, wincing as the baby at the next table started howling again. "You're really trying your luck, Avery baby."

I nudged her foot under the table. "Can you tell me? You pulled me out of school and dragged me out to the middle of nowhere."

"I didn't hear you complaining when you were gnawing on that chicken bone," she said dryly.

"Mom!"

We started laughing, and it felt good. So good. In that moment, it didn't feel like we were a mother and daughter who only knew how to argue. We felt like close friends, huddled in the corner of a dim restaurant, sharing secrets.

"Fine," Mom said. "Carole and I used to be best friends.

Like Arnie said, we were thick as thieves. We went everywhere together. We did everything together. My entire world," she said, voice shaking, "was the Zora and Carole Show. Everyone else was a spectator. Even when things were bad—really, really bad—Carole was there." Her eyes welled up, and I shoved my hands under my thighs, waiting patiently for her to go on.

She didn't say anything for a while. The music had shifted to a soulful ballad, and Mom stared at the disco ball twirling on the ceiling for several long beats. Sparkles washed over her tired face and tight coils. She opened her mouth, then closed it again. Seventeen years of being her daughter, and it wasn't until we moved to Bardell that she was at a loss for words so often.

"You don't remember much from your first visit to Bardell, do you?" she asked.

"No." No matter how hard I tried, there were only pinched memories that made no sense on their own.

Christmas lights. Screams. Clouds. A box shattering against a wall.

"Mama Letty and I had a fight," Mom said. "No surprise there. We never run out of things to argue about. But one of the biggest ones used to be about Carole. And how my mother treated the two of us growing up. Carole and I were best friends, yes. But there was a time when we were more than that, and your Mama Letty found out."

My heart felt like it was going to drop through the wooden chair and onto the floor. "You and Ms. Carole dated?"

"No, we never dated. But yes, we definitely loved each other." She swallowed, hard. "Not every love is romantic, Avery.

Not every love is given the chance to bloom beyond possibility."

"What do you mean?"

"I *mean*," Mom said, "two Black girls in love wasn't a thing in the eighties—not in this town. We didn't know what we were doing. We didn't know that we could ever *be*. And everything was ruined when Mama Letty found out." Her face screwed up with tears and she yanked a napkin from the metal dispenser. She didn't look like composed, poised Dr. Anderson. As she cried into the napkin, I saw flashes of a scared girl unsure of her own heart. So many things made sense now—from when I heard her crying in the shower after I came out to how the letter from Carole made time freeze to Mom always tugging at an earring in her presence.

"I was so lonely," Mom wept, "for so long. My childhood was nothing but a long stretch of loneliness, hiding from Mama Letty's drunken tirades and shutting myself in my room. Carole was the *only* bright spot. And she took that away from me."

"What happened?" I asked. "Did she catch you . . ." I raised my eyebrows, hoping she got my drift. She scoffed and sipped her water.

"God, no. Never. She only caught us dancing, but she put the pieces together. Forbid us to ever see each other again."

"Oh, Mom," I said softly.

Mom swallowed. "I have a lot of regrets, but choosing your father and having you isn't one of them. You have been my greatest adventure, my miracle. I don't know what my life would've looked like without you and your father."

"Maybe you would've ended up with Carole," I suggested.

Mom laughed and crumbled the used napkins. "I don't think that was ever in our cards." She blew her nose and looked back up at the disco ball.

"I'm far from perfect. Mama Letty is far from perfect. She's seen such unthinkable things, and I want you to know that just because we're still working at being a family doesn't mean we don't love you."

My own eyes burned with tears now. I reached for her hand again. She let me take it. And we sat there for a moment, listening to the skipping record and watching the disco ball spin in lazy circles. I was grateful for the dim lighting; I wasn't ready for Mom to see the shame on my face. I wasn't ready to admit I felt small and childish for wanting her and Mama Letty to get over problems that existed long before I was born. Problems that could potentially live on, even after Mama Letty died. It felt like Mom's heart had been cracked open, and all we could do was sit there and revel in the mess.

The banana pudding was soggy by the time Mr. Arnie made another round. As he gathered our dirty dishes, Mom rummaged around for her credit card. Mr. Arnie shook his head. "Zora, if you don't put that goddamn thing up."

"I have cash," she offered, but Mr. Arnie swatted away the bills.

"Just come back soon," he said softly. "And tell Letty and Carole I said hello."

Mom stood up and hugged him tightly. They swayed back and forth to the music, and when Mr. Arnie whispered something in her ear, she nodded on his shoulder and started to cry again. I looked away, toward the jukebox in the corner, to give them some privacy. My stomach was full and my mind was reeling. Even though a part of me knew something was up the moment I saw them outside the Draper, having Mom confess her feelings in the special place she and Carole used to share was yet another blow I didn't see coming.

After Mom and Mr. Arnie pulled apart, he placed his warm hand on my shoulder. He had gentle eyes and a smile that seemed like he was always in on the joke. "You look out for your mom, you hear me, young one? She's very special."

I smiled at her. "I know."

"You come back to Renny's anytime," he went on. "My door is always open. Well, except on Sundays because I need to sleep off Saturday night. Oh, and holidays are for me and my honey, and every third Wednesday I take the afternoons off to go into town to get a fresh cut, but *any* other time, my door is open for you!"

"Good to know," I said, laughing, and he crushed me into another hug.

"My sweet girls. You are loved so much. Please be gentle with yourselves. You hear that, Zora? I'm telling your daughter that y'all need to be gentle with yourselves!"

"We hear you, Arnie," Mom said with a smirk. "You don't have to scream."

The three of us stepped out into the shaded alcove together. It was the thick of afternoon, and it felt like the entire world was taking a nap. While Mr. Arnie took a couple of moments to whistle over the BMW, I wandered to the riverbank and watched the water slip by. I wondered if my wish to become a granddaughter Mama Letty would miss was buried somewhere deep in the silt.

In the car, Mom flicked through radio stations as we pulled out onto the main road. The Renaissance disappeared in a thick tangle of trees, sheltered from the rest of the world.

"So I guess now is as good a time as any to tell you Simone and I kissed last night," I said.

She looked over, completely unsurprised. "Does Carole know?"

I shook my head. "No one does. Just me and Simone. And apparently Mama Letty? And now you."

"What did I say about being careful, Avery?"

"It was one kiss!" But once I said the words aloud, I realized how much I didn't want them to be true.

"This is not DC."

"I *know*—"

"You don't know, Avery. If people saw you two together, do you know what could happen? Do you?"

"Fine, we'll be careful," I mumbled.

Marvin Gaye crooned as we drove on. I shot her a curious glance.

"So you're bisexual? Why didn't you ever tell me? Especially after *I* came out to *you*."

Mom's fingers tightened on the steering wheel. "I was afraid. I'm still . . . figuring it out. But yes, I would say I'm bisexual."

I told her I was proud of her, and a shy smile bloomed on

her face at the exact same words she said to me when I came out.

We passed a sign announcing that Bardell was twenty miles away. The road felt empty and open and endless.

"What about Simone? Do I tell her?" I asked. I'd been afraid to bring her name up. But didn't she deserve to know our moms' history as much as I did? What did this mean for us?

"It's your decision," Mom said, "if you want to tell her or not. I'm assuming Carole hasn't told her."

"Of course she hasn't." Then I told her about Simone's fears of coming out, her being afraid of Carole's wrath. "Simone has no idea. She deserves to know the truth, too."

"You're right."

I considered telling Simone and imagined her going to Carole. How would Carole respond? Would she be angry that I told her daughter about her history with Mom?

"And what about Jade?" I asked. "Do I tell her what Mama Letty told me? About what her grandfather and great-grandfather did?"

"These are tough questions." Mom tuned the radio station and landed on twangy country. She made a face and switched it back to the best of the seventies. "I don't know, Avery. I don't know."

I faced the window, a million questions still burning a hole in my brain.

"What other questions do you have?" Mom asked.

"I don't know where to start."

"You already have," she said with a grin.

"Okaaaay. What music did you and Carole dance to?"

She turned the radio up. "You're listening to it."

I read the name of the group scrolling across the screen on the dashboard. "The Stylistics. How romantic."

Mom started to sing along, and I hopped in to provide the background vocals. We took a break whenever I had another question—*Do you think Grandpa Ray would've accepted your sexuality? Did you ever meet Ms. Carole's husband? How does she feel now?*

Some questions were harder to answer than others—*I hope so. No, I never met her husband.* And *I'm not sure. I think she's happy?*

In those moments, it felt like the fighting and bickering were behind us. We followed Mr. Arnie's advice and were gentle with ourselves and each other. We drove toward the sun and took the long way home.

THE ASTRONAUTS

THE RENAISSANCE WAS not the kind of establishment one could rate on Yelp or Tripadvisor. In the span of its fifty-six-year existence, it would never reveal itself to eager tourists scouring the web for *authentic Southern experiences*. Cloaked in secrecy was always how Arthur "Arnie" Thomas intended for the Renaissance to operate. Since its inception, Arnie's home on the river was meant to be a landing place for tired, lonely souls. It could only be found if you followed the Bardell River long enough and you knew exactly what you were looking for. Quite simply, Renny's was invitation only.

Zora Rayla Harding and Carole Marie Thompson were sixteen years old when they discovered the Renaissance. Upon meeting them, Arnie recognized Raymond Harding in Zora's face and was reminded of a violent, bloody story he'd heard through the town grapevine sixteen years prior. It was then that Arnie made an immediate, silent vow to never let anything bad happen to these girls, not if he could help it. So every Saturday night, Zora and Carole could be found twirling on the sweaty dance floor, riding a wave of Teena Marie and Diana Ross, sparkling like disco balls. When they got tired, they caught their breath by the edge of the river under a curtain of stars. They had a routine. Zora would point to the moon and say, *One day, our footprints will be up there.* Carole would reply, *We'll work on the same rocket, become the first Black girl astronauts! They'll build monuments of us.* They'd laugh because they knew it was ridiculous. There was only one of them that truly wanted to learn the calculations required to break the exosphere and it wasn't Carole, and that was okay. It was fun enough to dream.

Even after the astronauts were long gone, even after the Saturday night soundtrack shifted from Janet Jackson to TLC, Missy Elliott to Janelle Monáe, Renny's barely changed. Its reputation as a safe haven for fatherless girls and the ones deemed *too flamboyant* or *too weird* or *too outside the box* became as ingrained as the names carved into the wall behind the makeshift stage. Arnie always said he never set out to provide anything other than a good time. But in reality, the gifts his establishment offered were the ones that kept giving long after Sunday mornings.

For example: After kissing Morris Rainey for the first time, Darnell Hitchens took the deepest breath he'd taken in eighteen years. With shaking hands, Tanya Grambling slipped on her friend's black silk dress and greeted herself for the first time in the scratched bathroom mirror. And although Zora Harding never made it to the moon, she knew from her nights at the Renaissance that you didn't always have to look to the stars for magic. Because magic was actually two shades of lipstick staining a shared straw in a glass Coke bottle. Magic was sweat-slick dancing to mantle-deep beats, magic was renaming constellations after Black women because who else could be worthy?

Magic was a riverside home with a big, beating heart.

16.

WHEN ONE CORNER of my universe righted itself, the other tilted. All of a sudden, I was good with Mom. But when we arrived back at Sweetness Lane, I felt as if I was back to square one with Mama Letty.

No matter how many times I tried to get her to talk over the next few days, she wouldn't budge. We were back to grunts and grumbles. Even Isaac's attempts to lure her from her bedroom with *Get Out* and *Candyman* DVDs didn't work. I wanted more than anything to beg her to share her side of the story of what happened between Ray and the Olivers. But Mom told me to give her space, so I fell back and stewed in my questions alone.

School wasn't much better. Whenever I looked at Jade, I heard Simone in my ear, asking me to keep whatever we had going on strictly between us. I saw Tallulah's jaw dropping, heard Mama Letty's comments about a murderer still being a murderer, and Mom's tearful side of the story. It was a constant tilt-a-whirl of emotions, the universe tilting and righting itself, tilting and righting.

On the opposite end, whenever I looked at Simone, I thought about Renny's and the earth-shattering news of our mothers. I sat on the story for days, trying and failing to figure out the best way to tell her. We stole time alone whenever we could, but in those rare, precious moments, talking was the last thing on our minds.

Twice she snuck over after Carole and my parents were asleep. We made out in my dark bedroom against my desk, and jumped at every floorboard creak and house-settling sigh. A few days later, Mom sent me to the store for a gallon of milk, and I hastily swung by Slice of Bardell so I could see her on her break. We even started planning our bathroom breaks at school, plotting so we'd be out of class at the same time. We would kiss in the cleanest empty stall we could find, the minutes never seeming long enough to do everything we wanted, stall never big enough to fit all our feelings. Kissing Simone was easy. Hiding it from Jade, however, proved to be much harder.

"Why don't we just tell her?" I asked a couple of days before Halloween. It was the middle of sixth period, and Simone and I were in the bathroom with our hands up each other's shirts. Simone peeled away and unlocked the stall.

"Because," she said, straightening her uniform in the mirror, "I don't think it's time." I sidled up to the sink next to her and worked on taming my curls. I needed another shave; the left side of my hair was growing in prickly, fast.

"Then when is the time?" I asked. I'd been working on mastering my casual tone when it came to the topic of whatever we were doing, but it was beginning to show its cracks.

I wanted to support her, but I didn't want to be her secret. I wanted to tell her about our mothers, but I didn't know how. My universe—tilting and righting, tilting and righting.

Simone scrubbed her hands vigorously. Then she held them under the hand dryer forever, even though we were pressed for time. When the dryer stopped, the bathroom was eerily quiet. She tugged at the hem of her skirt.

"Your reaction to me coming out was so positive."

I raised my eyebrows. "Uh. Yeah. I think it's great. Go gays."

"What if Jade's isn't like that?" she asked hesitantly.

"You're not giving her enough credit. She's going to be fine."

"But what if she's not? Especially after hiding it from her? And our No Dating rule?"

"What are you going to do, Simone?" I asked, exasperated. "She's your best friend. You're going to hide from her forever?"

"Not forever."

We stared at each other in the mirror for a moment longer before an underclassman walked in and started primping at the sink next to us.

"I need to get back to class," Simone mumbled. She left before the conversation could get any messier.

• • •

My grounding wasn't set to end for a few days, but Mom was in a great mood when the last weekend in October rolled around. While she attempted to make French toast, she blasted Cherrelle and serenaded Dad with a silicone spatula. There were a dozen bloodred roses in the middle of the Formica table, and I suddenly remembered it was their wedding anniversary.

"How many years has it been?" I asked, grabbing a bowl in preparation for the cereal I'd have when the French toast ultimately burned.

"Twenty-two glorious years," Dad sang. He twirled Mom around and accidentally bumped his hip into the oven door handle. They dissolved into giggles like children.

Surprisingly, the French toast survived the jam session. I was halfway through my second slice when Dad shared the best news I'd heard in a while.

"We're going away this weekend," he said, "to Savannah. For a romantic beachside getaway."

"And we're counting on *you* to be here for Mama Letty in the evenings," Mom added.

I shrugged. "I'm grounded until Sunday. Where am I going to go?"

My parents exchanged a look, and Hope showed her gorgeous, promising face.

"About that," Mom said, "we decided to end your punishment early."

"It's almost Halloween!" Dad said, as if that was reasoning enough.

"Enjoy the weekend with your friends," Mom said with a gentle smile. "Have fun. But we need you to be home by eleven because that's when Isaac's shifts are up. Do I make myself clear?"

I jumped up to hug her, and she laughed into my hair.

"I mean it, Avery baby. Home by eleven tonight *and* tomorrow. Okay?"

"Yes, yes, okay—"

"And the Georgetown deadline is the first. You're sure you turned it in?"

"Yeah," I said, checking my phone; it was almost time for Jade to pick me and Simone up for school. "Turned it in last week."

Mom didn't see the lie on my face. Guilt crept into my veins.

"Then I think you deserve some fun," she said. "Go be a kid."

• • •

It was the last weekend of the Bardell County Fair, and practically everyone in town was there. It was a quarter past five when Jade pulled into the fairground's grass parking lot, and we had to circle for ten minutes to find a spot.

Jade cut the engine and flipped her visor down to primp. We'd gotten ready in the bathrooms after school, Jade overprepared with the makeup and costumes in her car. Now the three of us looked like a gang of badass pirates.

"Avery, could you grab the water bottle?" Jade asked, smudging her black liner so her eyes looked even more hollowed out. I rummaged around the back seat and handed it to Simone, who twisted the top off and smelled it with a wrinkled expression.

"This smells like death." She flipped her eye patch down and tossed her locs over her shoulder. The tips were now neon green and adorned with gold charms. The effect was so stunning, I could barely keep my eyes off her the entire ride.

"It's my parents' good shit," Jade said with a frown. She took a timid sip and tried to control her pinched expression. "Okay. That's *strong*."

"What is it?" I asked.

"Tequila and orange juice," Jade replied. "I figured we'd get a little buzz to enjoy the carnival, then finish it off at the Perfect Spot afterward." She took another sip and coughed. "But yeah, it's pretty strong. Sorry." We all laughed and groaned, but the bottle made its way between us several times anyway.

By the time we emerged from the Jeep, the sun was setting and we were tipsy. As Jade led the way to the entrance, Simone trailed the tip of her plastic sword along my back, her scarlet-painted lips grinning seductively. As she got closer to my butt, I squealed and ran away.

"What's so funny?" Jade called over her shoulder.

"Nothing," we chimed.

The fair was a haunted Halloween wonderland. We bought wristbands and tickets at a booth covered in fake cobwebs and wandered inside, savoring the scent of fresh waffle cones and fried corn dogs. Screams escaped from the rides and haunted corn maze, and the lines were packed with kids we recognized from Beckwith. The air was chilly, and Simone and I showered Jade in praises for opting to make our costumes with long, puffy white sleeves. And while the two of them were wearing ankle-length red skirts, Jade made sure my costume had pants. *Because I know you hate dresses*, she'd teased as I slid into the black-and-white-striped leggings. It was Friday night, we looked amazing, I was no longer grounded, the tequila had softened my worries, and the sunset had washed everything in shades of violet and honey. Everything was perfect.

Jade insisted on riding the Ferris wheel first so we could enjoy the sunset, so the three of us squeezed into one car and marveled at the shrinking carnival. When we got to the top, Jade pointed to a peach-colored tent far below.

"ARRGHHH!" she yelled in a horrible impression of a pirate. "Shiver me timbers! Down below, you see? The tent where my parents be!"

"Tell me we're avoiding them," Simone said. "I cannot deal with your stepmom tonight."

"Nah," Jade replied. "I figured we'd let Avery and Tallulah fight to the death in the middle of the haunted corn maze."

We were still laughing when the Ferris wheel circled us back to the ground.

• • •

By eight, we'd exhausted most of the rides. Simone decided a funnel cake break was in order, so we nibbled on one while we browsed the local vendor tents, our fingers quickly becoming coated in powdered sugar. When we stopped by the Slice of Bardell tent for cheesy bread samples, Simone got roped into a conversation with one of her coworkers. Jade and I wandered off to the next tent alone, which turned out to be an antique store, full of odd trinkets and knickknacks. The woman behind the register was dressed like a witch. She introduced herself as the store's owner, Rhoda.

"Happy Halloween!" Rhoda said. "Welcome to Flashback Antiques!"

Jade picked up a creepy-looking doll from a wicker basket full of toys. "This is cute. I could do a lot with this." She started muttering to herself about a potential art project while I kept browsing. I stopped at a bin full of picture frames, and Rhoda swooped in.

"All one of a kind," she said, beaming proudly. "We're offering a great Halloween weekend sale. Two for the price of one. See any you like?"

I picked up a wooden frame with intricate etched flowers along the side. On the bottom, in swirling letters, it read *Love Forever*. It was corny, but oddly beautiful.

"Got a sweetie?" Rhoda asked. "Perfect frame for showing off a lovely couple."

"Maybe." I wasn't sure if it was the tequila or the funnel cake sugar rush to blame for my amazing mood, but I suddenly didn't want to walk away without buying something. "It *is* my parents' anniversary."

"Perfect gift! I'll wrap this up, and you pick another one for free!"

By the time Simone caught up with us, Jade had purchased her creepy doll. Rhoda wrapped my second frame—simple oak with no inscription—while I dug around my wallet for money.

"I leave y'all alone for two minutes," Simone said, resting her chin on my shoulder, "and you transform into antiquing grandmas."

"Antiquing," Rhoda said stiffly, adjusting her pointed hat, "is for all ages."

I handed Rhoda a twenty, and Jade and Simone giggled while she counted out my change. Then their laughter abruptly stopped, and when I turned around, I saw why. Lucas and

Tallulah Oliver had found us. Magical Halloween had been replaced with Fright Night terror.

"Girls!" Lucas said. "You all make marvelous pirates!"

"Thanks," Simone said. "And you're a . . . cop?"

Lucas tipped his faded hat to us. "I was a bit pressed for time, so I had to dig up my dad's old sheriff outfit. Glad it fit!"

My mouth went dry. I had the sharp, biting memory of Mama Letty at the train station, telling me about the men who took Ray. Who killed him. Evil men. I heard her raspy voice, choking out—

The goddamn sheriff and his men! They all had connections to the Klan back then. They killed him and covered it up so good no one ever found his body.

A murderer is still a murderer, Avery.

I felt a chilly gaze on my temple, and when I looked up, Tallulah was boring holes into my neck. In her slim black dress, long satin gloves, and outrageous jewelry, she resembled a red-haired actress straight from an old Hollywood film. An actress who was doing a very bad job at hiding her disdain for me.

"Elizabeth Jade," Tallulah said with a firm smile. "Can I speak to you for a moment?"

"You already are," Jade said dryly.

Tallulah looked to Lucas for help, but his attention had been compromised by the sizzling sausages being sliced for samples at the local butcher's tent. He excused himself, became lost in the crowd. Tallulah sighed at his worthlessness.

"I thought I told you," she said slowly, "that I no longer wanted you to hang around these girls." She spoke as if Simone and I were two skeleton props, simply there for decoration. Anxiety crawled in my stomach as I stared at the spot where Lucas had been, his broad shoulders stretching the tan sheriff's uniform. Everyone's voices felt so far away.

"—told you that you're not my mother, and you can't dictate who I choose to spend time with."

"You never used to be this disrespectful—"

"You don't know anything about me!"

"I know enough—"

I felt Simone pulling me away, pulling Jade away. Heard her saying, "Come on, we don't have to listen to this." Still, I could only hear Mama Letty, her warning on an incessant loop.

"Elizabeth Jade, come back here this instant!"

There was a blur and suddenly Jade's younger brothers, Johnny and Nolan, appeared in a sugar-rush frenzy, whirling around in their superhero costumes.

"Jade, can we go to the haunted corn maze?" Nolan pleaded.

"*Please!* We're too young to go on our own and Mom won't take us!" Johnny added, sticking his tongue out at Tallulah.

Jade gripped their hands and dragged them away. "Absolutely," she said, shooting Tallulah a death glare. "Come on."

"Elizabeth Jade, this conversation is *not finished*!" Tallulah's voice was swallowed by the crowd as we hurried away.

Johnny and Nolan took off in excited screeches, and the three of us had to struggle to keep up.

"That went well," I joked.

"I'm sorry," Jade moaned.

"And now we're babysitters," Simone grumbled.

Jade looped her arms through ours, and my bag full of picture frames whacked against our hips.

"We'll let them go through the maze once, and we're out of here," Jade promised. "I just needed to get away from her. What else was I supposed to do?"

"Run," Simone muttered.

The five of us joined the long, snaking line for the corn maze. Every two seconds, Jade had to warn Johnny and Nolan that there would be no maze if they didn't stop shoving each other. My heart was still pounding from Tallulah's frosty words and Lucas's disgusting costume. His dad's sheriff's costume. The same sheriff who was also in the Klan. The same sheriff who shoved my grandfather in the back of a patrol car, never to be seen again.

"You okay?" Simone asked in my ear.

I nodded because I couldn't speak. It took everything in me to force a smile when she stealthily grazed her fingers along my arm.

Creepy music box melodies poured from tinny speakers at the entrance. A pimpled boy from my chemistry class took our tickets in exchange for flashlights and waved the five of us in. Johnny and Nolan promptly took off, laughing as they wound their way through the swaying cornstalks.

"Slow down!" Jade yelled. But the boys weren't listening; they darted out of sight into a row of dark yellow-green shadows.

Jade sighed. "These two seriously make me reconsider ever having kids." She jogged after them, the beam from her flashlight bobbing.

Simone and I paused in the middle of the dirt path, listening to the screams from other people in the maze. When the cornstalks to our left started rustling, Simone shook her head and pulled me away.

"This scary shit ain't sitting right in my spirit," she said.

"Did you miss the memo that this was a *haunted* corn maze?" I asked with a giggle. Over her shoulder, I spotted a man in bloodstained overalls glowering at us. "Uh," I stuttered, "being scared is kind of the point."

Simone turned to see what had caught my attention and screamed, "Aw, hell no!" She gripped my hand and started running. Instead of following the path Jade had taken, she darted in the opposite direction. We passed a father consoling a trembling boy and a couple of bored teenage girls on their phones. Boots pounding the ground, we made several turns, using the flashlight and a thin sliver of moon to guide the way. When we reached a dead end, our feet were killing us, and we were out of breath.

"I think we're safe here," Simone said.

"I think this was an elaborate ruse to get me alone," I joked.

"How'd you know?" she purred against my lips. She kissed me in the shadows, our mouths a mixture of tequila and sugar. Her fingers tangled in my curls. "You sure you're okay?"

I kissed her again. "Yeah. That thing with Tallulah was . . . a lot."

"She's a bitch. Don't feel bad." She trailed her lips down my jawline, my neck. I relaxed slightly. I focused on the indigo clouds slipping past the moon and tried not to think about Lucas or Mama Letty or Ray or Tallulah.

"My parents are gone all weekend," I said quietly. "Maybe you can ..."

"Is this a proposition? Because if so, I accept." Her fingers trailed to my waistband, her touch warm against my skin.

"We should go," I whispered, but her fingers slipped lower, and my mouth clamped shut.

"Let me revel in you," she said, and so I did. Everything felt so good, I wanted to bottle up the moment so I could keep it forever.

We stumbled back into the cornstalks in a tangle, giggling into each other's mouths. I wrapped my hand around her neck and pulled her closer. She fumbled past my underwear and circled once, twice, three times. It felt better than anything I'd ever experienced, and all I wanted was more. All I wanted was her.

Then there was a rustle. The pattering of footsteps. Simone and I sprang apart, scrambled to our feet. At the end of the dirt path, a Superman and a tiny Hulk were gaping at us.

Johnny and Nolan.

"Hey, boys!" Simone called. Then, realizing her shirt was tangled and bunched, turned away from them. "Are you having fun?"

My blood ran cold when they didn't answer. I had no idea how much they'd seen. Seconds later, Jade appeared, completely out of breath.

"Y'all have one more time to run away from me before I—what? What's funny?"

Nolan pointed his green fist in our direction. "They were kissing!"

"What?" Jade looked over, and all the color drained from her face. Simone took two stumbling steps forward. I was frozen, watching the scene unfold like a movie.

"No, no, no," Simone said, "that's not what we were doing. That's not—"

"We *saw* you!" Johnny exclaimed, twirling around, little red cape flapping like fire. "We *saw* you kissing."

"We were playing." Simone's voice rose, cracked. "We were—"

Jade's expression was unreadable. Johnny and Nolan cackled like tiny evil villains. They ran around in circles, screaming, "*Avery and Simone, sitting in a tree! K-I-S-S-I—*"

"Shut up!" I screamed.

The boys froze. Panic, fear, and terror bubbled in my chest as I closed the distance between us and looked at Jade.

"We were wrestling," I lied fiercely. "They don't know what they're talking about."

Jade's eyes narrowed behind her glasses. Her hair looked white in the moonlight. "Look at your face," she whispered. Then she tugged Johnny's and Nolan's wrists and stormed away.

I turned to face Simone, and my heart dropped at the tears streaming down her cheeks. My arms extended for a hug, but she pushed me away and held out her phone.

"Look," she said, swiping up to the camera.

And I finally saw myself how Johnny and Nolan did. How Jade did.

Flushed cheeks. Tangled hair. Ruby-red lipstick staining my mouth, my jaw, and my neck like a bloody trail of evidence.

17.

WE HEADED FOR the warm glow of the emergency exit in a stony silence, swords and shopping bag trailing behind. We ended up in the corn maze's waiting area, where the thumping music and multicolored lights were harsh and bright.

"There she is," I said, pointing to the headful of white-blonde curls weaving around a candy apple booth. We followed her, dodging Harley Quinns and Disney princesses, Wonder Women, and Black Panthers. The strobing lights from the House of Mirrors had cast everything in a smoky red and gold glow. I was choking on the sugar-spun scent of cotton candy when we caught sight of her again, dropping Johnny and Nolan off at the Draper Hotel & Spa's tent.

"Shit," Simone mumbled as we observed the scene from a safe distance. Johnny and Nolan were yammering, yanking on Tallulah's dress, but she was too busy fussing at Jade to notice. Jade was yelling back, throwing her hands in the air, spinning around, stomping off. Simone and I followed her to the entrance gates, moving as if we were wading through a flood.

"Jade!" I yelled once we were in the parking lot. Her shoulders clenched, but she didn't turn around. Simone and I picked up the pace.

"Slow down!" Simone called. "We can explain."

"Explain what?" Jade yelled over her shoulder, walking faster.

When we reached the Jeep, Jade threw her sword in the back seat and glared at us. I'd seen her annoyed before, but never angry. Now, she was past angry. She was fuming.

"I can explain," Simone blurted.

Jade's face twisted. "I think your lipstick all over Avery's face tells me everything I need to know." Her hands trembled when she glared at me. "And for you to just lie to me? Do you think I'm an idiot?"

"No. I—"

"Avery was protecting me," Simone interrupted. "She wanted to tell you, *been* wanting to tell—"

"How long has this been going on?"

"Not long," I said. "We were trying to figure out the best way to tell you—"

"You should have told me! You're my best friends! How could you not have told me?" Her eyes welled with tears, and my throat tightened.

"I was afraid to tell you. I . . . actually *am* a lesbian," Simone said quietly. "I didn't know how you would respond. I told Avery because *she's* gay, and then we started to have feelings—"

"I don't give a shit that you're gay!" Jade yelled. A family climbing into their minivan a couple of spots over glanced at us curiously, but Jade's voice only rose as she barreled on.

"You've been hooking up behind my back? I feel like an idiot!"

"It's not about wanting to hide it from *you*!" Simone argued. "It's about *me* not being ready!"

"That's bullshit and you know it." Jade took a few breaths; her tears had smudged her black eye shadow even more. "Whatever. I don't want to fight. If y'all want to be together, then I'm not going to stop you."

"Let's go to the river like we planned," I suggested. "We can tell you everything."

"I don't feel like going to the river anymore," she said stiffly.

Suddenly, Simone gasped and choked back a sob. "Your brothers. They're going to tell Tallulah."

"*That's* all you care about right now?" Jade spat. She yanked open the Jeep's door, shaking her head. "You're more worried about my stepmom's reaction than mine. That's great. Just great."

"Tallulah will tell *my* mom," Simone said through tears. "*That's* what I'm worried about. And my entire life will be ruined, J!"

"My family's not *that* evil," she said with an eye roll. "You're being so dramatic."

A peal of laughter escaped me; I couldn't help it. Jade placed a hand on her hip and glared me down with a level of sass I didn't know she was capable of producing.

"You have something you want to share with the class?"

"Not that evil? Jade, be real."

"I *am* real! We tell you one half-baked story about my father—"

"This isn't about your stupid dad hiring a hitman!" My voice was climbing and people were staring, but I couldn't stop the fury spreading to every inch of my body. I had tunnel vision again, and Jade was the only one in my sights.

"This is about your grandfather and great-grandfather," I said, every syllable shaking. "And how they *murdered* my grandfather. But sure, your family isn't evil."

"What the fuck are you talking about?" Jade snarled. "Simone, what is she talking about?"

Simone glanced between us, wide eyes shining. "I don't know—"

"Mama Letty told me all about it." I stepped forward; gravel crunched beneath my boots. "She told me how my grandpa Ray was murdered by the Klan. By men in *your* family."

"What are you talking about?" Jade demanded, louder.

"I was in your house. I sliced cucumbers for their goddamn salad, and you want to tell me you had no idea?"

Jade started to cry, and I didn't feel bad at all. A fire-breathing dragon had taken control of my body, and all I wanted was to singe, burn, destroy.

"Your dad parading around in a sheriff's outfit like it's a fun costume! I should've known your family was all types of fucked-up when I saw you live on a *plantation*."

"I can't deal with this. I'm not dealing with this." Jade climbed into the Jeep and slammed the door. "Simone, are you coming?"

"I—" Simone looked back and forth, frozen. Jade rolled her eyes and started the engine.

"Fine. Choose her. Be like that. I'm leaving."

And that was it. I was gone. I was fire. I couldn't stop myself as I saw my leg swinging out to kick the Jeep's door, leaving a mud-streaked, dented scuff. I no longer saw Jade. I saw Kelsi. I saw Hikari. I saw Mom. I saw Mama Letty. I saw every single person who'd ever brushed my feelings to the side. I heard *Focus forward* and *I can't deal with this right now* and *You don't need to know everything* and *Get over it.*

I couldn't get over it. Not this time.

"Leave then!" I screamed. "Go about your fucking day like nothing ever happened! Turn your back on any hard feeling ever because leaving is easier!"

"You're crazy!" Jade yelled. "This has absolutely nothing to do with whatever shit you've made up about my family and everything to do with you and Simone lying to me! We had zero issues with our No Dating rule until *you* showed up!"

"Enough!" Simone yelled. "Jade, the only reason we have that stupid rule is because you got one shred of attention from some asshole guy and lost your mind—"

"And you *agreed* with me!"

"—but we're not freshmen anymore!"

"No. We're not." Jade's chin wobbled as she yanked the selenite ring off her middle finger and threw it at our feet. "I hope you two are really happy together." She leveled her gaze at me. "Never talk to me again."

"Right back at you," I snapped. Tears pricked my eyes, and I was back at the museum, watching my relationships with two of my closest friends go up in flames.

Jade flipped her blonde curls over her shoulder. "Happy Halloween," she yelled through the window. The wheels made a sickening crunch on the gravel as she backed up. She was off without a final look, tearing through the parking lot like a bat out of hell.

Simone and I watched the Jeep shrink smaller and smaller until it turned out of the lot, and she was gone.

● ● ●

It was approximately seven miles on foot from the Bardell County Fair to Sweetness Lane. For the first two, Simone and I didn't say a word.

For forty minutes, Simone alternated between crying and staring straight ahead, face stony. Our swords dragged behind us in the grass as we walked back to town. Every now and then, a car would pass, but no one stopped. I could no longer feel my feet in the pointed boots.

"I can't believe she left us," Simone mumbled. "I can't believe it."

"Really? Because I can." The heated words exchanged were loaded with things we'd never be able to take back. My dragon was still curled up, snorting fire between my rib cage.

"How could you not tell me?" she asked. "About the Olivers and your grandfather?"

"I didn't know how."

"This is crazy," she muttered, head tilting back to face the stars. "My brain doesn't even know what to focus on. My mom finding out I'm gay from Tallulah? Jade's grandfather murdering *your* grandfather?" She looked back down at Jade's ring, which she hadn't let go of since she'd scooped it from the parking lot. "We've never fought like that. Ever."

I said nothing. My plastic bag of picture frames smacked against my calf. How quickly I went from being on top of the world, kissing Simone, to feeling frigid and frozen. Like nothing.

Simone sniffed. "I knew I should've told her. I knew she would understand. She wouldn't care if I was gay, but God! She was so stuck on that No Dating rule for so long."

I wanted to ask, *Who cares?* Who cared about some stupid rule when my grandfather was dead? Who cared about what Jade thought when her family were the ones responsible for ruining Mama Letty's life and ending Ray's? Who cared?

"My life is ruined," she whispered, coming to a halt. Her tears broke through my chilliness and before I knew what I was doing, she was in my arms, sobbing into my chest.

"My mom is going to hate me," she cried. "Everything is ruined."

"It'll be okay. We'll fix this."

"Easy for you to say. You're already out and your parents are cool. My mom—" She cried and cried and cried.

I should've told her. Right then, I should've told her the story about our mothers. But a sedan had slowed and was pulling onto the shoulder a few yards in front of us. Simone straightened and wiped her tears with the red bandanna that had once been a headband for her locs. A woman in a pumpkin knit hat popped out of the driver's side.

"Avery? Simone? Is that y'all?"

We squinted in the dark, trying to make out the familiar voice. As we drew closer, my shoulders relaxed. It was our history teacher, Mrs. Newland.

"Thought that was y'all!" Mrs. Newland said cheerfully. "Looks like you're down a musketeer! Where's Ms. Oliver?"

"She had to leave early," Simone said limply.

"Well, come on. Me and my granddaughters were headed home, but we have room for two more."

I let Simone take the front seat and squeezed into the back with Mrs. Newland's two granddaughters. The one in the middle looked like she was about six and was dressed like Princess Elsa. She gave me a curious look as she picked at her turquoise snowflake skirt.

"Your costume's dirty," she said matter-of-factly.

"That's not nice, Anna," the older girl at the window scolded. She was dressed like an old-timey Southern belle, complete with a ridiculous ruffled pink hat. She shot me an apologetic glance.

"Sometimes things get dirty," I said with a shrug.

"Ain't that the truth!" Mrs. Newland said. "Where to, girls?"

• • •

Pumpkins with crooked smiles and gaping candy wrappers dotted the lawns of Sweetness Lane. I instructed Mrs. Newland to park halfway between Mama Letty's driveway and the Coles'.

"Thanks for the ride," Simone and I echoed as we climbed out.

"Of course, dears," Mrs. Newland replied. "I always look out for my students."

The granddaughters waved and they drove off, lurching slightly as Mrs. Newland swerved around a pothole.

"Guess I better enjoy my last few moments as a free woman," Simone muttered, glancing at her empty driveway. "I'm sure my mom will know by the time she gets home from work."

"You don't know that."

She leaned into me again, sniffling. "I can't believe this. What are we supposed to do? About Jade? About Mama Letty? About everything?"

"I don't know," I answered honestly.

"My mom is going to kill me. Or worse, ship me off to Bible Camp."

"I don't think Bible Camp operates in the fall," I said, patting her back. "Seems like more of a summer thing. You're probably safe until June."

"I'm glad you can make jokes at a time like this."

"I don't know what else to do," I said, and the dragon in my chest whimpered and vanished. There was no more anger, only sadness.

"Are you going to talk to Mama Letty?" Simone asked.

I shrugged.

"Well, if you don't hear from me tomorrow, it means my mom has murdered me. Please have sunflowers at my funeral."

"Please don't joke like that," I whispered, and her face fell. We hugged, tight.

"Keep me posted with everything," she said.

"You too."

She kissed me gently and started up her driveway, sword dragging limply behind her. My heart curdled like sour milk as I watched her front door close.

I headed inside in a daze. Isaac was getting ready to leave.

"There you are." he said. "Letty and I were taking bets on whether you'd be home by eleven or not. Looks like she owes me a soda."

"I don't owe you a damn thing!" Mama Letty called from her bedroom. Isaac and I laughed as he pulled on his jacket.

"She's all yours," Isaac said. "She's good on her medication. Might be a little nauseous. She ate a little, talked a lot of shit."

"So the usual?"

"Exactly. You have my number if there's any issues."

"We'll be fine." I waved him out. "Enjoy the rest of your night."

"Oh, I will. I'm catching a midnight showing of the *Rocky Horror Picture Show*, and it's gonna. Be. Epic."

After he left, I kicked off my boots, sighing in relief as my toes were freed. I set the picture frames on the couch and headed for Mama Letty's bedroom. We hadn't really talked in what felt like forever, so I hovered at the edge of the door, waiting for her to notice me. She was reading a piece of paper, eyes squinting behind reading glasses. Her room looked like a tornado had ripped through it with piles of clothes and stuff scattered everywhere.

"You gone stand there all day or come in?" she grunted.

I joined her on the bed and asked her what she was reading.

"Ray," she said simply. "Remember all them letters I told you about?" She motioned to a box at her feet. "Here they are."

My eyes burned as I picked one up. Ray's handwriting was a sloppy scrawl, like everything he had to say was urgent. The year was 1968. The opening line: *Dear Letty, I haven't been able to stop thinking about you.*

The sight of his words, the proof that he was once real, not just a story or a rumor or a mystery, but a real, breathing, flesh-and-bone human who once loved my grandmother broke something in me. I started crying, right there on Mama Letty's bed.

"The Olivers," I sobbed, "who killed him. It was the Olivers, right? It was them."

Mama Letty gently pried the letter from my hand. When I looked up, she was crying, too.

"Yeah, Fish. It was them."

"And nothing was ever done. There was never any justice."

"Never," Mama Letty said. "Never."

Everything escaped, like a dam breaching. I leaned into Mama Letty, and although she stiffened at first, she eventually softened back onto the headboard and held me.

"Y-y-y-you must've b-b-b-been so lonely," I sobbed. "And *angry*!" I couldn't understand it. I'd only held the news for a few weeks, a second in the grand scheme of time. This was Mama

Letty's life. The one defining thing was grief and trauma. How did she do it?

I cried, telling her how I'd been in their house, their plantation house. I saw where they ate their meals, I saw what kind of plates they used. I shook the oldest one's hand. I let them make me feel small.

"I don't know what to do," I cried. "What am I supposed to do, knowing this?"

Mama Letty stroked my curls and chuckled. "You see why your mama ain't wanna say anything?"

"I should've *known*! I should've known. I should've gotten to know you before. Now we don't have time—"

"Hush with that," Mama Letty scolded. "We got a little time left." And as if on cue, she started coughing and I had to sit up.

"Mama Letty, I don't know what to do."

She coughed and coughed and coughed. I helped her with a glass of water. When she was stable again, she patted the space on the bed next to her and told me to bring up the box of letters.

"Just stay with me," she rasped, "read some of his letters to me."

So I did. I got comfortable. I read Ray's big-hearted declarations of love, one right after another. I read one where he spoke of ending an engagement to a woman named Vivian. I read several where he detailed the sights he encountered on the train. We laughed when I read one where he said that even though Mama Letty was like a bat out of hell, he still thought she was the woman of his dreams.

Even when Mama Letty fell asleep well after two a.m., I stayed. I read the words of a man I'd never physically meet and reveled in the heartache and mess of it all. I stayed and Raymond Harding introduced himself to me, one word at a time.

18.

A SWEEPING CHILLINESS arrived overnight that lasted well into the next morning. Mama Letty and I started the day off quietly on the couch wrapped in a huge afghan, half watching a nature documentary on the ancient television. While she alternated between napping and working on a crossword puzzle, I alternated between wanting to cry thinking about Ray and checking my texts every five minutes, anxious for an update from Simone. The first one came at nine a.m.

Simone: She still doesn't know.

Then ten.

Simone: Still nothing!

Then eleven.

Simone: Omfg still nothing. It might . . . actually be okay?

It was like she was waiting for a bomb to go off and was continuously trying to keep me up to speed since my house was in the blast zone. By noon, she finally mustered up the courage to come over for a visit. She squeezed next to me on the couch and snuggled under the afghan.

"You look radiant today, Mama Letty," she said.

Mama Letty didn't look up from her crossword. "Liar."

Simone shot me a look, and I shook my head. Now was not the time for conversation.

When Mama Letty stepped out for a cigarette, Simone whispered, "Have you talked to her about your grandfather and the Olivers?"

"A little," I said hesitantly. I was exhausted from staying up late and reading Ray's letters, but it didn't feel right to tell Simone yet. Not when I was just now uncovering the full story. "Have you talked to your mom yet?"

"No," she said with a sigh. "She's going to work later, and I *know* she's going to see Tallulah." Her face fell. "Has Jade texted you?"

I faced the TV. "Nope."

"I texted her ten times. And called five. She must've blocked me."

I said nothing. I realized I was still simmering from the fight. Every time I thought about reaching out to apologize for the things I said and the way I acted, the memory of Mama Letty's story about Ray forced the urge away.

Simone rested her head on my shoulder. On the porch, Mama Letty lit a cigarette with trembling hands.

"Give it time," I said. "Things will blow over. At least your mom doesn't know."

"Yet," she grumbled. "I decided to pull a card this morning, you know. New month, new me? Needed some clarity. Guess what the universe slapped my ass with?"

"Haven't the faintest."

"Three of Swords," she said, leaning close, eyes bulging.

I pursed my lips. "I'm guessing that's . . . not good?"

She slapped her forehead and groaned. "No! Not good at all, DC."

• • •

Later that afternoon, I convinced Mama Letty to join me on the porch for a cup of coffee. While we sipped, Simone emerged from her house in her Slice of Bardell uniform, looking less than pleased to be heading to work. Carole, in her pressed Syrup shirt, followed.

"Good afternoon, ladies!" Carole called across the lawn.

Mama Letty lifted her hand, barely. I waved back, breathing a tiny sigh of relief she clearly still didn't know. They got into their car and drove down Sweetness Lane. Seconds later, my phone pinged with a message.

Simone: She still doesn't know . . . should I tell her and get it over with?

The mere thought of that made my hands clammy. I typed back quickly.

Avery: Maybe not now? You don't want to have the conversation right before you go to work. Feels like more of a sit-down talk.

Simone: Smart AND cute . . .

After sending a couple of heart emojis, I set my phone down. The neighborhood had settled into peaceful quiet. I took another sip of coffee and watched the old man that lived three houses down rake leaves into neat piles on his front lawn. I gave myself another push on the swing.

"Hey, Mama Letty?"

She grunted.

"I want you to know," I said slowly, "there's a good chance Ms. Carole might kill me in the next coming days." I was half serious, but Mama Letty gave a rare laugh.

"Why? 'Cause you and Simone got the hots for each other?"

My face warmed. "I wouldn't call it 'the hots' . . ."

Mama Letty smirked. "You forgot I saw y'all out here the other night sucking face?"

I curled into my oversized Georgetown sweatshirt. "And . . . you're okay with it?"

Mama Letty snorted. "Why wouldn't I be?"

My stomach burned with nerves for not only myself, but Mom, too. We hadn't talked about Mom and Carole yet. It felt like yet another thing on the long list of family traumas we were trying to work through.

"Mom told me," I said, looking at the ground. "About how awful you were to her and Carole."

The rocking chair groaned as Mama Letty sighed. She fiddled with the drawstring on her gray cotton jacket. "Not one of my finer moments, that's for sure."

I buried my knees into my sweatshirt. "So you're okay with me being gay but not Mom?"

Mama Letty's eyes were sad. "What happened between your

mother and Carole was a very long time ago. And I'm tired, Fish. I don't care 'bout who people love anymore. Back then, I thought I was protecting your mama. It was dangerous. If people found out, the same thing that happened to Ray could've happened to her. I ain't want that."

I knew it made sense, but I still couldn't shake Mom's grief in Renny's. How it must've felt to return there and recall a love deferred. Down the street, a man was gently coaching a young girl with puffy braids how to ride her bike without the training wheels. I smiled as the girl's yelps turned into excited screeches and she wobblily biked down the middle of the street, narrowly missing a pothole. Her face was pure delight flashing with terror, and I wondered if that's how Mom and Carole felt dancing at Renny's. How joy and fear could be two sides of the same coin.

"You never wanted to love again?" I asked after we watched the girl take her bike for a few more successful spins, much to the delight of her father.

Mama Letty laughed. "No. There was no one else for me but Ray. He was the only one. Losing him snatched the soul outta me."

"I'm sorry."

"For what?"

"That people didn't believe you. That nothing ever happened. That it took so long for me to get down here. Take your pick."

"I don't need no more apologies. I can't take them where I'm going."

My stomach sank at the words. Her rocking chair creaked

and creaked and creaked as she stared into her coffee. The sky was a brilliant blue, there was an overjoyed child laughing on the street, and my coffee was warm and perfect. All these simple pleasures, and it still wasn't enough to balance out the sorrow on our porch.

"I don't know what life would've been like if Ray had lived," Mama Letty said. "I don't know what life would've been like if your mother and Carole had acted on whatever feelings they had. You wouldn't be sittin' on this porch, that's for damn certain."

I smiled. "So many ifs."

"And you can't make a life outta a bunch of ifs. You can't do nothing with them. So what's the point of wondering?"

I shrugged. "It's fun to think about sometimes."

"No one's ever described me as fun."

I cocked my head. "Why, Mama Letty, I think you're a hoot and a half."

She tried to hide her smile with her mug.

"In fact," I said, wiggling my eyebrows, "I think you should have your own comedy special. Picture it. Letty Harding, one night only! Live at Bardell Theater!"

"I'd get booed off the stage," Mama Letty said, and we laughed into our mugs.

On the street, the little girl was still pumping her legs, perfecting her balance. The sparkly pink streamers on her handlebars flapped wildly.

"I've got it!" the girl screeched to no one, to everyone. "I'm going! I'm flying, Daddy!"

"I know that's right!" Mama Letty called out, and I whooped and cheered her on.

The smile on the girl's face was bright enough to be seen from the porch, fear morphed into glee. Her ride was shaky, but she was going somewhere. She was flying.

• • •

It was dark when the tapping began. I was in bed with my laptop, watching reruns of *Steven Universe*, when the familiar code of Simone's arrival turned into frantic knocking. I threw the covers off and stumbled to the window.

"She found out" was the first thing Simone said when I slid the glass pane over. She was still wearing her Slice of Bardell uniform, eyes bloodshot and puffy. Her chin wobbled as she held up her phone, the screen bright and jarring.

Carole: Tallulah told me about you and Avery. We'll be having a talk when I get home.

"What am I going to do?" she cried. "She's going to kill me."

I queued up Mom's breathing exercises. One, inhale. "She's not going to kill you." Two, exhale.

"You don't *know* that!" She looked over her shoulder, eyes frantic. "Can I—" She didn't need to finish the sentence. I held my hand out, and she hoisted herself inside and started pacing.

"I'm dead. She's going to kill me, and I'm going to be dead." Her hands were shaking, her knees were shaking. I gently guided her to my bed.

"How much time until she gets home?" I asked.

"She gets off at midnight. So I have four hours to pack my

bags and get the hell out of town. I can go to my dad's—ugh, no, that'd be the first place she'd look. Maybe I could go to my sister's. Or Jade's! Wait—"Then, seeming to remember Jade wasn't currently on speaking terms with us, her face crumpled. "Avery, what am I supposed to do?"

I was still trying to remember to breathe. To give myself something to do, I bent down, unlaced her shoes, and tugged them off. I pulled her into bed with me, shoving my laptop to the side.

"Can we run away together?" she asked, burrowing into me. "Please? Can we get on the first spaceship to Jupiter and never look back?"

I laughed and pulled the blanket over our heads, cocooning us in darkness. "Your request is my command." I mimed talking on a radio, complete with static. "Houston, this is Mission Space Blanket. First stop: Jupiter. Over."

"This is a really fuel-efficient spaceship."

"Only top-of-the-line for you." I kissed the tip of her nose. "To Jupiter."

Simone's fleeting smile crumpled. She pressed closer, and all I could smell was pizza.

"This was not how I pictured the first time in your bed," she said.

I traced her smile with the tip of my finger. "Nice to know you've thought about it."

"Of course I've thought about it. I thought there would be candles and nice music. Not us planning our journey to outer spacc to escape my mom." She wrinkled her nose. "When I'm smelling like cheese and pepperoni."

"I love those things."

Her eyes met mine in the darkness. It was starting to get hot, but I didn't want to be the one to break our blanket sanctuary.

"Everything's ruined," she said quietly. "Jade hates me, my mom is going to kill me—"

"She's not going to kill you."

"—and you're leaving." She swallowed. "After Mama Letty dies, you'll go back to DC, and I'll never see you again."

"Why don't we," I said, interlacing our fingers, "focus on one day at a time? One moment at a time. Besides, your mom is more likely to kill me than you."

"You?"

"I'm the out-of-town pansexual weirdo who rubbed rainbows off on you."

"You wish," she said with a snort.

In the next room, I could hear Isaac coaxing Mama Letty to take her evening pills. There seemed to be a lot of negotiating going on.

"Let's go for a walk," I said.

"I don't want to walk," Simone whined. "I want to get in a car and drive away and never stop."

"Well, considering neither of us have cars . . ."

"Mama Letty does." She sat up, bursting through the blanket fort. The fresh air was a cool relief.

"She'll let us borrow it," she said, gears turning. "I know she will."

I thought about my mom's warning to make sure I was home by eleven. "I don't know," I said, checking the time on my phone. It was almost eight.

"Avery. Please. I can't be in Bardell a moment longer. I feel like I'm dying here. I'll deal with all this shit once I get back, but please . . . can we go somewhere?"

"Where?"

"Anywhere," she said urgently. "I'll go anywhere with you. It's Saturday night. The world is our oyster." She kissed me, and that was all it took. My heart was pounding, but I was already picturing us in the car.

"It's Saturday night," I repeated. A slow smile spread across my lips as the game plan figured itself out effortlessly. "Okay. Meet me in the driveway in twenty minutes. Wear something cute."

19.

MAMA LETTY GRANTED us permission to use her car, so I met Simone in the driveway. She'd ditched the pizza uniform for a jean jacket and a long dress the color of seafoam with a slit up the thigh. Her locs were loose around her face, lips a deep purple. She wore a crown of sunflowers and white roses.

"I made this for you," she said, holding out a crown of delicate green leaves and gold star charms. "It was supposed to be for the winter formal but . . ." She looked down. "I know it's kind of corny—"

"I love it. Thank you." I placed it over my curls, and she smiled at me in the glow of the porch light. I opened the passenger door and helped her inside.

"To Jupiter, my sunflower," I said, mimicking the Draper's bellman.

We drove down Sweetness Lane with the windows cracked and the scratchy Ray Charles tape playing. Our escape plan was in motion.

With the lights of downtown fading behind us, it felt like

Simone and I were the only two humans alive. The breeze lifted our hair; our fingers intertwined over the cupholder. I drove past the WELCOME TO BARDELL sign while Simone's other hand danced outside the window. We were only going forty, but we didn't mind the slow pace. It kind of felt like the whole point.

"So where are we going?" she asked, giving my fingers an excited squeeze. "Should we have stopped for road trip snacks?"

"It's a surprise. And you said nothing about snacks, so you'll have to wait."

She kissed my cheek. "Snacks are always included, DC," she mumbled against my skin. "Damn, haven't you learned anything?"

"I will turn this car around."

"You will not."

I tapped the brake pedal teasingly, and she laughed.

We continued along the darkened highway, and I tried not to think about the mountain of problems waiting for us back on Sweetness Lane. I switched off the Ray Charles and asked Simone to play something from her phone. We sang along to Kehlani and let our hearts expand.

Tonight was about us.

• • •

The alcove by the river was packed with cars. I found a space near the base of a weeping willow tree and helped Simone out. She looked around in astonishment, gaping at a group of Black women in tight dresses climbing out of their SUV and two Black teenage boys kissing each other on the hood of a pickup truck.

"What is this sorcery?" she asked in reverence. "Avery, where are we?"

I grabbed her hand and kissed her, fully, on the mouth. "Follow me."

Simone and I headed for the Renaissance like royalty, heads held high in our flower crowns. I was glad I'd chosen to wear my nice black blazer over a white button-down shirt and dark ripped jeans. We climbed the steps, and when I caught a reflection of us in a window, I couldn't stop the wide grin from bursting across my cheeks. Simone noticed, too.

"We look good together," she said in my ear.

"We do indeed," I replied, and kissed her.

Mr. Arnie was stationed near the front door, wearing a pair of dark sunglasses. I didn't have time to wonder if he recognized me—as soon as he saw us, a huge smile split across his face.

"Well, if it isn't Dr. Zora Anderson's daughter!" He pushed people aside and escorted us to the front door. "And you brought company."

"This is Simone," I said. "Simone Cole."

Mr. Arnie whipped off his sunglasses and studied her with a gleam in his eyes. "Oh, I know who this is."

Simone arched an eyebrow. "You do?"

"Lookin' like your mama when she was seventeen," Mr. Arnie said. "Come on, girls, band's 'bout to come on." He waved us inside, into the aroma of sweat and smoke and soul food. On a stool by the front door, the server from my visit with Mom counted out bills and yelled a greeting over the music.

"No alcohol for these two, Khadija," Mr. Arnie said. "Don't think I won't hesitate to call your mamas if I catch either of you with a drink."

"Mr. Arnie!" I protested.

"Girl, you should know by now it's pointless to argue with me," Mr. Arnie yelled, heading back to tend to the line. "The rules are the rules! Now go on, have fun!"

Simone and I looked around the dark, cramped room. All the dining tables had been stacked away, making room for the dance floor, which was packed with Black people grinding, dipping, and twirling to "No Diggity." A live band was tuning their instruments on the small, cramped stage. There was a large ice chest near the kitchen, and a woman in a cheetah-print tank top grabbed a beer from inside and slipped the guy standing next to it a couple of dollars. Under the dim multicolored string lights, everyone looked like one beautiful brown blur.

"What is this place?" Simone asked as we squeezed into a corner near the band. She leaned in to be heard over the music, and her breath was hot in my ear.

"The Renaissance! Part restaurant, part dance club, apparently!"

"Your *mom* took you here?"

I nodded. "Our moms and Mr. Arnie go way back."

"My mom knows about this place, too? I feel like I'm in Wonderland." Simone adjusted her flower crown and looked around the packed room in awe. Everyone was dancing, laughing, drinking, calling out to each other, singing along, shaking their hips. Mr. Arnie moved toward the band, somehow managing to dance, sip a beer, and hold a conversation with everyone he passed all at the same time. I thought about Mom telling me about her history with Carole in this very room. I knew I needed to say something, but this moment—it was too perfect.

"You want a soda?" I asked.

She nodded, seemingly at a loss for words. I gave her hand a squeeze and weaved through the crowd toward the ice chest. I tried to give the man standing near it my money, but he shook his head and thrust two ice-cold root beers in my hand.

"You Zora's girl, right?" the man shouted over the music. When I nodded, he tipped his beer at me. "It's on me tonight."

"Thank you," I stammered.

"Your mama used to tear up this dance floor," he said with a whistle. "'Bout time you found your way here!"

There was a crackle of microphone feedback, and the music abruptly stopped. Mr. Arnie was standing on a chair, his pink T-shirt soaked to the bone.

"Alright, alright, good morning, good morning!" Mr. Arnie said to uproarious applause. "Saturday night at Renny's, how y'all feeling!"

Everyone clapped, whistled, yelled. I thanked the man by the ice chest and made my way back to Simone. The cold root beers were like heaven in the steaming hot room. Mr. Arnie used a towel to wipe the sweat off his forehead.

"Last Saturday of the month, and y'all don't know how to act! Halloween got y'all out here acting a fool. Alright, alright, y'all already know it's live music night, so grab a cutie and put ya goddamn hands together for Sheila Blue and the Bassline!"

Behind him, the all-Black band launched into a rousing rendition of Luther Vandross's "Never Too Much." There was a bassist with long blue braids, a guitarist and keyboardist that looked like twins, both of them with freckles and matching rainbow overalls, and a drummer whose face was covered with large neon green sunglasses. The lead singer was tall with a shaved head and colorful flower tattoos weaving up her neck. She wore a gold fringe dress and thigh-high white boots, and her voice was soulful and raspy. As more people filled the dance floor, I shot Simone a glance.

"Do you want to dance?" I asked, voice shaking.

Simone smiled so hard I could see all her teeth. "Of course, DC. What kind of date would this be if we drove all this way and didn't dance?" She pushed away from the wall, hips already winding, and inched her way toward the dance floor. She curled her finger over her shoulder, beckoning me. I followed her like I was being controlled by puppet strings.

Simone took the lead, and I quickly realized how different dancing at Renny's was compared to the two house parties I'd attended. At those, no one really *danced*. It was more of choosing someone to grind your butt on all night and hoping friction worked in your favor. And Kelsi was usually ready to leave right as the DJ was getting warmed up.

But at Renny's, there was no Kelsi. There was no drama. Only good vibes as the more skilled dancers conquered the center circle, dipping, twirling, and shimmying in a neon pink haze. Everyone on the perimeter, including me and Simone, cheered them on with loud applause and laughter. The room's energy was contagious, the bassline shaking the wooden floor beneath us. Sheila Blue and her band had an energy I'd never seen. Simone and I held on to our flower crowns and grinded and spun ourselves dizzy. After five songs, her dress and my blazer were soaked with sweat.

"We're going to slow it down a bit and give y'all some Meshell Ndegeocello realness!" Sheila Blue said after a fast-paced number that left everyone gasping and fanning themselves. "This song is called 'Beautiful,' and it's for anyone who's ever loved someone."

The crowd filled with murmurs of "Alright now!" and "Okay?!" My stomach dropped. I wasn't sure what Simone and I were, but I didn't think we were at slow-dancing-to-love-songs status yet. I started to head back to our corner, but Simone grabbed my hand. Her flower crown was lopsided.

"What's your rush, DC?" She pulled me close, our bodies slick and warm, and laced her fingers behind my neck. "You too good for a slow dance?" Her face was mere inches away, shining with sweat. I turned my head and hated myself immediately.

"Of course not," I said.

"Why you so tense then?"

"I don't—" I paused. I wanted to tell her that I was so happy it scared me. I'd never felt anything remotely close to this before. When I peeled away the hurt from my breakup with Kelsi, took off the aloof mask, I was just a lonely girl full of ache and insecurity and yearning. I wanted to tell her I was afraid she was going to change her mind, that maybe when morning came, she'd look at me in the light and decide we weren't worth the trouble. I wanted to tell her I was terrified that we weren't big enough to overcome the ugly fight with Jade or parents who didn't understand. I wanted to tell her how much it hurt to have to hide ourselves from the rest of the world sometimes, and I was so tired. I wanted to tell her I'd never reached this golden, transcendent place with Kelsi—with anyone—before, and how was I supposed to go live a life without her now that I'd had a taste?

I wanted to tell her I was afraid that maybe whatever we had was fated to be a reflection of our mothers: Beautiful. Fleeting. Gone.

But I couldn't say any of that. My tongue was too big for my own mouth. All my confidence had vanished. Simone's fingers on my cheeks brought me back to the glitter, smoke, and dark blue fog of the party.

"Dance with me, you beautiful human," she said.

"Are you sure you want to?"

Her fingers traced my jaw. Her face was awash in the purple sparkles reflecting off the disco ball. "I've never been more sure of anything in my life, Avery Anderson."

She melted into my arms, tucking her chin in the crook of my neck. We rocked together. My entire body was on fire.

"Relax," she said in my ear. "It's okay. We're okay here. Let's revel in it."

"I thought *I* was supposed to be taking care of you," I said, half joking.

"We can take turns."

Her words broke something inside me, and my throat tightened. My eyes screwed up with tears, and I was grateful for the darkness that hid them. My stomach was a hard knot as I struggled to hold it together. What was wrong with me? This was everything I wanted, and now I couldn't stop crying.

I tried to focus on the music. I tried to focus on the fact that inside Renny's, the outside world didn't matter. Simone and I weren't bad. We weren't alone. We made sense. Couples of all genders swayed around us, wrapped in the warmth of the dance floor. Across the room, Mr. Arnie was in the arms of the man from the ice chest, their foreheads gently resting against each other's. Next to us, two older women with gray hair swayed back and forth, hands on each other's waists. Simone and I weren't outsiders here. In fact, I'd never been somewhere I belonged more.

The song was nearing the end, but Sheila Blue's lyrics were going in one ear and out the other. I cried against Simone, and she pressed closer, leaving nothing between us. I felt her own tears against my skin. We didn't care how we looked. We held each other, dancing and crying in our flower crowns, hearts expanding with possibility.

Sheila Blue hit her final note, and the crowd hooted and hollered, demanding an encore. Mr. Arnie peeled away from his dance partner and took the mic, once again wiping the sweat from his forehead.

"Alright now, Sheila Blue is gonna take a break, but the night is just beginning!" Mr. Arnie said. His dance partner came up behind him and kissed his cheek. The crowd roared, and Mr. Arnie beamed.

"Y'all know why we call it the Renaissance?" Mr. Arnie yelled, and the crowd responded with laughter and "Go on, tell us again!" and "Go 'head, Arnie!"

"Renaissance means rebirth, baby!" He enunciated every syllable like a charismatic pastor, gripping the bedazzled microphone with a gleam in his eyes. "A re-vi-val after a dormant state! You might feel like the world out there don't love you, but here at Renny's, we know they really just asleep!"

"I know that's right!"

"Amen, amen!"

"Tell 'em, Arnie!"

"Y'all here 'cause you woke up and said good morning to yourselves! Can I get a good morning?"

"Good morning!" My and Simone's voices blended seamlessly with the rest of the crowd's.

"Turn to your neighbor and say, 'Good morning, it's so nice to meet you!'"

"Good morning, it's so nice to meet you," I said to a cute dimpled Black kid in a neon green crop top. They fluttered their false eyelashes and told me it was a pleasure to meet me as well.

Mr. Arnie was revving up for his finale, waving a rag over

his head like a helicopter. "Grab another drink, give us some goddamn tips, and know it's all love here at Renny's, baby! Be gentle tonight! Or be rough, but always with consent, my star children!"

Simone and I wiped tears away as we joined in the thunderous applause.

"Oops (Oh My)" started playing, and I glanced at the time on my phone. It was nearly ten, and the drive back to Bardell was forty-five minutes. We were cutting it close.

"We should go," I said reluctantly.

Simone looked like she was considering something. Her eyes were puffy from crying, and she was still as beautiful as ever. I used my thumb to wipe away a mascara track on her cheek.

"I think we should stay for a while," she said.

"Are you sure?"

"Everything's already broken, Avery. Let's have fun while we can."

I hesitated, looking between her face and the rest of the dance floor. Half of my heart was already in the parking lot, wanting to return Simone back to Bardell as soon as possible so Carole wouldn't have another thing to be angry about. But the other half, and ultimately the bigger half, was cradled in Simone's palms and never wanted to leave.

"Okay. Let's stay."

She kissed me so fast I didn't have time to react. "Come on," she said, and we made our way back into the heart of the dance floor.

• • •

We danced together all night.

By the second slow song—a cover of Tracy Chapman's "Give Me One Reason"—my nerves were gone. I reveled in the feeling of being in Simone's arms as we kissed, unashamed and often. During the more upbeat songs, we cheered for the dancers whose limbs seemed to move by magic. Before we knew it, three hours had passed in a haze of laughter, smoke, and sweat. At one a.m., we spilled out of a side door for some air and quiet by the river.

"This whole night has been a dream," Simone swooned as we climbed onto a large tree stump. We sat cross-legged, facing each other, our clothes soaked with sweat. The river glided by, its dark waters peeking through the trees on the bank. "And I've *finally* decided what your flower is."

"Do tell."

"Eucalyptus. Technically, it's a tree, but it's really a perfect fit for you."

I smiled. Asked her to tell me more.

"It's adaptable, like you. You thought you were going to come to Bardell and shrivel up like a raisin, but look at you. Out here thriving. And you're useful and . . . medicinal."

I laughed. "Thanks?"

"I'm serious! Being around you makes me . . . feel so calm. Like sipping a warm cup of tea or taking a bubble bath. You have a soothing spirit." She leaned in so our noses and flower crowns brushed. "Plus. Eucalyptus pairs lovely with sunflowers, if I do say so myself."

"I will happily be your useful eucalyptus," I said, and we kissed for the millionth time, lips sweet and sticky with root beer.

Down the riverbank, others were taking breaks from the dance floor, their silhouettes dotting the water's edge. The person in the crop top who told me good morning was a few yards away, leaning against a tree, entangled in the arms of someone. Simone braided our fingers together, our wire rings meeting in the middle.

"How in the world did your mom find out about this place?"

I searched her face in the moonlight. Her lipstick was smudged, and I swiped it away gently. "That's what I wanted to tell you," I said, "but I could never really find the right time."

"Tell me what?"

"My mom took me here and told me . . . something. And I don't know how you're going to take it."

She fell back slightly. "What is it?"

I took a deep breath and looked out at the river. The rhythmic hum of the water and breeze rustling the leaves calmed me. The glow from the dance floor told me everything would be okay.

"My mom used to come here with your mom," I said slowly, "like . . . on dates. They were never, like, formally together, but they had a thing. Years ago."

Simone's eyes widened as I relayed the entire story, from

what I saw that night outside the Draper to everything Mom told me during our lunch. By the time I was finished, her jaw was hanging open. She slid off the stump and walked to the river's edge. She stared at the water while I stared at her.

In that moment, riding the high of the night and memory of our mothers, I thought, *I might be in love with you.* I always thought falling in love would feel like an endless summer. Warm and whimsical, sugar-sweet sherbet and sparklers lighting the sky. But it was autumn now, and the world was still beautiful, and it all reminded me of her. I rested my hand on her back and thought yes, hearing her laugh felt like jumping into a lake on the first day of summer vacation. But it also felt like this, like being wrapped in the navy glow of a fall evening with golden leaves beneath our feet. It felt like an angel in a fresh layer of snow and a text message saying all schools were closed. Being around her felt like the opening of a tree bud after a long winter's sleep, and I wondered if that was what love *really* was. A four-season delight. Did our mothers feel that way, too?

But I didn't say any of that. I was too afraid. Instead, I asked if she was okay.

When she turned around, her face was a mixture of glee and shock. "Well, DC. I thought nothing would top you calling Jade's grandfather a murderer, yet here we are." She released a shaky laugh. "*God*, that makes so much sense! How did I not see this coming?"

I shrugged. "People are full of surprises."

"And my mom is full of shit. I . . . need some time to process this."

"Did you want to go home?"

"Hell no."

She laughed and pulled me back toward Renny's, back toward the music, back toward a haven.

20.

WE SHUT RENNY'S down.

It was almost four in the morning by the time Mr. Arnie yelled out, "Last call!" Simone and I joined the groans of the stragglers, none of us ready to return to the real world.

"We're here every Saturday night, y'all know that!" Mr. Arnie said when a man in snakeskin boots begged for one more song. "But y'all gotta get the hell outta here now because I'm an old man who needs his sleep!"

Mr. Arnie followed Simone and me outside to the cool early-morning air. On the porch, his sweetheart was smoking a cigarette.

"Jerome!" Mr. Arnie said. "These are Carole and Zora's girls! Girls, this is my honey, Jerome. We both knew your mothers very well."

"Avery filled me in on our mothers' clandestine affair," Simone said. "So it's true?"

Jerome whistled and nodded. "Oh yeah, it's true. Feels like

yesterday they were here, getting in trouble and dancing up a storm. They look like them—"

"Don't Avery look like Letty? With all these damn freckles?"

"*Exactly* like Letty, damn!" Jerome studied Simone's face. "And you got Carole all over you. She know you're here tonight?"

Simone looked down, seeming to remember the storm we were about to head back into. "No. She doesn't."

Mr. Arnie hummed sympathetically. "Give her time. She'll come around."

"And you," Jerome said, leveling his gaze at me, "don't let old Letty scare you. Old bat hates everything that moves, but she got her reasons. After everything that happened with Ray."

"You knew my grandfather, too?" I asked, heart lighting up.

"Of course!" Mr. Arnie said. "We knew Ray. Everyone loved him. Damn shame what happened."

It was a quick pinch, a subtle reminder that Ray was real. People knew him. Loved him. Mourned him. There were so many questions I wanted to ask, but Mr. Arnie was already moving on.

"If your mama asks," he said in a low voice, "I never saw you tonight."

I grinned. "Roger that."

"Get home safe," Jerome said. "Which one of y'all is driving?"

I raised my hand.

"Breath check!" Mr. Arnie yelled.

"Mr. Arnie!"

"And I *better* not smell any alcohol."

I crossed my arms and exhaled. He gave a satisfied nod.

"All clear. Now get y'all asses out of here so I can give my man some attention." Jerome tipped his fedora in our direction, and him and Mr. Arnie fell into each other's arms.

The stillness of Mama Letty's car was jarring. Simone and I were sweaty and stinky, our flower crowns were missing leaves, but we couldn't stop smiling.

"This might've been the best night of my life," she said as I started the car. I pulled out of the dirt parking lot, and we glanced at Renny's one last time before it disappeared in the trees. "Danced with a hottie all night. Found out my mom used to be gay. Seriously ten out of ten. Say we'll come back here again?"

"We'll be back," I promised, laughing. "But didn't I tell you? Better than Jupiter?"

"Better than Jupiter," she agreed, and entwined her fingers with mine.

• • •

As much as I wanted to take Mama Letty's car and keep driving until we hit California, I knew the storm upon our return was inevitable. Simone and I weren't surprised when we turned onto Sweetness Lane and saw Carole pacing on Mama Letty's porch. What did surprise us, however, was the BMW in the driveway.

My parents were home early.

"Shit," I whispered. I glanced at the clock on the dashboard; it was nearly five a.m. I parked behind the BMW and took a deep breath. Next to me, Simone shuddered.

"I'm about to throw up."

I gripped her fingers. "We'll be okay."

"You sure about that?" she asked, looking past me. When I turned, my insides froze. Carole was stomping across the yard and, even in the darkness, I could tell she was fuming. Simone and I dropped our hands, and I braced myself as Carole yanked the passenger door open.

"Get out." Her grip was deathly tight on Simone's wrist. "Now."

My mom appeared at the driver's door as if she'd materialized out of thin air. For a millisecond, I thought she would be our rescue, a calm voice of reason in all this. But that hope vanished when we locked eyes.

She wasn't upset. She was *pissed*. More furious than I'd ever seen in my life. She threw my door open, her entire body trembling.

"Get in the house," she said through gritted teeth. "Right. Now."

"Mom, I can explain—"

"Get in the fucking house!"

I scrambled out so fast I tripped over myself. As Carole pulled Simone into our house, my dad grimly watched the entire scene unfold from the porch.

In the living room, Mama Letty was in the oversized armchair, looking small and exhausted in her frayed yellow bathrobe. Carole pointed to the couch and told us to sit.

Simone and I obliged like robots.

Carole was still in her Syrup uniform, gripping her cell

phone so hard it looked like it was about to snap in half. Mom stood next to her, glaring. Dad manned the front door, as if he was preparing for a quick escape.

For a moment, all was silent.

"It is five in the morning," Carole said icily. "And no call? No text? Where have you been?"

"We went for a ride, Mama," Simone said. "We lost track of time."

"We're sorry," I added. "Our service was bad—"

"Don't speak," Mom snapped.

I sat back against the couch and stared at my lap. I tried to remember the warmth of Renny's, the joy that Simone and I had basked in not even an hour ago. But that riverside home felt so far away.

Mama Letty shifted in her armchair, light from the lamp illuminating her tired, wrinkled face. "I told y'all I gave them permission to use my car. It's okay."

"Nothing about this is okay," Carole said. "I had to find out from *my boss* that my daughter was kissing another girl? Do you know how that made me look? How that made me feel? Simone has *never* behaved this way! Not until your daughter tried to corrupt her!"

Dad stepped forward, floor creaking under his bare feet. "Why don't we all calm down—"

"Not now, Sam," Mom said. She leveled her gaze at Carole, fists curling. "We are not going to have this conversation if you're going to be throwing around accusations like that. My daughter has corrupted no one."

"It's not an accusation! Clearly they've been out all night doing God knows what!"

We watched Mom and Carole go back and forth like they were in the midst of a ferocious tennis match. I pulled my flower crown off slowly and set it on my lap. Simone quietly did the same.

"I don't know how you're raising *your* daughter," Carole said, "but Simone is a child of God. She is not like Avery."

"That's not true."

Simone's quiet voice cut through the tension like headlights through fog. Carole blinked and asked her to repeat herself.

"That's not true," Simone said louder. She looked at me and reached for my hand. I grabbed it, heart pounding.

"I'm gay, Mom," she said. "And apparently, once upon a time, so were you."

Carole's face dropped. Mama Letty said, "Oh boy," and propped her chin in her hand.

"What did you tell her?" Carole snarled at me. "What *lies* are you feeding my daughter?"

"They're not lies," I shot back. "My mom told me—"

"That was a long time ago. We were *children*. We didn't know what we were doing. We were confused little girls who didn't know right from wrong."

My heart broke in half when I saw how Mom's face fell. For a moment, there was nothing but anguish in her eyes. I saw the vulnerable girl from that afternoon in Renny's.

Then, the mask. The Dr. Zora Anderson mask.

"These girls *are* good," Mom said. "We can be mad at their

irresponsibility and missing curfew, but they are *not* bad because they like each other. You remember what we were like when we were girls at Renny's?"

Carole's eyes were about to pop out of their sockets. She whirled around to look at me. "You took my daughter to that disgusting place? Is that where y'all were at? *Renny's?*"

Anger rattled my chest. Even Simone's hand in mine didn't soothe me.

"How is it disgusting?" I snapped. Mama Letty's temper, somehow buried deep inside me my entire life, burned brighter. "Literally nothing about it is disgusting. It's a place full of love and music and people being their true selves—"

"Avery," Mom warned.

"You think Mr. Arnie and Jerome are disgusting? They said *nothing* but good things about you and how much they missed you." My heart was pounding, but my adrenaline was pushing me, driving me to keep going. "I didn't corrupt your daughter, Ms. Cole. You can be mad at a lot of things, but it's not fair for you to take your anger out on us just because you're repressed."

Simone's hand seized in mine. Carole's jaw dropped, and it reminded me so much of Tallulah that I almost laughed.

I *really* wasn't good with parents.

Carole stormed around the coffee table and yanked Simone up. Our hands dropped, and her sunflower crown fell to the floor.

"Go to the house now!"

"But Mama—"

"Simone Josephine Cole, I swear if you don't move in the

next five seconds, I will put my foot so far up your ass you won't sit for a week!"

Simone made a beeline for the front door, narrowly missing Dad as she barreled outside in a wave of tears. Carole looked around the living room in disgust.

"Stay away from my daughter," she told me. Then she glared at Mom. "And I'll be praying for you."

"Likewise," Mom snapped.

Carole stormed out, footsteps pounding on the porch.

When the coast was clear, Dad closed the front door with a gentle click. For a full minute, we sat in the hum of the refrigerator and the whining springs of Mama Letty's armchair as she shifted. For the first time, I realized Mom still had her silk nightgown on under her jeans and jacket.

"Well," Dad said with a gigantic sigh. "It's late. I think we all need a breather."

Mama Letty chuckled and pulled her cigarettes out. "Amen."

Any hope I had of Carole's departure simmering Mom's anger was quickly doused. In fact, her gaze was chillier than ever. My thighs were superglued to the couch.

"What part," she started slowly, "of an eleven-p.m. curfew was unclear to you? After you were just grounded for two weeks?"

"I know," I said quickly. "But Simone was upset and—"

"I don't care! We said eleven. We can't go away for one weekend without all hell breaking loose? We *trusted* you, Avery. So imagine my surprise when Carole is calling me at midnight, saying you and Simone are gone!"

"I told y'all," Mama Letty repeated dully, "I let them borrow my car."

Mom held up her hand. "Mama, please. Stay out of it. We all know you aren't exactly the authority on motherhood."

"And there it is!" Mama Letty twirled the cigarette between her fingers. "It always ends up here. I was a horrible mother, I know, I know."

"*Do* you know?" Mom cocked her head. "Honestly, do you? Do you want to know the thousands of dollars I've spent on therapy trying to undo all the shit you put me through?"

"Mom, stop," I said. "This isn't about Mama Letty. She had nothing to do with this." Everyone ignored me. It was like trying to contain a wildfire.

Mama Letty looked amused. "Why you here then? If I was so awful, why you here?"

"I'm trying." Mom brought her hand to her heart. "I'm trying to be a good mother. I'm trying to be a good daughter. That's more than I can say for you. You're a shell of a woman, I swear to God."

Mama Letty waved her hand. "I knew that saint act of yours was all bullshit."

"Will you shut the fuck up!"

Dad stepped forward, trying to calm Mom, but she pushed him away. "All my life you've been nothing but a miserable woman. Even two minutes from death and you're *still* as cruel as ever."

"Mom, stop!" I yelled, jumping up between them. "Please!"

"The only reason you're here is because I'm 'two minutes

from death,'" Mama Letty said. "You didn't care that damn bad when you left! You made your choice."

"No, Mama, you made that choice. You made that choice every day when I was a kid and you were checked out, drinking yourself silly. You made that choice when you told me I was disgusting when I even *hinted* I had a crush on Carole. You made that choice when you let my letters go unanswered. You read Dad's letters day in and day out. You have boxes, *mountains* of letters from him, but you never once replied to any of mine." Mom was full-on sobbing now. Tears formed in my own eyes as I watched the two generations of women before me look at each other with so much hate.

Mama Letty's hands trembled as she set her cigarette down on the coffee table. "Ray was murdered. My husband, your father, was murdered. And you never cared about that."

"Of course I cared," Mom said shakily, "but I was a child. What was I supposed to do? I couldn't be your therapist when I was too busy raising myself."

"Yeah, you raised yourself alright. You raised yourself, got all your fancy degrees, got your high-paying job, and married that fucking white man, and you ain't come back. You erase me out of Avery's life, you erased Ray out of her life. You abandoned me like everyone else in this town, and now want to come in on your white fucking horse and solve everything."

"That's enough," Dad said. "We all need to get some sleep. It's almost six in the morning." Sure enough, I could see the beginnings of a purple twilight creeping through the window.

Mom was still crying under Mama Letty's cruel gaze, and I was torn. Again. I didn't know how to fix something that stretched past decades I'd been alive. My mind was reeling. The perfect bubble Simone and I had created at the Renaissance wasn't deflated, it was shattered into a million pieces. Silence stretched painfully as Mom tightened her jacket as if she was getting ready to go somewhere.

"If you don't want us to be here, we will leave," she said after several tense beats. "If you want to die alone and miserable, then be my fucking guest."

I reeled away. "You don't mean that, Mom."

"And I don't want to hear a word out of you," she said to me. "You have completely broken my trust. You're grounded until further notice. No phone, no hanging out, no weekend plans, nothing. School and home, that's it."

My mouth dropped. "Are you serious?"

To prove her point, she reached into my back pocket and took my dead phone in one swift motion. She pointed it in my face. "Step one goddamn toe out of line," she said slowly, "and see what happens."

• • •

In the aftermath, I followed Mama Letty to her room and helped her get settled into bed. She looked utterly exhausted, and I felt nothing but guilt as I placed a glass of water on her nightstand. When I told her I was sorry, she rolled her eyes.

"Whatchu sorry for?"

"For taking the car. None of this would have happened if we hadn't missed curfew."

Mama Letty closed her eyes. For a terrifying second, I imagined she were dead.

"All of this would've happened whether you missed curfew or not. We'd been overdue for a fight."

"How can you joke about this? Don't you care about anything?"

Her eyes flew open. "Don't you dare. All them years and your mama ain't come back. *She's* the one who don't care."

I sat at the foot of the bed. "Is it true? That she used to write you letters, too?"

Mama Letty looked away, toward the window. Soft sunlight crept through the blinds.

"Mama Letty, how could you not write her back? After all this time?"

"I'm tired of this conversation, Fish."

"Well, so am I!"

"I already told you not everything is yours to fix."

Fatigue tugged at my eyelids. I thought about arguing. I thought about trying to figure out a way to make everything right. But I was tired, and so was she.

"Good night, Mama Letty." I was about to stand when she held out her hand.

"Wait."

I stopped.

"Before you go . . . could you read me one of Ray's letters?" Her face held so much anger, exhaustion, and pain I couldn't tell where one emotion ended and the others began. How could I say no?

I grabbed a letter at random from the box near her footboard and curled up next to her. I cleared my throat and started to read. This particular letter was written when Ray was in New York, trying to describe the hustle of the city and saying how much he wished Mama Letty was with him.

She was asleep by the time I finished.

But again, I stayed. I rested my head on the pillow next to her, eyes drooping with sleep, and hoped Simone was right. If I truly did have a eucalyptus spirit, maybe it would be able to soothe something by the time morning came.

THE RUNAWAY

PEOPLE FROM BARDELL often joked that you couldn't call yourself a true Bardell County local until you had left and somehow found your way back. It was one thing to be pushed into the world without a choice at Bardell County General; it was another to consider the oppressive heat, the deeply racist past, and the rural Walmart sprawl, and decide for yourself that it was worth sticking around. To have the option of Elsewhere and still choose—and love—Bardell anyway? Well, that was the mark of a true Bardell County, Georgian.

Eighteen-year-old Zora Rayla Harding shed Bardell like a snakeskin as soon as her Atlanta-bound bus crossed the county line. Over the twenty-five hours it took to get to Baltimore, Zora practiced saying *I'm from Georgia* with an impenetrable aloofness that would ultimately dissuade anyone at Johns Hopkins from pressing further. Zora knew delving into the specifics of a place had the potential to summon ghosts. So she left her mother's glazed eyes and gin-tinged words and the girl under the dogwood tree down in the Deep South where they belonged.

Years later, in therapy, Dr. Zora Anderson couldn't stop laughing when she realized that although big things had driven her away from Bardell, it was something microscopic that would ultimately call her back: cells. Billions of them. In her mother's breast. She laughed into her five-year-old daughter's curls on the airplane, laughed during the taxi ride when the driver refused to change the holiday music even though Christmas had passed, laughed when she arrived on Sweetness Lane sour-mouthed and exhausted. It wasn't until Zora uncovered a box full of answers in her mother's bedroom that she realized nothing was funny.

Carl Sagan's pale blue dot speech had always brought Zora comfort in the times she needed it the most. Whenever she found herself in the trenches of racist academia or staring down the nose of a white superior, Zora would cling to Carl's reminder that, in the grand scheme of the universe, all her problems were minuscule specks. She was merely a mote of dust, suspended in a sunbeam. It was only when Zora returned to Bardell County and was forced to reckon with the past that this narrative didn't work. When she realized the childhood memories and trauma and grief and loss were not dust, but rather the sun. And every time Zora returned home, she had no choice but to stare directly into the glaring beam.

21.

I DIDN'T WAKE up until mid-afternoon. I squinted against the sunlight streaming through the blinds and rolled over to see Mama Letty, propped on her pillows, reading one of Ray's letters.

"Surprised you ain't drown from all that drool."

I swiped a hand across my face and was about to reply when the horrible, crushing memory of the fight came back like a kick to the ribs.

Carole's biting words.

Mom's fury.

Simone's tears.

I rolled over and faced the wall, not moving until hours later when Mom knocked on the door to tell us dinner was ready.

Mama Letty and I joined my parents at the kitchen table, and it felt like the four of us were sets of tag-team wrestlers, waiting for our opponent to make a move. Dad unpacked Styrofoam containers of caramelized ribs, stewed greens, and black-eyed peas. Mom silently set four glasses of sweet tea out and, without looking at me, told me to wash my hands. Clearly, everything was ruined again, but I was too exhausted to even try and think of a way to fix it.

Dad put on a Temptations record to cover the awkward silence, and it felt way too happy for the occasion. It made me think about Renny's and Simone. I could still feel her lips on mine and our chests pressed together in the luminous purple glow. I started to smile at the memory, but then caught myself. There was a very good possibility there was no more *us*.

"Should we say grace?" Dad asked.

"No," Mom and Mama Letty said at the same time. Mama Letty cracked the smallest of smiles.

"No," Mom said again, shoulders relaxing slightly. "Let's just eat."

• • •

Instead of waiting to be disappointed that Jade was no longer driving us to school, I asked Dad to drop me off early on Monday morning. In history, I sat in my usual seat and braced myself for the sight of them.

Jade walked in right before the bell rang, and she was alone. She took one look at the empty desk next to me, and her cheeks flushed. I only caught a whiff of her vanilla perfume as she rushed by to sit in the back row.

Someone whistled behind me.

"Hey, new girl," Tim Joplin whispered in my ear. "Trouble in paradise?"

"Kiss my ass, Tim," I said with a sigh.

Mrs. Newland began her lesson, and I stared at the whiteboard with a clenched jaw, a dull pain burrowing in my chest. It was an ache that said maybe it would've been better to stick to my original plan. None of this would've happened if I listened to my get in, get out, focus forward motto. Maybe it would've been better to stay lonely.

For the rest of class, I kept one eye on the small window of the classroom door. And although my stomach dropped every time someone walked by in the hallway, Simone never showed.

• • •

Jade and I started giving each other wide berths, repelling like magnets the few times we passed in the hallway. She took permanent residence in the back row during history and vanished during lunch. Every time I thought about apologizing, the dragon in my chest from the Halloween fair reared its ugly head and forced the words back down.

Simone didn't return to school until Wednesday, and her face was stone when she walked into history. She said nothing as she took her usual seat next to me. It looked like she hadn't slept since Saturday, and all I wanted to do was kiss her and hold her if she needed to cry. I wanted us to take turns caring for each other, like she said in Renny's, but I wasn't sure if that was an option anymore. It felt like my fear of us not being able to weather the storm was slowly coming to life.

We hesitated at our desks when class ended, waiting for everyone to trickle out. Jade rushed by with her head down, clutching her books to her chest. Simone looked as sad as she did on Saturday night, wilting on my couch.

"I'm sorry I haven't texted or called," I said. "My mom took my phone."

"Same," she said. "When can we talk?"

"Lunch? Library?"

She nodded, and for a fleeting second, I thought we were going to walk to second period like we normally did. But then she gathered her books and left without another word. That sour feeling in my stomach returned with a vengeance.

• • •

I arrived at the library first and claimed a table tucked in the corner near the encyclopedias. Simone showed up moments later, without any food.

"Not hungry?" I asked.

"I don't have much of an appetite."

"You should still eat something." I cut my turkey sandwich in half and pushed it toward her, but she shook her head.

"I don't want it. I couldn't keep it down anyway."

"That bad?"

Her cold, heavy eyes met mine. "Yes, it's that bad, Avery. My mom took my phone and grounded me until the end of time. She told my dad. She even tried to convince my sister to come back and 'talk some sense' into me. That's how I *know* hell is freezing over."

I looked down, my appetite vanishing, too. "I'm so sorry."

"She's been praying over me nonstop. Praying for my healing, my salvation. Using herself as an example that if she could be 'cured' from impure thoughts, so could I. She's forcing me to go to church three times a week now. My life is over."

I took a deep breath. A group of freshmen, doing a horrible job of pretending they weren't eavesdropping, stifled giggles as they walked by. Simone rolled her eyes.

"This fucking school," she mumbled. "I hate it here so much."

"We could run away again," I said, trying to lighten the mood. "Maybe actually shoot for Jupiter this time?"

She tented her fingers. "I knew this would happen. My card tried to warn me."

"Your card?"

"The Three of Swords," she said, exasperated I wasn't keeping up. "It represents heartbreak and hardship."

"Ah."

She buried her head in her hands. "I don't know what to do. I'm so confused."

There was a pang again, deep in my chest.

She looked up, and I saw the scared girl who crawled into my bed a few nights ago. "You know I'm never going to leave Bardell. You know that."

"I don't know that. And neither do you."

Her eyes clouded over. "We don't have a future. So we might as well end this now."

That pang burrowed even deeper, but I forced myself to sit still and take it. If I wasn't so exhausted, I'd start crying.

"You're going to leave soon, and you'll end up dating someone who's already out, and we'll break up anyway," Simone went on, "so let's end it now."

"Why are you pushing me away?" My voice was strangled. I

could only see us in Renny's. Dancing. Kissing. Crying. "Why are you doing this? We don't have to break up."

"I didn't realize we were together."

"Wow." I sat back in my chair and looked around the library. My eyes fell to a colorful map on the wall, and I imagined being anywhere but here. "So that's it? None of the stuff from Renny's matters? I was making it all up?"

She wouldn't even look at me. "I don't see how it's going to work."

It hurt a hundred times more than my breakup with Kelsi. Then, I'd had anger, justification. Relief. Now, there was only a desperate pleading rising from somewhere deep within me. It was the feeling of a good thing—a *great* thing—slipping through my fingertips, and I could do nothing but watch it fall to the floor and shatter.

"So we can't even be friends?" I asked.

"I should go," she said, grabbing her backpack.

"Simone—" My voice cracked, and I couldn't think of anything I could say to make her stay. We stared at each other as the librarian tapped away on her computer.

"I'm sorry," she said.

She left, the glass door closing with a soft *whoosh*.

My throat was tight as I stared at her empty chair. It was like she'd never been there at all, and I had no idea what to do with the gap she left behind.

• • •

I spent the rest of the day on autopilot. Somehow, I made it through a calculus quiz, a group presentation in Spanish, and a lab practical in chemistry without breaking down. In English, an overly peppy counselor guided us through sample college applications, and I was reminded I'd completely let George-town's Early Action deadline pass me by. Six months ago, I would've had a panic attack at the mere thought. Early acceptance to Georgetown was part of the Plan. Now, I felt nothing. I stared out the window at the dreary sky and thought about the lecture I was in for when Mom found out I'd lied to her about yet another thing.

Dad picked me up after school. I climbed into the passenger seat without a word and threw my backpack on the floor. He raised an eyebrow.

"Rough day?"

"Just peachy."

He smiled. "Would ice cream help?"

I bit back a grin. He always knew how to cheer me up. "Maybe."

We drove to Scoops with Top 40 playing, and he treated us to two hot fudge sundaes. We ate them in the parking lot with the windows down and a wad of napkins between us. I watched the neon pink ice-cream cone sign flicker erratically, and imagined Simone and Jade making up a song about it.

"Don't tell your mother about this," Dad said, swirling his spoon around a ribbon of fudge. "She's picking up *salads* for dinner."

"I won't."

"Promise?" He held up his pinkie, and I wrapped mine in his.

"I don't need anything else for her to get mad at me about," I grumbled. I spooned up another dollop of ice cream, but it landed in a giant plop on my school polo. I set my sundae on the cupholder and started dabbing at the stain. "Great. Because this day couldn't get any worse." I rubbed harder and harder, but it was only making it worse.

"Hey, hey, hey." Dad grabbed my hand. "It's okay."

"It's *not* okay," I said, and surprised us both when I burst into gut-wrenching tears.

He hugged me awkwardly over the center console. "It's okay, Unsavory. We can get you another shirt."

"It's not about the shirt," I sobbed into his neck. "It's everything. It's Mom and Mama Letty. It's Jade. Simone broke up with me." Dad tensed, but he didn't say anything. He rubbed my back in slow circles and let me cry.

"Everything's a mess, Dad," I cried.

"Oh, I know," he cooed. "I know."

"I feel like I have no idea who I am anymore. I used to work hard but had no fun. Then I started to have fun, and everything exploded. I try to mind my business, and I miss out on Mama Letty's life. I try to get involved, and that leads to more fights!"

"Oh, sweetheart. I'm so sorry. This all sounds so hard."

"I don't talk to Hikari and Kelsi anymore—"

"They weren't that great to begin with."

"Dad!"

"I'm just saying," he said gently. "Kelsi never wanted to take her shoes off in the house, and you know how that bugs me and your mother."

I laughed despite myself. Dad peeled away and lifted my chin.

"I hear you," he said. "All of this sucks. Big time. But part of feeling like you don't know who you are is part of being human. I'm over fifty and there are still so many days where I feel unsure of myself."

"Is that supposed to make me feel better? Because it doesn't."

Dad's eyes sparkled. Against the drab parking lot and gray sky, they held a warmth I didn't know I needed.

"You're seventeen," he said. "You're not supposed to have it all figured out. That'll take away all the fun."

"I don't even know what I want out of life, Dad! The only things that made me happy since moving here were Simone and Jade, and now they're gone."

Dad sighed. "That *is* a problem, kid. We can't base our entire happiness on other people."

"I know that, Dr. Phil," I snapped. Then I stared at the floor mat in shame. "I'm sorry. I'm a mess."

Suddenly, Dad took the last remaining spoonful of his ice cream and smeared it right down the front of his favorite T-shirt.

"There. Now we're both messes."

I burst out laughing. "You didn't have to do that."

"And you don't have to use yourself as a human punching bag, yet here we are."

The ache in my heart eased slightly. "I wish I could hurry

up and figure out who I'm supposed to be. Outside of other people."

Dad frowned, and I knew whatever he had to say next was important. He only pulled out Serious Dad Face on rare occasions.

"It's okay to feel lost sometimes, Avery. It's okay to feel like you don't have the answers. You don't *need* to always have the answers, but you do need to give yourself some grace. It's okay to breathe sometimes. Why does everything have to be so urgent?"

"Because!" I wiped tears away. I didn't know how to tell him my whole life had felt urgent up until this point. And how could it not? What did he expect? I learned active shooter drills the same time I learned my ABCs, every summer was the hottest on record. The pandemic paused a majority of my high school years, and I'd been convinced the only way to make it up was to go, go, go full steam ahead. And now this. It was Mama Letty's last days, and there wasn't nearly enough time to make up everything I'd lost. Life was short. Everything was urgent, and who had time to breathe in all that?

"You're going to run yourself ragged," Dad said, "if you don't stop and look around and breathe sometimes. You *can't* get to know yourself if you can't sit with yourself for a while."

We sat in silence for a minute, my tears subsiding. We watched the Scoops sign flicker and buzz. We watched the drive-through line move at a glacial pace. The air smelled like fresh waffle cones. I took a deep breath and closed my eyes and tried to savor it.

"Hey, Dad?"

"Hmm?"

"You know Mom is gonna know we got ice cream because of our shirts?"

He sighed. "Yeah, I know."

I grinned. "I guess it was worth it though."

Dad laughed. "So worth it."

22.

OVER THE NEXT couple of weeks, autumn wrapped around Bardell like a cozy sweater. The days grew shorter, the air cooler. Crunchy leaves coated the sidewalks of Sweetness Lane.

At school, Jade, Simone, and I became so good at avoiding each other, it was like we'd never been friends in the first place. The times at the river, the party at the Draper, our plans for winter formal—they didn't matter anymore.

In class, I became a professional daydreamer. While the rest of the seniors buzzed on about college applications and military plans and gap years, I stared out the window and found shapes in the clouds. I looked at bare tree branches and saw wishes. I listened to rain on glass panes and drafted song lyrics. My grades began to slip, but I didn't care. I felt passionate about nothing, and I could only imagine the horror on Kelsi's and Hikari's faces if they could see me now.

Home wasn't much better. Mama Letty grew so tired she barely left her room anymore. One night in mid-November, I noticed a grim look on Isaac's face while Mama Letty hacked her way through *Train to Busan*. After he helped her to bed, I asked him what was wrong.

"I'm going to miss her," he'd said sadly. "She doesn't have much time left."

Mom avoided the subject of Mama Letty's health entirely by throwing herself into deep-cleaning the house from top to bottom. I came home from school one day to find her on her hands and knees, scouring the kitchen floor, even though the grime between the tiles seemed like it'd been a permanent fixture for decades. She bought shiny new appliances we didn't need—a blender, a food processor, an air fryer that took up half the counter. The junky living room transformed into a neat oasis fit for a home decor catalogue. My bedroom sparkled, the front porch was swept and free of cobwebs. The only room she didn't touch was Mama Letty's. It'd been weeks since their massive blowout fight, and they were still barely talking.

The weekend before Thanksgiving break was rainy and miserable. Mom, fresh out of things to clean, had moved onto reading self-help books. There was a neat stack on the coffee table with titles like *Moving Through Grief* and *Breaking the Trauma Cycle*. After I wandered into the kitchen for a snack, she beckoned me over to the couch with a gentle wave. I wearily joined her.

"What are you up to?" she asked.

"Studying?" Which was a lie, but I didn't know what she expected me to say. My punishment was still firm, I had no friends, and I hadn't seen my phone in weeks.

"I wanted to talk to you about something," she said. "It's about Thanksgiving."

I stared out the window and watched the rain drench the yard.

"Your father and I have been talking," she went on, "and we'd like to do something special for Mama Letty this Thanksgiving."

I snorted. "Because we all know how well *special plans* go over in this family."

Mom's face fell. "I know we haven't really talked about the fight. There were a lot of things said that night."

"So what?" I shrugged. "What does it matter? All we do is sweep it under the rug anyway. Pretend like it never happened."

"Avery." Mom sighed. "I'm trying to be patient with you. Please, let me talk." She pulled a photo from the inside of her book and handed it to me. It was a grainy photo of a couple at the beach, both of them wearing bathing suits. Their smiles were wide and frozen in time.

"Is that . . ." I peered closer. "Mama Letty?"

Mom nodded. "And Ray. It's the only photo I have of them."

My eyes widened, and my attitude vanished. "This is Ray?" My fingers traced the aged photo. It was weird to finally put a face to the name. All those times reading his letters in Mama Letty's bedroom, but I still hadn't seen a picture. There was a pinch of irritation that this was yet another thing Mom had kept from me for so long, but it was buoyed by Ray's smile. "This is my grandfather? Does Mama Letty know you have this?"

Mom grinned. "I swiped it many years ago. I doubt she remembers." She took the photo back and smiled fondly. "This was taken at Kisabee Island, not long before he died. Your father and I want to take Mama Letty back there."

"For Thanksgiving?"

Mom nodded. "We wanted to surprise her. What do you think?"

I hesitated. The stubborn part of me wanted to shrug again, act like I didn't care. I'd gotten so good at that lately. A trip to the beach wasn't going to fix the words that were shouted that night. It couldn't make up the years of neglect and pain. It wouldn't make us whole.

But underneath all of that was a stubbornness that couldn't let go of the possibility that maybe, just maybe, it could be a step in the right direction.

"If I say yes," I said, "can I have my phone back?"

Mom flicked my lip ring. "Girl, don't press your luck."

• • •

The morning before Thanksgiving brought a crisp, gorgeous blue sky. While Mom and Dad bustled around the house, preparing for the trip to Kisabee Island, I had the job of waking Mama Letty up and telling her the surprise. I knocked on her door and waited for her signature grunt. When it came, I threw open the door.

"Good morning, Mama Letty! I hope you're ready for a road trip!"

She was still in her pajamas, the television at the foot of her bed muted. The hollows under her eyes were dark and deep. "Hell you talking about?"

"We're going to Kisabee Island!" Mom shouted as she passed in the hallway. "Your bag's already packed!"

Mama Letty looked intrigued. "Kisabee Island?"

"Heard it holds a little history for you and Ray," I said, trying to sound nonchalant. "Figured it might be nice for you to see it again."

"We're going to Kisabee Island?"

My excitement dimmed when I noticed her bewildered expression. Maybe this wasn't a great idea after all. She was tired, and the last thing she needed was an exhausting road trip. I was about to tell Mom we should cancel the entire thing when Mama Letty smiled.

"It's 'bout time I get a break from this hellhole."

I laughed and kissed her cheek, fast enough she didn't have time to react. "The car's already packed. We're leaving in twenty."

• • •

Half an hour later, we were pulling out of the driveway. I tried not to look at the Cole house as we passed. I hadn't spoken to Simone in weeks, and I wondered how she was doing. I wanted to know if she'd applied to Spelman. If she remembered our night at Renny's with the same aching loneliness I felt. I stared at my bare middle finger and wondered if there would ever come a time I looked at it and didn't miss the sight of my sodalite ring. After our conversation in the library, I'd slipped it off and tucked it in the darkest corner of my closet so there was no way I could accidentally stumble across it.

We left Bardell with all the windows down, highway unfurling before us like a possibility. Halfway through the ride, Dad tried to start a singalong, an endeavor that was promptly squashed when Mama Letty said his voice was going to accelerate her journey to the grave. We all laughed, but there was a lingering sadness at the reminder that every day was numbered now. Mom must've felt the same way because I caught her wiping away tears.

We arrived at Kisabee Island in the early afternoon. Dad pulled into the driveway of a quaint light blue cottage overlooking the white sand beach. Sea salt whipped our faces as we emerged from the car. Mama Letty inhaled deeply.

"Feels like yesterday Ray and I were here." She smiled at us, almost shyly, and took a cautious step in the direction of the water. She put a hand over her eyes and gazed at the hypnotic Atlantic Ocean. It looked like it stretched forever.

"Is it how you remember it?" I asked. "I'm sorry it's not the same, but . . ."

Mama Letty shook her head and released a shaky exhale. "Don't apologize. This is exactly what I needed."

• • •

Mom made reservations at one of the nicest restaurants in town for our Thanksgiving meal. We dressed in our finest clothes—Dad in a fitted suit he usually saved for fancy wedding gigs, Mom in a gorgeous royal purple wrap dress. Mama Letty wore a simple pantsuit with a pale blue shawl. And I, figuring I no longer needed to save it for the winter formal, wore my only suit, a gray one with a hot-pink bow tie. Dad even cleaned up my side shave before we left.

At the restaurant, the four of us nabbed a table overlooking the water and treated ourselves to a buffet fit for royalty. There were crab legs, filet mignon, a shrimp cocktail tower, a chocolate fountain! We piled our plates high, and even though Mama Letty still didn't have much of an appetite, she picked at her food with a smile that hadn't left since we arrived in town.

"If Ray were here, what would be the first thing he'd eat?" I asked, shoveling a forkful of potato salad into my mouth.

"First of all," Mama Letty said, "if Ray was here, we wouldn't be having Thanksgiving in no hotel. This was Ray's favorite holiday. He wouldn't leave the cooking up to no one else."

"Okay . . ." So I amended my question and asked about his favorite dish to make.

"Mac and cheese." She closed her eyes, as if she could taste it. "No one could make mac and cheese like Ray."

I pointed to my plate with my fork. "I'm guessing this mac and cheese has nothing on Ray's."

She laughed. "Not even close."

My parents split a bottle of wine, and by the end of the meal, we were all giddy, our hearts lighter. Mom and Dad shared funny stories about their first couple of dates, telling us how Dad tried so hard to impress Mom with his piano skills. Mama Letty indulged us in stories about her and Ray and how they used to dance to Sam Cooke. During dessert, Mom pulled out the photo of Ray and Mama Letty at the beach and placed it in the middle of the table. Mama Letty gasped.

"*You* took this?" She held it up to the light like she was trying to figure out if it was real. "I thought I'd lost this!"

"It was one of the few things I took with me to college," Mom said. She took a large gulp of wine, and it was like we were all bracing ourselves for another fight. And maybe on another day, it would've led to one. But Mama Letty ran her finger along Ray's smile.

"This a great picture of him. Wasn't he handsome?"

"You said I look like him a little," I said proudly.

"You and Zora both do," Mama Letty said, and it felt like the biggest honor I could've asked for.

"I hearby dub Raymond Harding the official guest of honor at tonight's meal," Dad said, raising his wineglass. "To Ray!"

"Hear! Hear!" I toasted with my ginger ale.

"To Ray," Mom and Mama Letty echoed, and I thought my heart was going to burst from happiness right there at the dinner table.

Dad, being Dad, insisted we needed a photo to remember the occasion and flagged down a server. The four of us smiled for Mom's phone, our table piled with empty plates, the ocean reflecting behind us.

It was late when we got back to the cottage. While Dad went straight to bed in an exhausted and tipsy stupor, Mom and Mama Letty lingered on the porch, gazing at the expanse of white sand that led to the dark, infinite ocean.

"Did y'all want to go down?" I asked. "We can sit in the sand."

Mom hesitated, looking at Mama Letty as if for permission. Mama Letty wrapped her shawl around her shoulders.

"I'd like that," she said quietly. "If Zora don't mind."

"I don't mind," Mom said quickly. "Avery baby, could you grab something for us to sit on?"

I ran inside and grabbed two thick yellow throw blankets from the linen closet. When I returned, Mom and Mama Letty were still staring at the ocean, transfixed.

We walked down to the beach in silence. The moon was new, a shadowed ghost in the sky. Waves crashed on the shore, inviting us to come closer, listen to its song. We spread the blankets on the cool sand and for a full minute, did nothing but listen and breathe and sink into the opposite of urgent.

23.

"THERE IT IS, Mama. Your ocean view."

Mama Letty smiled. We'd settled on one blanket—Mama Letty in the middle—and wrapped the other around our shoulders. Our shoes were tossed in a pile as if the tide had brought them in.

"That was one hell of a last Thanksgiving," Mama Letty said after a couple of minutes.

Her words felt like a nail in a tire. During dinner, I'd almost convinced myself things were fine again. Or at least as close to perfect as we could get. Now, we were out in the open and the final chapter of Mama Letty's life was palpable under the infinite sky.

"We don't know if it'll be the last," I said. "There are miracles all the time."

Mama Letty and Mom smiled at me knowingly. They looked so much alike, I wanted to cry.

"It's the last one, Fish," Mama Letty said.

"Did I miss the origins of this Fish nonsense?" Mom asked.

"Mama Letty calls me that because of my lip ring," I said. "Don't you remember our first day in Bardell? When she said I looked like a fish on a hook?"

"Mama!" Mom scolded.

Mama Letty dug her toes in the sand. "I said what I said."

I rested my head on Mama Letty's shoulder and looked to the stars. I pointed to a familiar constellation. "What's that one, Mom?" I already knew, but I wanted to hear her voice.

"Cassiopeia," she answered. Mama Letty and I watched her finger trail along the sky as she pointed out more. Andromeda. Pegasus. Perseus.

"Your head was always in them stars as a little girl," Mama Letty said. "Shoulda known you'd be smart enough to make a living out of it."

"I couldn't imagine devoting my life to anything else. Avery's going to study astronomy, too. Isn't that right, baby?"

I swallowed, my gaze falling to the waves. Crashing against the shore, they sounded like the most gentle lullaby.

"I don't know anymore," I said. "I don't think so."

I could feel Mom shifting on the other side of Mama Letty. "Since when?"

I shrugged. Wrapped the blanket around my shoulders tighter.

"You'll figure it out," Mama Letty said. "You got all the time in the world." And it was yet another reminder that *her* time was limited.

"I'm going to miss you," I said, snuggling my head into the

crook of her neck. She stiffened, then relaxed. "I'm sorry we don't have more time together."

"Ah, don't be sorry. I'm gonna be with my Ray. I been waiting a long, long time."

My eyes burned. It wasn't fair. None of it was fair.

Mom cleared her throat. "I'm going to miss you, too, Mama," she said, voice trembling. "I know it hasn't always been easy. Hell, it's usually been hard. But . . . I love you. Avery and I love you very much."

"I know," Mama Letty said. "I . . . I love y'all, too."

The water ebbed and flowed. The sky was cloudless, and the stars were shining, and I wanted to cry because I didn't understand how a world so beautiful could also harbor so much pain.

"I wish I could've met him," I said. "Grandpa Ray."

"He woulda loved you," Mama Letty said. "He woulda loved both of y'all so much. I see him in y'all sometimes. Like when you let loose and dance and have fun, Zora. And when you waltzed up on that porch with your shaved head, Fish."

"Grandpa Ray would've shaved his head?" I asked.

"He woulda respected your audacity," Mama Letty said. "Ray always respected anyone going against the grind. Anyone with an attitude, Ray was determined to melt."

"No wonder he loved you," Mom muttered, and we laughed and laughed and laughed.

"We was like fire and ice, me and that man," Mama Letty said. "I'd never met someone so warm. So unbothered by the cruelness of the world. I thought I knew everything about myself until I met Ray. And he upended my world."

I started crying, quick and quietly. Her words echoed so much of how I felt with Simone and Jade. How meeting them proved maybe I didn't know anything about myself at all.

"What did you do?" I asked. Mom, always prepared, reached across Mama Letty with a tissue she'd yanked from her purse. "After Ray died? How did you go on after losing someone who changed your world like that?" I wasn't sure if the question made any sense.

Mama Letty sighed. "I didn't go on. For a long time, I didn't. I went through the motions, you know. Ate somehow. Got dressed somehow, went to work somehow. But I wasn't there for a long time. Zora . . . you know."

"Oh yeah," Mom said, and I could tell from the sound of her voice that she was crying, too. "I thought you were the meanest woman in the world. I hated you."

"I don't blame you."

"You were really miserable, Mama. Really miserable."

"I know it." Mama Letty coughed, and Mom handed her a tissue, too. We held on as she rode through the wave of a raspy coughing fit.

"I'm going to get some water," Mom said, and she left for the cottage, running across the sand barefoot. Her vibrant purple dress resembled a glowing apparition on the dark, empty beach.

Mama Letty crumpled the tissue in her fist and wiped her mouth. "Not gonna miss feeling like shit all the time," she said. I rubbed her back. She smiled at me. "Thanks, Fish."

"Thank *you*."

"For what?"

"For upending *my* world." I was choking on tears, and so was she. In that moment, I wanted nothing more than for time to stop like the cat clock I had no memory of picking out. I wanted to yank the batteries out of the world and stay forever on the beach, stop the ticking, stop the inevitable. But the stars kept burning, and the tide kept breaking on the shore.

"I don't know how I'm supposed to go on without you," I said. "It's not fair."

"Life ain't fair. I learned that the hard way. When Carl and Wallace Oliver shoved the man I loved into the back of that car." Sea breeze ruffled her short gray curls, and she closed her eyes to savor it. "I never saw him again after that day, but he ain't go nowhere. He always right here." She touched her heart, then mine. "Like I'm gone be right there in you when I'm gone."

"I hate them, Mama Letty," I sobbed. "I hate them so much. How could they get away with that? Carl hugged me!" And I shivered in the blanket at the memory of his rough hands scraping my forearms in the kitchen of Ivy Rose Plantation. "How could they do that to him? How?" I buried my face in Mama Letty's shoulder and cried, exhaustion seeping down to my bones.

It might've been minutes. Might've been hours. But when I looked up, eyes puffy and heavy, Mom had returned and Mama Letty was sipping from a water bottle. Mom had brought out another blanket, a thick aqua diamond–patterned one, and we spread it across our laps. Mama Letty handed me the bottle, and I took a grateful sip. The memory of the Olivers had transformed my tears to anger, and now all I wanted was to destroy something.

"Mom? Mama Letty?"

Mama Letty grunted while Mom said, "Yes, Avery baby?"

"Why didn't you tell me about the Olivers and the rumors? When I first met Jade? During the spa date at the Draper? How could you not tell me?"

"Oh, Avery." Mom sighed. "We've talked about this."

"Y'all have?" Mama Letty asked.

"Yes. I told her what I'd always known. That the story of what happened with the Olivers had never been proven—"

"It don't need to be *proven*," Mama Letty snapped. "My word should've always been good enough. I was the only one there that night! I know what I saw. Those men took Ray, and I never saw him again."

"Yes, and those stories were always told to me when you were too drunk to remember them the next morning," Mom said, equally as sharp. "You screamed this story in my face when I was four years old. When I was six. Then nine. Every day of my life, I walked on pins and needles—"

"Please don't fight," I begged, but neither of them were listening.

"—the *only* time you ever paid me any attention was when you were drunk and you wanted to scream about something," Mom continued. "You told that story in the same breath that you told me I was disgusting for dancing with Carole. Calling me names. Telling me I was an *uppity bitch* for wanting to go to college. You were *abusive*, Mama. You abused me for a very, very long time. So excuse me if I didn't have time to pick apart your truths from all the lies you spewed about me when I had to inevitably work through all that bullshit on my own!"

"Zora—" Mama Letty paused. I held my breath for the comeback, for the fire that was sure to follow. The ocean whispered and crashed, sang a song we couldn't understand.

"Zora," Mama Letty repeated. "I'm . . . sorry." Then she placed her forehead on Mom's, and both of them cried like they'd been waiting for it their entire lives.

• • •

Midnight came and went, and we stayed on the beach. We spent the minutes staring at the waves in silence and crying. Mom pointed out more constellations, and Mama Letty let us rest our heads on her shoulders.

I pieced together a sandcastle, one damp palmful of sand at a time. It was lopsided and sagging, and the only decorations I had were shells, but Mom and Mama Letty applauded wildly when I finished anyway.

"A castle fit for royalty," Mom said.

"Let's think of a name," I said. "What about . . . Zolevery Castle?"

"Zo who what now?" Mama Letty asked between laughter and coughs.

"It's a combination of our names!" I protested.

"Well, *I'm* going to go with Ara," Mom said, handing Mama Letty the water bottle again.

I wrinkled my nose. "What's that?"

"A constellation in the Southern Hemisphere," Mom replied. "It means the altar. It's sacred."

"Mama Letty, looks like you're the tiebreaker," I said.

She swallowed a gulp of water and made a face. Mom handed her a clean tissue.

"Both them names awful," Mama Letty said. "My vote is for Silver Meteor. Ray's train."

"I think Grandpa Ray deserves better than this sad castle," I said, placing another shell on a leaning turret.

"Ray deserved every damn thing," Mama Letty said, smiling off at the ocean. "He deserved monuments. Television specials, documentaries." Then she looked directly into my eyes. "Murals. He deserved all of that."

Mom rummaged around in her purse and pulled out the photo of Mama Letty and Ray on Kisabee Island so many years ago. She untangled herself from the blanket and joined me by the castle.

"I think," she said, propping the photo against the castle's front wall, "that Silver Meteor Castle is perfect. To Ray."

"To Ray," we echoed.

Behind us, the tide was receding. Still, I knew the water would eventually creep up again and claim the castle for itself, even if I stayed there all night and used myself as a buffer. I sighed and carved a window into one of the walls using my pinkie nail.

"We can always build another one," Mom said, as if reading my mind. When I looked up, she and Mama Letty were smiling, all of us tired and cried out.

"If this ain't the saddest party," Mama Letty said. "This is the opposite of how Ray would want the grand opening of his castle to be."

"I can turn on some music," Mom said. "I have my phone."

"You ain't got no music *I* like on there."

"I have this thing called Spotify," Mom said, standing and wiping sand off her dress. "If you can believe it, there's *millions* of songs on there."

"You mocking me? Sounds like you mocking me."

"I would never dream." Mom pulled her phone from her purse, shivering against the wind. "Alright. What's the request?"

Mama Letty narrowed her eyes. "You got any Sam Cooke?"

"That's easy."

Mama Letty still looked doubtful. "You got his Copa album? That was Ray's favorite."

Mom grinned. "Which song?"

"'You Send Me.'" And a smile burst on her face as soon as she heard the applause and opening notes and Sam saying, '*I ain't gone do it, honey. Naw . . . I ain't gone do it!*'" Me and Mom helped her to her feet. We each wrapped a blanket around our shoulders, and we gave Mama Letty the pretty aqua one.

"I ain't heard this song in forever," Mama Letty said.

"The wonders of technology," I sang.

"Come on," Mom said. "Let's dance."

We probably looked ridiculous—three figures wrapped in thick blankets, swaying on the beach under the star-streaked sky. Mama Letty's wrinkled face cracked open with delight when Mom spun her around. Then she laughed when I tripped on the edge of my blanket and fell into the sand, toppling half of the Silver Meteor Castle in the process.

"Clumsy ass!" Mama Letty cackled. "Just like Ray!"

"You okay, baby?" Mom asked, giggling too.

"Oh, don't mind me. I'm fine." I wrapped myself in the blanket like a burrito and stayed on the ground, staring up at them as Sam sang through his medleys. Mom and Mama Letty serenaded each other and swayed in their blankets, and I marveled at them. I reveled in them. I soaked it all up. And even though I wasn't able to stop time, I made a wish on the stars that I'd always be able to remember it. I breathed in the big, wonderful, awful world and realized when I smelled the salt it was the first time I'd felt peace in weeks.

Later, when we were walking back to the cottage, shoes dangling from our fingers and sand-covered blankets wrapped around our shoulders, Mama Letty pointed to the sky and said, "I hope he's waiting up there. Ray, I mean."

"I'm sure he is," I said through a yawn.

"Lord help that man," Mom joked.

We didn't have all the answers; we gave ourselves grace anyway. We went to bed, exhausted, hearts full. By morning, the ocean had claimed the castle.

• • •

Two nights later, Mom found Mama Letty wandering in the kitchen at three a.m., dizzy and disoriented. We rushed her to the hospital, and the entire ride, she talked about Ray as if he were in the car with us.

THE MERMAIDS

THE DAY AMELIA Oliver died was an unseasonably cold one for Bardell County, Georgia. Amelia was giddy when she woke and saw the temperatures were expected to dip into the low twenties, just in time for the Draper Hotel & Spa's Christmas party. She wished, foolishly, for snow. A light dusting would transform the hotel into a real winter wonderland. It'd be the perfect finishing touch to the event she'd been planning since September.

To Amelia's disappointment, it didn't snow that night. But the party didn't need it. Guests were delighted by the live band and prime rib carving station, the bubbling champagne fountain, the elaborate gingerbread house. Amelia was the only one who noticed something amiss, and that was only because it was personal—her husband and his mistress, resurfacing after an hour with flushed cheeks and tussled hair, as if they'd emerged from the ocean. This particular transgression hurt Amelia more than all the others because Lucas knew how much this night meant to her. He'd watched how she papered the town with event flyers, saw how she sacrificed sleep when the mistletoe soap favors were in danger of not being bagged on time. Still, he betrayed her. And Amelia needed a break.

She savored her cigarette on an empty bridge overlooking the Bardell River. It was a nasty habit Lucas hated, so as soon as she finished, she lit a second one. As the smoke curled, she stared into the river's depths and imagined becoming acquainted. She envisioned herself as a mermaid with long, flowing blonde hair, swimming away with a merman who only had eyes for her. Her tail would be blue, obviously. Blue like her daughter's eyes, seashell bra to match. She was flicking ash into the water, imagining herself singing a song that would lure Lucas to his death, when a shaking person stepped from the shadows, streetlight glinting off the silver of their gun.

Years later and eighty miles away, Todd Floyd was walking his goldendoodle, Mr. Biscuit, down the Kisabee Island boardwalk at one a.m. when he noticed something odd on the beach. Three blurs—one aqua, two yellow—twirling in the sand. For a fleeting second, he thought he was witnessing a miracle. Mermaids, right there on the beach! However, upon further inspection, he realized it was just three boring humans, laughing, shrouded in blankets. He passed them off as drunk tourists and told Mr. Biscuit to come on.

Little did he know, Todd Floyd *was* witnessing a miracle. It was a rare thing, those mermaids on Kisabee Beach. Historic, actually. It was the first and last time the three of them ever danced together. It was the night the oldest mermaid finally apologized, and the middle mermaid finally accepted it. Later, the youngest mermaid would uncover treasure chests full of gems and deadly secrets. But that night, she was in awe of the mermaids who came before her, simply grateful when she realized she was happiest outside in nature. The memory of this night would stay with the youngest mermaid for the rest of her life, bubbling to the surface anytime she dove into water.

24.

"**WHERE DO WE** start?"

"Avery and I can start cleaning if you wanted to run to the store for new bedsheets."

"Okay. Do we need anything else?"

"Another bottle of disinfectant spray? And more trash bags."

"Check *annnnd* check. Anything else? A candy bar for all your hard work, Unsavory?"

"Avery? Avery baby—"

Mom shook my shoulder, and I blinked twice. I wasn't on the beach, watching Mama Letty dance and cry. We weren't rushing to the hospital. We were in Bardell, in Mama Letty's bedroom. My parents' faces sharpened.

"Sorry," I said. "Um, no candy bar for me. I'm good."

"I'm going to get you one anyway," Dad sang as he left.

Mom stared at me, face etched in concern. "You were spacing out again. You okay?"

I hesitated, but there was no point lying to her. "I was thinking about us at the beach. What if . . ." The worries I'd had for days bubbled up again. "What if it was because we stayed out too late? It was cold—"

"Hey," Mom said firmly. "Stop that. We talked about this already. None of this is your fault."

I blinked faster, looking around the room. "I'm worried about not finishing in time."

Mom pulled me in for a hug. "We're going to finish. Mama Letty will be home tomorrow to the cleanest room she's ever seen."

I closed my eyes, returning to the night on the beach. All that joy. How quickly things changed in only a couple of days.

Unfortunately, there's nothing we can do at this point, the doctors in Kisabee Island told us.

A week. Two if we were lucky.

When we returned to Bardell, Mama Letty's regular doctors echoed the same timeline but decided to keep her overnight to monitor her pain levels.

"I'm not ready to say goodbye," I said, the words muffled against Mom's shoulder. Her spine went rigid.

"Me either, Avery baby," she said finally. "I don't think we'll ever be ready. All we can do is make her as comfortable as possible."

I swallowed down tears and nodded. "Okay."

"Let's get to work," Mom said.

• • •

We cleaned Mama Letty's bedroom to Mom's favorite throwback station.

Luther Vandross crooned while Mom stripped the bed and

threw Mama Letty's comforter in the laundry. She dusted every nook and cranny of the ancient wooden headboard.

Earth, Wind & Fire played as we cleaned under the bed. We threw out decaying paper plates with crusted food and crumpled soda cans, forgotten socks with holes in them and dust bunnies the size of my hand. We found a pair of sunglasses with one of the lenses missing, and we cackled with laughter when Mom donned them and sang along to Isaac Hayes's "Theme from Shaft."

I Windexed the hell out of the window, determined to leave no streaks behind, and sang along to Whitney Houston.

It wasn't until we got to the boxes of letters at the end of her bed that we turned the music off. Mom lifted the lid on one, and her face softened.

"Want to read some?" she asked.

I nodded, and she placed the box between us. We read quietly to ourselves, reading lines aloud that struck us.

"'You lit up the room last night when you were dancing . . .'"

"'I love you, lady in blue . . .'"

"'I'm in Philadelphia this weekend. We'll go sometime together . . .'"

"'Letty June Prince, I'm going to marry you one day . . .'"

"He really loved her," I said.

"He really did," Mom agreed.

We talked about what our world would look like if Ray were alive. We imagined him and Mama Letty dancing at their fiftieth wedding anniversary. I imagined holidays with all of us gathered around a Christmas tree. A family reunion with too many relatives to count, Ray wielding tongs near the grill with a big belly and a giant smile.

Later, Dad returned with cleaning products, fresh sheets, and a brand-new memory foam pillow. He made the bed, then the three of us tackled the closet together. We cleaned out every corner. Threw out magazines that were over a decade old. When we came across another box with a stack of letters in them, I assumed they were more of Ray's. Then Mom sucked in a breath as she picked one up.

"These are mine. The ones I sent her in college." The envelope was ripped open. The return address was in Baltimore. Mom snorted, but her eyes welled up again. "Nice to see she *did* read them, even if she never responded."

I shuffled through some of the letters, all of them holding Mom's words in her neat, skinny handwriting. I caught glimpses of sentences.

I miss you so much! I was . . .

I'd love to show you around Baltimore . . .

Please write back. I don't . . .

Merry Christmas, Mama . . .

There was a weight in my chest as Mom struggled to follow her breathing exercise. Dad massaged her shoulders.

"Maybe we should take a break," he suggested. "We're almost done, and you've been working for a while. Come on, I brought some snacks."

"No, it's okay," Mom said, sniffling. "I just gotta get through this, and I'll be okay."

I touched her elbow gently. We were sweaty and smelled like

lemon disinfectant spray. "Mom. Rest for a moment. Come on, the floor is clean now." I laid down on the freshly vacuumed carpet and spread my limbs. "Oooh, so comfortable!" I sang. "So clean!"

With a giggle, Mom flopped down next to me. We stared at the ceiling together as Dad left to grab some snacks.

"Do you think she'll like her new clean room?" I asked.

"Not at all. She'll fuss us all out for not consulting with her first and say the new pillows feel like shit."

"You're so right."

"I know." Mom took a deep breath and turned toward me. She looked tired; new wrinkles had sprouted around her eyes, and I hadn't seen her wear lipstick in weeks. I was struck by how different she looked compared to when we first arrived in Bardell. I wondered how I looked to her, if she could see my emotions on my face as easily as I saw hers.

"You really think she'll hate it?" I asked.

A ghost of a smile crossed her lips. "No. I actually think she'll love it, but she'll be too stubborn to admit it."

"A true Mama Letty response. At least she's consistent."

She pushed a curl away from my face. "Consistent until the end."

• • •

We finished around dinnertime, after the sun had set. We stood at the bedroom's threshold to survey our work.

Every surface had been wiped clean. The windows were sparkling and streak-free, offering a lovely view of the lawn. The floor was clear and crisscrossed with neat lines from the vacuum. The bed had clean, crisp sheets. Fresh red poinsettias adorned the dresser. A box of Ray's letters was in easy reach of the bed.

"What do you think?" Dad asked. "Is this a bedroom fit for a queen or what?"

Mom and I shared a grin behind his back.

They went off to open a bottle of wine, but I stayed behind, taking another look around the room. It looked good—great even—but none of it mattered without Mama Letty's presence. The mess was gone, but it felt almost too clean, too spacious. The next time Mama Letty stepped into the room could very well be the last. It needed a final touch. When I realized what it was, I ran to the kitchen and asked to borrow the car.

"You're still grounded," Mom said without looking up.

"But it's for Mama Letty!"

"The last time you borrowed a car, you disappeared until five in the morning and caused a massive family blowout."

"Let us not forget," Dad said solemnly from the Formica tale. Mom whacked him with a dish towel, but nodded at the keys on the counter and told me to make it quick.

• • •

After I ran my errand, I rushed to my bedroom, envelope from the pharmacy tucked under my arm. The bag from Flashback Antiques hadn't moved from my desk in over a month. I sat and pulled out the two frames.

I'd barely thought about them after I bought them at the county fair. At the time, I thought they'd be perfect for a photo of me and Simone, maybe my parents. But as I pulled the freshly printed photo out and slid it into the simple oak frame, I realized it never could've held anything else. I secured the back with the tiny metal flaps and sat it upright. The quality wasn't perfect, but it was as good as it got.

My family after our Thanksgiving feast stared back. Mom looked like she was about to blink and there was definitely something between Dad's two front teeth. My hair was frizzy, and there was a stain on Mama Letty's pantsuit. But there we were, forever frozen in time for someone to remember. A stranger would simply see a family out to dinner. But I saw us toasting to Ray, surrounded by abundance. I saw me, Mom, and Mama Letty dancing on the beach under a million stars.

The photo of Mama Letty and Ray at Kisabee Island was a touch too small for the *Love Forever* frame. So I surrounded it with a simple white mat, and it didn't look half bad. I secured it and turned it around for inspection, and there was a knock on my window. I almost yelled until I realized it was only Simone, wearing an oversized blue hoodie. I slid the glass pane up.

"You scared the shit out of me!" I hissed.

"Sorry. Can I come in?"

I gazed past her shoulder. "Where's your mom?"

"At work."

I hesitated. "Now is not really a good time. We're getting ready to have dinner."

Her face fell. "Oh. Okay."

We hadn't talked in weeks, and it showed. We couldn't look each other in the eyes for longer than a few seconds. My hardened heart splintered slightly as she tugged at the end of her locs.

"I wanted to see how you're doing," she said. "I'm guessing you still don't have your phone back."

I shook my head. "Nope. Still on punishment."

"Same," she said with a sigh.

The awkwardness pained me. I had a flash of us dancing at Renny's, entwined and kissing without a second thought. We were strangers again.

"How was your Thanksgiving?" she asked.

"It was okay. We went to Kisabee Island. Mama Letty . . ."

Simone's eyes bugged. "Mama Letty what? Is she okay?"

"She has about a week or two left."

Her face crumpled. "I'm so sorry. Is she home?"

"No. She's at the hospital for one more night. She'll be back in the morning." I smiled faintly. "We cleaned her bedroom today."

"Holy shit. That must've taken hours."

"You have no idea."

A gust of wind blew, and Simone shivered in her hoodie. My heart—my weak, pushover heart—shuddered. I pushed aside the photos and held out a hand.

"Come on," I said. "Get inside before you turn into an icicle."

Simone climbed in. At the last second, her foot slipped, and we tumbled to the floor together. Every atom in my body thrummed when I caught a delicious whiff of her signature almond body butter. She rolled off and sat up with a nervous chuckle.

"I didn't do that on purpose," she said.

I hummed. "Sure you didn't."

She smacked me with the sleeve of her hoodie. "Don't flatter yourself, DC."

"Wouldn't dream of it."

She bit her plump bottom lip and looked away. Her eyes fell on the picture frames, which apparently had clattered to the ground in our fall. She picked them up gently, and her smile bloomed as she took in a younger Mama Letty. "*This* is the infamous Ray? He's so cute! And let me find out Mama Letty was a bad bitch back in the day."

"I'll be sure to pass on your regards."

She moved on to the Thanksgiving photo. "This is the happiest I've ever seen Mama Letty my entire life. Nice suit, by the way."

I stared at the photo upside down. "Figured I might as well put it to good use since I won't be going to the winter formal."

Simone set the photo down on the carpet and shrugged. "Winter formal is overrated. Jade doesn't even want to go anymore."

"You're friends again?" It was a shot to the heart. They'd made up without me, of course. I wasn't sure why I was surprised.

She cast her eyes down. "Not really. I don't know how to move forward, but she stopped by when I was working, and we talked a little. She said she misses you." She hesitated. "So do I."

"I'm still not ready to talk to her."

"I know, I get it. Everything that's happened has been . . .

a lot. But she was telling me that she talked to Mrs. Newland and—"

Suddenly, my bedroom door flew open. Simone and I bolted upright as Mom stepped in, holding her cell phone in a death grip. Her face was twisted in fury.

"Mom, we weren't—"

"Mrs. Anderson—"

But Mom didn't seem to care about Simone's presence. In fact, the look in her eyes wasn't anger at all. It was fear.

"It's time. We need to go."

Simone looked around frantically as Mom rushed off. My stomach dropped as I grabbed the photos.

"I'm coming with you," Simone said. "I'll call my mom. Avery?"

My mouth was dry. I was going to throw up. I couldn't move. Mama Letty couldn't die now. She was supposed to come home first. That was the Plan.

"Avery. Come on." Simone found my hand, like habit. Together we raced to the car, and all I could do was hold on.

25.

THE RIDE TO Bardell County General was a bad dream I couldn't wake up from. Even with the calming jazz on the radio, even with Simone's hand in mine, even with Dad's gentle reminders to breathe, I was trapped in a nightmare. It was the night in Kisabee Island all over again, when I was in the back seat with Mama Letty, so sure we were about to lose her.

But she didn't die that night. She lived. She made it back to Bardell. She was due home in the morning. She couldn't die. Not now. She had to see the work we'd done. She had to complain about the pillows. She was supposed to turn her lip up and tell us she preferred lilies when she smelled the poinsettias on the dresser. She was supposed to admire the photos I was going to place on the nightstand. We were supposed to have time for more stories.

Now, the frames dug into my stomach as we sped through downtown. Simone's hand was warm in mine, but I felt like I was composed of static.

"Can you please go faster, Sam?" Mom was in full Dr. Anderson mode: composed, in charge.

"We're going to make it, Z," he said, pressing the gas.

"I know we will," she said stiffly. "Simone, did you call your mom?" She seemed to have forgotten she'd already let Simone borrow her cell phone as soon as we got in the car.

"Yes, ma'am," Simone said quietly. "She's going to meet us there."

Mom nodded and told Dad to drive faster.

Bardell County General was tiny in comparison to the hospital where Grandma Jean died, but I had the same awful feeling rattle my chest as soon as I saw it. Dad dropped us off, and Mom, Simone, and I hightailed it inside the automatic sliding doors. A sleepy-looking receptionist instructed us where to go, and we took off in a full sprint down the hall. I clutched the photos to my chest.

I had to hold on. Mama Letty had to hold on.

I'd always hated hospitals. Partly because of the overwhelming bleach stench, the fluorescent lighting, the identical taupe hallways that were so easy to get lost in. The vending machines never had any good snacks, and the televisions were always tuned in to something that wasn't worth watching. But more than anything, I hated being in hospitals because the only time I'd ever been in them ended with someone dying. And Mama Letty couldn't die tonight. Not when the doctors had told us she had a week left. It didn't make any sense.

Mama Letty was in room 205. Outside of her door was a nurse with long black hair and a somber smile.

"She's still here," the nurse said. "You made it."

I could've cried; Simone looked like she was close. Mom stopped abruptly and placed a shaking hand on her chest. She was still in her cleaning clothes and dirty sneakers.

The nurse guided us inside. "It's okay. She's here."

And she was. She was propped up on pillows with wires hanging from her like vines in a garden. Her eyes were closed, and she looked skinnier than she did when I last saw her this morning. Her curls were flat against her head.

"Letty," the nurse said. "Letty, your family is here." She placed a gentle hand on Mom's shoulder. "She may not respond, but she can hear you. Take all the time you need."

Mom rushed to her side. "Mama? Mama, can you hear me?" When she didn't answer, Mom's chin quivered. I wanted to join her, but my feet were two cement blocks. Simone slipped her hand in mine and nodded toward the bed. Together, we inched closer.

Mama Letty still hadn't responded. Mom brushed her hair away from her face. "Mama, I'm here. Avery's here, Simone's here, Sam will be here."

"So will my mom," Simone chimed in. "Carole's on her way."

"We love you so much," Mom said. "We love you so much." She repeated it over and over and still, Mama Letty didn't stir. The photos weighed a thousand pounds.

"I love—" I started, but my voice broke. I couldn't finish the sentence. My eyes burned. I looked at the floor and watched the flecks in the tile blur together.

"We're here, Mama. We love you so much," Mom repeated. "Avery, come here."

I looked up and swallowed hard. I clutched the photos to my chest and reluctantly dropped Simone's hand. I joined Mom by Mama Letty's side. I looked for somewhere to set the photos, but there wasn't any place besides the windowsill, and that felt too far away.

"They told . . ." My voice died, again. I didn't know how to say it without sounding ridiculous. She wasn't supposed to die here. This wasn't her home. This wasn't her bedroom. We had already set everything up for her to die peacefully at home. It's what she deserved. Not this cold, unfamiliar room. I couldn't even be happy that, at the very least, we were with her instead of saying goodbye through the phone. Like Hikari had to do, like so many other people had to do. Jade never got to say goodbye to her mother, Simone never got to say goodbye to her brother, Ray was taken in an instant. At least I got to say goodbye. I was one of the lucky ones, and it still didn't feel fair.

None of this was fair.

Where were her crossword puzzles? Her one last cigarette? What was the last thing I even said to her? *See you tomorrow?* The fucking doctors told us a week.

They told us a week.

They told us a week.

Mom was still talking, but I couldn't hear her. My eyes found everything in the room but Mama Letty. There was a painting on the wall above the bed, a shitty stock image of a flowered field. A television bolted to the ceiling in the corner. The bathroom sign was scratched. It clearly needed to be replaced.

"Avery."

I looked at the bed, the lump in my throat nearly doubling in size when I realized Mama Letty's eyes were still closed. Why weren't they opening?

"Avery, show her the pictures," Mom pleaded, and I could tell by the pinch in her tone it wasn't the first time she'd asked.

I needed to focus. I needed to breathe. I gingerly placed the photos by her side. Mom grabbed one.

"Here we are at Thanksgiving," she said. "We were right there by the ocean. Remember all the good food?" She picked up the other photo. "And here you are at Kisabee Island with Ray. You looked so beautiful, Mama." She glanced at me with a pleading expression, begging me to say something. The lump in my throat swelled.

Simone came to her other side. "Mama Letty, it's Simone. I love you so much. Remember when you used to bring me Burger King after school? Remember when you bandaged my knee when I fell out of the tree in my yard?"

My throat burned. Everything hurt. This couldn't be happening. Why couldn't I get it together and say something? Why was I being a baby?

Dad arrived, out of breath. Sweat shone on his forehead, and his hair was disheveled. He hugged me and Mom and shakily said, "We made it." He didn't ask how Mama Letty was doing. The look on Mom's face said it all.

"Say something, Avery baby," Mom said. "Please."

I opened my mouth. Again, nothing came out. I was frozen. Stuck on a layer of thin ice over water and afraid any sudden movement would plunge me into the cold. Of course I wanted to say something. I wanted to say too much, and there wasn't enough time, and I didn't know where to start.

I wanted to tell her it wasn't fair. I wanted to tell her I wished I'd spent every summer in Bardell. How when she smiled it felt like I'd earned something important. I wanted to tell her I would miss the smell of her cigarettes. How I hoped the sound of her grunt would be permanently etched in my brain. I wanted to tell her we still had letters to read, horror movies to watch, Sam Cooke songs to dance to, train stations to break into.

But, at the end of it, the only thing I could say was, "I love you." Then the ice broke, the tears came, and I was drowning.

• • •

She lasted two and a half more hours. By ten p.m., Letty June Harding was dead.

Carole, who'd arrived not long after Dad, ushered Simone out to give us some privacy, but their sobs echoed in the hallway. A doctor with a salt-and-pepper beard stopped by to confirm the death and gave us the same pitiful look I was sure he gave people every day. Then the kind nurse removed the IVs and tubes.

"Take as much time as you need," she said. "Let us know when you're ready."

Dad thanked her. Mom laid her head down next to Mama Letty and sobbed.

I'd already cried so much, all I felt was a gaping emptiness as I stared at her in disbelief. She looked like she was sleeping. I half expected her to wake up and cuss us out for all the noise.

"I'm sorry, Mama." Mom's voice was muffled from the sheets. She looked up with bloodshot eyes and brought Mama Letty's palm to her lips. "I'm so sorry."

Dad and I rubbed Mom's back as she cried, but my arm felt like it was being controlled by an on-and-off switch. This went on for what felt like hours.

Eventually, Simone and Carole rejoined us. Carole, still in her rumpled Syrup uniform, took one look at Mama Letty and burst into tears again.

"She was like a mother to me," Carole sobbed. Simone leaned against her, furiously wiping away tears.

All of us in the same room again felt like a sick joke. If we weren't fighting, we were mourning. Carole looked at me through her tears, and I recoiled, remembering the snipes we shot at each other.

"Your grandmother was an amazing woman," Carole said. I tucked my lip in, biting down on the piercing, and nodded to the floor. I thought I'd gotten all my tears out, but I was wrong.

Mom brushed Mama Letty's curls away from her face. "I hope she's home. My God, I hope she's home."

No one asked Mom where she thought home was.

Maybe we all had our own versions.

In mine, Ray was waiting for Mama Letty. They were young again. They still loved to dance. They had plans for a future—vacations to Kisabee Island, train tickets to New York City. Ray would point out landmarks along the way, and Mama Letty would tell him to hush, she was trying to sleep. They attended Mom's parent-teacher conferences and helped her move into her dorm at Johns Hopkins. Every summer, they welcomed me to Sweetness Lane, and I found myself in both their faces.

They never, ever encountered the Olivers.

They were in love.

They were alive.

THE RIVER

THE BARDELL RIVER was a humble river. Unlike the Mighty Mississippi, it had no nickname and no songs were named in its honor. But the people who lived near its banks liked that. If there was ever an apt description of life in Bardell County, Georgia, one only had to look to the slow-moving waters in their backyard. Much like Bardell residents, it was a river that liked to take its time. There was no rush as it twisted through several counties, flowing east toward the Atlantic. Sometimes, unless you really looked, the river appeared to not be moving at all. It was always flowing, yet somehow constant. And Bardell folks admired consistency.

The river was home to many things: largemouth bass, white catfish. Mussels perfect for a stew. Oars long forgotten, a treasure trove of coins. It was home to plastic bottles that never disintegrated.

It was home to charred remains that did.

Its fresh waters held the salt of lovers' tears. People used its surface as a mirror. It provided the soundtrack on nights when words didn't come easy. It swallowed the wishes of girls and carried them somewhere bigger than itself.

The Bardell River didn't care what you looked like. Or how much money you made. Or who you loved. Or how you died. It welcomed everyone equally. Dark waters saying, *Come home to me.*

Come home to nature.
Come home to God.
Come home to yourself.

26.

THE FUNERAL WAS exactly a week later, on the first Saturday in December. I woke up to a dreary sky and a too-quiet house I still wasn't used to.

My parents and I ate cereal at the Formica table, the Marvelettes playing on the radio. The music couldn't mask the noises that were no longer there. There were no more body-rattling coughs. No more grunts, no more *swishes* from turning pages in a crossword puzzle book. No more slow unwrapping of cellophane, no more flicks from the lighter. I looked up at the unmoving cat clock, and felt so angry that we never fixed it before she died. I looked at the refrigerator and took in the magnets of faded pieces of fruit and peeling dental calendars from the mid-aughts. I wanted to cry when I thought of our stainless steel refrigerator in DC, covered in mementos from Niagara Falls, Cape Cod, Yellowstone, Miami. Mama Letty deserved so many more magnets, so many more memories. I pushed away from the table and went to her room to cry. I sank down on the floor at the foot of her bed and buried my head into my knees.

Mom knocked softly. "Avery?"

"She deserved so many more magnets," I said, and then I started to cry because I knew it made no sense, and I didn't know how to explain it. Mom joined me on the floor and wrapped me in her arms.

"I know, baby, I know. Cry it out."

We were supposed to be getting ready, but I couldn't move. I dug my fingers into the carpet, so angry that we'd cleaned her room and wiped away every trace of her. I cried when I realized I might never find another one of her silver hairs because we'd washed her old sheets, and she never had a chance to sleep in the new ones.

There was another knock and Dad entered, clutching a small box with a sheepish smile.

"Mind if I join you?"

I nodded against Mom's shoulder. He sat across from us on the carpet and placed the box in the middle. **DO NOT OPEN UNTIL I'M IN THE GROUND** was written on the piece of masking tape that secured the flaps together.

"I could very well be setting myself up to be haunted by Mama Letty," Dad said, "or at the very least, cursed for the rest of my life. But I'm willing to take a chance because I love you both from A to Z."

"Sam, what is this?" Mom asked.

"A little while ago, Letty gave me this box with strict instructions to not pass it on until after her funeral. I know I'm technically cheating but . . ." He smiled and pushed the box forward. "I think she'd understand if I broke the rules."

"She really is gonna haunt your ass," Mom said, but she grabbed the box anyway and passed it to me. "Do the honors, Avery baby."

I peeled the tape away cautiously, opening the flaps and reeling away as if something was going to come crawling out. I released a breath when I realized the only things inside were small black-and-white speckled notebooks—lots of them. Identical to the one I'd seen tucked in her crossword puzzle book one night. She never did let me in on what was written inside. On the top were two white envelopes with names in shaky blue marker.

"This is yours," I said, handing her the one with *Zora* on it. I smiled and rolled my eyes at the one that said *Fish*.

Mom clutched her letter to her chest. "I'll give you some privacy." She kissed my forehead and left with Dad, but not before I caught her wiping away a tear.

As soon as I was alone, I ripped my envelope open. My breath caught in my throat at the sight of her shaky scrawl.

Dear Avery,

If you're reading this, I'm dead. Sorry about that. I know funerals are the worst, and I'm sorry you just had to attend mine.

Last night, you asked me why I never wrote your mother back. I didn't tell you at the time, but you had asked the wrong question. I always wrote your mother back. The real question is why I never sent them. If you'd asked that, I'd tell you that stamps are expensive (did you laugh? I hope you laughed). But the real reason is that I was afraid of facing all the ugly things I've done, and I have been for a very long time.

These are my journals. My life. I'd never been good with words until I fell in love with your grandpa Ray. We spent two years exchanging letters, and in that time, I fell in love with writing. But I never shared my words with anyone, not until now. I know we missed out on a lot. Hopefully these notebooks can fill in the gaps.

I am not a perfect woman, Avery. I've done a lot of horrible, awful things. As I'm writing this, I'm not sure if it's even right to share them. I told you not everything is yours to hold, so I think this way is easiest. Read the journals, if you want. Find out everything you need to know. Or not. I think you're grown enough to decide what's right for yourself.

This is it, Fish. I don't have any money to leave behind or a big fancy house. I'm sorry about that. The only thing I can give you are these words, and I'm not sure if they'll ever be enough. You are remarkable, and I'm sorry I couldn't find the strength to say those words aloud. You're so much like Ray. Curious with a big heart. But that attitude of yours? Is all me.

Thank you for taking me to the train station. Thank you for reminding me there's still some good in the world.

Hug your mother for me. And tell your hippie father I said thanks for passing along this message.

Live, Avery. Live for me.

I love you,
Letty June Harding

• • •

The letter ripped me in half. I read it over and over, allowing Mama Letty's words to wash over me like a baptism. I missed her so much it hurt. The ache was deep, so deep I couldn't sit upright, so I slumped and rested my head on the floor.

The underside of Mama Letty's bed was blurry through my tears. Still, I noticed a cigarette butt we must've missed when vacuuming. I grabbed it and held it to my nose, stupidly hoping I could catch a whiff of her. There was nothing but ash. I buried my face in her comforter and smelled only laundry detergent. Shoved my face against the floor and cried and cried and cried.

I stayed there until Dad called out that we were leaving in twenty minutes and I needed to get ready. I started to peel myself off the floor and suddenly became eye level with a small wooden box, wedged between the bed and nightstand.

Thinking it was more of Ray's letters, I wiggled it out gently, as if it were a Jenga block. I ran my hand over the smooth, unfinished top. I recognized it. It was the same box Mama Letty had snatched from my bedroom on our first day in Bardell. I smiled as I flipped open the clasp, remembering her chilliness those first few weeks. How hard I'd had to work to melt her down.

I opened the box. Instead of being filled with Ray's familiar scrawl, I was met with newspaper clippings—dozens of them. I sifted through, trying to make sense of them, headlines popping out like jump scares.

LUCAS OLIVER NAMED NEW OWNER
OF DRAPER HOTEL

BELOVED BARDELL SHERIFF
WALLACE OLIVER HANGS HAT
AFTER FORTY-TWO YEARS OF SERVICE

DRAPER HOTEL & SPA NAMED
BEST HOTEL IN GEORGIA

WEDDING BELLS FOR
LUCAS OLIVER & AMELIA BARNETT

There were so many. Every last one about the Olivers in some way. I held up a wrinkled, water-stained flyer with a candy cane border.

THE DRAPER HOTEL & SPA PRESENTS:
A SOUTHERN CHARM CHRISTMAS PARTY!

And when I looked down again, the shimmer of silver. Everything froze as I pushed aside more clippings and touched the barrel of a gun.

"Avery, did you hear your father? We're lea—"

The door was opening too quickly, and my brain was moving too slowly. I couldn't speak. Couldn't say a word as Mom crossed the room and hovered above me. Why would Mama Letty need a gun? For protection? Why were there so many news clippings about the Olivers?

Why did this look like a box full of evidence?

For ten seconds, there was nothing but Dad's whistles drifting from the living room.

"Where did you find that?" Mom asked, voice low.

I pointed to the side of the bed. I couldn't speak.

Mom grabbed the box. The closing snap of the clasp was like a gunshot.

"Go get ready, baby."

I looked at her, brain murky and confused. I looked at the box of journals at my feet. I looked at my shaking hands.

"Avery," Mom said. "Let's go. Please."

It was all there, threatening to boil over to the surface. I was five. Was it Christmas? I heard screams. Saw a gold-wrapped present hitting the wall. Mama Letty gripping a box like the one in Mom's hands.

A murderer is a murderer, Avery.

I stood. I somehow made it across the room. When I looked back, Mom was tucking the box under her arm and gazing at herself in the mirror above the dresser like she didn't recognize the person staring back.

I thought about asking the question on the tip of my tongue. What did all of this mean? Surely it wasn't the absurd conclusion I was thinking. Mama Letty was a lot of things. But a murderer?

"Go, Avery," Mom said again.

And I realized that even if I somehow found the strength to ask the question, I wasn't sure I wanted to know the answer.

So I left.

• • •

Mama Letty had never been a churchgoer. She didn't want a formal service, didn't want the bells and whistles. She wanted to keep it short and sweet.

Mom and I were silent on the way to the funeral home. Dad tried to lighten the mood, but it was impossible. The world was void of color. Nothing made sense. Everything made sense.

At the viewing, I didn't care that people were eyeing my suit or my side shave or my lip ring. I simply stood there and accepted condolences. Said thank you when people told me they were so sorry. Tried to hold in my screams when Sam Cooke played. I thought about Christmas lights and long-ago fights and pale blue dots and dances on the beach.

The crowd was bigger than expected. Mr. Arnie and Jerome showed up in snappy suits. Isaac was barely able to hold back his tears when he saw the casket. Several women who played bingo with Mama Letty long ago showed up in large, colorful hats.

There were other people I didn't recognize and some people Mom remembered from her youth. Soon, the room was full of laughter and chatter, and there was a short line waiting to view Mama Letty and say goodbye.

Carole and Simone arrived in similar black dresses. Simone's locs were piled high in a bun, and her lips were the same shade of purple they'd been the night of Renny's. I braced myself as they drew closer.

"I'm so sorry for your loss," Carole said.

"*Our* loss," Mom replied. "Thank you for coming."

"Letty always had the worst timing," Carole said. Then they both laughed, like it was some sort of inside joke.

"I'm sorry, Cee," Mom said.

She and Carole looked at each other for a long moment. Then they hugged, fighting back tears. Dad, Simone, and I looked away.

"Why don't you and Simone go nab me a plate of meat-balls?" Dad asked. "And take your time."

Simone and I took the hint and scurried across the room as our mothers' cries intensified. We joined the buffet queue behind two of the bingo ladies.

At first, we didn't say anything. We hadn't been alone since she snuck into my room, and the tension from that conversation apparently hadn't gone anywhere. My mind was busy, thoughts rattling around like a pinball machine.

"You still grounded?" Simone finally asked.

"I don't think so. You?"

"She's eased up a bit."

We inched forward, straight into a cloud of old lady perfume. Simone wrinkled her nose and glanced over her shoulder.

"She's still praying for me. But she stopped forcing me to go to church three times a week. Now I only have to go on Sundays."

I raised my eyebrows. "What changed her mind?"

"My sister, actually. I guess my mom thought Shayla would totally be on her side, but she wasn't. She told my mom she was going to lose me if she kept it up. I mean," she lowered her voice even further, "all you've gotta do is look at Mama Letty and *your* mom to see that."

"Damn. Go Shayla."

"My mom and I are going to see her in Atlanta for Christmas, and she said we could go visit Spelman. It wouldn't be an official tour, but at least I could see the campus."

Excitement shattered my cool demeanor, my grief. I threw my arms around her in a huge hug. "That's so amazing!"

"I still have to get in. Nothing's set in stone."

"You'll get in," I said surely.

The food line stalled. At the front, Mr. Arnie and Jerome squabbled over who would get the last slice of pound cake, neither of them believing when the caterer said a second cake was on the way. Simone and I watched in amusement.

"I was wondering," Simone said slowly when the line started moving again, "do you think you could look over my essay? I totally get if you don't want to, but I figured I'd ask since you're such a nerd." She grabbed a paper plate and slapped on a helping of potato salad.

"Hmmm, insulting me at my grandmother's funeral," I said. "How could I say no to an offer like that?"

She shot me a sideways grin. "I missed you."

We helped ourselves to a little bit of everything and nabbed two chairs in the corner. Two slices of cornbread dangerously teetered off the side of Simone's plate.

"Gotta keep up these cornbread thighs!" Simone said, happily patting her stomach. "Can't disappoint Mama Letty."

We were halfway through our food when Jade showed up, clutching a bouquet of ivory peonies. Even from thirty feet away, I could tell her hands were shaking. Simone and I watched as she exchanged words with Mom and Carole and then set her flowers down among the others near Mama Letty's casket.

"Did you know she was coming?" I asked Simone.

She shook her head. "No idea."

Jade made her way to us. She was wearing a black sweater dress, her mother's locket resting in the hollow of her neck. I shivered, looked away.

"Hi," she said quietly once she reached us. "I'm sorry I can't stay long. Tallulah's outside." She pulled at the end of her messy fishtail braid. "I'm so sorry for your loss, Avery."

"Thanks," I replied, mouth dry.

"I'm assuming you're not going to the winter formal tonight?" she asked.

In the midst of the funeral preparations, the dance had completely slipped my mind. "Don't think your stepmother would appreciate that," I said coolly.

"I don't blame you. I'm going to show my face for some people in the historical society but—" She sighed. "Sorry. I'm rambling. I know things got majorly messed up. And I'm sorry."

I stared at the glob of pasta salad on my plate. I couldn't speak, could barely think.

"I wanted to give you this," Jade continued, handing me a folded piece of paper. "You don't have to read it now. But it's my proposal. For the Faces of Bardell monument project. Um, I did a lot of research after we talked. Um—"

Her eyes were shining. I looked over at Simone, but she was intensely focused on her cornbread.

"I went to Mrs. Newland and asked her about amending my application," Jade went on. "And I submitted an application to honor your grandparents instead."

My heart pounded as I unfolded the paper slowly. I skimmed the page, catching glimpses of birth dates and Letty June Harding, Raymond Harding, and mentions of Amtrak. My heart pounded when I saw Mama Letty's death date, only seven short days prior.

"Why did you do this?" I asked.

"My mom will always be remembered," she said. "But um, so many other people won't. I guess I didn't know what else to do. I don't know if it'll get approved, but I had to do something. I'm sorry."

"I'm sorry, too," I said.

"Me too," Simone said.

Jade swallowed and pushed her glasses up. "It's completely

understandable if y'all say no. But I've missed you both so much. I know now is *not* the time for a big apology session, but . . . if y'all wanted to go to the river sometime, I'd really, really like that."

Simone and I looked at each other, hesitating. Then, she said slowly, "I don't know. I *do* have a couple of wishes I need to make on Tree."

A classic James Brown song started up, and Mr. Arnie whooped in the center of the room. We all giggled as he and Jerome started shimmying their shoulders.

"A night at the Perfect Spot does sound enticing," I said. I could already hear the river and feel Tree's sturdiness beneath me. "I guess I'm in need of some wishing, too."

"Text me," Jade said, and with a wave, she was gone.

Simone and I were quiet for a while. She picked at a chicken wing. "Do you want to be alone tonight?"

"No," I answered honestly. The past week had been nothing but a lonely stretch of silence. The thought of returning to the quiet and potentially running into *that* box again made my skin crawl. "No, I don't."

She shrugged. "Maybe we can go to the river tonight? I'm off work."

Mr. Arnie and Jerome were still dancing in the middle of the room. Mr. Arnie caught my eye and winked. I was reminded of Renny's warmth and how once upon a time, everything felt possible. I turned back to Simone.

"Yeah, I think I'd like that," I said. "I think I'd like that a lot."

• • •

After all the food had been eaten and all the guests left and the tears had been shed, Mom, Dad, and I finally got a quiet moment alone with Mama Letty.

We gathered around her casket. Mom tenderly adjusted the gold brooch on her emerald-green dress. It was the fanciest thing I'd ever seen her wear. Between her crossed hands, the photo of her and Ray at Kisabee Island rested on her stomach.

"She would've hated this entire thing," Mom said. "All these people making a fuss, staring at her and crying."

Dad shivered. "I can almost feel her spirit in the room, cussing us out."

I'd done so well the entire service. I hadn't cried at all. But soon, the lid of the casket would be closed and Mama Letty would be in the earth forever, and the thought made my eyes well up. Now all I had were her letters and my memories. Some questions would never be answered now.

Maybe it was better that way.

"I miss her already," I said.

"She's with Ray now," Dad said.

"Lord, help that man," Mom said.

We were half laughing, half crying. We said goodbye one last time.

27.

"OKAY. I OFFICIALLY feel underdressed. You"—I took in Simone's curvy figure—"look amazing."

Simone giggled. "Oh, you mean this old thing?" She twirled on my porch, showing off her form-fitting floor-length red gown. She flipped her curled locs over her shoulder. The tips were now silver. "I just threw this on."

"I thought we weren't *actually* going to the dance?"

"We're not. I dressed up for me."

I glanced at the time. We had ten minutes until Jade arrived. More than enough time for me to throw my suit from the funeral back on.

"You don't have to change!" Simone insisted. "You know I'm a little extra."

"A *little*?"

"Okay, maybe you should go change since those sweats are mad raggedy," she shot back.

I burst into laughter and invited her inside. "Give me a moment, Your Highness."

Eight minutes later, I wandered back into the living room in my suit. Simone and my parents were on the couch, and they all smiled when they saw me.

"You look stunning, Unsavory," Dad said.

"Dad, please. This is the third time I've worn this suit this month."

"Third time this month, and your bow tie is still crooked," Mom said with a sigh. "Come here."

"Actually," Simone stood up slowly, "I got you something." She opened her tiny gold clutch and pulled out a bright red bow tie.

My heart swelled. "Matching the bow tie to your dress, huh?"

"Don't go getting cocky, DC." With a little instruction from Mom, Simone tied it around my collar. Mom's eyes welled when she saw us.

"Let me go get my phone," she said.

"Mom," I whined. "We're not actually going to the dance."

"Girl, if you don't hush up and let me have this!" Mom called. She sounded so much like Mama Letty, we all had to laugh. When she returned, Simone and I smiled wide in a variety of different poses, Dad in the background pretending to be the paparazzi. When Jade honked, Simone and I made a beeline for the door.

"Be safe and have fun!" Mom called.

We walked down the driveway, our fingertips brushing. The night air was clear and cool.

"I'm sorry my mom was so embarrassing," I said as we drew

closer to the Jeep. Jade was checking her lip gloss in the visor mirror.

"She wasn't embarrassing," Simone said, entangling her fingers with mine. "She wanted us to know we're worth remembering."

Before we climbed into the Jeep, Carole hesitantly stepped outside. For a second, I thought she'd come to object. But then I saw her phone in her hands.

"Do you have time for some pictures?" she called across the lawn.

Simone and I exchanged a glance. She looked like she was on the verge of happy tears. "Yes, Mama," she said, "Of course we have time."

We made our way to her. I told her we had all the time in the world.

• • •

The Draper's parking lot was packed. Couples in formal wear waited outside the revolving front door as Mrs. Newland and another teacher checked tickets. Jade found a spot and cut the engine. She was wearing contacts, and it was strange to see her without her glasses. Her soft blonde curls fell in gorgeous waves, and her gold dress was covered in sequins.

"I'm going in to show my face to the historical society for a minute," she said. "Then we're out of here."

"Give Tallulah our regards," I said dryly.

We laughed, but it was hesitant. We were still working our way back to us.

After Jade left, Simone turned around in the passenger seat, licking chip dust off her fingers. She'd already opened half the snacks we were taking to the river.

"Wanna go for a walk?"

"As long as you bring the chips," I said.

We made our way through the parking lot, ignoring the few curious looks we got from our classmates. We walked in the opposite direction of the Draper, the dull base of a country rock song softening the further we got.

"You sure you don't want to go?" I asked. "Last chance."

"I'm good. I don't want nothing to do with that energy." Simone munched on another chip. "My card this week told me to mind my business."

"Which card?"

"The Hermit."

"Ah."

She looked at me sideways as we approached the bridge overlooking the Bardell River. "You got no clue what I'm talking about, right?"

"Not at all."

"You're such an earth sign." She sighed, and we laughed when I admitted, after all this time, I still didn't know what that meant either.

We leaned against the barrier rail and stared down at the river's dark currents, taking turns digging our hands into the chips.

"I'm going to whip you into astrological shape," she muttered. "You can't be running back to DC all uncultured."

I grinned and popped a chip in my mouth. "I look forward to the lessons."

She bit back a grin; so did I. Flirting with her came so easy. It felt nice after being weighed down with grief.

"You took your ring off," Simone said.

I looked at my bare finger and shrugged. "Do you blame me?"

"Guess not. If you broke up with me, I'd take off your ring, too."

I gasped. "But, Simone. I thought we weren't even together! How could we possibly break up?"

She shoved my shoulder. "Keep it up, DC, and I'll throw your ass into this river."

"I'd love to see you try."

We dug around in the chip bag and stared at the river, the stars. There were so many things on my mind, but all I wanted to do was sink into the familiar scent of Simone's almond body butter.

"You look really beautiful tonight," I said.

She grinned, dimples deepening. "So do you. Very handsome."

"It's the bow tie."

"I've got good taste, huh?"

"I'd say so."

Simone tossed a chip into the water, and we watched it bob on the surface before being slowly swept away. "I'm sorry for cutting you off like I did. I panicked. I . . . I guess I wanted to leave you before you had the chance to leave me."

"That's very . . ." I whispered, "what's your astrological sign again?"

"Cancer," she said, laughing.

"That's very Cancer of you."

She shoved me again. "You don't even know what that means!"

I rested my elbow on the rail and propped my chin in my hand. "I got time."

"Cancers are water signs. We're emotional and intuitive. We're authentic. In touch with our emotions."

"The Cancer sunflower," I said, marveling at her in all her glory.

She bit her lip. "The Capricorn eucalyptus." She rested her hand on the railing next to mine. "We do make a pretty good match if I say so myself." Her fingers inched closer to mine.

"We do," I agreed, and I opened my palm. Her hand slid in mine. Like habit.

"What are we going to do?" she asked quietly.

"About?"

"We have limited time! Now that Mama Letty has passed, who's to say y'all won't move back to DC over the holiday break? Especially when there's nothing left here."

I ran my thumb over hers. "You're here."

She snorted. "Cornball."

"Says the girl who bought me a matching bow tie."

"I will throw that bow tie into the river, Avery Anderson, if you keep playing with me!"

I laughed and wrapped my arms around her waist. We leaned against the cool railing and buried our faces in each other's necks.

"We don't have to have the answers figured out tonight," I said into her ear.

She relaxed against me. "I missed you so much. I missed the way you smell."

"I smell like Doritos."

"Mmm." She smacked her lips loudly. "My favorite."

I brushed her locs from her neck and placed a kiss on her collarbone. "I missed you, too," I whispered.

She shivered and pulled me closer. "Can you promise me one thing?"

"Possibly."

She peeled away. "If you *do* end up running away from Bardell, could you please not be like your mom and stay away for a zillion years?"

I hummed. "A zillion *is* a mighty long time. Would you settle for a billion?"

"Avery!"

I leaned my forehead against hers. "I'm not going anywhere. And even when *we* leave, and I say *we* because you're getting into Spelman—"

"God, I hope."

"—we'll always be connected."

She bit her lip. "Do you promise?"

I nodded. "I promise. There's no one else I'd rather get caught making out with in a haunted corn maze."

"I swear to God, when I catch those little goblins again, I'm gonna whoop their asses."

"I'd pay admission to see that."

I brought my hands to her cheeks. I let myself revel in her deep brown eyes as the water slipped by below us.

"Kiss me, you beautiful human," she whispered.

So I did, and it was everything.

In that moment, nothing in the world mattered besides Simone. I didn't think about the healing we still had to do, the grief we would always carry. I didn't think about the hard conversations that lay ahead or the thousands of words I had to read. I didn't think about what would happen when we would inevitably leave Bardell one day. My heart was a mess, and it was full and beautiful.

Simone pulled me closer, and the world went on. But I was there, in that moment, and nothing was urgent. We sank into a calm so still, someone passing by might've mistaken us for statues. A tangle of red and Black, brown and glitter, gold and gleam. The plaque might've read, SUNFLOWER & EUCALYPTUS. Or TWO GIRLS IN LOVE. Or perhaps, simply, LIFE GOES ON.

But if they looked closer, they would've seen our chests rising. They would've noticed our blinking eyes. They would've seen a living, breathing example of something marvelous and worthy of remembrance.

They would have seen us.

THE MONUMENTS

ELIZABETH JADE OLIVER'S proposal to honor Ray and Letty June Harding died in a Bardell Historical Society meeting, four to three. *There's not enough evidence to prove these people are worthy of monuments*, Mayor Ryan Gruber said before casting the deciding vote. Thus, five statues went up in downtown Bardell, four of them for white people. The last one was for Gloria Mitchell, the first Black student to integrate the public high school. *She was an inspiration*, Mayor Gruber said during the ribbon-cutting ceremony. *Truly worthy of such an honor.*

Those monuments stood for decades, even as other ones around Bardell County crumbled. Simone Cole never got the chance to fulfill her promise of tearing Richard Beckwith's statue down—a group of white freshmen beat her to it when she was completing her third semester at Spelman. Elizabeth Jade Oliver left for art school in New York City and did not return to Bardell for many years. Thus, Amelia Oliver's mural faded into the bricks of the Draper Hotel. It was eventually painted over at the suggestion of Tallulah Oliver, who claimed guests would prefer a more *uplifting* image. And on the wall of a riverside home, Avery Anderson's initials disappeared under a wave of new signatures, new names, new memories. She wouldn't mind. She knew from her time working in national forests that sometimes things required an annihilation in order to renew themselves.

But.

Other monuments were left behind, if you knew what you were looking for. There was one on Sweetness Lane in the form of a dogwood tree in honor of two girls who once sat at its base and wondered how the other's lip gloss tasted. Over the Bardell River, there was a crooked oak branch in honor of Simone Cole, who once picked at its bark and prayed for the day she'd feel safe enough to come out. Eighty miles away, on the shores of Kisabee Island, grains of sand that once stood in honor of Raymond Harding became so embedded in the fabric of the beach that they never really left.

After it happened, Letty June Harding went home. With the first of what would be three cancer diagnoses and flyers for the Draper Hotel & Spa Christmas party riding shotgun, Letty informed Ray that although she didn't get the men who killed him, she thought she got someone better. Someone who would hurt more. She played Ray Charles, shivering because it was twenty-two degrees and her heater hadn't worked in years. On her drive, she passed several monuments, but she was too high on adrenaline and horror to notice. There was the train station where her man made the choice to stay. The bus station bench where her teenage daughter looked to the stars and decided she was done. The corner of Sweetness Lane and Maple Drive where that same daughter would vow to take Letty's secret to her grave. And when she pulled into her driveway, Letty gazed at the porch swing where her granddaughter would eventually fall in love and realize what it meant to come home.

Letty sat in her car and waited in the dark for hours. For what, she wasn't sure. God. Justice. Relief. The red and blue lights of a cop car. Or maybe, she was waiting for someone to cross the frosted dead winter grass and knock on her foggy window so she could write her testament in the condensation. Telling whoever wanted to witness, *See me.*

See me.

See me.

ACKNOWLEDGMENTS

A LIFETIME OF gratitude to Yasmin Curtis, my best friend, my first reader. We've come a long way from elementary school days, giggling at our earnest handwritten stories at Crestview Park. Thank you for always believing, for reading every word, and for being my BCBB for life. The first one was always for you.

Publishing is a roller coaster, and I'm so grateful for the people who've made every high and low of this ride worth it.

To Mekisha Telfer: I knew from our first phone call that you were meant to work on this book. You are the definition of a dream editor. Let's do this again?

To Suzie Townsend and Stephanie Kim: I truly landed some of the best agents in the business. Thank you for advocating for my career and believing in me, especially during the times I didn't believe in myself.

The wonderful people I've worked with at New Leaf Literary: Dani Segelbaum, Sophia Ramos, Katherine Curtis, Pouya Shahbazian, Victoria Hendersen, Veronica Grijalva, and Meredith

Barnes. Kate Sullivan, thank you for your vision and thoughtful edits and for always pushing me to make my writing the best it could be.

To the folks at Roaring Brook and Macmillan who helped usher this book into the world: Connie Hsu, Allison Verost, Ilana Worrell, Taylor Pitts, John Nora, Beth Clark, Michelle Gengaro, Sarah Kaufman, Lindsay Wagner, Hayley Jozwiak, Jacqueline Hornberger, Kelly Markus, Ronnie Ambrose, Molly B. Ellis, Mariel Dawson, Mary Van Akin, Kelsey Marrujo, Chantal Gersch, Teresa Ferraiolo, Katie Quinn, Nicole Schaefer, Megan McDonald, Johanna Allen, Jaime Bode, Jennifer Edwards, Kristen Luby, and Jessica Weil. To have a group of folks who love Avery and Simone and Mama Letty as much as I do is a dream come true.

To Laylie Frazier for creating such a beautiful cover.

To Alex Hightower for providing feedback that ultimately changed this story for the better.

To the authors who graciously took their time to provide early reads and blurbs: Maika and Maritza Moulite, Kelly Quindlen, Kim Johnson, Kyrie McCauley and Brandy Colbert. I appreciate you all so much.

To the amazing people writing has brought me: thank you to the Lit Squad for literally making me laugh every single day. Shout-out to the Black Mermaids for the endless support and insight. Special thanks to Sami Ellis, Bethany Baptiste, Camille Baker, Elnora Gunter, Britney S. Lewis, Shauna Robinson, Aislinn Brophy, Gabi Burton Leah Johnson, Morgan Rogers, J. Elle, Adrienne Tooley, Meryl Wilsner, Dahlia Adler, Alexandra

Villasante, Linda Epstein, Addie Tsai, Muriel Leung, Andrew Rincón, Gabriella Burnham, Sam Cohen, Wei Tchou, Amanda Galvan Huynh, Lisa Factora-Borchers, Jimena Lucero, Kei Kai-Ro, Kirin Khan, Mei Ramirez, Victoria Newton Ford, Lamar Giles, Irene Reed, Katherine Nazarro and Leila Meglio at Porter Square Books, and K.S. Watts. Thank you to Melody Simpson and the tremendous work you do with Melanin in YA.

To Trisha Tobias: look at your stepbook taking baby steps into the world! I will forever be grateful that Pitch Wars brought us together. Thank you for plucking me out of obscurity (haaaa). You are the best mentor/advocate/editor I could've ever asked for. I know this novel is nothing like the one we sent into the world over three years ago, but I still hope it makes you proud.

To Jen St. Jude and Octavia Saenz: my fellow Aquarian weirdos, how I love you so. Jen, thank you for always making time to read everything I write (even if I'm convinced it's awful), for being the first person I turn to with a publishing crisis, for always being down to make a mean spreadsheet. Octavia, your sheer existence inspires me. Thank you for always encouraging me to let loose and get weird in my work. 306 for life!

To Keiko Wright and Kathy Zhang: thank you for your support and hospitality and for always being down for a getaway from the city. Beach day at Riis soon? Also thank you to Whitney Porter for providing a quiet place to land when I needed it the most.

Thank you to the institutions that have uplifted my work by gifting me time and space to write: Sundress Academy for the Arts, the Highlights Foundation, Baldwin for the Arts, and

MacDowell (the Sorosis Studio will always have a special place in my heart!). Thank you to Amazon Literary for the generous gift of the James Baldwin Fellowship, an honor I'm still pinching myself over.

Thank you to Lambda Literary for uplifting queer artists for over three decades. My time at the 2018 Emerging Writers Retreat changed my life. To my mentor, Emily Danforth, thank you for your continued guidance and for being so damn cool. To my YA cohort—it was an honor to study and learn alongside all of you, and I can't wait for your novels to grace my bookshelf. Thank you to the following people for donating to my fundraiser so I could attend the retreat in the first place: LaCheryl Ball, Kevin Sharp, Stanley Hudson, Chelsea Vicente, Sarah Laidler, Kathy Ball, Eliseo Valenzuela, Rue and Lauren Lavender, and Monika Cofer-Eimer (Rest in peace).

Gratitude for the teachers whose lessons stayed with me long after I left the classroom: Rebecca Newland, Tim Seibles, Sheri Reynolds, and Sebrina Lindsay-Law.

To my friends: Lexi Mingo-Smith for relentlessly pursuing your own dreams and inspiring me to do the same, for the hours of FaceTime calls, for the fall party traditions. Shatika Dodson for always making me laugh until I cry, for listening to my publishing woes even if you had no idea what I was talking about, for being ready to fight if needed. To Allison Vazquez for your unwavering faith and eight hugs a day. To Meghan Horvath for over a decade of friendship, even across all the miles. To Gabrielle Rodriguez and La Espirista for creating a sobriety group full of beautiful humans who kept me grounded throughout 2021.

To my father, brother, and grandmother for your relentless support and love. Mom, thank you for always encouraging me to follow my dreams, for your patience during the times I poked and prodded you for our family history. Thank you for the unforgettable road trip down south, for always believing I could do anything I set my mind to, and for being my bestest mostest.

To Kay: You are the dreamiest curmudgeon queer of my heart. Thank you for making sure I'm always fed, for reminding me to drink water, for telling me yes, I can do this, for celebrating my wins, for mourning my losses, for being a poet in a tent who watches *Gilmore Girls*. I am so grateful to have found a home in you and Biggie in this lawless place. I love you.

Love to all queer, trans, and nonbinary people of color, especially queer Black people. We are magical, y'all.

Finally, thank you, dear reader, whoever you may be. You deserve monuments, too.